P9-ARK-627

LEONIDAS OF SPARTA

A Boy of the Agoge

Leonidas of Sparta: A Boy of the Agoge

Copyright © 2010 Helena P. Schrader. All rights reserved. No part of this book may be reproduced or retransmitted in any form or by any means without the written permission of the publisher.

Published by Wheatmark®
610 East Delano Street, Suite 104
Tucson, Arizona 85705 U.S.A.
www.wheatmark.com

International Standard Book Number: 978-1-60494-474-7
Library of Congress Control Number: 2010930441

SPARTA

Late 6th Century BC
Cast of Characters
(Those marked with * are historical figures)

The Agiads
  King Anaxandridas*
  Taygete, his first wife
  Chilonis, his second wife
  Cleomenes*, his firstborn son, by Chilonis
  Dorieus*, his secondborn son, by Taygete
  Leonidas*, his thirdborn son, by Taygete, twin to Cleombrotus
  Cleombrotus*, his thirdborn son, by Taygete, twin to Leonidas
  Gyrtias, Cleomenes' wife
  Agis, eldest son of Cleomenes
  Gorgo,* daughter of Cleomenes
  Dido, nurse to Leonidas
  Polyxo, nurse to Cleombrotus

The Eurypontids
  King Ariston*
  Demaratus,* his son and heir
  Leotychidas,* cousin of Demaratus, next in line to the throne
  Percalus, wife to Demaratus

In the Agoge
  Gitiades, Leonidas' first eirene
  Ephorus, elected herd leader
  Prokles, son of Eurybiades, herd member

Alkander, son of Charmos, herd member
Timon, herd member

Other Spartans

Hilaira, Prokles' sister
Philippos, Prokles' father
Lysandridas, Prokles' grandfather
Leonis, Prokles' grandmother
Lathria, Timon's sister
Euryleon, youth in Leonidas' unit
Eirana, daughter of Kyranios
Kyranios, divisional commander
Nikostratos, Spartan treasurer

INTRODUCTION AND ACKNOWLEDGEMENTS

THE DEATH OF LEONIDAS DEATH IS legendary. His last days have inspired great works of art and popular enthusiasm. The stand of "the 300" at Thermopylae has been harnessed to a hundred modern causes pitting East against West, and Leonidas with his 300 Spartans have come to symbolize what is good and noble in war: self-sacrifice for the sake of one's country and family. But who was Leonidas? And what was he before he became the incarnation of Freedom fighting Tyranny?

Herodotus gives us some tantalizing tidbits—the story of his father's forced second marriage, the tensions between his elder brothers, the precociousness of his wife. But he is silent on many key points, from the date of Leonidas' birth to his role in Sparta prior to becoming king. Only one thing about his early life do we know for certain: because he was not the heir apparent to the Agiad throne, he would have been subjected to the full Spartan agoge. Knowing that, knowing how he ended, and building on fascinating insights into his personality provided by the few sayings attributed to him, I have created a young Leonidas.

Nothing in this novel contradicts known facts about Leonidas— not even the late date of his birth. It is true that most historians prefer to think he was born "shortly" after Dorieus, as Herodotus says; but the fact that he personally led the Spartan advance guard to Thermopylae and fought in the front line for three days of fierce fighting, supports my thesis that he was not already an old man at the time of the battle. The fact that his son was still quite young at the time of his death is another undeniable historical fact that supports the postulated later birth date of Leonidas. I have made Leonidas roughly eight years younger than most historians postulate and from ten to fifteen years older than most popular portrayals of him in art and film.

That said, the novel is quite candidly fiction.

I wish to thank my editor, Christina Dickson, for encouraging me to publish this short work as a stand-alone Part I of a Leonidas trilogy, and for patiently correcting all my persistent spelling errors and inconsistencies in form and usage. I wish to thank my cover designer, Charles Whall, for putting up with my changing visions and nit-picking of his highly effective and evocative design. Without their hard work, this book would not have been finished. I look forward to working with both of them on the next two books in the trilogy: *Leonidas of Sparta: A Peerless Peer* and *Leonidas of Sparta: The Dispensable King*.

PROLOGUE

AS SOON AS IT BECAME EVIDENT that the Gods wanted a human sacrifice, Leonidas knew it would be he. The priest appointed by his co-monarch Leotychidas, delivered the Delphic Oracle, reading in his deep, resonant voice:

Hear your fate, O dwellers in Sparta of the wide spaces,
Either your famed, great town must be sacked by Perseus' sons,
Or, if that be not, the whole of Lacedaemon
Shall mourn the death of a king of the house of Herakles.
For not the strength of lions or of bulls shall hold him,
Strength against strength; for he has the power of Zeus,
And will not be checked till one of these two he has consumed.

And every single man in the Council chamber turned to look at Leonidas. No one looked at Leotychidas, who was no less Sparta's king and no less a descendent of Herakles. They looked at Leonidas.

Delphi was rarely as unambiguous as in this oracle, and the cynical part of Leonidas' brain wondered just what it had cost Leotychidas to extract this message. Of course he'd taken a chance. He couldn't have been 100% certain that *everyone* would look to Leonidas. But his gamble had paid off. The Council was unanimous in expecting Leonidas to dutifully play the role of the sacrificial lamb.

He supposed he ought to be honoured. Since the sons of Herakles had come to Laconia and set up their capital on the banks of the Eurotas, no Spartan king had left his body on a field of battle. For sixteen generations, Sparta's kings had ruled over a city-state that consolidated its rule first in Laconia, then conquered Messenia, established its pre-eminence throughout the Peloponnese, and was now the acknowledged leader of all freedom-loving Hellenes. Only the cowards, those who had paid tribute to the Persian emperor, did not acknowledge Sparta's primacy. Even the richest and most populous of Hellas' cities, mighty Athens, acceded to Sparta the right to lead in this desperate coalition against the Persian invaders.

To lead meant to set an example, and for twelve years Sparta had set an example of defiance to the Persians. But defiance was mere bravado and bluster unless it was backed by the willingness to sacrifice life itself. Cities whose citizens are not prepared to die for their freedom deserved slavery. Leonidas did not doubt that the majority of Sparta's citizens—and their wives—would prefer to die than surrender their freedom. And what was a Spartan king other than a leading citizen? What *good* was a Spartan king unwilling to make the ultimate sacrifice for the sake of his city?

If the Gods would spare Lacedaemon from sack and slavery at the cheap price of his own life, then so be it.

"All right, then," Leonidas agreed. "But let's not make it a futile sacrifice. Any defence on land that does not simultaneously prevent the Persian fleet from simply bypassing our position and landing troops in our rear is worthless. We have to fight north of the Isthmus, or we will lose Athens and her fleet. Since Tempe proved untenable, the next best position is Thermopylae, with the fleet at Artemision."

"You can't take a full call-up that far north! It would denude the city! What if the Athenians fail us and Persian fleet breaks through or outmanoeuvres them?" Leotychidas (who fancied himself an expert in naval affairs) protested.

"And there's Argos to consider. They're only waiting for the chance to strike. Argos and Achaea," Orthryades added.

"Especially if the Allies go north with you. Without Tegea to worry about, Argos and Achaea are sure to fall upon us," Talthybius agreed.

"It's at least a five or six days' march to Thermopylae! If you take the whole army that far north, it could never come back in an emergency. At least from the Isthmus we could be home in two days if we're needed here," Alcidas added.

"Who said anything about a full call-up?" Leonidas snapped back. "I'll hold Thermopylae with the Guard alone, if you want me to."

"No hubris, brother. We can spare you more than that," Leotychidas retorted flippantly.

"Two thousand hoplites," Leonidas countered, adding up in his mind what the Allies were likely to bring. He thought he could count on their old Peloponnesian allies for at least 3,000 troops and the newer allies, those whose homes were directly threatened, for about that again. 8,000 heavies ought to be enough to hold the pass at Thermopylae almost indefinitely.

"Of course." There was a general murmur of assent and the nodding of many grey heads around the Council chamber.

"Well then. You don't need me here any more. I'll get on with the business of our defence." Leonidas stood, and something strange happened. The ephor Technarchos came to his feet. Traditionally the ephors did not rise in the presence of the kings. They represented the Assembly, and to symbolise the equality between the kings and the Peers, they showed no deference to the monarchs. But Technarchos stood, and after only a moment's hesitation the other four ephors followed his lead, and then every member of the Council, ending with a somewhat disoriented Leotychidas, also got to his feet. Leonidas acknowledged the gesture with a nod of his head, and continued out of the Council chamber into the blinding light of a hot summer day.

The Council House was located directly on the agora and opposite the Ephorate. It was fronted by a broad, double colonnade and raised a half-dozen feet above the paving stones of the square. Leonidas paused in the shade of the colonnade, grateful for a light breeze that ran its fingers through his hair and fluttered the short sleeves and skirt of his chiton where it was not encased in airtight leather and bronze. The sun was high, almost directly overhead, and most of the merchants had closed up their stalls for a midday break. The helots from the surrounding countryside were packing their wagons and hitching up their mules to return home.

HELENA P. SCHRADER

Leonidas let his gaze sweep around the marketplace, mentally caressing each familiar landmark in a prelude to farewell. The statues to Apollo and Artemis marked the boundaries of the "dancing floor" where he, like every other Spartan youth, had in his time danced in honour of the Gods. There were the two ancient and (after seeing Athens) rather dowdy temples to the Market Zeus and Market Athena. Far more impressive was the temple that housed bones stolen from Tegea just fifteen Olympiads ago and allegedly belonging to Orestes. This was an impressive modern temple completely encircled by a colonnade in the Ionian fashion, but Leonidas' eye fell on the older sanctuary to the Fates beside it.

Was it fate or intrigue that had brought him to this juncture? And would his death really prevent this somewhat haphazard and amorphous—but fiercely beloved—city from being sacked and turned to ashes? Could he with his death really ensure that the acrid smoke of burning crops did not smear the air above the Eurotas? It hardly seemed credible.

Leonidas descended the steps from the Council House and made his way over the hot paving stones toward the tree-lined "Going Away" street that led northwards out of the city. At this time of day, the shutters on shops and houses were closed against the heat of the sun, offering rather grim exteriors. Spartan tradition and custom did not encourage the painting or decoration of houses. As a result, unlike other cities, the facades here were not brightly painted, but simply whitewashed. Nor were the door frames elaborately carved and decorated; they were made simply of tarred beams. Even the roofs here lacked the decorative tiles that in the wealthier cities of Hellas were increasingly used not just on temples but on private homes as well.

In recent years, Leonidas had travelled extensively; he had been in Corinth, Athens, Crete, and Alexandria. Leonidas knew that other Hellenes looked down on Sparta as little more than a rag-tag collection of villages. The very fact that there was no protective city wall was often used to suggest that Sparta was not a "proper" city at all. But to Leonidas, this very openness was much of Sparta's charm. Unlike other cities, in Sparta there was no stark contrast between the wide, paved public streets and the cramped jumble of back alleys. Although Sparta's paved streets were not monumentally wide, the back streets were hardly narrower. Because Sparta had no walls, it had room to expand. Rather than cramming houses closer and closer together, new houses were simply built on the fringe, stretching farther out into the broad plain around the city. And the houses behind their simple facades were spacious and well lit. Leonidas had been in homes of prominent citizens in other cities where the light of day hardly ever penetrated, but the houses he passed now had citrus, almond, and cypress trees reaching skywards over the walls—clear indications of the large, sunny courtyards and gardens that graced them.

He heard high-pitched voices behind him and the patter of feet. He glanced over his shoulder and stepped aside just in time to let a herd of little boys dash past him. They were barefoot, their heads shaved, and their chitons so ragged from constant wear that they seemed hardly to cover their nakedness. Their bodies were thin as only the bodies of fast-growing boys can be when they never got quite enough to eat. In other cities, the slaves dressed better, but nowhere did boys enjoy so much freedom and have so much say over their own lives.

Clearly two boys were contending for the lead and their fellows were chasing after them, shouting encouragement to their favourites. One of the boys noticed Leonidas before the others and abruptly tried to stop, causing his supporters to groan and curse and demand an explanation. But then the other boy also caught sight of Leonidas and tried to stop, too. Half the boys careened into one another, and one of the boys even fell over in the confusion.

"Father!" the first boy called out respectfully. "Is it true? There is an oracle from Delphi about the Persians?"

They were all looking up at him now, their chests still heaving from the exertion of running, sweat glistening on their thin limbs, but their big eyes fixed on him alertly. Leonidas estimated that they were no more than nine or ten years old. They were certainly still at an age when half the day was theirs to play with and when they were not yet learning how to wield even wooden swords and wicker shields. They were so young, he thought, that they would undoubtedly be spared the sword if the Persians came. Instead they would be herded off into slavery—some of them would undoubtedly be castrated for service as eunuchs or sold as prostitutes in the markets of Asia. If his death could really save them from such a fate, he wished he could give it a thousand times!

"There is an oracle," Leonidas confirmed, reluctant to share it with them.

"What does it say, father? Will our Allies fight, or will we have to fight the Persians alone?"

They unmanned him with that utter confidence in their own unshakeable defiance, and it took him a moment to answer. "It did not answer that particular question; but I am confident that our allies will stand by us, as we will be defending their freedom, too."

"But to defend Athens, we'll have to fight north of the Isthmus," one of the boys protested. It was one of the boys who had been leading the informal race.

"Are you the pack leader?" Leonidas addressed the boy.

He nodded, and dutifully introduced himself: "Leonymos, son of Gylippus, father."

"What would you rather, young Leonymos: to fight together with the Athenians, Boioteans, Thespians, and Plataeans north of the Isthmus—or to stand at the Isthmus with our Peloponnesian friends, while the Persians land ten times ten thousand men in the Gulf of Laconia and slaughter and burn their way up the valley of the Eurotas?"

Their eyes widened in astonishment. They had never thought of that.

"The Persians have a fleet—far greater than Athens or Corinth or Crete or all the Hellene cities together. They can carry more men than all the cities of the Peloponnese have together and land them anywhere they like. Without Athens and her fleet, we have no way to stop them."

"But will the Athenians *fight*, father?" another boy asked anxiously.

"They fought—and won—at Marathon."

"But will they fight under *your* command, father?"

How could even these little boys be so certain that the command was his? But there was no point questioning them on the point. They would have heard it from their fathers or older brothers, or the Peers in the syssitia where they served as mess boys. "There's only one way of finding out, isn't there? Now that's enough, boys." Leonidas cut the interrogation short. "Carry on."

They gazed at him, clearly still full of questions (and not a little excited to have him all to themselves for once), but the order had been too explicit. So they nodded and thanked him and started off at a trot. Then someone shouted a challenge and they broke into a mad dash again, apparently for the bridge.

Leondidas followed them at a more decorous pace. On the bridge across the Eurotas he stopped and took a deep breath. The river itself was at its weakest this time of year—a meandering, shallow stream upon a broad bed of sand. But from here he had a good view of the broad basin of fertile land that formed the heart of Lacedaemon. Straight ahead to the south and as far as the eye could see was the broad, rich plain of the Eurotas valley. Sparta, and beyond it Amyclae, backed up against the west bank of the river. Near at hand were a number of bathhouses with long piers leading to the deepest part of the river, and there were a number of boys jumping off the ends of these with loud, happy squeals he could hear even from this distance. Farther downriver there were tanneries, factories, and sawmills built hard upon or into the river itself. But beyond the town the barley fields stretched into the hazy distance. It was enough, even without Messenia, to ensure that no one in Lacedaemon went hungry.

Behind him, to the north, the valley narrowed rapidly between the foothills of the Taygetos and the Parnon ranges. The lower slopes of these steep hills were covered with olive and almond orchards, while the upper slopes were dotted with grazing sheep and goats. To the west, beyond the acropolis and city of Sparta, the Taygetos range reared up majestic and haughty, rising rapidly to 8,000-foot peaks. To the east, just beyond the river, were the drill fields at the foot of the comparatively moderate slopes of the Parnon range. Here the vineyards gradually ascended toward these mountains, lost in purple haze.

Leonidas brought his eyes back to the drill fields. These were being used at the moment by youths of the agoge. Nearby was one of the younger cohorts of the upper classes, identifiable by the fact that they were using wooden weapons and were still very inept at manoeuvres. In fact, they could hardly keep their lines and files straight when they advanced, much less perform any reverses or turns. There was nothing shameful in that. There was only one way to learn, and that was drill, drill, and more drill. It was odd the way foreigners seemed to imagine the Spartans were uniquely made for war, when in fact, one on one, they were no better than other men. It was only practise that made them good soldiers—hard, gruelling, boring, unrelenting drill. How he had hated it most of his life!

Leonidas left the bridge, heading toward the drill fields. He had barely started along the road between the fields and the river, heading for the oldest of all Sparta's sanctuaries, the Meneleon, when the eirene in charge of the boys on the drill field recognised him. With a shout, he called to his charges to halt and come to attention. The youths drew themselves into a semblance of order. Leonidas halted and waited. The eirene came and presented arms in front of him respectfully. "Sir!"

"Oh, it's you, Simonidas." Leonidas recognised him with a smile.

"Would you do us the honour of reviewing us, sir?" the eirene asked.

"If you want," Leonidas agreed. With Simonidas a respectful pace behind him, he walked along the line of youths standing at attention. They were a skinny, bony, dirty lot, and with their shaved heads they looked very young. They were at an awkward age, really—rebellious, sullen, overconfident, impudent. The Persians might decide either to kill them as potential troublemakers or to enslave them in some capacity where they could be best controlled—the galleys and mines sprang to mind. Leonidas again told himself that if his death could spare them such a fate, he would die smiling.

"How old are your charges, Simonides?" he asked the eirene.

"Fourteen, sir."

That made them only two years older than his own son. He held his breath for a second as, with a sharp stab of regret, he realised that Pleistarchos would never stand here like this. He would not be given the chance. He would be king before the year was out, and they would yank him out of the agoge after that.

The thought made Leonidas' throat dry as he, out of respect for the youths, pointed out every one of their faults, one after another.

There were many, and not one of the youths escaped unscathed. Then he nodded to Simonidas, and continued on his way.

The Meneleon stood on a steep hill that loomed up quite abruptly from the floodplain of the Eurotas like an advance sentry of the Parnos range. It was built in honour of the Mycenaean king made famous by the *Iliad*, and was said to stand on the foundations of his palace. Certainly there were ancient graves in the area. Leonidas felt certain that, whether or not this had been the exact site of Menelaus' palace, it had been part of the Achaean city of Sparta. Leonidas leaned forward into his stride to make it up the steep road to the ancient sanctuary. Half way up the road he realised he had come without any kind of offering, and faltered. But then he remembered that *he* was the sacrifice, and there was no need for any surrogate at this stage.

The temple was very ancient, with no windows, only the entrance fronted by two columns. It seemed dark as Hades after the bright glare of the sun. Leonidas paused for his vision to adjust, and his ears registered before his eyes that someone else was also here.

"The news must be bad," a voice said from the darkness.

"Gorgo?" He couldn't quite believe it—and then again, he did. It was his wife. She was, as always, one step ahead of him.

She had been sitting on a bench. Now she rose and came towards him. She walked with the surefooted self-assurance that had scandalized all of Athens when he took her there a few years back. Gorgo had never been deemed a beauty. Her mouth was too wide, her jaw too prominent, and her hair too red. Now she was 33 and there were smile lines running from her nostrils to the corners of her mouth, crows' feet around her eyes, and a certain sagging about her neck. But she had bright, well-spaced eyes that met his now, knowing as much as asking.

Leonidas opened his arms and she walked into them. That was all. He held her. After a long time he answered her question. "No. The news was not bad. Lacedaemon can—and will—be spared. We will not suffer the fate of Troy."

"At what price?"

"Blood."

"You don't have to be a seer to know that!" Gorgo retorted with a short flash of annoyance. She pulled back from him to look him in the face again. She was almost as tall as he. Their eyes met and she understood. "You mean *your* blood."

"Yes."

She stared at him mutely.

He felt obliged to explain. "I can't remember the exact wording, but the gist of it was that either Sparta would lose a king in battle or the city itself would fall."

"In that case, Leotychidas would do just as well." Her tone was endearingly tart.

Leonidas pulled her back into his arms. She tried to resist, angry with him; but he was stronger, and she did not want to be angry with him. The thought that she would soon lose him made her stop struggling and cling to him instead.

As soon as she had surrendered, Leonidas lifted one hand and shoved back her veil so he could run his fingers through her thick, tangled hair. Then he bent and kissed her on the lips. They were trembling from the effort not to cry.

"It had to be me, Beloved, because I am superfluous. I always have been—from the very day I was born the younger twin to a father with two wives and two near-grown heirs. My whole life, if you like, has been nothing but marking time in order to be ready to fulfil this destiny of losing it."

CHAPTER 1

THE FIRST SEVEN YEARS LEONIDAS RARELY saw either of his parents. In fact, when he was still a toddler it had surprised him to learn that the exalted personages who occasionally swept in and out of his life, surrounded by an elaborate entourage, had anything particular to do with him. He and his twin brother Cleombrotus were fed, clothed, washed, and disciplined by their respective nannies, Dido and Polyxo. These were buxom, sturdy girls with black hair and eyes, and apparently sisters.

Polyxo and Dido competed as fiercely as mothers with regard to their charges, each claiming to have the finest boy. Polyxo had all the obvious advantages, because Cleombrotus weighed a pound more than Leonidas at birth and he grew faster. By the time the twins were two, Cleombrotus could knock Leonidas over with relative ease—which he frequently did. Dido, however, insisted that her little charge was nevertheless the better of the brothers because while Cleombrotus had brute force, Leonidas had tenacity and cunning. He might get knocked down, but he did not let that defeat him. Quite the contrary, he would at once seek to drag his brother down on top of him. He did not always succeed; but like a good hunting dog, once he had hold of his prey he could not be shaken off easily.

Polyxo and Dido had once rushed after the sound of high-pitched screaming to find Cleombrotus trying to run down a long flight of stairs to escape Leonidas. But Leonidas clung to his leg so fiercely that he tripped his brother. They both fell all the way down the marble stairs, Leonidas still clinging grimly to Cleombrotus' leg, to land at the scandalized feet of their mother, Taygete.

Taygete was a regal personage. She was tall and slender, and despite her 50 years of age, she was as straight as a battle spear. Her hair, pulled back behind a diadem of ivory, was the colour of iron. And so were her eyes. Leonidas never forgot the way she levelled those merciless grey eyes on him and then lifted her head to demand in an icy voice of Polyxo and Dido: "What in the name of the Dioscuri is going on here? Are these not princes of the Agiad house? I will not have them rolling about in the dirt like helot brats. If you cannot raise your charges in a befitting manner, I will find better nurses for them. The likes of you can be found in any marketplace of any perioikoi town all across Lacedaemon!"

The girls were terrified—and so was Leonidas. He staggered to his feet, bruised and bleeding, and tried to grab hold of Dido. His mother reached out and yanked him free of the nurse with a single gesture. Taygete's hands and arms were as hard as her eyes. She had trained at the bow and javelin all her life. Leonidas went flying halfway across the hall to land with an audible thump. Dido gasped in sympathy but did not dare move.

"Have I made myself clear?" Taygete asked the terrified helot girls.

"Yes, ma'am," they answered in unison.

Taygete turned on her heel and departed, her magnificent purple silk peplos billowing out behind her.

Dido came and collected Leonidas into her arms. She was weeping, and he soon found himself comforting her, rather than the other way around. It was then that she tried to explain things to him.

Taygete, his mother, was the neice and wife of King Anaxandridas, Leonidas' father. She had been barren for many years after her marriage, and she reached the age of 30 without her womb quickening once. By then King Anaxandridas was in his mid-forties and the ephors and Council of Elders became increasingly concerned. They searched the heavens for a sign, and the stars said that the Agiad King must marry another woman or the Agiad house would die out. So the ephors had demanded that King Anaxandridas put aside his barren wife and take a new bride.

"Your father," Dido explained, "being very fond of your mother, flatly refused to do so. He called the suggestion improper and pointed out that his wife was without blame. After much thought and discussion, the ephors and the Council of Elders agreed that the stars had advised only that King Anaxandridas need marry *another* woman, not that he must divorce his current wife. They decided to make an exception to the law to allow him to take a *second* wife. Although your father at first resisted this suggestion, after some time he gave in and submitted to the will of the Council and ephors. The ephors then selected a maiden descended directly from the wise Chilon himself. (When you get older and go to the agoge, you'll hear all about him.) And to your mother's great dismay, your father not only married her, but bedded her as well.

"In fact, within a very short period of time, your father's second wife, who is called Chilonis after her famous ancestor, became pregnant. One year after your father had taken her to wife, she produced a son, your half-brother Cleomenes." Leonidas thought: oh, no, not *another* brother!

Dido continued with the story, "but no sooner had Cleomenes been presented to the ephors and found sound and healthy, than your mother found herself pregnant, although she was nearer to 40 than 30 by this time. There were many people who did not believe her. They thought she was making it all up and would try to deceive the people by putting another woman's child into her bed and presenting it as her own. So the ephors insisted on being present at the birth – right in the birthing chamber!

"But perhaps it was a good thing after all, because the ephors saw for themselves that there was no deceit, and your mother had indeed produced a fine son. In fact, she presented them with a bigger and healthier son than the boy of the other wife."

"What about me?" Leonidas asked, hurt and distressed that even his own Dido would speak only of his bigger, stronger brother.

"Oh, this was more than ten years before you and Cleombrotus were born!" Dido explained with a little laugh and a hug. "I was speaking of your brother Dorieus."

Yet *another* brother! Leonidas thought in despair.

"After that, your mother felt she had been vindicated of all blame in the affair, and no one ever expected to her to have another child, but ten years after Dorieus was born, she became pregnant again. And at the end of her time, you and Cleombrotus came into the world."

"Why don't I ever see my other brothers?" Leonidas asked, rather hoping that they lived on the far side of the Taygetos, or beyond the Pillars of Herakles, or anywhere where he would never have to encounter them. Cleombrotus was trouble enough.

"Dorieus is already in the agoge, but he visits his parents on holidays. Cleomenes lives in his mother's household on the far side of the Eurotas. Your mother will not let him or his mother cross the threshold of this house. When your father wishes to see them, he must go to them."

———

At age seven, Cleombrotus and Leonidas were enrolled in the agoge. Dido had warned him this would happen, and she had always looked sad when she told him, but she hadn't been able to tell him very much about it. She was a helot, after all, and no one in her family had ever been allowed to go to the agoge. Nor could Leonidas' father tell him much – if he had dared ask him - because the heir apparent to the throne was exempt from attending the agoge and so King Anaxandridas had never gone. As for Dorieus, he didn't waste time talking to his youngest brothers, so neither of the twins had any idea what to expect except that it meant leaving home and living in the agoge barracks with other boys their age.

One day just after the winter solstice, their father came for them dressed in his armour and scarlet cloak. He was already a great age by then, much more than three score. He had white hair that he wore braided in the Spartan fashion, but it was so thin that his plaits were tiny little strings, and his scalp was almost completely bare. The skin of his scalp was flecked with brown. He could no longer stand upright; the weight of his breastplate appeared to be too great for his shoulders and dragged him forward. He kept himself partially upright by using a T-shaped walking stick that he propped under his right armpit.

Without a word he signalled his twin sons, who had been told to be ready for him, and with one on either side of him he walked out of the palace. At once they were caught in the cold wind that blew down off the Taygetos. Leonidas clutched his himation tighter around him, but his father shook his head. "Better get used to the cold, boy. You'll not be allowed to keep such a thick himation in the agoge."

Leonidas gazed up at the old man, who he knew was his father but who was still a stranger to him, and started to become alarmed.

The king led his sons to an imposing building standing directly on the Agora, opposite the dancing floor and at right angles to the Council House and the Ephorate. Although given the same prominence as these buildings, it lacked the lovely colonnade and elegant portico of the government buildings. Instead, the entrance was supported by three ancient Kouros. All had once been painted but were now naked stone, except for some remnants of colour in the curls of their hair. Boys of various ages with shaved heads and rough, black himations came and went in groups. Leonidas noticed that despite the snow lying in the shadows, the boys were all barefoot. This was going to be terrible, he registered.

They entered an office. An elderly man in Spartan scarlet sat behind a desk. Several middle-aged men stood about discussing things earnestly. At the sight of King Anaxandridas, the others fell silent, and the elderly man behind the desk got to his feet respectfully.

"Here they are," the king announced simply. "My youngest boys."

All eyes were drawn to the two boys, whom Anaxandridas now pushed forward.

"You'd never know they were twins!" one of the men exclaimed.

Hardly a brilliant observation, Leonidas thought. Brotus was dark-haired and dark-eyed, with a stubborn set to his jaw and a compact body that—as one of the men immediately observed—made him look a good year older than his twin. Leondias was not blond, just brown, but he was much lighter in colour than his brother and his eyes were hazel. He was also ten pounds lighter and two inches shorter than Cleombrotus.

"Who's this fine fellow here?" They all focused on Brotus.

"Cleombrotus," the king said.

"Then this is Leonidas." The oldest of the men walked around his desk and stepped closer to look intently at Leonidas. Leonidas wanted to step back, but he felt his father's hand on his shoulder. In a vice-like grip it held him in place. Leonidas stared rather terrified up into the headmaster's face, but Leonidas decided that whatever the man thought of him (and he did not say), he did not seem hostile.

The king took his leave. It was the last time Leonidas ever saw him up close. A little more than a year later he was dead.

The two boys were left in the cold room, surrounded by strangers.

"I think we best separate them, sir, at least at first." one of the younger men suggested. "Twins have a tendency to be dependent on one another."

The Paidonomos, or headmaster, nodded. He looked from one boy to the other, evidently considering something, and then nodded. "Put Cleombrotus in Herripidas' and Leonidas in Gitiades' unit."

Leonidas was taken out of the administrative building and down the street to an even less assuming building. Here he was taken along a long corridor to a simple room furnished with what looked liked shelves running around the perimeter at knee and shoulder height—except there were ladders leading up to the upper shelves. There were wicker bins or baskets under the lower shelves. Already there were a half dozen other boys his own age in the room. All looked as bewildered and uncertain as he felt. There was also a young man there. He was tall and well formed, but not a citizen yet because he wore a black rather than a scarlet cloak. Also, his face and head were shaven. Leonidas knew enough about the agoge to know this young man must be one of the so-called eirenes. The eirenes were 20-year-olds who had just graduated from the agoge themselves. They were required to spend one year as a unit leader of younger boys before being enrolled in the ranks of the citizens and army at age 21.

The man escorting Leonidas addressed this eirene: "Gitiades, here's another one for you: Leonidas, son of Anaxandridas."

"King Anaxandridas?"

"That's right."

That made the other boys look over and stare. The older man was gone, and Gitiades addressed Leonidas. "You're nothing special here. Remember that. Just one of the herd. And you can get out of those fancy clothes—all of you!" he ordered his charges collectively. "Put them in that bin over there." He pointed. Shyly the seven-year-olds took off the chitons and himations lovingly made by mothers, aunts, and sisters, and put them into the indicated basket. The room was unheated and it was cold standing around naked, but Gitiades seemed unconcerned. "Line up over there." The boys did as they were told, while yet another couple of boys arrived and were ordered to strip as well.

Gitiades arranged the boys in order of height. Leonidas was second from the last. "Remember your place! Whenever I ask you to line up, do it in this order. Later, your position in rank and file will be based on which of you deserves praise and which of you deserves humiliation. That!" he pointed—"the outer right-hand wing—is the place of honour. It is the position of officers, because the man who stands there has only his own sword to protect him. That—the outer left-hand wing—is the place of disgrace. The man there is sheltered behind the shield of all his comrades; it is therefore the coward's or bungler's post."

Leonidas thought that simplified things somewhat. Everyone knew that the enemy might come from any direction. In an instant the army might have to about face, and suddenly the man on the outer right found himself on the outer left and vice versa. But Gitiades was obviously not going to accept any objections, certainly not from the boy second from the left-hand post of "disgrace".

Gitiades next handed each boy a couple of unbleached chitons from a stack on a nearby shelf. Leonidas had never felt such rough wool in his life. It felt as if it were half hemp. The boys were told to put one of these on, which they gladly did because of the cold. Only the cloth scratched the skin so that Leonidas wasn't sure it was an improvement. Gitiades next handed out himations of dirty brown, natural wool, just one a piece this time. The weave of these garments was so loose that the cold seemed to come right through them. Leonidas sighed inwardly, knowing that these were to be his only clothes for a full year – only to be replaced next year by a new set of identical clothes. Not until he graduated from "little boy" to youth at age 14 would he get a better chiton and a black cloak, along with his first set of leather training armour. At 17, after enduring the test of Artemis Orthia, he would at last be given real weapons and armour, and the clothes that went with them. At 19, as a meleirene, he would be issued real hoplite clothes and equipment, only in black rather than scarlet, and rather than attending classes would serve the army as messenger, watch-keeper and the like. At 20 he would become an eirene like Gitiades, and finally be allowed shoes again. Only when he attained his citizenship at age 21 and went on active duty with the army would he at last be given Spartan scarlet for his battle chiton and himation and be free to wear whatever he liked off duty. Fourteen years seemed an interminable period to Leonidas: it was twice as long as he had lived already.

The next thing that happened was even more unpleasant. One after another, the boys had their hair shaved off. Long hair was the mark and privilege of full citizens, the men over 31. That was the age at which men at last went off active duty and into the reserves, and therefore also became eligible for public office. The men on active service were allowed to grow their hair only as long as the back of their helmet. The boys of the agoge went shaved, while the eirenes— in accordance with their transitional status—were in the process of growing out their hair after 14 years of going about shaved.

By now there were eleven of them in the little group. Gitiades had them line up again, and assigned them each a bunk. The taller boys got the upper bunks, and Leonidas had a lower bunk near the back door that, by the smell of things, led to the latrines. Clearly this was another post of relative disgrace. They were informed that at the next new moon from this day they would be allowed to elect their own "herd leader", after which they would be given the mornings from breakfast to lunch free to fend for themselves "productively" (whatever that meant). Until then, Gitiades announced, he was going to introduce them to their new environment, from the sports and running fields, to the classrooms and the syssitia, where they would serve as mess-boys.

———

By the end of his first month in the agoge, Leonidas knew that he was going to survive. Unlike some of the other boys, he had not been terribly spoilt at home. Dido had lavished as much love on him as she could, but her authority had been very circumscribed. Furthermore, Brotus had always cast a large shadow, filling each day with uncertainty. At the agoge, Leonidas faced no similar bully.

The elected herd leader, Ephorus, was a bit of a show-off, faster than the rest of them and confident of his superiority. He took a certain pride in pointing out to Leonidas that he was faster and stronger than a "son of Herakles", but he didn't actually hurt Leonidas as Brotus frequently had done. At worst, he gave him a shove or shouted something like, "Eat my dust, son of Herakles!" Leonidas shrugged it off.

As for the other boys, they were mostly just as unsure of themselves as he was. The bulk of them followed Ephorus' lead and tried to win Gitiades' approval by fawning on him a bit. One of the boys, Prokles, seemed a bit stand-offish and almost rebellious, refusing to pander to Gitiades' every whim and sometimes challenging Ephorus. Timon, the only boy shorter than Leonidas, distinguished himself by being rather sullen and aggressive, apparently determined to get out of his position of "disgrace". But he really didn't have much to worry about, because it soon became evident that Alkander was destined to be the herd dunce.

Alkander was taller than Leonidas, but he seemed strangely uncoordinated. He tripped frequently and knocked things over. He even had a slight stutter, which the others mercilessly mocked. This had the effect of making him speak less and less often—and when he did speak, the stutter was worse than ever. Initially, Leonidas was glad that there was someone worse than he, who consistently landed in the position of "disgrace", but after a while he found himself just feeling sorry for Alkander.

By then, of course, his brothers had found out that he, unlike Brotus, had not been elected herd leader. When Brotus saw Leonidas following around behind another boy, he'd charged over and throttled him for "disgracing the Agiads". As this was pretty much what Leonidas had expected from Brotus, he wasn't terribly upset by it. What came as a complete surprise was that his entire herd took this as an insult to *them*. Ephorus roared to the attack, knocking Brotus down, and soon it was a full-scale free-for-all between the two herds. The brawling seven-year-olds attracted a crowd, with older age-

cohorts from the agoge and even citizens standing about shouting
encouragement. It ended pretty much in a draw, with every one of
them bleeding someplace or other and their chitons very much the
worse for the "engagement". But there wasn't one who didn't feel very
proud of himself. Leonidas had never felt so happy in his life. He was
no longer alone in the world; he had comrades.

Dorieus took a different tack, and it was far more humiliating.
Leonidas had seen little of Dorieus over the years. Although Dorieus
always returned to the palace during the frequent holidays, he was so
much a favourite with their mother Taygete that she never wanted her
younger boys around when Dorieus was there. As a result, Leonidas
had seen his oldest brother only at a distance, or for brief encounters
of no substance in the corridors or courtyards of the palace. It came as
a horrible shock to have Dorieus stop him in the middle of the agora
in full view of citizens, matrons, and even perioikoi and helots.

Leonidas and his herd had been lurking around the stalls of the
agora, hoping for handouts to supplement the boring diet of the
agoge. Meals at school were, in Leonidas' opinion, dismal, and the
portions skimpy. At the agora there were almost always some helots
with kindly hearts who weren't above giving boys bruised fruit, burnt
crusts, or other less marketable wares. Leonidas had his eye on a meat
pasty that had fallen off the counter of a pastry stall and been pecked
at by some sparrows. He was sure the vendor wouldn't sell it to a real
customer, and if he could just—

"Leonidas, son of Anaxandridas, is that you?" Dorieus called out
in loud voice that turned everyone's head.

A seven-year-old Spartan boy is at the very bottom rung in the
long ladder that ended with the men over sixty. They are required to
show "respect" for every other Spartiate, male or female, who is older
than they. (Children under the age of seven were still "infants" and
not expected to know their manners yet, so they were exempt from
duty and discipline.) What this meant, among other things, was that
the younger boys had to give way to their elders in the streets, to
stand up for their elders if they were sitting, and to give up their seats
to them if requested. They were also strictly admonished to hold their
tongue in the presence of their elders unless directly spoken to. In
the latter case, however, they were required to address adult females

with "ma'am" and adult males of active-service age with "sir," and all men old enough for the reserves with "father." Unfortunately, since anyone of an older age-cohort and especially the eirenes or citizens had a "responsibility" for training the boys and youth in the agoge, they also had a right to stop and question any boy.

At the sound of his name, Leonidas jumped guiltily and turned around to face his older brother.

Dorieus was beautiful. In fact, he seemed to embody manly beauty in the abstract, as if he were a direct throwback to Herakles himself. He was tall for his age. His shoulders were as broad as a grown man's. His arms and legs were a melody of entwined muscle. His belly was flat and hard as if it were made of bronze. He was now an awesome 18 years of age, and so Leonidas had to stand with his hands at his sides and his eyes at his feet and call him "sir". "Yes, sir," he said dutifully.

Dorieus came to stand directly before him. His head was shaved, too, of course, but he was wearing training armour, carried a shield slung on his back, and a real sword hung from his baldric—something Leonidas couldn't even dream about for another ten years.

"Is it true what I hear? That you were not elected herd leader?" Dorieus had been herd leader of his unit ever since he had been enrolled in the agoge. He had won the contest of Artemis Orthia at 16. He had innumerable prizes for running, wrestling, javelin, and discus. Dorieus was quite simply the most splendid of all the young men still in the agoge—not excepting even those youths in the age-cohorts ahead of him.

"Yes, sir," Leonidas answered the question.

"And why not?"

"Ask the others, sir. They were the ones who voted." Even as he answered, Leonidas stiffened his stomach muscles and braced for the blow Brotus would have given him for such an impudent retort.

Dorieus was made of different stuff. "That was a very facile answer, boy, and you know it. Try again."

"Ephorus is faster and stronger than I am, sir."

"Then why aren't you in the gymnasium improving your strength rather than loitering around the agora looking for handouts like a mongrel dog?"

Everyone in the whole agora (it seemed like the whole city to Leonidas) was listening to them.

"Because, sir, if I get that meat pasty over there, I will have far more strength than if I try to exercise in the gym when I'm half starved to death."

The pastry vendor laughed outright, but Dorieus was unimpressed. "You are either a fool or you are trying to provoke me. The leanest dogs run fastest, and the hungriest lion makes the kill."

"How do you know that the hungriest lion makes the kill, sir? Have you talked to one?"

"Now I know you are just trying to provoke me, little brother, but I won't play your silly game. You disgrace our house and our mother, just as Brotus told me you did." Dorieus turned on his heel and departed, everyone in the agora making way for him as if before a reigning king. Leonidas stood in his wake, feeling very small and silly and worthless.

Someone jostled his arm. He looked over alarmed, but it was only the pasty vendor. "Here you go, lad." He offered him one of the good pasties—not the one picked at by the birds. "Eat up and enjoy it. Don't let that pompous ass get you down."

The vendor was a helot, of course. Leonidas knew that his brother would be appalled if he turned around and saw what Leonidas did next, but he didn't care. He took the pastry and smiled up at the vendor. "Thank you! I won't forget this. When I grow up and have money, I'll buy only from you!"

The vendor laughed. His front teeth were missing. "Is that a promise, little Leonidas? Will you make me a purveyor of the Agiad royal house one day?"

"Well, I can't do *that*," Leonidas admitted with evident regret. "I'm never going to be king. But I'll buy all my own pasties from you," Leonidas assured him solemnly. He *was* serious, even though the helot seemed to think this was all an enormous joke.

By the time the third of his brothers, Cleomenes, took notice of his failure to win election from the other seven-year-olds in his "herd", Leonidas was rather tired of the whole thing. Besides, he had been raised to look down on this half-brother as something distinctly "inferior" and "distasteful". Cleomenes was King Anaxandridas' son by "that other woman". Although the ephors had made a great show of setting aside Spartan marriage law and allowing King Anaxandridas to take a second wife, Leonidas had been raised in his mother's household, and she insisted that the ephors ("nothing but a rude coterie of jumped-up royal servants") had no such authority. How could five ordinary citizens (who were not even priests and without the sanction of Delphi!) simply set aside Spartan law? This question, when asked indignantly by the Agiad queen, was clearly rhetorical, and Leonidas had never heard anyone dare to answer her. Even his father, on the one occasion when Leonidas happened to hear her raise this beloved topic in his presence, had only shrugged. The ageing king had been too weary to fight with his queen over this bitter issue.

If the ephors had no right to set Spartan law aside, then "that other woman" was *not* King Anaxandridas' wife, but his concubine. Ergo, the child this concubine bore was a bastard—pure and simple. Taygete never referred to Cleomenes by any other term than "that bastard" —although the adjectives used to describe "the bastard" varied over time.

At first, on the basis of helot rumours, Taygete had been led to believe that Cleomenes was "sickly" and so he had been "that feeble bastard." Then it was rumoured that he was rather wild and self-willed, so she called him that "unruly bastard." When as a little boy of about 10 it was reported in the City that he had been caught telling some minor lie or other, he became "that deceitful bastard." And because, as the heir apparent to the Agiad throne, he was exempt from flogging, she called him "that cowardly bastard" – although obviously Cleomenes had no choice in the matter. Following an incident in which he allegedly showed disrespect for the Gods in one way or another, he became "that impious bastard". So it was this "feeble, unruly, deceitful, cowardly and impious bastard" that confronted Leonidas just outside the monument to Lycurgus one fine early-summer morning of Leonidas' first year in the agoge.

Leonidas like most of his fellow "little boys" did their best to avoid interrogations from their elders about what they had (or had not) learned so far by avoiding their elders altogether. At the sight of someone older, most boys tried to dart out of the way without being noticed. Leonidas was no exception. Unfortunately, just when he thought he'd made his escape, a mocking voice called after him: "Well if it isn't my littlest brother Leonidas! Trying to run away like a coward too. Come here, boy!"

With an inward sigh, Leonidas stopped, turned around, and, when he stood a yard away from his tormentor, dutifully stopped and faced him. "Sir?"

Cleomenes was a year older than Dorieus and hence 19 years old and should have been a so-called meleirene. But Cleomenes, as the heir-apparent to the Agiad throne, was exempted from the agoge. He therefore did not wear his hair shaved, nor was he barefoot. He was dressed in a simple but fine chiton, probably of angora wool. Although Leonidas was supposed to keep his eyes down, he couldn't resist one glance at the face of this feeble-unruly-deceitful-impious coward. To his embarrassment, he met his brother's eyes, which were examining him with discomfiting intensity.

Cleomenes could not be called beautiful by any means. He did not have Dorieus' even features or his broad shoulders and muscular arms and legs. He was tanned and by no means fat, but there was nevertheless a softness about him. Furthermore, his shoulders were narrow and his joints all seemed too large for his limbs, suggesting that his muscles were underdeveloped. His face, too, was somehow misshapen without being actually deformed. He had his father's too-large nose, his teeth were too prominent, and his eyes set too close together.

But these eyes were very sharp, and they seemed to miss nothing as they drilled into Leonidas. "So you're the runt of the family, are you?"

Leonidas viewed this as a rhetorical question and said nothing, but Cleomenes snapped his fingers. "I asked you a question, boy."

"Yes, sir."

"Yes, sir, what?"

"I'm the runt of the family, sir."

"Couldn't even get elected herd leader, I heard."

"No, sir."

"I like that." Cleomenes answered with a smile that was anything but friendly. "At least you won't have any populist delusions like your elder brother."

Leonidas wasn't sure what he was talking about and held his tongue. Cleomenes' eyes narrowed. "I must say one thing for you, however. You don't look as dumb as your brothers." He paused as if expecting Leonidas to protest, but Leonidas had no intention of making that mistake. So Cleomenes continued with a mixture of provocation and satisfaction. "You're not so dumb, are you, little Leonidas?"

Although this too seemed rhetorical, Leonidas did not want to risk another rebuke and answered dutifully, "I wouldn't know, sir."

"If you are half as clever as you look, you'll remember one thing: you are the product of incest, the product of a boneheaded sire cross-bred with a dim-witted dam. I, in contrast, am descended through *my* mother from Chilon the Wise, honoured throughout the civilized world for his intelligence. You won't outwit me, little Leonidas."

Leonidas shook his head dutifully, noting that the "feeble-unruly-deceitful-impious-cowardly bastard" clearly had a lot of unpleasant titles for his half-brothers as well.

———

But by far the worst consequence of not getting elected herd leader was his reception at home on the first holiday thereafter. Except on those festivals where the age-cohorts of the agoge were involved directly in rituals (the Hyacinthia, the Gymnopaedia, Artemis Orthia, and the like), the children of the agoge were sent home during the holidays. Although Leonidas had come to enjoy the agoge more than he had expected, still he looked forward to going home that first holiday. He looked forward to as much food as he could eat, to honey and raisin cakes, to sleeping as late as he wanted, to taking a proper bath in the heated palace bathhouse, and most of all, to telling all his adventures to Dido.

It did not surprise him that his arrival aroused little attention. Dorieus was already home and with the king and queen. The king was ill, and both Brotus and Leonidas were told they would be sent for when he wanted to see them. (He never did.) Brotus went straight to the kitchens, while Leonidas went in search of Dido. He couldn't find her. Finally he asked someone.

"Dido?" they answered as if they had never heard of her.

"My nurse," Leonidas insisted, frowning with frustration.

"But she was sent home as soon as you went into the agoge," the astonished servant answered.

"Home?"

"Back to her family."

"But where is that?"

"Good heavens, how should I know? I think she came from Boiai, or was it Kotyrta? I really don't know."

Boiai and Kotyrta were perioikoi towns out on the Malea peninsula—farther than Leonidas could ever get on his own.

Without Dido, the palace was empty. More than that: it was hostile. Because of his father's illness, everyone tiptoed about and talked in whispers. Leonidas had the feeling that whenever he tried to do anything, someone hissed at him to be quiet. His mother and Dorieus were almost always closeted together, apparently in earnest discussions about something. Brotus, fortunately, considered it beneath his dignity to harass Leonidas, and generally ran off and joined his friends. Leonidas hardly knew what to do with himself and hung about listless and bored, wishing for the holiday to end.

And end it did, but not before he had attracted the attention of his mother. Coming upon him sailing twig-and-leaf triremes in the central fountain of the "diplomatic" peristyle, she paused just long enough to remark to Dorieus: "It's no wonder really that that boy was not elected herd-leader like Brotus. Brotus is a natural leader – big and vigorous and strong-willied. But Leonidas has always been weak and backward. Sometimes, I wonder that the Elders let him live at all, don't you? He's completely superfluous."

CHAPTER 2

Ages 8 and 9

As seven-year-olds, the boys of the agoge had been eased into the routine of the agoge. They had been taught the rules and restrictions on the use of public facilities, from the baths and gymnasiums to the sports fields and running tracks. They had learned to form ranks and files and to stand at attention. They had been taught how to greet and respond to their elders. They had been tested in basic literacy, and those who were behind the others had been taught their letters. Likewise, all the boys were required to swim, and those who could not were taught how. They had also been taught by the cooks of the various syssitia how to set tables and clear them away, how to serve wine and water, and they had been taught the rules of conversation in preparation for serving as mess-boys. They had been given free run inside the city during the morning, and taken on hikes to the surrounding countryside in the afternoon. But real lessons did not start until the next year, when the boys turned eight.

At age eight the boys of the agoge started to learn the duties of citizenship. This meant that, first and foremost, they started to learn by heart the laws and constitution of Lacedaemon. The laws and constitution were viewed as the most fundamental part of Spartan education and society. The boys of the agoge not only learned to recite the laws, but were expected to discuss their purpose, virtue, and effectiveness.

Almost of equal importance, at age eight the boys were formed into a chorus and started to learn the songs of Sparta's famous poets, particularly Terpander, Tyrtaios, and Alkman. The entire age-cohort was brought together into one chorus for this purpose and for once, one's position was not determined by overall prowess, but purely by musical ability. The singing masters were very strict, however. They carried canes, and they were quick to use them if the boys were inattentive or sang off key. Although Leonidas' voice was at best average, he was lucky to have a good ear for a melody. He found singing easy and pleasurable—and it rather pleased him that Brotus was absolutely useless at it. Brotus just couldn't hear the differences in pitch, and almost always sang flat. While Leonidas secretly rejoiced in this fact, he felt badly that poor Alkander also proved inept at singing, in this case due to his stutter. It seemed so unfair that he could not excel even at this skill that required no physical strength or agility. Alkander usually left chorus with welts on the back of his shaved head from the chorus-master's cane.

Another subject that Leonidas loved was botany. Now when they took their hikes outside of the city, they were taught to identify the plants they saw. They were taught which plants were poisonous; which could be used to ease pain or bleeding, to close or loosen the bowels, to help sleep or keep sleep at bay; and much, much more. At the same time they were introduced to the fundamentals of tracking. Trapping was on the agenda for the next year, and they would start hunting when they were ten. But this was the beginning.

At sports, wrestling and javelin was added to the programme along with the running, jumping, swimming and rope climbing they had had the previous year. They would not be given bows until they were nine, discus the year after, and would start boxing at ten. But Leonidas soon excelled in wrestling; after all, he'd been doing it with Brotus for as long as he could remember. He rapidly demonstrated to his trainers that he could master larger and heavier opponents, and it was clear that with proper training he would be a very good wrestler indeed. For the first time in his life, Leonidas found himself the object of widespread praise and applause, and his status in his unit improved correspondingly.

Not that he was elected leader. Ephorus still held that honour, and with right. Quite aside from still being the fastest of them and excellent at javelin, he was a quick learner, had a beautiful voice, and everyone young and old liked him. Leonidas remained inwardly indebted to him for taking his side in his fight with Brotus.

However, the best thing about turning eight, as far as Leonidas was concerned, was that the boys were now allowed out of the kitchen and into the dining room of the syssitia. Throughout the previous year they had worked in the hot, steamy kitchens just making up the tables, clearing them, and washing up; now at last they were allowed to actually serve the Peers at dinner. This was the first opportunity they had to learn at first hand about this fundamental institution of Spartan citizenship.

Lycurgus' laws required that all citizens belong to a syssitia, or dining club. Each citizen chose the syssitia to which he wished to apply, but all the existing members had to agree by secret ballot before an applicant was accepted. Each citizen was then required to eat dinner at the syssitia into which he was accepted every evening for the rest of his life—unless he was excused in advance or out hunting. A citizen who was absent from his syssitia without a valid reason was fined. Each member was furthermore required to contribute a set quantity of barley, cheese, figs, oil, and wine, and either share from the game taken while hunting or contribute money to buy fish.

There was much controversy over why Lycurgus had included these dining clubs in his laws. Some people said it was to weaken the family and increase the bonds between men. Others said it was to build up ties across age groups, because so much of the rest of Spartan life was organised by age-cohort. Still others insisted that it was a means of ensuring that each man ate no more and no less than his neighbour, thereby reinforcing the effects of the land reform and stressing the equality of all citizens. Others suggested that the purpose was to ensure that Sparta's soldiers ate a healthy and well-balanced diet designed to maintain their physical prowess even into old age, rather than being spoilt by doting wives or hired cooks. All agreed that the syssitia ensured that men drank wine only in moderate quantities and well-mixed with water, because the mess-boys were strictly prohibited form serving neat wine even if it was called for, besides which the members all had to get home (or back to barracks) in the darkened streets after dinner.

Whatever its objective at initiation, it had become a deeply entrenched feature of Spartan society. The mess halls lined the road from Sparta all the way to Amyclae, and each reputedly had a distinctive character, albeit one that changed over time as members died and new young men joined. Within the clubs, men were supposed to be able to speak their minds openly about any topic without fear that their opinions would be carried outside the walls.

The reason Leonidas was so curious about the syssitia was quite simply that he had never experienced the company of men before. His ancient and ailing father had had little to do with him, and in the agoge he was with boys his own age and his eirene. The syssitia was thus his first exposure to grown men. He was anxious to learn what he could from them, and a little nervous that he would attract negative attention.

While working in the kitchen as a seven-year-old, he had noticed that some of the older boys working in the messes occasionally returned to the kitchen flushed and agitated. Once he had seen a boy reduced to tears. It wasn't the actual serving that was difficult, but the fact that the members of the mess had the right to ask the boys any question they wanted. Although technically the boys had the right to refuse to answer, that was obviously not an option that would win them respect. On the other hand, Leonidas had often heard peals of laughter coming from the messes, and boys had frequently returned to the kitchens still grinning. Joking and banter was very much encouraged, and the trick was to be part of it rather than the butt of it.

There were always two boys assigned to a mess at any one time. Whether by design or chance, Leonidas and Alkander were assigned to serve together. Alkander was very nervous, so much so that he started dropping and knocking things over while they were still in the kitchen getting the tables set up. At first Leonidas was annoyed because he had to clean up after Alkander, but he felt sorry for him, too. "Th-th-they're g-g-going to make f-f-fun of me," Alkander predicted miserably. As this seemed more than likely, Leonidas didn't answer. In fact, part of him was rather glad that Alkander would probably work as a kind of lightning rod deflecting any unkind ridicule away from him.

They made their appearance in the mess, dutifully reporting to the eldest member, or chairman, first. This was a venerable old man who had lost an eye in the battle against Tegea ten Olympiads earlier. Alkander got his name out without stuttering, and attention turned to Leonidas.

"Ah ha. The youngest Agiad," the old man declared, his one eye focusing hard on Leonidas. "Well, all right. You know what to do?" They nodded. "Then get on with it."

They brought water and towels to all the members as they arrived, and were introduced to each by the chairman. They also got the first course of black broth out to everyone without incident, but during the second course someone decided to ask Leonidas what he thought the qualities of a good Spartan king were.

"Courage, father," Leonidas replied without hesitation. It was a safe bet; no one in Sparta could ever suggest that there was ever a time when courage wasn't a virtue.

"That is a quality required of every citizen," the man scoffed. "We are talking of our kings. What do they need *besides* what every citizen must have?"

Leonidas thought for a moment and decided: "Good judgement, father."

"Certainly. And what more?"

Lacking further inspiration, Leonidas tried to remember all the things his mother said Cleomenes lacked. "Prowess at sports and arms, father."

"Well enough. What more?"

"Dignity, father."

"I suppose, yes. And?"

"Ah, self-discipline, father."

"Not bad. What else?"

"Piety, father."

"Oh, very good. I'll bet you heard *that* one from your mother, didn't you, boy?"

"Ah, yes, father," Leonidas admitted.

For some reason, everyone in the room burst out laughing. Although Leonidas didn't get the joke, he was relieved to note that the atmosphere was far from hostile.

Another man took up the interrogation in a distinctly friendly, even paternal, tone. "Tell us this then, son of the Heraklid: why are Spartan men the only Hellenes who wear their hair long?"

Leonidas didn't have a clue. He thought for a second and then tried: "Ah, so the boys of the agoge will know who to address as father rather than just 'sir', father?"

To Leonidas' amazement and relief they all burst out laughing again, this time more heartily than before; and when the guffaws had faded into chuckles, they turned their attention to Alkander.

"Tell us, Alkander, son of Demarmenus, what is Sparta's worst enemy?"

"Argos, sir," Alkander got out without stuttering. (He rarely had trouble with vowels.)

"Argos? Argos? That ridiculous mud-heap filled with braggarts and ass-lickers? Argos is not an enemy, boy; it is a training field. The only reason we haven't razed Argos to the ground is so you boys will still have someone to practise your weapons on before you face a real enemy. Try again: What is Sparta's worst enemy?"

Leonidas was very glad he was not on the spot. He hadn't any idea what the man wanted.

Alkander tried again, "Athens, sir."

"Athens? A bunch of shopkeepers and whoremongers! They're more interested in a good play than a good fight. Not worth the mention. Come on; use your brains, boy. What is our worst enemy?"

Alkander swallowed hard, and Leonidas could see he was sweating miserably. His throat was working, too, as he tried to suppress his stutter. "Persia, sir?"

"He has a point there," one of the younger members of the syssitia suggested; but the questioner was not satisfied.

He frowned and retorted to his peer rather than to Alkander, "What do we care who rules Asia? As long as they don't try to set foot in the Peloponnese, they can carry on painting themselves like women and castrating little boys. It only denies them men they may one day need." He turned again on Alkander. "You are barking up the wrong tree, boy. Let me ask the question a different way: Is there any army in the world that Sparta needs fear?"

"No, sir."

"That's better. So what should we fear?"

"I d-d-d-don't know, sir," Alkander was forced to admit, and Leonidas wanted to groan in sympathy. The stutter had come.

"What was that?" the Peer asked sharply, cocking his ear toward Alkander.

"I d-d-d-don't know, sir."

"You don't know."

"No, sir."

"Do you know, son of Anaxandridas?" The man turned on Leonidas.

"No, sir."

"I see. Two equally ignorant whelps."

"Why don't you enlighten them, Phormion, so we can get on with the meal? Some of us are hungry."

"Hungry? You're not hungry. You're in a hurry to get home to your wife."

"If you had my wife, you'd be in a hurry to get home to her, too."

"Don't tempt me."

"Get the next course, boys," the syssitia elder ordered, and Leonidas and Alkander dashed gratefully back to the kitchen. From the dining room waves of laughter came in quick succession. The boys filled up the next tables and dutifully rolled these out. The conversation around them faded, and again the attention focused on them. "Leonidas, where does Lacedaemon end?"

"In which direction, sir?"

"Any direction."

"Well, to the south it ends at the Gulf of Laconia, and—"

"Really? What about Kythera?"

"Oh."

"Come now. Think harder. Where would we be if the Sons of Herakles had accepted that all they owned was the plot of earth they were born on?"

Leonidas considered that for a second, and then asked cautiously, "You mean, sir, that our borders are what we make them?"

"Well done! Or as we prefer to word it: as far as the reach of our spears."

Leonidas liked that.

"Now let's try the other question again, you two. What does Sparta most have to fear?"

Leonidas and Alkander looked at one another. Leonidas still didn't know what the man was looking for, but Alkander had evidently been thinking about it and very cautiously suggested: "D-d-d-disobedience to our l-l-laws."

There was a moment of tense silence. There was no question that the boy stuttered and that was not to be applauded, but the answer had been good. One of the men started rapping his knuckles on his table and declared, "Well said, Alkander." And the others joined in nodding and saying this was a good answer. In relief the boys fled to the kitchen, their ordeal over for this night.

———

That summer Leonidas' father died. Of course King Anaxandridas was very old and it had been obvious he was dying for a long time, so it didn't come as a surprise to anyone. What surprised Leonidas' family was that the Council and the ephors and the Assembly acknowledged Cleomenes as king without a second thought.

Not that *Leonidas* was surprised. It seemed perfectly obvious to him that since Cleomenes was the firstborn, and since he had been treated as the heir apparent all his life, he would become king when the time came. After all, Leonidas had quickly noted that he was only referred to as "that (whatever) bastard" by Taygete and her household; everyone else referred to him as "Prince Cleomenes." (Leonidas noted, too, that the title "Prince" was not awarded either Cleombrotus or himself, although Dorieus sometimes enjoyed it.)

However, it was soon evident that Taygete and Dorieus himself had convinced themselves that Dorieus would be chosen over Cleomenes, because he had proved such an outstanding model of manly virtue throughout his upbringing. He was now 18 and again at the top of his class in every sport worth speaking about—notably discus and javelin and running in armour. How could the Spartans, Taygete asked in outraged disbelief, prefer a "weakling" like Cleomenes over a strong young man like Dorieus? Sparta's kings commanded her armies in the field. Dorieus had all the virtues one wanted in a commander, and Cleomenes had none.

Taygete's raging and grief clearly unhinged her. For the first time in her life she neglected her public duties, and her appearance at her husband's funeral aroused indignant and unkind comment. It was all too obvious that she was not grieving over her husband's death, but rather her son's slight. Far worse, as always, she publicly slighted "that other woman". But in the eyes of the city, "that other woman" was a widow no less than she, and more importantly she was now the mother of the reigning king. Voices of indignation were raised, particularly among the women, and Leonidas was ashamed of his mother.

Leonidas, of course, took part in all the funeral rituals in his designated place—which was behind his brothers, of course. Since he hardly knew his father, he was not particularly affected by his death, and the elaborate mourning rituals were simply another set of rules (like those for the agoge, for sports, and for serving in the syssitia) that he had to memorise. He felt little different from the "official" mourners and helots, who were all required to "lament aloud" although they couldn't have cared less if the king were dead. Because of the law that required two representatives, one male and one female, of every family to attend the funeral, the largest crowd of people that Leonidas had ever seen in his life assembled for his father's funeral. Everyone was dressed in black—even he was allowed a decent chiton and himation rather than his agoge clothing for the occasion—and they all keened and hit their foreheads in grief. It would almost have been comical if it hadn't all been so solemn.

After the funeral, things got worse. For eight days after the funeral, the entire city observed mourning. This meant that all public assemblies were forbidden; the market was closed, and so was the agoge. This would have been bad enough—since Leonidas dreaded the thought of spending eight whole days at home with his mother even under normal circumstances—but in her present state of agitation, the thought was outright alarming. And then came the real blow: they had hardly returned from the funeral to the palace before a messenger arrived from *King* Cleomenes announcing that he was

moving into the palace, as was his right, immediately. He gave his
stepmother and her children just three hours to remove themselves.

Dorieus was furious. He stormed out to confront Cleomenes,
while Taygete went into hysterics, declaring they would have to drag
her out by her hair! She was not leaving her home for "that vainglorious bastard"! The household, meanwhile, demonstrated an acute
sense of self-preservation, and at once started clearing out the goods
and chattels of the "deposed" branch of the family while studiously
ignoring all Taygete's orders to the contrary. Since no one was paying
any attention to Leonidas, he had ample opportunity to observe the
apparent chaos around him very alertly. It seemed to him that with
the exception of his mother's old maid and one or two other elderly
servants, no one showed much sympathy for his mother. Here and
there he even noticed suppressed smirks and overheard murmured
exchanges that suggested a goodly portion of the staff was taking
outright pleasure in Taygete's humiliation. It was an important lesson,
one which Leonidas took well to heart.

Whatever transpired between Dorieus and Cleomenes, the former
returned red-faced with agitation and blustering about revenge, but
he had obtained only a 24-hour reprieve. Taygete turned her rage on
her eldest son, and pounded his chest with her fists as she shouted at
him that he had failed her. Since he was wearing a breastplate, she
did herself more hurt than Dorieus, and he withstood her onslaught
as stoically as he had borne the various floggings he had endured.
Eventually, Taygete exhausted herself and collapsed in Dorieus' arms,
a broken woman.

They had to carry her out of the palace on a litter the next
morning. She was swathed in black veils and the curtains of the litter
were kept closed. Dorieus had arranged for her to move into one
of the larger town houses, one which belonged to the Agiads and
was usually used to house state guests from other cities. But Taygete
refused this, insisting on going to one of her country estates.

This meant that they had to organise a wagon and then spend the
whole day on the road before arriving at a rather run-down manor
that was ill prepared for royal guests, having only had a few hours'
notice. Taygete was taken straight to bed, and Dorieus then called his
younger brothers to him. He was very grim. He clenched his teeth

and fists in anger. "We must avenge this humiliation!" he declared. "Right now none of us are of age, but you must swear by the Twins and on the bones of Orestes that you will avenge our mother! They can't do this to us! I will be king of Sparta! As soon as I am of age, I will lay claim to my birthright! Swear! Swear you will avenge our mother!"

Leonidas did not see that he had a great deal of choice. He and Cleombrotus solemnly swore on the house altar (which was dedicated to some lesser god), but called—at Dorieus' insistence—on Orestes to be witness of their pledge that they would avenge their mother and not acknowledge Cleomenes as rightful king of Sparta.

The remaining seven days of the "holiday" were a long drawn-out nightmare, dominated by an alternately weeping and hysterically shouting mother and a grimly fuming elder brother. It was even too much for Brotus, and for the first time in their lives the twins became allies. Together they fled the house as much as possible, seeking relief "hunting" (without success) in the foothills of the Taygetos. Leonidas had never been so glad to get back to the agoge.

———

Unfortunately, the next holiday came around all too soon. He was again faced with the very grim prospect of having to spend three days with his mother, and he had heard that things had not notably improved at home. In fact, throughout the city it was rumoured that the ageing queen was going slowly mad. It was said that she wandered about her little farmhouse having wild conversations with ghosts or the Gods—in any event, with beings no one else could see.

While the other boys excitedly packed together their knapsacks and chattered happily about all the things they were going to do (and eat) at home, Leonidas sat morosely on the doorstep of the agoge barracks, wondering if his mother would even remember to send a donkey cart to come fetch him and Brotus, or if they would be expected to walk the whole 16 miles to her farm.

Suddenly Prokles was standing beside him, his knapsack over one shoulder. "Would you rather come home with me?" he asked simply.

"Yes, I'd love to!" Leonidas agreed at once. He had met Prokles' parents on several occasions because Prokles' father, Philippos, was still on active service and so lived in barracks just a couple blocks away, while his mother kept a small apartment in the city. Here she was raising Prokles' two younger siblings. Prokles and Leonidas had dropped by to see her more than once, and she had always had a smile and something nice to supplement their monotonous school diet.

Prokles shrugged as if he didn't care one way or another, and then said, "Come on then. My granddad's waiting already."

Leonidas jumped up and followed after the other boy with a mixture of relief and tardy apprehension. The thought of spending a holiday with Prokles' kindly mother had prompted Leonidas' ready acceptance. Prokles' grandparents were something else again.

Although Leonidas had never met them, after 16 months of living side by side with Prokles he knew enough to be intimidated. Prokles' grandfather had driven the winning four-horse chariot at no less than two Olympic Games and subsequently won 14 various pan-Hellenic races with his own horses. His wife was famous in her own right, for once having ridden from Tegea on a racehorse with word that the tyrant Onomastros had seized power and the reasonable citizens of Tegea would welcome Spartan intervention. Leonidas was rather intimidated by such historic personages.

A chariot with two magnificent chestnut stallions waited in the crowded street in front of the agoge, and Prokles ran straight for it, leaving Leonidas in his wake. "May I bring a friend along?" he called out, already grabbing the edge of the chariot and swinging himself up agilely beside his grandfather.

The man holding the reins looked over at Leonidas, who was hanging back uncertainly. He had a hideous scar in the middle of his forehead where (as Leonidas knew from Prokles) the flailing hooves of a Tegean cavalry horse had found their mark almost half of a century earlier. Prokles' grandfather had awoken in Tegean captivity, a slave. It was almost four years before his father had bought his freedom and brought him home. Now he was a man of 62 years, still slight of build and wiry. The hands that held the reins of his fretful horses were scarred by work in the Tegean quarries. His grey eyes met Leonidas' and he smiled. "Hello there. And who might you be?"

"Leonidas, father."

"The Agiad?"

"Yes, father."

"What will your mother think if you don't come home for the holiday, young Leonidas, son of Anaxandridas?"

"I don't think she'll notice, father," Leonidas mumbled truthfully, as he looked down ashamed. What must a man think of a boy whose own mother didn't want him?

"Come on, then; climb aboard." Leonidas didn't hesitate any longer, and he felt the grip of the older man helping him. "Ever ridden in a chariot before, boy?"

"No, father."

"Right; then come stand here next to me and hold on. Don't be ashamed. You have to get a feel for them. Prokles has had lots of practise."

What followed was even more fun than the agoge. Prokles' grandfather, Lysandridas, had a lovely kleros on the western side of the narrowing valley of the Eurotas north of Sparta. The house was built into the side of a steep hill so that the house appeared to be only one storey from the road, but the back of the house was two and a half storeys high. The back terrace offered a wonderful view across the orchards to the valley and the Parnon range. Prokles' grandmother was a severe-looking woman with straight grey hair that she wore pulled severely back at her neck. She was thin and tough, and not at all *gentle*; but there was nothing cold about her, either. In her own matter-of-fact way, she made Leonidas feel so welcome it was almost as if he'd been coming here all his life.

That very first evening, the whole family—including the helots—gathered on the warm tiles of the back terrace. The helot women were spinning, and one of the men was sharpening farm implements with a hand stone. Lysandridas himself had a stack of leather tack and a bucket of warm water. Prokles started helping without being asked, and Lysandridas showed Leonidas how it was done. Prokles' grandmother brought wine and water in solid pottery jugs and then settled herself down with a lyre, which she played very softly so as not to disturb conversation.

Leonidas at last ventured to ask, "Will you tell me about your Olympic victories, father?"

Lysandridas laughed. "If you like; but as you will see, the fates are fickle, and victory and defeat lay side by ide. My greatest victory was one that Sparta chooses to ignore—because I was driving for Tegea. It is good to strive for excellence, but sometimes I think it would be better if we did not put so much emphasis on winning."

But that was too much philosophising for the eight-year-old audience, and so Lysandridas told the boys what they wanted to hear: about the excitement and the close calls and the funny ways of foreigners. They sat until the last light had drained out of the sky and the stars were bright in the moonless night. Far too soon, as far as Leonidas was concerned, the Olympic champion stood and announced it was time for bed.

Leonidas followed Prokles up an outside stairway and along a gallery to a room that Prokles had to himself most of the time. There was a large window with shutters to keep out the heat of the sun, but warmth lingered in the room nevertheless. There were a carved chest, hooks on the wall, and a broad bed with linen hangings and covers. On a table stood a wash basin and a pitcher with cool water. The boys washed themselves perfunctorily and had just climbed into bed when there was a knock at the door. Lysandridas opened it and stuck his head in: "I presume you want to help me with the horses tomorrow, young Leonidas?"

"Yes, father—but I know nothing about them."

"I'll teach you everything you need to know," the older man promised, adding, "I am sorry that your mother has been turned out and is said to be ill."

"Thank you, father."

The door closed and then opened again. "Which does not mean I support your brother Dorieus in his impudent claim to the throne. The ephors' decision to give your father the granddaughter of Chilon the Wise to wife was correct and indisputable. I knew Chilon personally, and he was a man of awesome intelligence combined with exceptional human warmth and humour. His granddaughter has many of those same qualities, and the Agiad house can only profit from her blood. I expect much of the young king. Now, enough. Get a good night's sleep. You will have a busy day tomorrow if you want to start learning about horses."

And indeed he did. By the time Leonidas returned to the agoge after the holiday, Leonidas was firmly in love with horses, and Prokles was his best friend.

———

Leonidas and Prokles were soon inseparable. They not only spent their holidays together—sometimes riding from dawn to dusk—but they sat together in class, slept side by side at night, wrestled, raced, and swam together, and even stood together in chorus, managing always to match their accomplishments so perfectly that there could be no official objection.

As nine-year-olds the boys of the agoge were taught how to skin and gut their catch and cure the fur. Because they were allowed to keep whatever they trapped for their own use, trapping had an immediate positive effect on the diet of the boys. Their meals were increasingly supplemented by rabbit, hare, squirrel, or even by sweets, fish, and other delicacies purchased with the proceeds of the sale of fur. Leonidas and Prokles trapped as a team, building and placing their traps together and sharing the yield equally.

As nine-year-olds they were also taken on their first overnight camping trips. These were important exercises in moving in the countryside at night, in making their own beds from the ubiquitous river reeds, in carrying fire all day so they could make a fire at night, in locating a camp for proximity to water, good visibility, and defensibility, and also in watchkeeping. By the end of the summer, when the first autumn thunderstorms drenched the countryside and the nights turned cold, the boys felt very proud of their ability to keep their fires going even in this weather. But they were glad, too, when the "season" ended and they again spent all their nights in the relative warmth and safety of the agoge barracks.

CHAPTER 3

Ages 10 and 11

As they became ten-year-olds their training continued to increase in difficulty, with archery and hunting added to the program. The length of the overnights extended to three days and then four, and finally five in the fall. It was on returning from one of these longer camping cum hunting expeditions that Leonidas learned that his mother had died. He was given leave to attend her funeral.

She had given orders to be buried on her estate rather than beside her husband, whom she blamed for her humiliation. If King Anaxandridas, she reasoned, had not given in to the pressure of the ephors—or at least not slept with "that other woman"—then she would never have been driven from her home, and her son would be king of Sparta. In a lucid moment before her death she had asked to be buried beneath a chestnut tree, and it was here that her body was interred.

The funeral was the first time that her three sons had collected together in a long time. Brotus was now a good four inches taller than Leonidas and much heavier. He was burnt almost black from a summer of frequent camping and outdoor sports. Leonidas looked light beside him not only because his skin just didn't tan as darkly, but also because his eyebrows were bleached in the nearly continuous exposure to the summer sun and the fuzz of hair on his shaved scalp was almost invisible. Dorieus, however, put both his younger brothers in the shade. He had graduated top of his class and had served his year as a meleirene with his usual unblemished record of excellence. As an eirene, he had had charge of a class of 18-year-olds—a privilege accorded only the eirenes deemed capable of such unruly charges so close in age—and here again he excelled and was deemed the finest of all the eirenes. This past winter he had finally become a citizen, and now awed his younger brothers in Spartan scarlet and a full head of hair.

But Dorieus was not a happy man. Unlike the younger boys, he had been very close to his mother, and he grieved sincerely. More importantly, he felt a burning sense of guilt because he had failed to avenge her humiliation. Now, even if he one day became king of Sparta, his mother would never see it. In his guilt-stricken grief, he again made his brothers swear that they would never accept Cleomenes as the Agiad king. Then they all returned to the city.

Within a week Leonidas was confronted with the consequences of his brother's grief. He entered the syssitia in which he was then serving, oblivious of the scandal his brother had caused that same afternoon by failing to rise in the presence of King Cleomenes. His brother's pointed and public mark of disrespect for a reigning king made Leonidas the target of a barrage of hostile questions. What in the name of the Twins had he been taught at his mother's knee about the Spartan Constitution? Didn't he realise that the ephors swore to preserve the kingdom only as long as the kings upheld Lycurgus' laws? Wasn't he aware that the ephors consulted the heavens every nine years and that they had a clear warning that the Agiad line would die out unless his father took a second wife? Or more bluntly: just who the hell did Dorieus (and implicitly Leonidas) think he was to challenge the ephors and Council and Assembly?

The furore did not die down. Leonidas soon learned that Dorieus was not as isolated as the questions that first night had made it seem. In fact, there were a score of young men who supported Dorieus, calling Cleomenes not only illegitimate but weak and inadequate. These angry young men all consistently refused to stand for Cleomenes, and interrupted him when he spoke, and openly declared they would not follow this "weakling" in battle.

Shortly afterwards, the rotation of mess duties took Leonidas and Alkander to the mess of the Eurypontid King Ariston. Leonidas was at once confronted with open glee over the dissention in the Agiad House. "Squabbling like a pack of hounds, aren't you, boy?"

"Yes, father," Leonidas agreed readily, determined not to get drawn into any sort of defence of his brother. He had served in this mess once before, the previous year, and he disliked the Eurypontid King Ariston not only on principle, but because he seemed to be a thoroughly selfish and self-satisfied man with no redeeming qualities. Furthermore, Leonidas had heard from his mother that the Eurypontid had tricked and betrayed even his "best friend" in order to steal his wife. Although Spartan law explicitly "allowed" a woman to be "shared" between two Spartan citizens for the sake of siring sons, it was supposed to occur only with the consent of all parties. King Ariston, however, had allegedly tricked a man who owed him much money into promising "anything" Ariston asked. Ariston had then asked for his wife. The man and his wife had allegedly both begged to be released from the promise, but Ariston's lust outweighed his sense (as Leonidas' mother had worded it) and he had taken the woman to be his queen. From that time onwards Ariston did not have many friends, and his messmates were mere sycophants who flattered him and agreed with whatever he said. Leonidas hated the atmosphere in this syssitia, much preferring those messes where the men treated each others as equals, comrades, and friends.

"Aha, so you admit that the entire Agiad house is nothing but a pack of squabbling dogs."

"Yes, father," Leonidas agreed again, determined to just get this night over with as quickly as possible.

"Well, then, boy, from now on you can go on all fours and answer with 'woof' for 'no' and 'woof woof' for 'yes'."

Leonidas just stared at the older man, unable to believe his ears.

"I gave you an order, boy! Go on! Get down."

"No, father."

"What did you say?"

"No, father."

"I gave you an order, whelp!"

"Not one I have to obey!" Leonidas flung back, losing his self control and refusing to add the compulsory "father", either.

"What did you just say, boy?" The Eurypontid's eyes narrowed at him, and although he was reclining on his coach with a kylix in his hand, he seemed to tense like a cat preparing to spring.

"I don't have to crawl on all fours and bark like a dog. I'm Spartan! In fact, I am every bit as good as you are."

An uproar errupted from the other members of the mess, and the Eurypontid king threw his entire kylix of watered wine in Leonidas' face. Leonidas stood for a moment with the wine dripping off his nose and running down his cheeks and neck. Then he turned and ran out of the mess.

"Going out to cry, little whelp?" someone shouted after him.

"Running back to your mother's womb, baby?" another hooted.

But King Ariston shouted for him to come back.

The helot cook caught Leonidas by arm and advised him urgently to return. "You can't win, boy. Go in and do what they want of you. It'll be over in a moment or two! If you run away, they'll take this to the Paidonomos. You'll get flogged! Don't be a fool, boy. It'll hurt you less to say 'woof, woof' a couple of times than to have your back torn open by the cane!"

"But he doesn't have the right to ask that of me!" Leonidas insisted, with all the intensity of a child confronted with something that is *not* fair. For three years he had memorised the Laws of Lycurgus. For three years they had taught him that the Spartan Constitution was designed to ensure that all citizens were *treated* equally. The land reform, the common education, the uniforms at school and in the army, the equal portions at the messes—everything was designed to ensure equality of status for all Peers.

Furthermore, Leonidas had also been taught for three years that all the discipline of the agoge was carefully instituted because no other city in the world took such an intense and protective interest in its youth. The agoge was harsh, his instructors and eirenes and the men at the syssitia said, but it was fair. It had been explained that the very rigourousness of their training was a privilege reserved only for future citizens. Helots and perioikoi were not subject to the discipline nor put through the tests because they would never be citizens, never stand shoulder to shoulder in the phalanx, nor vote at Assembly, nor have the right to be elected to office, Ephorate, or Council.

In short, it had been drummed into him that as sons of Peers and as future Peers, the boys of the agoge had a right to respect. Citizens were not allowed to strike the boys or otherwise force them to do anything. That was the exclusive prerogative of the officials of the agoge, and only after "due process" in which the boys were given a chance to defend themselves. Certainly no citizen had the right to humiliate the boys of the agoge in ways incompatible with their dignity as future Peers.

But no sooner was Leonidas out of the oppressively hot syssitia and the mocking circle of hostile faces than he became afraid of his own courage. In the sobering chill of the night air, the cook's warning rang in his ears, and the thought of a flogging made his bladder weak. He started running for his agoge barracks, anxious to tell his side of the story to his eirene before the Eurypontid king could report him to the headmaster.

Leonidas' eirene, Lysimachos, was in the eirenes' mess with his colleagues. He was anything but happy to be interrupted during this short interval of free time. "What the hell are you doing here, Leo? Dinner can't be over yet."

"Please, sir. I need to talk to you about something," Leonidas explained, still standing in the doorway and signalling for his eirene to come over to him. "Just for a moment, sir."

"You look like you need a pee. Go take care of that first and then come back for me."

Five minutes later Leonidas found himself breathlessly relating what had transpired. But even as he told the story, he knew he was not going to get any help from his eirene. Lysimachos, son of Megakles, was not exactly the top of his class. The best youths were always assigned the most senior age-cohorts, because it was assumed they were the most difficult to manage. By the time the Paidono-mos assigned the eirenes to the ten-year-old and younger age-cohorts, only the "dregs" were left. But whereas Gitiades and the other two eirenes who had commanded Leonidas' unit the previous three years had at least taken their duties seriously, this youth didn't seem to give a damn what his elders thought of him. He let the boys of his unit wait on him hand and foot and claimed the best of everything for himself. He certainly did not lead by example, and Leonidas had been looking forward to the change of eirene at year's end even before this incident. Now he found himself the object of Lysimachos's outrage.

"You did what?!" the youth demanded furiously of Leonidas.

"I walked out, sir—"

"You don't have the right to do that!"

"But they wanted me to crawl on the floor and bark like a dog!" Leonidas protested.

"So what?"

"Well, they don't have the *right* to make me do that! I'm not a helot. I'm every bit as good as King Ariston!"

"Oh don't give me that shit! You're a little boy! You have to do what any Peer asks of you—let alone a ruling king and his household cronies. Are you out of your mind?! I've never known you to be a troublemaker before! You've always been so sensible up to now! What in the Name of Zeus got into you? By all the Gods! If the Paidonomos finds out about this, he'll have my hide!" Suddenly the young man was afraid for himself. He grabbed Leonidas and shook him hard. "You go back there and apologise for what you did. Grovel, do you hear me?! Go down on your knees and grovel for forgiveness—"

"NO! NEVER!" Leonidas told the eirene and fled.

Leonidas was very, very frightened now. He knew he was in trouble, and he knew that no one was going to help him. He ran in search of Prokles, who was returning from his own mess duties at another mess.

When Prokles heard what Leonidas had done, he gasped. "By all the Gods! You are in deep shit, Leo!"

"But surely you can see I couldn't do what he asked of me?" Leonidas protested again, more distressed than ever to discover that even his best friend did not support him.

"I'm not saying you should have crawled or barked, but you shouldn't have fled. What did Alkander do?"

"What *could* he do? They weren't addressing him."

"Well, he could have distracted attention from you—dropped a tray or knocked over a krater or something!" Prokles declared contemptuously.

Leonidas sighed. He didn't doubt that Prokles would have done something like that if he had been in the syssitia, but you couldn't ask that of Alkander. Alkander was still always last in sports and his stutter was, if anything, worse. No one listened to what he said, and his only function in the unit seemed to be to serve as a ready example of all things contemptible. It was unreasonable to expect him to actively risk more ridicule and abuse just to protect Leonidas. Leonidas *didn't* expect it of him.

"You're right. You can't expect help from that trembler," Prokles echoed Leonidas' thoughts. "I'll see if I can catch my dad at his syssitia before he heads home. Maybe he'll know of something you can do."

But Leonidas was summoned to report to the Paidonomos before Prokles returned. Leonidas had not been in the office of the Paidonomos since the day his father brought him to the agoge, which seemed like ages ago. Here by the light of torches he was confronted not only with the Paidonomos, but also the deputy headmaster for the younger age-cohorts, several of the officials of the agoge, the Mastigophoroi (the men who would actually carry out any flogging that was ordered), and the Eurypontid chief steward as well. The latter was one of the men who had witnessed the whole incident and had delivered the king's complaint to the Paidonomos. Leonidas was aware that his knees were shaking, a disgraceful display of fear that made things even worse.

The Paidonomos announced to Leonidas, his eirene Lysimachos, and Alkander, all of whom had been summoned at the same time, that a complaint had been lodged against Leonidas for "impudent" behaviour to "none other than the Eurypontid king". The Paidonomos then asked Lysimachos for an explanation. As was to be expected, the eirene proclaimed complete ignorance of both the charges and the incident. He put on a great show of being taken completely by surprise. In one sense it was a kind of defence, because at least he said he'd never had any trouble with or complaints about Leonidas before now. Still, he ended by saying that of course if Leonidas had "taken a bad example from his rebellious and arrogant older brother", they must "act vigorously" to "nip his impudence in the bud". Adding, "A good flogging would no doubt do him good."

Finally Leonidas was asked directly to explain himself. He had not been taught to dissemble and said straight out: "King Ariston ordered me to get down on my knees and crawl around on the floor like a dog, answering only with 'woof' or 'woof, woof'." Leonidas was so afraid of the flogging he expected that he spoke in a rush of air that made him talk too fast. He was bright red with agitation and his breathing was irregular.

"Ridiculous! The boy is not only impudent, he is a liar." This judgement came from the Eurypontid official. The steward then went on to describe what had happened at the mess, saying that Leonidas had strutted into the mess arrogantly declaiming that he didn't have to serve anyone there or even address them as "sir" or "father" because he was "as good as any of them". The steward concluded his narrative by saying, "Then he just turned around and strolled out."

"That's not true!" Leonidas burst out furiously, yet at the same time feeling helpless against these incriminating lies. "Father!" he pleaded, turning to the Paidonomos. "It's not true. I admit, at the end, after he'd ordered me to crawl on the floor and bark like a dog, I—I didn't—I couldn't bring myself—to call him 'father'. But only after he'd ordered me to crawl on all fours and bark like a dog."

"Why on earth would we give you such a ridiculous order?" the Eurypontid steward asked, in a tone of voice that made it seem utterly inconceivable. "You are making this whole thing up to protect yourself from the flogging you deserve."

"You can flog me if you like, but I won't crawl on the floor and bark like a dog! Father," Leonidas shouted in despair.

"Why on earth would anyone want you to?" the steward asked back in a tone of injured rationality. "The boy is obviously as mad as his mother. He must be hallucinating things."

"No, f-f-f-father. He's n-n-n-not!" Alkander broke in.

Everyone had forgotten the other boy was even there. Every head in the room swung around to look at him in astonishment. After four years in the agoge, Alkander had a reputation. Everyone in the room knew that Alkander was a hopeless case. He was still tall for his age, but he was last in every race. He could barely get up a rope. He was downed in wrestling with hardly a fight. His javelin and arrows always fell short, and the singing masters had given up on him entirely and ordered him to keep silent. Most importantly, because he was known to be a stutterer, he was automatically assumed to be the lowest form of Spartan life: a "trembler", or coward.

"Did you wish to speak, Alkander, son of Demarmenus?"

"Yes, sir. Leonidas isn't m-m-making anything up, f-f-f-father. He w-w-was ordered to go on all f-f-f-fours and b-b-bark." Alkander's breath was exhausted after this effort and he fell silent, but his throat was working in agitation and his face glistened with sweat in the torchlight. His fists opened and closed at his side.

"The boy is just trying to cover up for his friend." The Eury-pontid steward dismissed Alkander with a contemptuous wave of his hand.

The Paidonomos' eyes shifted sharply to the steward, but settled on Alkander again to ask: "Why on earth would a king order a boy of the agoge—much less an Agiad prince—to behave like a dog?"

So he was a prince after all, Leonidas noted, somewhat to his surprise and encouraged by this unexpected honour.

"B-b-because K-K-King Ariston c-c-claimed the Agiads were f-f-fighting—"

"This is agony to listen to! Can't the boy be taught to speak properly—"

The Paidonomos silenced the steward with a single look. Turning back to Alkander he prompted, "Go on."

"—he said the Agiads were f-f-fighting among th-th-themselves like d-d-dogs."

"Which indeed they are!" the steward agreed.

"Thank you. That will be all. Return to barracks." The Paidonomos dismissed the boys and their eirene.

Out in the hall, Leonidas wanted to thank Alkander. He was awed by the courage the weak boy had shown in speaking up like that to the Paidonomos even when he hadn't been addressed, but Lysima-chos silenced him before he even got a word out by announcing: "You were lucky this time. Don't think they'll go so easy on you next time around!" After that, no further comment seemed appropriate.

The following spring Dorieus left Sparta with almost 200 followers, most of them perioikoi, to found a colony in North Africa. Leonidas did not know the details of the stormy confrontations between his older brother and the ephors, but he knew that the whole enterprise was viewed as ill conceived and foolhardy. In his haste, his brother even neglected to consult Delphi. The handful of young Spartiates who accompanied him were of good family but reputedly all "hotheads"—at least that was what the older men in the syssitia said when they lectured Leonidas on his brother's wilfulness and rashness.

Part of Leonidas was glad to see Dorieus go. The six months since he had publicly refused to acknowledge Cleomenes as king had brought only hardship to Leonidas. But he also felt a chill of growing isolation. Even if Dorieus hadn't been much of a brother to him, he was better than nothing. Now the only relative he had in the world—unless you counted his hated half-brother Cleomenes —was his twin brother Brotus.

True, it had been four years since Brotus had been the bane of his existence, but the twins were still anything but close. In fact, they were almost exact opposites of one another. While Brotus excelled at sports of strength like sprinting, jumping, and especially boxing, Leonidas was better at sports where skill, judgement, or tenacity helped more than strength—wrestling, archery, and long-distance running. While Brotus was useless in chorus, Leonidas was increasingly recognised as gifted. Brotus was impatient with writing, had a poor memory for for poetry, and generally did poorly in any classroom subject; while Leonidas was one of the best "scholars", with a neat and admired handwriting. On the other hand, Brotus could track almost anything, and was reputed to have the "nose of a dog," while Leonidas was too easily distracted by plants and weather and other things to track properly; without Prokles, Leonidas would rarely have had extra rations. In short, Leonidas found little comfort in the fact that Brotus was his last remaining relative in Lacedaemon.

———

In the spring of Leonidas' eleventh year, King Cleomenes married. The young king (he was 23 at the time) chose a maiden of surpassing beauty, and inevitably the jokes in the syssitia were about the marriage of Aphrodite to Hephaestus. Everyone seemed to think it was very funny, and the ribald jokes were often beyond the understanding of the youngest mess-boys. In fact, Leonidas was frequently sent out of the room when the jokes about his half-brother's marriage became too explicit. But while the bride's beauty was cause for amusement, her age was the source of disapproval. In Sparta, girls generally weren't viewed as marriageable until they were at least 18, and usually 19 or 20. But given the king's own youth, he would have been forgiven that modest breach of convention in marrying a 16-year-old, if he hadn't also "stolen" an heiress.

This last fact aroused widespread and intense anger. Heatedly men pointed out that by marrying an heiress, the king, who was very rich already, concentrated even more wealth in his own hands— wealth that *should* have gone to an ordinary citizen instead. This was the first time Leonidas was made explicitly conscious of the fact that the reality of Spartan equality was far from the ideal laid down by Lycurgus and which they had so dutifully learned in school. But he didn't pay it much attention.

The next lesson was harder still. It came the same year when Prokles and Leonidas went off for one of their all-day rides during a holiday in the late summer. The weather was very hot and dry, as it had been for an inordinately long time that year. Everywhere the grass was brown and crisp rather than green and soft, and on the upper pastures the goats and sheep had sometimes grazed so much that dust blew at the slightest breeze. The shepherds moved the herds higher and farther to keep them from ruining the pastures altogether. Prokles' father and grandfather wore frowns much of the time, saying that the hay harvest had been bad and they would have to buy imported hay to get the horses through the winter—or sell some of the horses off sooner. At least the stream that bounded their kleros to the south was still running, albeit very low. Many other mountain streams, particularly from the Parnon range, which was not as high and had less snow in winter than the Taygetos, had dried up altogether. Even the Eurotas was unusually lazy and shallow.

When the boys set off for a ride, Lysandridas warned the boys to stay close to the Eurotas so the horses would always have somewhere to drink, and admonished them not to ride too fast in the heat. Leonidas could sense that the horse breeder would have preferred to order the boys to stay home, but the old man also knew how much the boys were looking forward to this outing before returning to the discipline of the agoge on the following day. His solution was to loan them the use of older horses, weathered veterans past their prime who could be relied on not to overexert themselves.

Prokles and Leonidas avoided Sparta to ensure no officious Peer would commandeer their horses (as they had the right to do), and crossed the river well north of Sparta. They continued to the north, riding cross-country to avoid the dusty roads and keeping to the edge of the orchards and vineyards that were planted on the lower foothills of Parnos. They absolved their consciences by telling themselves that as long as they had the Eurotas in *sight*, they were following instructions.

By noon, however, they were desperately thirsty, and the water in the goatskins they carried on their backs was so hot that it was almost undrinkable. Now the Eurotas looked a very long ways away—although it was still technically visible. The boys at once started to look around for an alternative, namely a mountain spring or village fountain where they could water themselves and their horses. They decided to turn east into the Parnon range, climbing towards a village they could see about a mile ahead of them. Even before they reached the village, however, they were met by a stocky woman carrying an empty jug on her head. She was obviously going to fetch water. They pulled up and called out to her, "Hello." (She was a helot and not entitled to the title of "ma'am".) "Can you tell us the nearest place to get water?" they asked her.

The woman's hair was streaked with grey, and her face was weathered by the sun to a leathery hide creased with wrinkles. Her feet were bare and the soles looked as hard as the soles of sandals. She squinted up at the two boys on their fine horses, obviously Spartiate sons by their shaved heads, and her expression was vaguely hostile. She made Leonidas feel uncomfortable, and his skin crept despite the hot sun.

"There is still water at Seliasia," the woman announced, finally answering the boys' question, and she pointed vaguely. Leonidas and Prokles followed the direction of her finger with their eyes. This was farther northeast, deeper into the valley of another tributary to the Eurotas. They thanked the woman and headed in the direction she had indicated.

It took them almost half an hour to reach the village the woman had pointed out, but they had no difficulty finding the fountain: there was a long line standing in front of it. Most of the people in line were helot women and girls, but with a cry of surprise, Leonidas noticed Alkander.

"Alkander!" he called out, and urged his horse forward past half the line to reach their classmate. Prokles followed.

Alkander looked up, and his expression was one of shock and then shame. He looked down, his face closed and blank, as it was whenever he was being upbraided for his failings or mocked for his incompetence.

Leonidas jumped down from his mount, taking in the fact that Alkander was still wearing his agoge clothes, only he'd unpinned the chiton on his right shoulder so it hung around his waist leaving his shoulder bare—just like a helot. He was also carrying a knapsack loaded with a large amphora, and held a second in his arms.

"Don't you have water on your kleros?" Leonidas asked in shock, putting two and two together.

"No," Alkander answered, so softly that Leonidas read his lips more than heard his words.

"How far away is it?" Leonidas asked next, looking about at the increasingly rugged countryside, which was hardly suitable to cultivation.

"Two miles," Alkander gestured vaguely.

"You're going to carry those amphorae full of water for two miles?" Leonidas asked, incredulous.

"Of course."

Leonidas looked at Prokles. Obviously a Spartan hoplite was expected to march 40 miles in a day, but never in full panoply; there were baggage wagons for that. While on an advance or patrol, a hoplite *might* have to march four or five miles in armour, but even then the armour was distributed more or less equally over the whole body. Trying to carry a 20-gallon amphora in one's arms while carrying another on one's back was a very different proposition. Besides, Alkander was only an eleven-year-old boy, and by no means the strongest of them.

"I can take the knapsack on my back, and we can rig up a saddle-bag for the other one," Leonidas suggested spontaneously.

Alkander stared up at him as if he didn't understand what Leonidas had said. "You mean, help me carry it home?"

"We've got horses," Leonidas pointed out.

Alkander did not seem particularly grateful. He looked at the horses and then at the fountain house, and he swallowed. He shuffled forward with the line. Leonidas looked over at Prokles with a question in his eyes, and Prokles shrugged. They kept beside Alkander, moving forward as he did but not talking. When he went into the fountain house, Prokles stayed with the horses while Leonidas went inside with Alkander. First Leonidas refilled Prokles' and his own goatskins with fresh, cool water from the basin while Alkander filled first the amphora in his rucksack and then the one he held in his arms. These being large amphorae, Leonidas had time to take the goatskins out to the horses and water them by hand twice before taking some water out for Prokles and himself. He refilled the goatskins a last time and then, as the second of Alkander's amphora started to overflow, he reached out and took it in his own arms. It was staggeringly heavy. He struggled to get it out of the fountain house, down the steps, and on to the street, where Prokles was waiting with the horses. It was impossible to imagine carrying it two miles.

"We can tie two old barley sacks together and hang one on either side of Penny's withers." Prokles had worked out the transport problem while he waited. Together the three boys obtained from one of the villagers some old, rather ragged barley sacks and hemp rope. They lashed the sacks together with the rope so that the rope lay across the withers of the mare Leonidas had been riding and a sack hung down on either side. They hoisted an amphora into each sack (with only a little spillage) and then turned Penny around. Penny did not like this awkward burden and balked. Prokles had to employ all his powers of persuasion with the insulted racehorse, most notably riding ahead with the other horse. Rather than be left behind, Penny at last moved forward.

It took them nearly an hour, with frequent strikes by Penny, before they reached their destination. Leonidas had been so busy concentrating on coaxing the stubborn mare forward without upsetting the load and worrying about the chafing on her withers from the hemp rope (the hair was rubbed off and Penny was starting to bleed by the end) that he did not notice Alkander's kleros until they were almost there. In fact, Alkander said, "Here we are," and Leonidas looked about bewildered. There wasn't a kleros anywhere in sight, just a helot cottage of dirty stucco with a thatched roof and a rough porch supported by rough-hewn wooden pillars.

Prokles was staring, too, and not just at the cottage but also at the woman who emerged from it. She did not look very different from the helot woman they had encountered on the road. Her hair was thin and greying, her skin dark, her feet bare. In fact, both Leonidas and Prokles assumed she *was* a helot until Alkander addressed her. "Mom, that's Prokles and this is Leonidas. They helped me bring the water."

Leonidas was too shocked by discovering this was Alkander's mother and this filthy cottage was his home to register that Alkander had not stuttered once.

The woman came nearer, modestly pulling the back of her peplos up over her head. "Leonidas? The Agiad?"

"Yes, ma'am," Leonidas answered dutifully.

"I'm honoured. Alkander has told me so much about you. I am honoured," she repeated, sounding more stunned than honoured. "I wasn't expecting you," she said next. "I have nothing in the house."

"Don't worry about that, ma'am. We just came to deliver the water."

"But you must come in," she insisted. "I'll find something. Come in."

Meanwhile Prokles and Alkander had between them taken the amphorae out of their sacks and removed the offending improvised saddlebags from Penny's back. Prokles was inspecting the damage to his grandfather's horse with horror and apprehension. The poor mare had been rubbed bloody in three places. His grandfather would have every reason to cane them both, Prokles was thinking. Alkander had one of the amphorae in his arms, so Leonidas took the other one and followed him into the cottage.

Inside it was even worse than outside. First of all, the room was windowless. The only light came from the door by which they entered. The air inside was thick with smoke from a smouldering hearth-fire that heated the temperature in the room far beyond the heat outside, making it feel as if they were inside a bread-oven. Leonidas broke out into a sweat at once. The floor was packed dirt and, from what he could see in the dim, smoky light, the cottage was filled with a jumble of junk. The woman tried to clear a place for them at a table and brought wooden plates that she wiped clean with a rag. Leonidas was famished, but the thought of eating anything here turned his stomach. The woman, or he ought to say Alkander's mother, set a chipped kothon in front of him and poured a finger of wine into it. She then looked around for water, and Leonidas hastened to offer water from his own goatskin. Prokles entered and joined them, a wary look on his face.

"Alkander has told me so much about you," the woman repeated, setting bread before them. It looked rather burned, but Leonidas' hunger got the better of him and he took some of it. "He says you are the only one in the whole agoge who is nice to him."

Leonidas was embarrassed, because he wasn't really nice to Alkander. The most you could say was that he wasn't particularly mean to him, either. "Do you live alone here, ma'am?" he asked to change the subject. He remembered vaguely that Alkander's mother was widowed, but he thought he remembered Alkander mentioning a sister.

"Yes, since my daughter moved away."

"Did she marry?" Leonidas asked innocently.

Alkander scowled and his mother turned away. "I'll get you some apples," she announced and left the cottage.

Leonidas looked at Alkander. "What happened to your sister?"

"What is it to you?" Alkander snapped back. "You can see how it is for us here! My mother has almost nothing for herself after she pays my agoge fees. The kleros won't support anyone else."

"But....you mean this is it? All of it?"

"Of course! Do you think we'd be here if we had a fine house someplace else?" Alkander was angry.

"But…" Leonidas looked helplessly at Prokles.

"Where are your helots?" Prokles asked.

"They live further down the road. In a better house, if you must know. There are lots of them, so they could build and fix it up more. My Mom's alone with me in the agoge."

Leonidas and Prokles looked at one another, still dumbfounded and confused. "But how did you get so poor?"

"How? How did you get so rich? Your brother just married an heiress, and so did your father. The rich get richer, while the rest of us have almost nothing left." He was so bitter and so angry and so ashamed that he was red-faced—but he still wasn't stuttering.

"I'm no richer than you are," Leonidas protested. "I wear the same clothes and eat the same food as you—"

"Only as long as you're in the agoge!" Alkander interrupted. "When you come of age, you'll take over huge estates scattered all over Lacedaemon."

This was the first Leonidas had heard of that, and he didn't believe it. "That can't be. My half-brother even threw us out of our home when he became king!"

"And where did you go? To one of your mother's many estates! Where do you think your agoge fees come from every month?"

Leonidas was appalled to realise he'd never given it a thought.

Alkander seemed ashamed of his outburst, and he rushed outside into the fresh air. Leonidas and Prokles looked at each other, and then got up and went out. Alkander was standing with his back to them and his mother was evidently trying to comfort him, but he kept shaking his head and waving her away.

She turned, saw that the other two boys had come out of the house, and put on a smile. "Please stay a little longer. I can go and fetch—"

"We can't stay, ma'am," Prokles answered with a nod toward the sun. "We have to get the horses back to my granddad. Thank you for your hospitality, ma'am." Prokles started untethering the horses, but Leonidas kept gazing at Alkander's back. The chiton still hung from his left shoulder, exposing one scrawny shoulder blade.

"See you tomorrow then, Alkander," he addressed the other boy.

Alkander spun around, and his face was struggling with emotions. "No, you won't! The harvest was horrible. My mom can't scrape together the agoge fees any more. I won't be there tomorrow or ever again."

"But if you don't finish the agoge, you'll never get citizenship!" Leonidas protested.

"Are you stupid or what!? I can't afford the syssitia fees, either! I'll never be a citizen. Never! I never fit in anyway, and you won't care if I'm gone."

Leonidas was shocked and stunned. He could find no words, except a rather weak denial. "That's not true. I'll miss you. I've never forgot how you saved me from a flogging last winter. I—"

"Just go away and leave me alone!"

Prokles brought Penny over to Leonidas and handed him the reins. Reluctantly Leonidas mounted. Why hadn't he ever thanked Alkander properly for helping when he was in trouble with King Ariston? Why hadn't he made more of an effort to help Alkander with things generally? Why hadn't he stopped the others from mocking him? Alkander wasn't *really* worthless. What difference did it make if he stuttered: what he *said* usually made sense, if one just let him finish—and listened to him. And while he was poor at sport, Leonidas was certain that somehow or other he would have brought his mother the water today even without help. Even more importantly, he had shown real courage in the Paidonomos' office. Suddenly it was clear to Leonidas that Alkander wasn't worthless at all, but a boy with intelligence, tenacity, and courage. He felt horribly guilty for not befriending him.

All the way home, Prokles and Leonidas discussed Alkander. Prokles was less positive about him, but he agreed it was unfair for him to get thrown out of the agoge.

"But how did he get to be so poor?" Leonidas asked in baffled outrage. "Lycurgus' Laws guarantee every citizen sufficient land to support a man and his family. That was what the Land Reform was all about. That is the point of all our laws against hoarding and owning gold and silver and about eating in common messes and going to the same school and wearing the same clothes! The whole basis of our

Constitution is equality of wealth so that we compete against each other only with respect to courage and virtue."

Prokles looked over at his friend a little askance. "You can't really believe all that crap! Just look around you."

When they got back to Lysandridas' kleros, Prokles was most concerned with the ugly sores on Penny's withers, and he talked long and fast to explain them to his frowning grandfather; but Leonidas was still upset about Alkander.

"His mother lives in a mud-floored helot cottage and now she can't afford to pay his agoge fees any more, so he won't be coming back to school. How is that possible, father? I thought our Laws and the Land Reform were supposed to ensure that every citizen has enough land to support himself and his family. How could Alkander's family have become so poor?"

Lysandridas looked up from the injured mare and considered Leonidas seriously. After a moment, he replied, "Good questions, Leonidas." Then he turned to his grandson and gave him orders to fetch and apply an ointment to the raw places on the mare's withers. At last he turned his attention back to Leonidas. "So you want to know why we no longer live by Lycurgus' Laws?"

"But I thought we did!" Leonidas protested.

Lysandridas shrugged. "We say we do. Maybe even most of us pretend we do most of the time. We have preserved many of the Laws, but—as you have so vividly witnessed—we have circumvented others."

"But when, father? And why?"

"Why? Because of two fundamental aspects of human nature that no one—not even Lycurgus or Chilon—can legislate away: greed and love. Greed for wealth and love of all our children, whether they be girls or boys, firstborn or last born. Lycurgus hoped to make new men with his new laws, but only the Gods can make new men." He sounded tired, and Leonidas remembered that he was now over sixty. "As for when we started bending the Laws—" He shrugged again and sank down on to a bale of hay to gaze at Leonidas solemnly. "I would say it has been a creeping process, so slow and steady that we hardly even noticed it. Your family is hardly typical, so let me take my family as an example.

"At the time of the Land Reform in the reign of your forefather Polydorus, this kleros was carved out of a great estate. It was the same size as other kleroi, but it had no house, no well, no barley fields, no vineyards or orchards. It was just pasture land. And while the land was equally redistributed, the livestock was not. That was why Lycurgus' laws said that any Peer could 'borrow' the ox, the horse, the hunting dogs, or the bull of a fellow Peer. This was to enable New Citizens without hunting dogs or horses or oxen to borrow these beasts long enough to hunt and plough or get their heifers serviced.

"And at first the system worked. The New Citizens, like my forebear—Agesandros, son of Medon—had terraces made to plant barley and planted the orchards amidst the barley. The kleros—like the others that had been newly created—became self-sufficient and even prosperous. But it took good management, and not all men have wives equally skilled in agriculture and accounting. Some men found it hard to make their kleros yield enough, but by then we had won the Second Messenian War and there were vast new lands to be distributed.

"And here is where the Laws certainly were consciously circumvented. Instead of dividing up Messenia into equal plots and giving every Peer a second kleros, the lands in Messenia were treated as spoils of war. I hate to say this to you, Leonidas, but the problem started with the kings. They wanted a 'royal portion'. But the Assembly felt that the men who had won the war in Messenia had a better right to reward—including, incidentally, my own great-grandfather, Agesandros. So in addition to the kings, who got their 'royal portions', the officers and the Guard and other men who had distinguished themselves in the war for whatever reason got rather larger estates than the ordinary citizen. Still, every citizen profited so much from the newly acquired and extraordinarily fertile lands in Messenia that nobody seemed to notice—and certainly didn't care—that Lycurgus' principles had been violated.

"And then we violated them further by allowing these acquired lands to be given away or settled upon daughters. Only the original Laconian kleroi are strictly held by the Lacedaemonian government and allotted to citizens as they come of age. All the other lands can be deeded as their owners wish. And the Laconian kleroi can only be redistributed after a widow dies with no heirs. So some estates were held out of circulation, while new citizens came of age with no place to go.

"You must try to understand that when we first circumvented the Laws, we did so not out of venal self-interest but out of love; because, you see, younger sons were coming of age and found that there was no state kleros available or only ones of marginal fertility. Keep in mind that even a good state kleros is really only large enough to support one hoplite and his family. That means an adult man and maybe one or two boys in the agoge. But what happens when those sons grow up and have sons of their own? One kleros is not enough to support three or five adult men and their growing boys. Theoretically, of course, adults get new kleroi of their own, but that is only possible when the population is not growing. When Land Reform took place there were just 6,000 citizens. Now we are nearly 9,000. Good for the army, but where are those extra kleros supposed to come from?

"I'll tell you. Roughly five Olympiads ago, marginal land—not already claimed by families—was turned into 3,000 additional kleroi, but these were very poor from the start. Parents therefore tried to provide for their younger sons—and for their daughters and sons-in-law—from their acquired land."

"But how could Alkander's family become so *poor*?" Leonidas insisted, still not understanding that his friend could be living like a helot despite being the son of a Spartiate Peer.

Lysandridas drew a deep breath. "I don't know exactly, but it could be that his grandfather was a younger son, for whom there was nothing extra from private lands and who was then given a marginal kleros. Or, maybe his forefathers were spendthrifts who sold off their private land for some other passion—like hunting dogs or to build a house. It is notable, incidentally, that the more inequitable the distribution of wealth has actually become, the more rigorous the laws enforcing the *appearance* of equality have become. When my great-grandfather built this house after the Second Messenian war, there was no disapprobation attached to the use of tiled floors, marble facing, or even frescoes on the walls. My great-grandmother proudly wore fine jewellery, because the laws against hoarding were applied only to coinage, not decoration. Even in my own youth, people bought and displayed decorative pottery, bronze, and ivory work in their homes and on their persons."

The old man was getting distracted, and Leonidas had to bring him back to the topic. "But Alkander's mother is living in a helot hut—with a dirt floor and open hearth and no water at all—much less fountains and latrines like here."

"Yes, you told me; but we don't know that there wasn't a house once. Maybe there was once a fine house that was lost in a fire, or sold off for short-term gain to pay for something else. Or maybe there were simply too many children, and the lands were divided up into smaller and smaller portions until none was large enough to support a family any more."

"But what about his *kleros*, which legally *has* to be large enough to support a citizen and his family?" Leonidas insisted.

Lysandridas sighed and shook his head. "The reality, Leonidas, is that the good land has somehow become concentrated in the hands of families that have a talent for that kind of thing, and only the marginal estates are still at the disposal of the city. It is very rare for an old kleros of any agricultural value to become vacant. That is, for a citizen and his widow to die without a male heir who can take it over. Officially, the city still "assigns" the kleros to that male heir, but it is unthinkable that a fine kleros would be allotted to another man's son as long as the former resident has citizen sons—or sons-in-law.

"Consider this kleros. It is a very pretty piece with a lovely house, but it does not pay for my own and my son Philippos' syssitia fees, much less Prokles' agoge fees. We only manage all that because we annually sell off our best colts and fillies. But horse breeding is risky. If we have a few bad years and no winners come from our stables, we won't be able to command the prices necessary to support three citizens—much less Prokles' younger brother.

"I strongly suspect that your friend Alkander's father was a younger son. That the kleros assigned him was marginal to start with, and that his wife—for whatever reason—mismanaged it to the point of ruin."

"But it's unfair that Alkander will lose his citizenship! The Laws were supposed to prevent that!"

Lysandridas raised his hands helplessly. "I'm sorry to have to tell you this, Leonidas, but much in life isn't fair."

"And there is nothing anyone can do to help him?" Leonidas persisted, angry that his city was not as fair and just as he had—until now—been led to believe.

"I didn't say that. It is becoming increasingly common for wealthy citizens to pay the agoge fees of poor relations. If Alkander has a wealthy grandfather or uncle or even cousin, he would be allowed to pay Alkander's fees, at least for the agoge. Then at 21 he would be entitled to a kleros of his own, which need not be the run-down one his mother is living on—assuming she dies first and it has already been given away. Remember that the laws do not permit a widow to be expelled from her kleros; which is why they usually go to sons, sons-in-law, or grandsons, because most widows are happy to share with relatives."

Leonidas did not think Alkander had any rich relatives. In fact, thinking back on the few things Alkander had said about his family, it was clear in retrospect that he had long feared that exactly this would happen—but Leonidas had not taken any interest in his hints until now. "And can't anyone else pay the fees? I mean someone *not* a relative?"

"I don't know. Maybe. I don't think anyone has ever wanted to," Lysandridas admitted.

"I want to," Leonidas announced. "If it's true that I have lands of my own, than why can't I sponsor Alkander?"

Lysandridas considered Leonidas for a moment and then, putting his hands on his knees, pushed himself to his feet. "That would be a great responsibility, Leonidas. You would, I believe, be held responsible for him in every way, and have to pay any debts he incurred or make good any damages he caused. It would almost be like a temporary adoption until he came of age. Do you really want to take on that much responsibility at your age?"

Leonidas thought about it for a minute, slightly intimidated. But he couldn't imagine Alkander making debts or causing damages. He felt so guilty about not being nice to him in the past that he decided simply, "Yes. If it means Alkander can come back to school and become a citizen as the Laws of Lycurgus intended."

Lysandridas waited for another moment, giving Leonidas a chance to change his mind. When he didn't, he said: "If you really want to do this, then I will put it to the ephors for you."

"Would you, father? At least ask if it is possible, because I want to help Alkander, but I don't really know if I can afford it—"

Lysandridas laughed a little bitterly. "You can afford it, Leonidas. Believe me, the Agiads can afford it."

CHAPTER 4

Age 12

LEONIDAS' SPONSORSHIP OF ALKANDER ISOLATED HIM in his class somewhat. On the one hand, it reminded the other boys that Leonidas was indeed an Agiad prince, and at the same time it associated him with the class "dunce". Leonidas felt on the one hand obliged to "protect" his protégé from unfair abuse and ridicule, and on the other embarrassed by his incompetence. This, in turn, induced Leonidas (and a somewhat reluctant but loyal Prokles) to try to help Alkander improve his performance.

It soon became evident that Alkander's greatest weakness was despair. Over the years he had become increasingly convinced that he would never make it through the agoge, and so he had inwardly given up really trying. With encouragement, he started to overcome many of his handicaps. His wrestling and running improved noticeably, and he never stuttered when the three boys were alone together. Javelin, discus, and particularly boxing (a sport Leonidas also hated) remained very difficult for him, and his stuttering returned whenever he was under pressure—which of course meant whenever the chorus masters, instructors, or other boys focused their unkind attention on him. Nevertheless, the bonds between the three boys increased steadily.

The bonds were, of course, reinforced by the fact that neither Leonidas nor Alkander had homes they *wanted* to go home to. Leonidas was a full orphan, and his closest adult relative was a man whom he had sworn not to accept as his king, much less treat as his brother. Alkander's father had been dead for as long as he could remember and, having once escaped the humiliation of his mother's poverty, he had no strong desire to return to it. Fortunately, Prokles' parents and grandparents were willing and able to "adopt" the other boys into their family circle. Thus Leonidas and Alkander spent holidays with Prokles' family, learning to ride and watching Lysandridas and Philippos train the racehorses, helping out in the stables, and enjoying the superb cooking of Prokles' mother and grandmother.

But being "adopted" by Prokles' family had its obligations, too— as the boys soon discovered when summer thunderstorms broke over Laconia with a vengeance. It was the worst thing that could have happened agriculturally, of course, because the rain ran off the parched countryside, tearing away the topsoil rather than soaking in deep. The torrents, gullies, and streams frothed with dirty, fast-moving water and swept many sheep and goats to their deaths. The barn and low-lying paddocks at Prokles' kleros also flooded, and all three boys worked through the night to get the horses up to safety on high ground. It meant going AWOL from the agoge and they all risked a flogging for doing it, but the safety of the horses came first. They were almost disappointed when, reporting to duty the next morning, bedraggled and exhausted but very proud to have played their part, their eirene winked at them and ignored their absence entirely. But he was a nice, easy-going youth anyway, and he too loved horses.

———

Another kind of "family obligation" confronted them when the hot, sunny weather returned and the boys flocked to the Eurotas for a good swim, something they had been unable to enjoy during either the summer drought or the violent rains. The rules of the agoge did not prohibit the boys outright from using the baths, but the fact of the matter was that most citizens disliked being disturbed by hordes of rambunctious and noisy young boys and youths while taking their ease at the baths. In consequence, boys were made to feel unwelcome—if not by the citizens themselves, then by the bath slaves. They were encouraged instead to cleanse and refresh themselves after sports in the Eurotas itself. A long pier had been built out into the deepest part of the river as a platform for jumping and diving into the river. On a day like this it was crowded.

Prokles, Leonidas, and Alkander had to squeeze their way past other boys—many of them older, bigger and stronger—to get out to the floating dock in the middle of the river. This was always a bit risky. Older boys weren't supposed to take advantage of their strength and better-honed fighting skills to displace little boys; but on the other hand, "little boys" were supposed to show respect for their "elders". It was a fine line. Prokles insisted that Leonidas should lead the way. He had an ingratiating smile, and people seemed more inclined to indulge him than either Prokles or Alkander. They had almost reached their objective, having talked their way past what seemed like hundreds of other boys, when suddenly a high-pitched voice started screaming: "Prokles! Prokles!"

Startled, they stopped in their tracks and looked around, bewildered. The shouting was coming from the water, and looking toward the sound they saw a wet head with plastered-down, dark hair.

"Oh, God!" Prokles groaned. "It's Hilaira." Hilaira, as Leonidas and Alkander knew well by now, was Prokles' younger sister. She was now eight years old. "Just ignore her!" Prokles ordered, and the boys continued toward the float.

But Hilaira was not so easily brushed off. She swam beside them and as soon as they reached the float, she swam straight up to it and took hold of the rope around the outside. She shook her wet hair out of her face as she surfaced. "Prokles! Didn't you hear me?!" she demanded.

"What do you want *now*?" Prokles retorted, frowning.

Hilaira answered by pulling herself up on to the float. This was not good. There was not really room for her on the float, and the youths around them were not at all pleased to have another wet body flop down among them. There were mutterings of disapproval, and had Hilaria been a boy she would have found herself shoved back into the river. As it was, when the boys registered it was just a girl, they resigned themselves to her presence, because it was beneath their dignity to push a girl back into the water. Instead, they cast angry—almost threatening—looks at Prokles, Leonidas, and Alkander.

Prokles seriously considered pushing his sister off the float himself, but settled for asking irritably, "What do you want?"

"I want you to promise to watch me race at Hyacinthia next month."

"Is that all?" Prokles groaned. "Why didn't you just stop by the barracks?"

"You forgot last year," Hilaira pointed out.

Prokles rolled his eyes. He hadn't really forgotten; he'd just been more interested in other events than girls' races. "OK. OK." He brushed his sister off now. "We'll be there."

"Promise?" Hilaira insisted, this time including both Leonidas and Alkander with her eyes.

"Yeah, yeah," Prokles answered, and Leonidas and Alkander nodded concurrence dutifully.

"I have *witnesses*," Hilaria pointed out, grinning, spreading out her arms to indicate all the other youths and boys packed on the float.

This got her a loud laugh, and several of the others hooted and agreed out loud. "She's got you there, Prokles!" someone shouted.

"What's your name, nymph?" another called out.

Hilaira just giggled and slipped back into the water to swim away.

"You better watch that one, Prokles," one of the older youths warned. "She'll be turning the city on its head in a few years."

———

At the Feast of the Hyacinthia, the boys were very busy. This festival, although it included the usual sports competitions, was most famous for the musical performances and dancing, especially the women's dances. In fact, increasingly almost as many tourists flooded into Sparta for this festival just to hear the singing and see the dancing as came for the more famous Gymnopaedia. Although Alkander was excused from the chorus altogether, both Leonidas and Prokles were required to perform.

By the end of the first day of the festival, Leonidas and Prokles' chorus was still in competition, and throughout the second day the excitement grew. This was quite different from athletic competition because no one was on his own; only the whole chorus could win or lose. That created an intense but highly intoxicating team spirit, with the boys encouraging one another and particularly their soloist, Ephorus. Furthermore, the results were far less clear-cut. Sports were objective, but choral singing was not, and the judges often seemed undecided or divided among themselves. When the soloist of their rival chorus lost his voice towards the very end of the second day, the victory went to Ephorus and his chorus.

Now, for the first time in their lives, Leonidas and the others were allowed to perform in the theatre itself, along with the winning youth and men's choruses. The boys were sent to change into fresh new chitons and himations specially kept for the occasion at the Temple to Apollo in Amyclae, while torches and lamps were lit along the aisles of the theatre.

Finally, well after dark, with the crowds packed into the very last row of seats, the boys filed in for their grand performance. The tension was almost unbearable. Because the boys were placed in the middle, between the youths and men, Leonidas found himself standing almost directly in front of the two ruling kings. Ariston was looking rather ill, he noted with spiteful satisfaction; he sat bent over and the expression on his face was sour, as if he had stomach troubles. Cleomenes, by contrast, was looking very smug, with his beautiful bride beside him.

More interesting in many ways, however, were the foreigners in the crowd. Leonidas was fascinated by the sight of men in very outlandish dress that could only have come from Asia somewhere, and there were Egyptians too in their stiff headdresses, and Ethiopians in leopard skins, and lots of other Greeks in bright-coloured himations and jewellery.

After the choral performance, the boys were free to watch the last event of the day, the dancing. Dancing was not done in the theatre but directly in the agora, on what was known as the "dancing floor" between the main civic buildings.

The women danced first, to the evident pleasure of particularly the foreign guests, who couldn't seem to get a good enough glimpse of the performers and kept treading on everyone's toes and shifting about trying to see better. The boys, however, were rather bored by the women, and waited impatiently for the last event: the sword dance.

This was performed by torchlight, which glowed on the broad breastplates of the dancers and was reflected on their polished battle helmets like glimmering inner fire, or dramatically flashed on the honed blades of the swords and on the fast-moving bronze greaves. All the dancers wore their helmets down over their faces; so that as they moved in and out, weaving back and forth, it was impossible to tell them apart. They were equally anonymous, inhuman really, and ominous. Leonidas and his friends watched in awe and fascination as the dancers performed to the wail of the pipes alone. Leonidas was entranced. This dancing in full armour required a precision of movement as perfect as in a phalanx and as strenuous as running. Sometimes when the dance pattern brought the dancers closer to the audience, you could hear how heavily they were breathing, and yet their movements were so perfectly controlled that their swords never clashed or struck—except in unison and on cue. Leonidas hoped that one day he would be one of these dancers.

It was getting close to midnight before, exhausted from the long, eventful day, the boys found their way back to their barracks and fell into bed. Their laurel wreaths were put carefully away in their baskets, souvenirs for life; but their new chitons and himations were folded up, collected, and returned to the temple.

The next two days of the festival were taken up with sports competitions, and the boys were free to entertain themselves except when competing. Philippos, Prokles' father, was driving a chariot in both the four- and the two-horse events, and the three twelve-year-old friends helped him when they could. Furthermore, Prokles and Leonidas were themselves riding in horse races; and Leonidas was competing in wrestling, Prokles in javelin, and Alkander in long-distance running, respectively. In all the excitement, it would have been easy to forget Hilaira—if Alkander hadn't kept reminding them.

"Don't forget your sister, Prokles," Alkander insisted, as the time approached for her event at the end of the second day.

Prokles scowled. "Do we have to go? If we do, we'll *never* be able to get good seats for the armoured race. They'll all be taken." The foot race in armour was the last event of the last day and very popular.

Crowds were already streaming toward the main stadium where it was scheduled to be held, and staking out their places.

"You promised," Alkander reminded Prokles.

"I could try to hold places for all of us," Leonidas suggested.

"No, we better stick together. We'd never be able to find you in that crowd."

So together they went to the smaller of the "race courses", where the foot races of lesser importance were held. To the boy's surprise, although it was only a "little girls'" event, there was an astonishingly large crowd here as well—and it was composed primarily of foreigners. "What are all the strangers doing here?" Leonidas asked generally.

Prokles' mother and grandmother caught sight of them and waved vigorously. The three boys hurried over to join them. The women had secured a good spot close to the finish line and at the very front. "I thought you had forgotten!" Prokles' mother declared, clearly relieved, and looked rather admonishingly at her eldest son. "This means so much to your sister."

"Does Hilaira have *any* chance of winning?" Prokles asked sceptically.

"She certainly does," his mother told him firmly.

"Why are there so many strangers here?" Leonidas asked again, because he noted that almost everyone around, although Greek, was speaking a different dialect—mostly Ionic.

"Oh, that's because they don't have maiden races in other cities," Prokles' grandmother explained. "In fact, they don't let their maidens out of their houses at all." Leonis knew what she was talking about, because she had lived in Tegea for a time when Lysandridas was in exile there.

"So how do they go to school?" Prokles wanted to know.

"They don't."

"They don't go to school?" Leonidas was shocked. "Not at all?"

"No—"

"And that is the proper way of things!" one of the men standing near them insisted, butting into the conversation firmly. He addressed himself to the boys rather than the women. "Everything a girl needs to know in life, she can learn at her mother's knee in the safety and seclusion of her own home. By letting girls run around in public view, you only encourage licentiousness and disobedience! The less a girl sees and hears, the better she is."

The three Spartan boys stared at the stranger in open bafflement. Because he looked at least 40 and by his rich clothes and carefully coifed hair appeared to be a man of wealth, they dared not contradict him.

It was Prokles' grandmother who answered him sharply. "If it is such a scandal, why are you here?"

"See! That's just what I mean!" the man declared, still addressing the boys. "Silence, SILENCE, is a woman's greatest virtue." Then, turning on Leonis, he sneered at her. "Flaunting your bodies is not half so bad as the way you chatter and interfere in men's affairs!"

"If you are afraid of a woman's words, go back where you came from!" Leonis retored.

"I intend to do just that!" the man said indignantly and would have turned away, but Leonidas stopped him.

"Excuse me, sir."

The other man looked back. "Yes?"

"May I ask where you are from, sir?"

"I am from the great city of Athens!" the man proclaimed, loudly enough to make others start to take notice.

"Oh!"

Leonidas looked so surprised that the man's curiosity was aroused. "Does that surprise you?"

"It does, sir."

"Why?" the man asked, perplexed. He evidently felt that his nationality should have been obvious from his clothes and accent.

Leonidas hesitated. He glanced a little uncertainly at Prokles' grandmother. She could not know what he was going to say, but she awaited it expectantly. "It's only that I was taught that Athens was a great and powerful city, sir."

"As indeed it is, boy—nothing like this provincial pig-sty you *call* a city! Why, your whole acropolis wouldn't qualify as more than a collection of third-rate district temples in Athens, and your agora could fit inside ours three times over!"

"I accept your word for it, sir, but it surprises me nevertheless— although I knew you had walls...." Leonidas trailed off enticingly.

"What surprises you, boy?" the man asked impatiently, frowning, sensing something behind Leonidas' words that he could not identify yet.

"It surprises me that you are so easily frightened."

"Frightened?!" the Athenian demanded, flabbergasted and uncomprehending.

"I mean"—Leonidas still sounded baffled and respectful, because it was a guise he had long since honed to perfection in the syssitia— "if you fear even the words of women, how you must tremble before the spears of men."

The man's jaw dropped in shocked outrage, and there was no knowing what he would have said if around him other spectators, both domestic and foreign, hadn't hooted with laughter. Angrily the Athenian pushed away into the crowd, with a loud sneer of "Whores and their whelps!" tossed over his shoulder.

Prokles leapt after him, apparently intent on making him retract this insult, but his mother caught him by the neck of his chiton. "Leave it! Leonidas won the round, and he knows it. Here's your sister now."

The seven competitors were lining up on the chalked starting line. They were barefoot and wore knee-length chitons, which were pinned at their left shoulder but left their right shoulder bare. Since they were all children still, it was impossible to speak of "bare breasts", although the foreigners around them whispered this word with obvious relish and were craning their necks for a better look. Leonidas, Alkander, and Prokles exchanged a look that dismissed these men as "dumb".

A high-pitched whistle called the competitors on to their marks. On their faces was the same grim determination that could have been found on the faces of their brothers—or on the pan-Hellenic athletes at Olympia. To these girls, this race was just as important. Another whistle set them loose. They bounded forward with the lightness of young deer, and in an instant all you could see was their backs. Prokles just had time to shout out after his sister: "Come on, Hilaira!" At the far end of the course they had to stop themselves and turn, and then work up to maximum speed to come tearing back. While the girls had seemed well matched on the outward run, bunched very close together, on the return they started to spread out. Two girls lagged quite far behind, apparently already giving up. Three more ran with waning strength, and the two leaders competed two-thirds of the distance, until Hilaira pulled out into the forefront with so much mastery that the race was won long before she crossed the finish line. By that time Prokles and his friends were jumping up and down and cheering wildly.

As she slowed down after finish line, she was audibly gasping for breath and glistening with sweat over her entire body. Her hair around her hairline was soaked with it, and she doubled over, grabbing her knees to keep herself from falling over dizzy from the exertion.

Now the commentary of the gawking foreigners was even harsher than before. "Poor thing!" was the kindest remark. Another remarked that it was "completely unnatural", while a third found the spectacle "downright disgusting". A fourth foreign spectator, however, actually grabbed Alkander by the arm and asked him pointedly, "Do you mean to tell me you'd actually want to *marry* a girl who'd run around like this with her breasts bared for all the world to see?"

"Why not?" Alkander managed in reply, afraid to say more for fear of stuttering.

He was rescued by Prokles' mother, who turned on the boys and urged: "Go give Hilaira your congratulations. It means more to her than my praise."

The boys obeyed readily enough, and soon afterwards met up with Prokles' father and grandfather. As a family they joined the crowd for the armoured race, but saw little of it because of their poor seats. Then they shared in the feast of the sacrificial beasts and, exhausted from yet a fourth day of excitement, went to bed.

It was only then that it occurred to Leonidas that Alkander had a sister, too. He stopped abruptly as he folded up his chiton into a pillow. "Alkander?"

"Yeah?"

"Don't you have a sister?"

No answer.

"I thought your mother said—"

"Shhh!"

They were in the barracks, and Leonidas took the hint. He said no more, and just finished stripping and climbed into bed. But he didn't forget about it. One day after the Hyacinthia was over and they were back to their routines, he asked Alkander about his sister when they were alone together. "Don't you have a sister, Alkander?"

"Yes."

"But where is she?"

"You know my mother couldn't afford the agoge fees!" Alkander hissed angrily.

"I know. But where is she now?"

You could see Alkander didn't want to say. He struggled long with himself, trying to find ways of not answering, or maybe lying, or just telling Leonidas to mind his own business. But how could he do that when Leonidas was like an adopted brother to him? So at last he admitted, "She's been p-p-put out t-t-to service."

"Service?"

"My mother f-f-found a job for her with a f-f-family in K-K-Kardamyle."

"Job? What kind of job?"

"What do you th-th-think?!" Alkander snapped. "It's a large f-f-family. She looks after the ch-ch-children and waits on the l-l-lady of the house."

Leonidas was appalled. She was a servant. After a moment he said: "I don't think that's a good idea. Can't we bring her back?"

"Where? To my mother? She probably gets more to eat where she is!"

"But, Alkander, she's my sister now. How old is she?"

"Fifteen."

Leonidas sighed. That complicated things. She was too young to marry. He was going to have to get some advice on this. So he let things rest for the moment, and they didn't talk of it again.

———

The most significant event of Leonidas' twelfth year, however, occurred at the very end of it. Just before the snows came and the passes closed for the year, the twelve-year-olds were sent on a "test" hunting expedition, an important exercise intended to prepare them for that all-important test of their ability to survive entirely on their own at age 13. Before entering the ranks of the "youths" at age 14, all the "little boys" had to prove that they had learned enough self-sufficiency to keep themselves alive without the benefit of civilisation for a period of 40 days. This so-called Phouxir, or "fox time" (because they lived by their wits like foxes), marked the end of childhood and the graduation to the official status of "youth."

During the Phouxir, the boys were allowed the help of neither other humans nor domesticated animals such as hunting dogs. Thus, hunting (without dogs) was a vitally important aspect of their training in the years preceding the "fox time". Without dogs, of course, tracking became particularly important; and Leonidas, very aware of his own inadequacies in this skill, was beginning to get nervous about passing the Phouxir test. It had been one thing to rely on Prokles, as long as it had simply been a matter of enlivening the dull diet of the agoge; but if it was to determine whether he survived and passed the "fox time", Leonidas decided he ought to try to improve his own skills.

This preliminary test involved living off the wilderness for just ten days, one-fourth of the time they would have to endure a year later. Leonidas proclaimed his determination to do it all without Prokles' help. What he hadn't reckoned with was Alkander. Although the boys were not officially prohibited at this stage from banding together, it was frowned upon; and while Prokles happily went off on his own with a shrug, Alkander declared he would stay with Leonidas. Leonidas tried to talk his new protégé into attaching himself to Prokles, but Alkander declared simply, "Prokles doesn't want me. Are you saying you don't want me, either?"

Trapped, Leonidas took Alkander along with him. They were not, however, a particularly effective team. After three days, they had still failed to kill anything edible and were getting very hungry. After five days of living on nuts, berries, mushrooms, and dried grass, they were famished. It was Alkander's idea to try to steal a smoked ham from the kitchen of an outlying kleros. They were caught red-handed by the geese.

Not only did the geese warn the helot residents of the intruders—the geese actually attacked them and made their escape impossible. Within minutes they were locked up in a windowless, slimy underground storeroom invested with vile creatures they did not see but could hear, feel, and smell in the dark. The next morning—hungrier, filthier and more discouraged than ever—they were turned over to the agoge authorities.

The disgrace, of course, was having been caught. If they had got away with the theft, it would all have been viewed as a legitimate tactic for survival. After all, hoplites cut off from their units in enemy territory also stole what they could to stay alive—albeit at high risk. Thus, while theft at other times was a contemptible indignity that lowered a Spartiate to the level of helots and foreigners, theft during survival training was deemed legitimate. Punishment for getting caught, however, was a reminder of the consequences of getting caught in a real wartime situation. A Spartiate hoplite, caught stealing in enemy territory, would be killed or sold into slavery.

By the time Leonidas was taken down to the sandpits by the banks of the Eurotas where the public floggings took place, he was at the end of his twelve-year-old strength in more ways than one. First, he was half-starved from six days in the wilderness with not one proper meal. Second, he was miserably disappointed that he had failed to feed himself by legitimate means. Third, he was frustrated that he had been so inept at thieving. And fourth, he felt guilty for dragging poor Alkander into the whole mess with him. He was famished, exhausted, and feeling utterly worthless when they made him strip off his chiton and, naked in the chill of an autumn morning, he turned to face the Eurotas. He stood barefoot in dew-cooled sand and gripped a bar of poplar, which was laid at right angles to two six-foot high stakes as if for high jumping. Alkander was beside him, facing the same punishment.

As the crowds and the officials gathered, cutting canes from the reeds and preparing for the flogging, Leonidas's terror grew to immeasurable proportions. If it weren't for the fact that he had had very little to drink in the last 24 hours, he would have wet himself right there in front of everyone. The sound of the Paidonomos' assistants testing the canes they would use made his insides cramp up, and he thought he was going to be sick. The only consoling fact was that at least his mother was already dead and Brotus was not around to ridicule him—and then Cleomenes arrived with his bride.

Leondidas had never really hated Cleomenes until this moment;

but the realisation that he had come to watch Leonidas' humiliation turned his dull, second-hand dislike of the "usurping bastard" into personal hatred. After all, both his full brothers had stood here themselves, but Cleomenes had been exempt.

To make matters even worse, Cleomenes' bride was at least eight months pregnant by now. She stood about with her distended belly prominently displayed, apparently very proud of herself for already being on the way towards providing the Agiads with their next king.

"I don't think I can stand this!" Leonidas whispered to Alkander beside him, through gritted teeth.

"You have to!" Alkander answered in like fashion.

The mastigophoroi, the young men who were to carry out the punishment, took up their positions with their canes. An unbearable stillness fell over the crowd. Leonidas could hear the cane whistle through the air, and then it cracked on his naked back, and the sting of it made his whole body leap in outrage. He clung grimly to the wooden bar, biting down to keep from emitting any sort of cry. The next blow followed. And the next. And the next. Gradually, Leonidas' body lost the strength to leap and start each time the cane struck at him. Soon he only wanted to sink down into the soft sand, just down and away. Escape. Surrender.

He could stop the ordeal at any moment just by letting go of the bar and sinking into the sand. It would be so simple, but it would be a disgrace. His mother wasn't even here, and yet he felt her ice-cold eyes boring into his raw back and making it cold, even as the welts turned red and hot. She hated him just for wanting to quit. But she hated him anyway. She had always said he was a useless whelp. He should have been killed at birth. He was no use to anyone. Completely superfluous.

"Leonidas!" Alkander hissed his name through his gritted teeth. "Leonidas!"

"What?!" Leonidas hissed back.

"Stand up!"

"Why?!"

"You're an Agiad."

"So what!" Leonidas replied, but he had stiffened his knees again already.

"You have to let me go down first!" Alkander insisted next.

"Why?!"

"It's what they expect. I'm a worthless *mothake*." Alkander referred to himself by the somewhat derogatory term reserved for the youths who, like himself, were to poor to pay their fees and were sponsored by someone wealthier. "If you go down first, you will *never* live it down."

Leonidas wanted to scream at Alkander to drop, surrender, to spare them both any further agony, but Alkander was (as Leonidas was learning) incredibly tenacious. There were many skills he simply did not have, but enduring pain was not a function of physical strength, dexterity or skill—it was sheer willpower. Alkander had more than enough of that when he wanted.

By now Leonidas could feel moisture running off his back. He did not know if it was sweat or blood, but the sense of simply not being able to endure any more was mounting. "Alkander! I *can't* take any more."

"Of course you can. I can."

"Why?!"

"To prove them all wrong!"

"I have to suffer so you can prove them wrong?!" Leonidas demanded.

"Just a little longer!"

"I can't!"

"Yes, you can!"

"I can't!"

"Please!"

Leonidas was unconsciously writhing, his body desperately trying to evade further abuse, while his mind kept his hands clasped to the bar and his feet in place. Someone called for him to "stand firm or surrender".

"I'm going down!" Leonidas hissed at Alkander.

"No! Just a few more!"

"Why?!"

"To prove them wrong!"

Again Leonidas forced himself to endure a little longer. But it really was getting unbearable. For Alkander, too. Later they would fight over who finally gasped out: "Now."

They dropped face first into the cool, soft sand, the ordeal over at last.

The pain didn't stop, really. It was so bad, Leonidas could still feel it; but then there were people standing around him, and their bodies shielded him from the bitter wind off the Eurotas. Someone solicitously lifted Leonidas' head from the sand and offered him water, wonderful, sweet water. Someone else was gently enfolding him in a himation. "Well done, Leonidas," he heard them say. "Very credible." Someone else was on his other side. "I'm going to put an ointment on your back now," the voice announced. "It will cool the wounds and prevent infection. Just lie still and try to relax."

Alkander was receiving the same treatment.

They had passed this test with honour and together. It was the final seal on their friendship.

CHAPTER 5

Age 13

THE 13-YEAR-OLD AGE-COHORT WAS THE LAST in which the boys were classed as "little boys." It was the last during which they served as mess-boys in the syssitia, and the last in which they had their mornings free to roam about under their elected leaders. Starting at 14, they became "youths" and, just as the sons of tradesmen generally entered their apprenticeship with a master at that age, the sons of Spartiates began trade-training as well. From 14 onwards, the skills and arts of war became the predominant focus of their education.

This in turn meant that by the time the boys crossed the threshold to "youth", they were supposed to already have the general education required of future citizens. At the end of their 13th year the boys were not only expected to be able to read and write, but also to have a firm grasp of the essence of precise and sparing speech, to have a foundation in the laws of their city, to know the fundamentals of botany and biology (as these pertained to their needs for survival in the world around them), to be familiar with all major works of song and poetry of importance to the city, as well as to be versed in the history and geography of the known world. In addition, they were supposed to have learned how to trap, track, and hunt, as well as have started training in all major sports. Most importantly, the boys were supposed to have developed a high degree of self-confidence that would enable them to become proud, independent, and free citizens at maturity.

In the following seven years they would be taught to bend their own will to that of the collective, to merge their individual strength with that of their fellow citizens, and to create strength and power greater than the sum of the parts. But in this last year of their semi-freedom, the most important lesson that the authorities wanted the boys to take with them into the next stage of training was a sense of individual self-sufficiency. This was why the survival training of the "fox time" fell in the 13th year and why the boys were encouraged to do a great deal on their own, without supervision.

It was in this spirit that Prokles, Leonidas, and Alkander borrowed horses from Lysandridas and set off for the port of Gytheon during the long holiday following the feast of the Gymnopaedia. None of the boys had ever seen the sea, and this was the ostensible purpose of the great adventure. By now Leonidas was almost as good a rider as Prokles, and both boys could be entrusted with fine horses; while Alkander, although not yet an adept rider, was good enough to be trusted with an ageing mare of sensible temperament.

The boys packed into knapsacks rations of fresh bread, oil, cheese, and fresh fruits from the kleros. They also loaded carrots and oats for the horses, along with grooming and eating utensils for themselves and their horses. They threw in various other things that might come in handy, from rope and fish hooks to coins. Philippos, Prokles' father, also provided them with the addresses of two perioikoi merchants in Gytheon and the address of a reputable livery stable there.

Full of enthusiasm, the three 13-year-olds set off at the crack of dawn, skirting the city to avoid officious or over-curious citizens, and made off down the Eurotas valley for the sea. Leonidas and Prokles sometimes could not resist racing a bit ahead on their high-strung horses, but they always waited for Alkander in the shade a little ways down the road. Then the three would ride together at a leisurely pace, talking as they always did. They felt very grown up to be making a trip like this to another city, and they were also acutely conscious of the responsibility they had for the well-being of the horses.

They had been given good instructions and warned of the dangers of losing their way. If they missed the turn-off for Gytheon at Athrochorion or again at Krokeai, they would end up on the passes over the Taygetos. These were dangerous for boys their age, as there were outlaws in the mountains, mostly runaway helots, who clothed themselves in patriotic pathos and called themselves "rebels". And there were also bears, boar, and wildcats in the forests of the Taygetos—beasts that the 13-year-olds might dream of hunting, but for which their small, light javelins and bows were no match.

Only once did they make a wrong turn, ending on a track that became steeper and rougher until it was obvious that they had lost the main road. They retraced their steps, found the correct fork, and continued. This, and perhaps a tendency to dally over snacks along the way, meant that it was getting dark when they finally crested the last hill and the gently curving coastland of the Laconian gulf unfolded before them. The haze blurred the horizon somewhat, and with the sun behind them, it was a moment before they understood what they were seeing. But when Leonidas noticed what could only be fishing boats dotting the expanse of shimmering silver, he shouted with excitement and led his friends in a last race down toward the broad, sandy beach.

The horses, too, were excited by the unusual scents brought on the evening breeze. Although tired from the long day, they pricked up their ears and flared their nostrils in excitement. When asked by their young riders to leave the road, which now paralleled the coast leading to the walled city of Gytheon to the west, they hesitated only briefly before plunging excitedly down and across the sand. Their racing blood overcame them, and soon Leonidas and Prokles were tearing headlong down the beach while Alkander's mare loped along behind, too lazy to race but unwilling to be left behind entirely. When the two lead horses encountered the frothing and hissing waves as they came ashore, however, they spun about on their haunches in abrupt alarm and ran back the way they'd come—leaving Leonidas and Prokles dumped in the damp sand.

Uninjured on the soft sand, both boys shook themselves as they got back to their feet and then—overcome by the excitement of it all—they stripped off their clothes and plunged into the water. The water came as a bit of a shock to Leonidas, used as he was to the warmer waters of the Eurotas, but he had plunged in so completely that he soon adjusted to the cold. Meanwhile, Alkander had reached the water's edge and jumped down to join his friends in the water. They swam out for a bit, shouting to each other in excitement as the first waves lifted them off the bottom.

Shortly afterwards Leonidas noticed, far in the distance, a large square that caught the pink rays of the setting sun. After a few moments of wondering and guessing, the boys concluded it could only be the sail of a great ship, although—hard as they tried—they could not make out her hull in the fading light. They speculated excitedly on where it was from and where it was headed, and Leonidas won a first glimpse of the vast possibilities of sea travel. Whereas the mountains, rivers, and deserts defined the routes that man must travel overland, funnelling and directing their steps, making it impossible to go directly where one wished, the sea appeared absolutely free of obstruction. It would be several years before Leonidas learned about winds and tides and the difficulties sailors faced in setting a true course and holding it. At that moment, a 13-year-old boy looked out and saw a flat surface and a ship that could sail wherever it wished.

When they started to get cold and tired, they went back ashore to find their discarded chitons. Meanwhile, the horses had collected on the banks of a little creek that emptied fresh water into the bay from the swampy wetlands. It was lined with tall, green grass and the horses were grazing contentedly. The boys joined them there, lying on their bellies to cup up the cool fresh water from the stream with their hands.

After quenching their thirst, they had to decide where to spend the night. Leonidas, who found the sight, sound, and smell of the sea intoxicating, suggested they spend the night out here on the beach; but Prokles pointed out that in Gytheon they could put the horses up in a proper livery stable and then buy themselves a hot meal. He concluded his argument by saying, "… and then we can go down to the harbour. There might be all sorts of ships in it."

This won over Leonidas instantly, and so they remounted and rode along the road to the town. This being a perioikoi town, it was walled and there were armed sentries at the gates. At the sight of three boys in the distinctive homespun, undyed chitons and shaved heads of the Spartan agoge, the sentries called out jovially, "Where away! What have we here? Not runaways, are you, boys?"

"Of course, not! We're on holiday," Prokles told the impudent sentries angrily.

"Sure you are!" the sentries laughed. "Well, just see that you keep out of trouble! Two triremes put in this afternoon with a half-dozen Spartiates aboard."

Prokles regally waved the advice aside and the boys continued into the city. They really were on holiday, and since they had the permission of Philippos to be here (and the other boys were orphans), they had nothing to fear from Spartiates. On the other hand, the news that two triremes were in port was exciting. This was the best they could have hoped for, and they were now in a hurry to find the livery stables recommended for the horses and get down to the port. Asking directions, they readily found the stables, turned over the horses to professional care, and plunged back out into this strange city as fast as they could.

The perioikoi had no laws against night lighting as Sparta did. The boys found a city where lamps burned over doorways and inside litters, or torches were carried through the streets, thrilling and exotic. Furthermore, although they were used to the fact that perioikoi dressed more lavishly and gaudily than Spartiates, being in a perioikoi town meant that rather than the perioikoi providing a splash of colour among the dour Spartiates, they were themselves an insignificant drop of blandness in a city populated by lavishly dressed men.

Soon the smells of the street-side kitchens and stands overpowered them. Many cookhouses opened their windows on to the street and sold to passers-by. The smell of warm bread, grilled goat and lamb, fried onions, coriander, rosemary, and cumin made their mouths water, and they could not resist stopping to eat. They had been given coins by Lysandridas (who could remember being young and had anticipated this eventuality), and they eagerly bought chunks of grilled lamb, onions, and cooked carrots all folded into a thin pocket of fresh bread. In their inexperience, they paid three times the normal price without even haggling or batting an eye; but although they sniffed at the wine, they were afraid to try it. It smelled far too strong, and they had only a little water to mix with it.

Instead they continued down to the harbour. This was easy. All they had to do was follow any street that sloped downwards. Here, collected behind a strong sea wall that extended out into the bay like a protective arm, were a collection of ships lying side by side. The bulk of the vessels were fishing boats and merchantmen with rounded bows and at most one bank of oars; but moored to the outer side of the sea wall were two giant, two-masted, sharp-nosed triremes. The boys were drawn to them like bees to honey.

They lay bow to stern, their oars shipped and their sails stowed. Their springs and lines creaked as they rose and fell on the swells. In wonder, the boys wandered up and down the sea wall, admiring them. They were disappointed that there was no one aboard to whom they could put any questions, but they paced them off, determining that one was a good 20 feet longer than the other. They were just debating whether they could risk going aboard one and exploring it when they noticed that people were gathering on the quay in increasing numbers, and with a little gasp of surprise Leonidas realised that yet another trireme was making straight toward the harbour entrance.

Even as he watched, the sails were being hauled up into their tackle, and yet there was no slackening of pace. Although the ship was close enough for one to hear the hiss of the more-than-a-hundred oars as they dipped into the water and the steady wail of the pipes from below deck. She was moving so fast that a bow wave curled back from the bronze-cloaked tip of the battering ram. Leonidas felt instinctive fear at the sight of the dangerous instrument pointed apparently straight at him. Then in the next instant it veered just enough to aim directly for the mouth of the harbour and—still travelling at high speed—plunged through the narrow gap in the sea wall. The awesome battering ram was pointed at the cluster of merchantmen tied to the quays, and Leonidas started running toward the end of the sea wall to get a better look of the inevitable crash.

Before he could fully grasp what had happened, the port oars were halted in the air, water dripping from them, and the starboard oars started to turn the bows around. Then, in perfect unison, the port oars again dipped into the water—backwatering. Now the great trireme pivoted around, and an instant later went in alongside the inside of the sea wall with just feet to spare. The oars were shipped and she glided into the tiny space, while barefoot sailors along her deck jumped ashore with lines. They dug in their heels and brought her to a halt just before her ram crashed into the side of the quay.

"Show-off!" a man mumbled on Leonidas' left, and he looked up. The man beside him appeared to be a sailor, or rather a marine. He was in a simple chiton with a leather breastplate. He wore a full beard, greaves, and a helmet shoved back on his neck, but he was barefoot and he seemed to have salt in his hair and beard—and very likely in his veins as well, Leonidas thought.

"Is it one of ours, sir?" Leonidas asked anxiously.

"That?!" The marine glanced down at Leonidas, torn between contempt for so much ignorance and pleasure at the opportunity to show off. Recognising his audience as three boys of the Spartan agoge, he quickly gave in to the latter. "Not on your life. We haven't got a crew in all of Lacedaemon who could pull off a manoeuvre like that. She's Samian."

He pointed out to his ignorant audience the fresh paint that gave this ship gunnels that gleamed even in the near darkness, and the large glinting "eyes" beside her prow. He praised the size and strength of the reinforcements on the ram. He assured them that her mast was tall and the yard broad, and said she had set a sail with a coiled snake device that suggested she came from the Samian tyrant, Marandros, himself. The fuss being made about a fat man, who now emerged from the deckhouse wearing very elaborate clothes and heavy gold jewellery, seemed to support this thesis. In fact, there was a large delegation of dignitaries on the quay to greet this traveller and his extensive entourage, and after much bowing and apparently the exchange of gifts, the fat man was offered a litter and then carried away, surrounded by an escort of soldiers carrying torches and trailed by his own numerous entourage.

Only after the commotion for the stranger had died down did Leonidas risk asking the strange marine about the other ships. "What about these triremes?" he asked. "Are they ours?"

"These poor wrecks?" the man answered with a contemptuous look at the ships Leonidas and his friends had found splendid just a few minutes earlier. "I don't know who they belong to. Whoever owns them, they brought back the remnants of that ill-fated expedition to Libya."

"You mean the colonists under Dorieus, son of Anaxandridas?" Leonidas asked in alarm.

"That's right—the fools who set off without consulting Delphi! What could you expect of such an impudent expedition? Got just what they deserved: run off the African continent by Carthage. Carthage isn't about to let some Spartan princeling get a foothold on its continent—no matter how small and insignificant the colony might have been. They drove him off, killing many of his companions, followers, and slaves. All the colonists who remained could fit aboard these two poor ships. Lucky to get off at all."

"What of Dorieus? Did he make it back?"

"The Spartan prince, you mean? Unfortunately—not that he looked much like a prince in his rags. But he still had all his limbs, as far as I could see—and a black woman, too. Yes, Dorieus made it back, all right—more's the pity. He wasted the lives of not a few good men, and from what I heard in the taverns last night, all he can talk about is revenge. Mad, that's what he is, obsessed with being a king! Who needs kings nowadays? You'd be better off in Sparta without them—much less exporting them. Mark my words, lad, that one will cause trouble in Sparta still. It would have been better for everyone if the Carthaginians had put an end to him."

The marine was right. Before Dorieus had been in Sparta more than a week, he was making trouble again. On the one hand he resumed his old tactics of openly denying Cleomenes respect, and on the other he lambasted the Assembly for sending him off with so little support and then "abandoning" him. He claimed to have sent pleas for help, which the ephors steadfastly claimed not to have received. Dorieus conceded that one ship might have been lost, but three? He found this incredible. So did some of his peers. From what Leonidas and his friends overheard in the syssitia and from what Philippos reported, a significant minority of the Peers felt Dorieus had been unfairly treated.

This sentiment was assisted by the fact that his arch-rival, King Cleomenes, had not done anything to win over the citizens' affection or respect during Dorieus' absence. Although he was still young and not actively disliked, there was nevertheless a faction that found him suspiciously self-indulgent. There was his choice of wife on one hand—which was very greedy; and now he could to be seen entertaining—and being entertained by—the Samian ambassador in an "unfittingly" lavish manner.

In fact, it was rumoured throughout the city (and not the least loudly by the perioikoi who ran the major stalls on the agora) that the Samian ambassador had arrived in Gytheon with a ship "loaded with treasure". Precisely because Leonidas had seen that magnificent ship, he tended to believe the claims. Furthermore, the perioikoi merchant who had the corner stall just behind the temple to the Horse-breeding Poseidon said that the Samian ambassador had brought chests full of ivory, gold, and silver into the city under the cover of darkness and guarded by crack troops.

"You can be sure he intends to buy something with all that loot— and it ain't Lacedaemonian pottery!" The merchant gestured contemptuously toward the stalls across the street with their humdrum offerings of household goods. Leonidas had been told that at the time of the Tegean wars, Lacedaemonian pottery had found markets in the entire world, but today the best pots came from Corinth and Athens. Even the Spartans preferred these imports to their own simple wares.

"But what could he want to buy?" Leondias pressed his informant. This was a merchant of horse and chariot tack who knew Prokles and his friends from frequent dealings with Prokles' father and grandfather. The boys sometimes hung around his shop in their spare time, helping to polish his wares in exchange for a good meal and gossip like this.

"Why, what Sparta makes best!" the merchant replied with a chuckle.

The three boys gazed at him, still not understanding—until Alkander ventured cautiously, "You mean our soldiers?"

"Exactly!"

"We aren't mercenaries!" Leonidas protested indignantly.

"But you have to go wherever your kings lead. Why do you think the Samian ambassador spends most of his time at the Agiad royal palace? It's not to admire the king's young heir, fine as he might be. Though, of course, it could be because of his wife...." The merchant laughed at his own joke, but Leonidas was distracted by the reference to the Agiad heir.

Cleomenes' beautiful bride had delivered a healthy son to her husband and the city shortly after the winter solstice. He had been named Agis, after the founder of the dynasty, as if to reinforce Cleomenes' own claim to the throne. This son, whatever name he carried, had certainly strengthened Cleomenes' position.

Admittedly, Dorieus had a son, too, but he had been born of an African woman. As such, the boy had no claim to citizenship, much less the throne. Still, Leonidas suspected his brother had brought the woman and baby with him to prove to everyone that he—unlike his father—was already potent at the young age of 24. He had obviously hoped that Cleomenes would be childless and had hoped his proven potency would furnish further evidence of his superiority over his rival. But young Agis, born of a beautiful and noble Spartan bride, made his own half-black baby an embarrassment rather than an asset. The African woman was hastily sent back to Gytheon with her embarrassing child, and it was said that Dorieus was looking for a "good" Spartan maiden to take to wife.

Prokles, meanwhile, was asking the periokoi merchant: "What do they want our army for?"

"Why, to fight the Persians," the perioikoi answered, as if this should have been obvious.

"What have the Persians to do with us?" Prokles wanted to know.

"Surely you know—provincial as you boys are—that they have enslaved almost all the Greek cities of Ionia?!"

"Is Samos enslaved?" Leonidas asked, remembering the magnificent ship and all the alleged treasure the Samian ambassador had brought.

"They are subjects of the Persian king. They may not live like chattel slaves nor even like our helots, but they are not truly free men," the merchant insisted firmly.

"Of course not," Alkander retorted with a shrug. "They have a tyrant."

"Isn't it the tyrant that sent the ambassador?" Leonidas was beginning to think he was confused in some way.

"Of course it was the tyrant that sent the ambassador. But Marandros is a Greek tyrant, and he does not like being under the Persian yoke."

The three boys just gazed at the merchant with various expressions of disbelief and confusion on their faces. It didn't entirely make sense to them, and it was soon evident that they were not alone in this.

When, not long afterwards, King Cleomenes announced to the Assembly that Marandros wanted a Spartan army to help "free" Ionia from the Persians, the debate among the adults was not substantially different from that which the boys had had. There were those who felt the Persians were a growing threat, devouring one city—or indeed whole nations—after another, that had to be stopped sooner or later. Others insisted that what happened on the other side of the Aegean was not any business of Sparta's. Others, more practical or more subtle, simply pointed out that Sparta did not have the ships to transport an army to Samos. To this the Samian ambassador replied that Samos would provide the bottoms, but this offer only made the old men in the assembly even more suspicious. It would mean that the Spartans would also have no way to return home—unless and until their Samian "hosts" provided the ships. That seemed a very risky proposition indeed, the old men insisted firmly, implying that by accepting Samian bottoms for transport, the Spartan army would be effectively "kidnapped" by a foreigner for his own purposes. Sentiment started to swing against support for Samos.

By now two factions had emerged. One faction was led by Dorieus, fervently advocating support for Samos as a means of establishing Sparta's reputation abroad. The other faction's most eloquent spokesman was Demaratus, the heir to the ailing Eurypontid King Ariston. Demaratus argued that it would be absolute madness to embark upon a foreign expedition in foreign bottoms to take on the most powerful nation on earth.

Dorieus mocked Demaratus for doubting that Spartan arms would prevail, which of course caused the Eurypontid to make disparaging remarks about the success of Dorieus' own expedition.

Dorieus responded with an unseemly display of temper, blaming—again—the ephors for abandoning him. While Dorieus was criticised for losing his temper, he nevertheless seemed to be gaining sympathy for the cause of supporting Samos. After all, people started saying, after Spartan humiliation at the hands of Carthage, Sparta could not "afford" to be seen as frightened of any foreign power. Sparta's reputation would be damaged and even the Allies of the League would start to question Sparta's right to leadership, if it did not demonstrate the "unquestionable prowess of its magnificent army". (There always seemed to be elements in the Assembly that devoured such phrases, even though they were at odds with a culture that demanded modesty and brevity of its individual citizens.)

It was at this stage that Cleomenes put an end to the whole debate, however, by peremptorily and unilaterally sending the Samian ambassador packing. He sent him away with high-sounding words about Spartan arms not being for sale, but Leonidas couldn't help but think he only sided with Demaratus to foil his hated rival Dorieus.

After all the excitement had died down with the departure of the Samian ambassador, Leonidas was startled to be stopped by Dorieus as he came off the race track after a long run. Dorieus had not previously made any effort to contact him, and Leonidas had observed him only from a distance—not keen to draw attention to himself, either. Since his return, Dorieus had outfitted himself in new clothes and armour, and he was again a splendid sight in the eyes of his little brother. Leonidas was at a particular disadvantage under the circumstances; he was naked, dripping wet with sweat, and gasping for breath.

His elder brother seemed to look him up and down and find him wanting. "I hear you still aren't herd leader," were his first words.

Bent over and holding on to his knees as he tried to get his breath back, Leonidas admitted this was true. "Yes, sir."

"Why?"

"Ephorus is a good leader, sir."

"And you aren't," Dorieus concluded.

Leonidas held his tongue. He had no idea whether he was a good leader or not, but he hadn't forgotten what the marine in Gytheon had said about this brother, either.

"I also hear you adopted a *mothake*," Dorieus continued.

Apparently he had taken some interest in his youngest brother after all, Leonidas thought, and readily answered, "Yes, sir." He was proud of paying Alkander's agoge fees.

"A weak stutterer, who did not deserve to be in the agoge in the first place!" Dorieus dismissed Leonidas' friend.

"That's not true, sir!" Leonidas responded hotly, and then got hold of himself before he could truly get in trouble. Meeting his brother's eyes, he insisted firmly, "Alkander is as good as any of us, and smarter than most. Sir."

"A stutterer?" Dorieus retorted, incredulous.

"He only stutters when he's nervous—"

"Oh, a nervous boy as well! May the Gods protect the men who have to stand with him in a phalanx—but then, that will be you, won't it?" his brother seemed to sneer.

"I would be happy to stand with Alkander in line of battle," Leonidas replied steadfastly.

Dorieus laughed outright. "All this courage from a boy who's never even stood in a phalanx in drill, much less in battle."

Leonidas had no answer to that; it was true.

"At least you've grown some," Dorieus observed. This too was true. Leonidas had suddenly started growing, and although Brotus was growing, too, it was no longer at so fast a pace. Leonidas was starting to catch up on his twin.

"I do not intend to let things rest where they are," Dorieus announced next. "I am going to Delphi and will get a judgment—a judgment that I can show the Assembly—and then see if the ephors can stop me."

Leonidas wondered how he could be so sure Delphi would support him, but he held his tongue. His brother nodded goodbye (or was it "dismissed") and then turned his back and was gone. Leonidas was glad when a few days later he set off for Delphi.

———

By then the summer was over, and the time had come for the 13-year-olds to prove they had learned the skills taught to them over the last seven years by living "outside society" for 40 days and 40 nights. The rules of the exercise prohibited them from carrying any weapons except the small sickle-shaped hand tool they had learned to use for a variety of tasks. They were likewise prohibited from taking dogs or beasts of burden with them. Nor could they take money or extra clothing. If they were sighted in a city or town, they were subject to immediate arrest, and—unless they could escape—they were deemed to have failed this all-important test. Depending on how serious the breach of the rules was, a boy could be held back a year and thereby forced to suffer the almost unbearable indignity of remaining a "little boy" for a year longer; or, theoretically, a boy could be expelled from the agoge altogether—but no one could remember that ever happening. It *was* said, however, that boys had died during their "fox time", usually the victim of wild animals they wounded but failed to kill, or in a rare case or two from outright starvation.

Of course, neither the officials of the agoge nor Spartan society at large was really as naïve as official policy pretended. Everyone knew that the boys could and did find warmth, shelter, and even food in the homes and gardens of "sympathisers" and, of course, they helped themselves to anything left about carelessly. As a result, wise house-wives and helot tenants guarded carefully anything they did not want stolen during the annual "fox season". But officially, the boys were supposed to live entirely like men cut off from their units in enemy territory—by hunting (without dogs), trapping, and living off the wilderness.

Given their poor performance the previous year, Alkander and Leonidas were both somewhat nervous about enduring this all-important test. Prokles, on the contrary, was completely unconcerned. In fact, he seemed to be openly looking forward to the ordeal. When his mother showed all three boys a hollow trunk where she promised to leave "emergency rations" for them, and told them to leave a certain shutter of the salt-house off one hinge if they needed more, Prokles announced confidently, "Don't worry about me, Mom;" adding to Leonidas and Alkander, "You can take all the stuff you want. I won't need it."

Of course both Alkander and Leonidas knew that Prokles was the best trapper among them, but his confidence still seemed somewhat exaggerated. After all, it had been another exceptionally hot and dry summer, and although not quite as bad as the year they found Alkander at the fountain, there was less game in the forests than was usual at this time of the year. Nevertheless, there was nothing they could do but hope Prokles was right and thank his mother earnestly.

"Now don't you worry," she answered. "I'm not going to let any of you starve; just be very careful when you come to get the stuff. The dogs will recognise you, of course, and won't bark, but you never know who might be visiting for some reason. Come only after dark and be as quiet as you can." They had no need for her admonishments. They were determined not to get caught, even if it meant half starving to death.

Over the centuries, the boys facing this ordeal had devised many different strategies for survival. There were some who had whole networks of "helpers" (nannies and married sisters, grandmothers and aunts), who promised to provide a veritable feast of "emergency rations" at various points. Others had hidden bows away in secret places and planned to hunt their way through the 40 days. There were boys who planned to live primarily by scrounging, and others who bragged that they had become adept at theft. Leonidas hoped to survive primarily by trapping and scavenging.

Although the boys were not supposed to keep together and would in fact be left by their eirenes at different spots all across Laconia, Leonidas, Prokles, and Alkander (like many of their fellows) had agreed on a place to meet in three days' time. No matter where they were left, they were confident that they could find their way to this particular glen partway up into the Taygetos. They had often camped out there during summer hunting trips with Philippos, who now promised to leave burning embers under the ash in the pit there every few days. Leonidas liked to think that he would get along without either the food or the fire, but it was a comfort to know that they would be there for him if necessary.

Leonidas also made sacrifices to several of the Gods on the evening before the full moon when the "fox time" started. It was always a good idea, he thought, to sacrifice to Zeus and Athena; but the main sacrifice he saved for the Dioskouroi, Kastor and Polydeukes. Being a twin himself, Leonidas felt a strong affinity to the Divine Twins, and particularly to Kastor, "breaker of horses". The fact that Polydeukes, like his own twin Brotus, was a boxer, tended to make him identify even more strongly with Kastor, and it was to him that he brought a wooden horse that he had spent most of the summer carving.

When the day came for the 13-year-olds to set off on their "fox time", Leonidas' unit was marched to the southeast, the exact opposite direction from Prokles' kleros. Alkander was dropped off, then another two-hour march beyond him Leonidas was left on his own, and Prokles continued with the rest of the unit, now winding up into the Parnon range.

Leonidas found himself not far from the kleros on which his mother was buried; and thanking the Twins for their protection, decided to take advantage of this unexpected good fortune. Not only did he know his way very well around this particular kleros, including knowing the location in the cellars where meat was cured and dried fruits packed, he also knew the helots. He did not think they would turn him in if they caught him.

He was right. The old man who came roaring down into the cellar was tamed instantly with a simple, "It's just me, Polypeites."

The old man held up a torch, growling, "Who's 'me'?!"

"Leonidas, son of Anaxan—"

"Is it really you, Master Leo? What are you doing snooping around in the cellar like a thief! Why didn't you come call on us proper?! We haven't seen you in such a long time. Come up to the hearth and have a nice chat with me and my wife."

"I really can't risk that, Polypeites. I'm not supposed to talk to anyone—much less enjoy a cozy fire."

"Why's that?" The old man sounded completely baffled.

"Well, it's the Phouxir—"

"What?! Are you that old already? I could have sworn you weren't a day over ten. Thirteen?" He held up the torch higher, coming nearer. "Well, you have grown. Getting almost as big as Brotus now, aren't you? We never see anything of him, either."

"We don't have a lot of free time in the agoge," Leonidas tried to explain, for the first time in his life feeling guilty for neglecting the helots here. It had truly never occurred to him that they might miss him.

"No, I know. It's a harsh life they put you through," the old man agreed, shaking his head in sympathy. "But you should come see us now and again. My wife often talks of how nice it was when you and your brother used to come here for holidays."

Leonidas promised to come again during a holiday—provided he survived the fox time—and the old man took the hint and provided him with a hearty package of hard sausage, dried figs, and fresh bread. Leonidas then set out under cover of darkness, making for the rendezvous with Alkander and Prokles.

Two days later, he found Alkander waiting for him in the designated glen. He shared what was left of his provisions, and they talked about their adventures until they fell asleep. Woken when the shadows reached them, they discovered that Prokles had still not joined them, but they did not worry. After all, he had clearly been taken farther away and would need more time to get back. Meanwhile, they were hungry and it was time to set up traps. Since they knew this area quite well from hunting here, they were already pretty much in agreement on where they wanted to set up their traps. Working together, they laid six traps, and then Alkander volunteered to go down and see what Prokles' mother had left for them in the hollow tree, while Leonidas collected mushrooms and nuts. Alkander came back with a hard cheese and fresh apples, which they devoured at once before settling in for the day.

When after five more days there was still no sign of Prokles, Leonidas and Alkander started to worry. They were certain that he would be able to find the glen, since he had chosen it himself as the meeting place. They would have liked to go out looking for him, but had no idea where he had been left, and so in which direction they ought to look. After much debate, they agreed that the only thing they could do was continue waiting for him here.

Meanwhile they were coping quite well. Their traps were yielding at a rate of one small animal every other day or so, and their mushroom and chestnut staples kept them going between times—that or another cheese from Prokles' mother. They had even managed to light a fire on two occasions from the embers Philippos left them. Eating the meat cooked was a wonderful luxury, and they were soon spending more time and energy on collecting firewood and keeping a fire going than in actually trapping or collecting nuts, berries, and mushrooms.

By the time the moon was waxing again, they had convinced themselves that it was just a matter of sitting it out; and despite a certain
nagging worry about the absent Prokles, they were quite content.

And then the rains came.

Of course, rains were usual during the Phouxir, and they had
thought they were ready for them. In fact, after the first drenching
day that killed their fire, they realised that they were woefully unpre-
pared. The forest around their glen offered shelter from the sun, soft
bedding, and hiding from other people if needed, but not shelter
from the rain. They had no change of clothes, and once they were
drenched through, they were wet even in the intervals when it didn't
rain. After three days of this they were so miserable, they seriously
talked of going down and seeking shelter in the salt-house of the
kleros; but knowing that the kleroi of boys undergoing the fox time
were frequently "visited" by officials of the agoge discouraged them.
After all, it was no secret that Prokles' mother had all but adopted
Leonidas and Alkander. The authorities were certain to keep a close
eye on her—particularly in weather like this. Instead, they took to
sheltering in the mouth of a cave. This gave them some protection
from the rain itself, but the cold, dank air that came out of the cave
behind them gave them both colds.

And the rain kept coming. It came in what seemed like ever
heavier clouds, and the earth could no longer absorb it. The little
stream near the glen where they had collected their water broke its
banks and ran ever faster. It was too dangerous to drink at it now, as
the banks kept breaking away and it swept everything it could grasp
along with it—saplings, soil, and rocks. The boys collected rainwater
for drinking, and watched in horror as the little stream turned into a
raging torrent.

Then just before sunset on the 29th day of their ordeal, a horrible
thunderstorm, worse than anything they had ever experienced in their
whole lives, burst over the Taygetos range and hurled hail and deluges
of water upon them with unspeakable fury. The thunder cracked
overhead, and the lightning came so incessantly it was impossible
to count the interval between lightning and thunder. The light just
flickered brighter and duller while the thunder cracked and rumbled
without pause. The hail that crashed through foliage tore away not

only the leaves, but whole twigs, and flung birds and squirrels down to the earth, bludgeoned to death by the balls of ice. The wind was meanwhile tearing the branches off the trees, and then with horrible cracking and crunching, whole trees started to break under the fury of the storm.

Caught away from the cave entrance and afraid to move in the raging world around them, Leonidas and Alkander took shelter against a huge rock, sitting on the down slope of the rock with their backs against it. The rock had a slight overhang that offered them no real shelter from the rain, but kept the falling branches and trees from crashing directly on to their heads. They clung to each other, terrified of the storm that seemed to be tearing the whole world apart and afraid to admit it. Leonidas kept asking himself what they could possibly have done to offend Zeus this much. And for a while he thought the storm would never end, or could only end in absolute destruction—the opening of the earth and the swallowing of everything.

After an immeasurable time, however, Leonidas realised that not only had the hail stopped and the thunder and lightning moved farther east, but that the rain and wind were easing, too. And then he heard it: someone was calling for help.

"Alkander! Listen!"

Alkander had heard it, too. They lifted their heads and held their breath. "It's from the stream!" Alkander was already struggling to his feet.

The ground around them was treacherous. Not only was it littered with branches torn from the trees, it was slippery, and they stumbled and slid frequently as they made their way toward the cries for help.

The voice calling was high-pitched and desperate, and although it was not identifiable, they both knew instinctively that it was one of them—one of the 13-year-olds out here in the wilderness on his own. By now it was completely dark. Any lingering dusk was obscured by the thick clouds still over the Taygetos; and the rain, which had eased to a steady pelting, further reduced visibility. The flashes of lightning came less frequently now and lit up a landscape already transformed from just a few hours ago. The rushing torrent of the little stream had torn away whole boulders and cut a new path down the face of the mountain. And there, in the middle of the new torrent, clinging desperately to a lone oak tree that stood on what had become an island in the deluge, was a naked boy.

It wasn't Prokles. In fact, the boy wasn't from their own unit at all, but that didn't matter. He was clinging desperately to the trunk of the tree, and it seemed obvious to him and to Leonidas and Alkander that his strength could not last much longer. Leonidas and Alkander worked their way to the closest point on the new bank of the stream and called out to the other boy. "Climb higher! Get into the branches of the tree!"

"I can't!" the boy screamed back. "I've tried! Help me!"

Alkander and Leonidas looked at one another in horror. It was impossible for either of them to step into the racing waters unless they were secured to the bank by a rope or some other means. If they stepped into the water on their own, they would only be flushed away to their death. "Should I run down to Prokles' kleros?" Alkander asked.

"Help me!" the boy kept screaming. "Help! I'm losing my grip! Help!"

"That will take too long. Surely there's a strong branch we could hold out to him," Leonidas countered. They started to look around for a branch long and strong enough for them to hold it out across the stream. If the other boy could hold on to the far end, they thought, they could then drag him ashore.

To their amazement, they saw another boy coming towards them in the darkness. After a moment they recognised Prokles.

"Where did you come from?" Leonidas wanted to know.

"Later! We've got to save that other boy first!"

Alkander found a suitable branch, and together they got it dislodged from the tangle of underbrush and with their little scythes, cut the last sinews that held it still to its trunk. The boy, clinging to the trunk of the oak tree, was still screaming hysterically, and they shouted to him to catch hold of the tip of the branch when they held it out to him. He was clearly reluctant to let go of the living oak tree to trust this branch; but by his own admission, he could not hold on to the tree much longer. He flung himself toward the offered branch, throwing himself on it more than taking hold of it, and none of the boys were prepared for what happened.

The force of the water was so great that the boy's body was whipped around in circles as he clung desperately to the branch. The sudden twisting of the branch in their own hands wrenched it completely clean out of Alkander's hands, and he fell over backwards. Leonidas and Prokles couldn't hold it alone, and they were dragged forward. The earth gave way under Leonidas' feet, and he plunged into the stream himself. He was barely rescued from being swept downstream by Prokles grabbing him, and then Prokles and Alkander together dragging him out of the water.

The shock and exertion left all three boys gasping for air, and Leonidas himself choking up water that he had swallowed in his short dousing. Yet despite the terror at their own near disaster, they could not lose track of the fact that the other boy was lost. His wail of despair filled the darkness and then ended abruptly.

"By all the Gods!" Leonidas cried out, trying to get to his feet. Prokles and Alkander just left him behind as they ran downstream along the banks, stumbling and tripping over stones, roots and branches, in the direction of the sudden silence.

Leonidas limped after them. He'd hurt his ankle when he was plunged into the stream.

Prokles screamed out of the darkness ahead of him. "I've found him! Here! Come quick."

Alkander and Leonidas followed the voice of their friend. Prokles was lying flat on his belly in the cluttered muck beside the stream and reaching out toward a white thing that, as Leonidas came closer, resolved itself into the body of the other boy. He was draped over the root of a tree, his limbs entangled in other rubbish, and the water surged over his head. Leonidas was certain he was dead.

Together the three boys dragged the body ashore, and then—as they had been taught to do—they turned him on his stomach and pulled his arms behind him to try to expel the water from his lungs. With a cough that made Leonidas' hair stand on end, the other boy gave a sign of life, and now Alkander took over, pumping rhythmically on the other boy's shoulders until the coughing came again.

By the time they had brought him back to life, however, they had

had time to see his other injuries. One leg was broken clean through, and his head was bleeding profusely from a horrible gash where he must have crashed against a rock before being snagged by the root. They had managed to restart his breathing, but he was groaning and vomiting now, obviously in terrible pain, and they were terrified.

"We've got to get help," Leonidas decided.

The other two boys stared at him. To go to anyone for help was to break the rules, and they would not graduate.

"If we don't, Koiris" (they had identified the victim by now) "will die," Leonidas told them.

The other two boys looked at the victim, whimpering in only semi-conscious misery, and they could not doubt it. In fact, Prokles replied bluntly, "I think he's going to die anyway."

"We can't assume that."

"We can't carry him all the way to Sparta, either."

"No, we'll have to take him to Paidaretos kleros." Although the boys were close enough to Prokles' kleros to go down to the hollow tree, it was not in fact the closest kleros to the glen or their present location. On the other hand, Paidaretos was a very unpleasant elderly Spartiate, whom the boys instinctively distrusted.

"He's as like to slam the door in our faces as help!" Prokles protested.

"Well, then, we could try to go to Cleitagora's," Leonidas suggested. This was the widow who occupied the next nearest kleros, the one just before Prokles'.

"All right," Prokles agreed. "We better make a stretcher."

Working in the dark and rain, the boys tore what was left of their himations into cords with which to bind branches together into a stretcher. When they went to move Koiris on to the stretcher, however, he screamed so shrilly that they lost courage and backed off. But they had to get him on the stretcher. They made a second attempt. He screamed again. They stopped, looked at one another, and then, gritting their teeth, they moved him on to the stretcher despite his screams and wails.

The trip down to Cleitagora's kleros in the dark and rain was a different nightmare. The lightning and thunder were now far away, and only the drenching rain was left. Leonidas' ankle was killing him and swelling up rapidly. The other two boys shouldered the stretcher and told him to lead the way. But the darkness was so impenetrable that they stumbled and tripped frequently. And each time they did, Koiris screamed or whimpered. They hated him a little by the time they finally staggered into the driveway of Cleitagora's kleros, where they were greeted by the furious baying of her hounds sounding the alarm.

Lights emerged at once as shutters were thrown open both at the helot cottages and the main house. Then a door opened and a huge hunting hound came bounding toward them, barking viciously.

The boys set down the stretcher and froze. The great hound circled them, his teeth bared, while he emitted a low, ominous growl from his throat. One false move and they would be dead. "Who's there?" an elderly woman called out.

As usual, his friends looked at Leonidas, and Leonidas spoke up. "Leonidas, son of Anaxandridas, ma'am. One of my age-cohort, Koiris, son of Polymedes, has been seriously injured, ma'am. He needs a doctor. Please can we bring him—"

The woman was already beside them, silencing her dog with a single command. "Take him inside at once. Go on! Hurry up!" She pointed toward the open door, and the boys shouldered their burden a last time and went forward into the large, warm hearth-room.

After almost a month in the wilderness, that fire-warmed room in the rainstorm was more wonderful than the finest palace of the Persian emperor. The floor was tiled, the roof beamed, the walls hung with woven hangings that kept out the cold and the damp. The smell of the wood fire mixed with the scents of a meal of meat and onions and rosemary.

As the boys entered, two other women came to their feet, but the boys didn't take much notice of them. They were following the staccato instructions of their hostess. "Put the stretcher down there! Right there!" Then over her shoulder to one of the women: "Fetch me a torch or a lamp!" To the boys again, "What happened?"

"We don't know for sure, ma'am" (as usual, the boys left the talking to Leonidas). "Just after the worst of the thunderstorm, we heard cries for help. We found Koiris clinging to an oak tree in the middle of the stream. We tried to reach a large branch across to him, but we lost hold of the branch. He was swept farther downstream until he was caught on a root. We dragged him ashore, but he had nearly drowned, and you can see he hit his head on something and his leg is broken."

Cleitagora was inspecting the naked boy closely as Leonidas spoke. "What were you doing out in weather like this in the first place?" she asked sharply without looking up from her inspection.

"It's the Phouxir, ma'am."

"What? You're 13?" She looked at the three bedraggled boys and snorted rather contemptuously, but then she turned to the other woman who was standing over the stretcher as well. To Leonidas' dismay he recognised this second woman as "that other woman", his father's second wife and the mother of King Cleomenes.

"We have to get a doctor at once," Cleitagora announced. "This boy's eye is totally crushed."

In horror, Leonidas looked at Koiris' eye. In the darkness they had not been able to see the extent of the damage, noting only the gash to his head that was bleeding profusely.

"I'll go down to Lysandridas' kleros and have him send a horseman for a doctor," Chilonis answered, pulling her shawl up over her head and heading out into the rain and darkness.

Cleitagora meanwhile ordered the other woman, who was evidently a helot, to fetch poppy seed and wine. She administered this to Koiris, and then turned her sharp eyes on the other three boys. Her eyes made them all squirm uncomfortably, aware of their filth, the rags they were wearing—and the fact that they had no right to be here.

"Let me see that hand!" she ordered, pointing at Alkander, and Alkander timidly held out his left hand. "Two fingers are broken," she told him after a short examination. "How did that happen?"

"When the b-b-branch t-t-tore l-l-loose in my hands. It t-t-twisted around...." Alkander fell silent, ashamed.

"And your ankle?" she asked Leonidas.

"When the earth gave away under me, ma'am..."

She shook her head in evident disapproval. "Go with my woman here to the kitchen and get out of your wet things. Amycla, let them clean themselves off in hot water and hang their chitons out to dry.

Bind up this boy's fingers and that boy's ankle. Give them some warm milk and broth as well." Then, directing her remarks to the boys again, she advised firmly, "When the doctor comes, you best have 'disappeared' out the back again. I'll tell the doctor 'someone' just called out and left your friend at my doorstep."

And that was exactly what they did. When they heard horses and voices in the drive, they ducked out the back door of the kitchens into the yard—by the smell of things they were near the pigpen and chicken coop. It had stopped raining, however, and the moon was actually starting to show through the ragged clouds. By the light of the moon they climbed over the fence of the yard and disappeared into the underbrush.

Only now, as they trudged back along the side of the road, keeping to the trees and undergrowth, did Leonidas again ask: "Prokles, where did you suddenly come from?"

"I'll show you."

Just before dawn they passed through the glen that Leonidas and Alkander had used as their base these past four weeks, and continued up the slope until around the fold of the mountain they found the entrance to another cave. Prokles led them confidently into the cave—down a steep, now slippery incline, around a pit, and into a tunnel. They had to crawl on all fours for a short distance and then found themselves in a large, spacious room—in which the remnants of a fire still flickered.

Not only was there a fire, there was a reed bed, complete with blankets; there were sacks apparently full of provisions; there were two skinned hares hanging out by their hind feet, a bow, and a quiver of arrows. "Have you been living here all along?" Leonidas wanted to know.

"Of course. I found it two years ago. I've been planning and provisioning it ever since."

Leonidas was at a loss for words. Part of him was shocked that Prokles had broken the rules to this extent. Part of him admired him for it. And another part of him was angry that Prokles hadn't let him in on the secret from the start.

"You always want to do things by the rules, Leo," Prokles declared, as if reading his thoughts. "I would have brought you here if you had ever been in real trouble, but you seemed to be getting along just fine."

"You mean you knew we were at the glen?"

"Of course; I used to watch you from a distance and even listen to your conversations sometimes," Prokles admitted with a little self-conscious grin.

Leonidas felt like a perfect fool.

"And what brought you out last night?" Alkander wanted to know.

"The storm. I'd never heard anything like it, and I stood in the cave entrance watching it. Then just when I was about to go back inside, I thought I heard someone calling for help. I thought it might be one of you and followed the sound of the cries. Let's get some sleep now. Tomorrow night you can go fetch stuff to make up your own beds."

And so they made themselves as comfortable as they could and fell asleep almost at once.

———

At the end of their 40 days, the 13-year-olds emerged from wherever they had been hiding and returned to the agoge. They were mustered on the drill fields by unit in the state in which they returned—filthy, in rags, their hair already growing out, scratched and bruised, or even with broken bones as in Alkander's case. The Paidonomos inspected them, looking at each boy with a penetrating glance that seemed to see exactly who had cheated most. Many of the boys, like Leonidas and his friends, had lost their himations. A few were completely naked. Some of the boys really looked terrible—skin and bones, or badly cut up. Some, like Prokles, hardly looked the worse for wear at all.

The Paidonomos stepped on to the stones from which the commanding officers and sometimes the kings addressed the army. Slowly the excited chattering among the boys died away, and they waited expectantly. The Paidonomos congratulated the boys in front of him for passing the survival test. He assured them that all mustered here would graduate to "youth" at the winter solstice.

The Paidonomos then announced that three boys had been caught "breaking the rules". He was not more specific, and boys would have to use their own network to find out the details—in which, of course, they were morbidly interested. Then the Paidonomos raised his voice, and Leonidas thought it quivered slightly. "Five others of your age-cohort will also not be with you when you receive your new himations. They lost their lives in the terrible storm last month." When the Paidonomos intoned the name of Koiris, Leonidas felt as if he had been kicked in the gut. They had failed after all.

CHAPTER 6

Age 14

AT 14 THE BOYS OF THE agoge were given their first set of leather training armour, and wooden swords and spears. They were taught the fundamentals of their use and were also taught the basic building blocks of formation drill: to advance, halt, turn, and reverse. They had to learn to do all this to the signal of pipes.

Of course, the first thing they learned was that all these things that looked so easy when performed by their fathers on the drill fields were surprisingly difficult. It required endless hours of drill to get it right, and Leonidas was not alone in wishing (sometimes) that he was still only a "little boy" enjoying half a day of freedom and self-government, rather than spending his time in mind-dulling, body-aching drill on the dusty fields beyond the Eurotas day after day after day.

Naturally, the 14-year-olds only got use of the drill fields when it suited the older age-cohorts. The men on active service, unless there was some special exercise, generally used the fields in the freshness of the early morning. Only after they were dismissed and went home did the youths of the agoge have access to the fields. The older agoge classes might take the fields immediately after the adults left, in the heat of the noonday sun, or they might leave that "honour" to

the younger cohorts. The drill instructors, who were officers of the
reserve, were intent on ensuring that the boys developed the endurance and skill necessary to fight in the heat of the day as well as in the
dark of night. Drill, therefore, could be scheduled at any time of the
day or night, and it took precedence over all other activities.

Holidays became even more important under the circumstances,
and Leonidas counted the days between holidays, already looking
forward to the next when he returned to barracks from the last. As
before, the holidays were usually spent with Prokles' family; and when
Philippos asked the boys if they wanted to come with him to Prasiai
on the Gulf of Argos to help deliver a colt he had sold to a Lydian
horse breeder, the boys jumped at the chance.

With great excitement, the party consisting of Philippos and
Lysandridas with their attendants, the chief groom and two assistant
grooms, and the three boys set off on horseback. The colt that they
had sold was on a lead, and they also had four pack mules with feed,
grooming equipment, and emergency medical supplies for both man
and beast.

They followed the road to Chryssapha and crossed the Parnon
range over the pass to Kosmas, and then descended down to the Gulf
of Argos. As before, Leonidas was thrilled by the sight of the sea. He
couldn't get over the sheer limitlessness of the water when he stood at
the shore and could see into infinity without anything getting in his
line of vision.

The port was exciting, too. This east-coast port received more
ships bound for the busy harbours of the Aegean and Ionian coastline
than did Gytheon. In the inn where they took lodgings, they saw
men from Naxos and Miletos, Chalkis and Andros. There were even
Medes, looking very outlandish and speaking a completely incomprehensible language, stopping at the inn.

The Spartans shared their table with some Athenians. Indeed, the
two Athenians actually sought them out, asking if they were Spartiates
and then asking if they could join them. Leonidas held his breath and
all eyes turned to Lysandridas, as the oldest man present. Leonidas
had been very curious about Athenians ever since his last encounter
at the Hyacinthia, and he was afraid that Lysandridas would decline;
but Lysandridas graciously invited the Athenians to join them.

The landlord arrived almost at once with large jugs of both white and red wine, and took the Athenians' orders for a meal. The introductions were made. The Athenians identified themselves as Alcmaeonidae, which meant nothing to Leonidas, but his elders nodded knowingly. Even to Leonidas it was obvious that they were very rich. They wore heavy gold signet rings, and broad armbands of gold on their upper arms; and the pins that held their himations in place were as large as a man's fist and studded with jewels, as were their belts. The Athenians wore long silk chitons with magnificently embroidered borders, and their sandals had turquoise and coral beads on them. Leonidas was very grateful he was not in his agoge attire, but instead wearing a proper linen chiton and a bright blue himation of good quality. Although he tucked his bare feet deeper under his chair to hide them, nothing could hide his shaved head, and for the first time in his life he was ashamed of it.

Meanwhile, the Spartan adults introduced themselves. When Lysandridas gave his name, the Athenians evinced surprise.

"Not *the* Lysandridas, son of Teleklos, who twice drove the four-horse to victory at Olympia?" Apparently the Athenians knew about horses, Leonidas concluded.

Lysandridas admitted that this was he, and now the Athenians grew even more animated and friendly. "Noble Lysandridas, weren't you also instrumental in bringing down the Tegean tyrant Onomastros?" This had nothing to do with horses or sports, and it seemed strange to Leonidas that they had come up with such a silly notion. Prokles' grandfather had been a slave in Tegea, not a citizen active in politics.

Lysandridas exchanged a glance with his son before admitting, "I played a very minor role."

Leonidas stared at the old man, wondering what more he didn't know about his past.

"But surely you, as a man who has opposed tyranny, must understand the plight of Athens?"

"I do not envy you living under Hippias," Lysandridas said dryly. "Is it true his brother was murdered on the open streets?"

"It is true—and now Hippias' hard fist has grown even heavier." The Athenians agreed intently. "At least that is what we have been told." The adults nodded; what else would one expect? The Athenian continued, "Sparta has freed many cities oppressed by tyrants. Why won't it come to the rescue of the queen of all Greek cities?"

"Athens is a long way from Sparta," Philippos said dryly, and a touch sharply.

"A day beyond Corinth—surely that is nothing to an army that boasts of being able to cover 500 miles in 10 days."

"Who boasts that?" Philippos asked, more sharply still. Boasting was not Spartan custom.

"I heard it said that your young king, Cleomenes, made the claim," the Athenian insisted with an air of injured innocence.

"Oh." Lysandridas glanced at Leonidas, and then remarked, "Cleomenes is young and full of ambition—as a young man should be. But he has not taken the army anywhere."

"But you cannot approve of tyranny. Spartan foreign policy has consistently opposed tyranny. The leading citizens of Athens would show themselves grateful for any assistance Sparta gave them in ridding them of Hippias. *Very* grateful indeed."

"Last year the Samians sought to buy our help to expel the Persians. This year it was the Scythians. King Cleomenes sent them both away empty-handed—and they, too, offered huge rewards. I do not think our army is for sale—no matter how grateful anyone might be," Philippos replied firmly.

"Nor did we free Tegea for gold," Lysandridas added as a reminder.

The Athenians glanced at one another, and then one hastened to assure the stuffy Spartiates, "We did not mean to imply Sparta was mercenary; but as the oldest democracy in the world, surely you have a moral obligation to protect democracy wherever freedom-loving Greeks are struggling to restore it?"

"That is surely beyond the power of so small a city as Sparta. We have just one-fifth your number of citizens," Philippos insisted.

"And ten times that number of perioikoi—not to mention your helots and the entire wealth of Messenia, your forests and mines."

"We have neither silver nor fleet, much less gold. Sparta is poor compared to many other cities."

"Poor in riches, which you scorn, but rich in courage—at least that was what we were led to believe...."

"Courage, no less than gold, should not be squandered."

"Isn't helping a friend in need the noblest use of courage—short of fighting for one's own city and children?"

"Sparta will fight for her allies no less than for herself; but to my knowledge, Athens does not belong to the League."

"Can Sparta not look beyond the horizon of the Peloponnese?"

"When Croesus came to us asking friendship, we were happy to give it—far away as Lydia is—because it was the will of Delphi. If only Croesus had heeded the oracle more precisely, he might still stand between Ionia and the Persian menace. As it was, we had no chance to even come to his aid."

"Are you are saying that you require an order from Delphi to set foot outside of the Peloponnese?" The Athenian leaned forward as he asked this, evidently acutely interested in the answer.

Lysandridas and his son exchanged an uneasy glance, and Lysandridas answered for them. "It was at the advice of Delphi that we adopted our Constitution, and at the advice of Delphi that we became involved in Tegea. If it is the will of Apollo that we assist Athens, I do not think the Spartan kings or Assembly would risk refusal."

"Your new Eurypontid king, Demaratus, what is he like?" the Athenian asked next, reaching out to help himself to more wine as if relaxing after the previous exchange.

"Demaratus is an excellent charioteer," Lysandridas remarked. "I believe he plans to drive his own team at the next Olympiad."

The Athenians looked pleased. "Then we will undoubtedly see him there—as I presume we will see you?" The conversation turned to horses.

The next morning was spent making the final arrangements for the transport of the colt, and Lysandridas and Philippos were closeted with the agent representing the distant buyer. Bored with all the details of who paid what when and to whom, the boys wandered out to the waterfront.

Leonidas was drawn to the exotic, brightly painted merchant vessel that was identified as "Persian". Not knowing very much about ships, it was hard for him to define what made it seem so different from the various Greek vessels tied up around her, but there was certainly *something* different about her. Maybe it was the smell of exotic spices that seemed to emanate from her, or the woven baskets on the deck filled with dark nuts he had never seen before. Or the huge, heavily muscled man on the foredeck with a live snake draped across his shoulders.

Leonidas and his friends stared so intently at the man with the snake that they jumped in surprise when suddenly a voice close behind them asked, "Would you like to come aboard and look around?"

They turned sharply and discovered a tall man with a thick, oiled black beard and carefully coifed hair standing at the end of the gangplank. He spoke to them in Greek, but it was heavily accented. By his bright-coloured clothes festooned with beads and bronze balls, he was clearly foreign. Looking closer, the Spartan boys were appalled to notice that he had even painted his face. Dark lines outlined his eyes, and both lips and cheeks were rouged like a perioikoi woman.

Discomfort warred with curiosity about the ship. The man seemed to understand this. He smiled more graciously. "This is one of the finest merchant ships in the Great King's entire fleet. She has sailed from one end of his nearly endless Empire to the other—and she is filled with treasure. Let me show some of it to you." He gestured with his elegant, manicured hand for the boys to proceed aboard the ship.

Alkander shook his head, and backed away. Prokles and Leonidas, however, looked at one another. There was an unspoken dare in the air. They each challenged the other to show fear, and as was usual in such contests, Prokles took the risk first. He stepped on to the gangway, effectively forcing Leonidas to follow or be a "coward" in his own eyes.

Directly behind them came the Persian, purring to them in his strange voice. "Have you ever been aboard a Persian vessel before?" he asked, as he stepped on to the deck and made a signal to the man with the snake. The latter at once disappeared below deck.

Leonidas and Prokles shook their heads in answer to his question.

"I have many surprises for you then." He winked to them conspiratorially. "First let me show you around deck." As he showed them the various cargoes he had stowed on deck he chatted easily with them, trying to draw them out a bit. Where did they come from?

Laconia. What did their fathers do for a living? Leonidas answered that his father was dead and Prokles said his "had a farm". They were both vaguely aware that they shouldn't be here, and didn't want to be readily identifiable. The Persian seemed impressed to learn they were only 14. "My, you look bigger and stronger than that to me. Do you do a lot of sports?" The boys agreed that they did. The man smiled and nodded, and invited them to come below deck. "This is where we keep all our *real* treasures," he told them.

They descended a steep gangway that led down to the next lower deck. This deck was still above the waterline, and though the wooden ladder continued to descend to the oar and then into the darkness of the hold, at first they found themselves in a rather pleasant area with portholes open on both sides, admitting a cooling cross-breeze. Light flooded in from one row of portholes, and the sound of the open sea from the other. Great wooden chests, apparently filled with cargo, crammed the space right up to a curtain far towards the bows that apparently separated the accommodations. Behind them was a wooden partition.

Their host knocked on the door in the partition and was answered. He apparently announced their presence, because a moment later the door opened and a rather fat man, also with black curly beard and hair and a puffy, painted face, stood glaring at them. "My captain," their host indicated the fat man as he bowed deeply. The fat man frowned slightly, but then signalled the boys into his cabin.

At the threshold, Leonidas felt a shudder of alarm. Every instinct in his body said he should retreat, but Prokles again took the lead and boldly walked into the cabin of the Persian ship captain.

The captain was by no means as friendly as his mate. He glowered at the boys and then walked around them. Leonidas felt as if he was being inspected, but not in the way troops are inspected by their officers—rather like a horse at a horse-market. His stomach muscles started to cramp up. "Prokles, it's time we got back to your father. He must be—"

The mate was between them and the door, which he slammed shut with a foot. He was grinning. "You're on Persian territory, boys."

"No, we're not. We're still tied to the Lacedaemonian shore," Leonidas countered, in a cold sweat.

"Ships have the nationality of their flag. You might as well be in Sardis."

Leonidas made a plunge for the door; the mate backhanded him and then raised his knee into his groin. The pain knocked his breath and his vision away as he crumpled to the floor, but he wasn't out entirely. He heard Prokles also make an escape attempt, and heard him gasp and groan and fall. The captain made some remark and the mate laughed at it. A moment later Leonidas' hands were wrenched behind his back and tied so firmly he could feel them swelling. Prokles and he were dragged out of the captain's cabin and shoved down the ladder, past the oar-deck, to the hold. Here it was dark, dank, and terrifying.

Worse, they were shoved forward into a very small cage where they could not stand. The door of the cage was slammed and locked shut. It had evidently most recently been used for transporting fowl, because the floor of the cage was covered with dried bird shit.

The mate bent down to grin between the bars at them. "See what nice treasures I have here? Two pretty boys to please the tastes of many a master. Too old for castration, perhaps; but pretty, healthy boys equally suited to the perfumed couch or the oar-bench! You will bring me a very good price." He laughed and left them in the dark.

It had all taken less than two minutes.

"Alkander will bring my dad," Prokles managed to cough out after a moment.

Leonidas nodded. He had to believe that, but the sound of shouting and feet running directly overhead terrified him. It sounded to him as if they were getting ready to cast off. Now it struck him that everywhere the chests had been full of cargo—even the deck cargo was loaded. The mate had evidently been returning from some mission ashore. Perhaps they had been awaiting only his return before putting to sea. The shouting was clearly increasing, and with a tiny, insignificant lurch, the boat moved under them. First only a tiny bit, but then more and more.

"They're putting to sea!" Prokles cried out horror. Together they threw themselves at the door of the cage and beat at it with their shoulders. It was utterly hopeless. Bent over and with their hands pulled behind their backs, they couldn't deliver serious blows. All they succeeded in doing was bruising themselves.

Prokles fell on to the floor of their cage gasping, "Poseidon! Help us! Get us out of here! Help!"

Leonidas bit his tongue, but he prayed nevertheless. Castor, Castor, Castor. Nothing more articulate—only a plea to his protector, the protector of sea-travellers and guests.

Over their heads they could hear the oars being shoved out. Under their feet the ship rocked very gently in the relatively calm waters of the harbour. Then with a dull thud, a drum started. The oars fell into the water with a loud slap and hiss just beside their heads. The vessel seemed to surge forward, and now they could hear the water gurgling past the hull and the slushing sound of the prow cutting into the water. With each drumbeat came a new surge forward, then a lag, then a surge. Yard for yard, thud for thud, they were being taken away from everything they knew.

It had happened so fast that they still couldn't fully grasp it. Leonidas found himself going over in his mind how he had come to be here, and asking himself how he could have been so stupid. Alkander had clearly seen the danger. Prokles and he had come aboard in part *because* they were frightened. They had been frightened—and afraid to admit it. They had to prove to each other and themselves that they could overcome their fear. And this was where it had got them. There had to be a lesson in that, but Leonidas couldn't see it entirely. Overcoming fear was something they had to be able to do— like going to the pits for a flogging or standing in formation when the enemy charges you.

By now he had lost the feeling in his fingers, and the pain in his shoulders was becoming severe. He started to wonder how long they were going to be kept in the cage. As "valuable" cargo, surely they couldn't be kept in these conditions for the entire journey. They would have to be given water and food. They were worthless dead.

"When they let us out of here, we've got to act tame," Prokles told him, apparently sharing his thoughts. "We've got to lure them into a sense of security, so they think they don't have to lock us up. That's the only way we're going to get our hands on weapons."

Leonidas nodded, "Agreed."

"The fact that they've got us down here shows they are afraid we *could* get away," Prokles continued.

Leonidas wanted to believe him, but he found himself unable to picture escape on the vast ocean. Where could they run to or hide on a ship at sea? "When your dad finds the ship gone, what will he do?"

"Inform the harbour master, I guess."

"And then?"

"They'll come after us."

"How? Even if they can get someone to lend them a ship, how will they know where to go?" Leonidas was picturing that vast ocean without any obstacles. Once a ship was out of sight, it could go anywhere, and how was anyone to find it again in all that endless ocean?

"I don't know," Prokles admitted.

They fell silent. Leonidas tried to find a more comfortable position, but the numbness seemed to be creeping up his arms from his fingertips. Before long, hunger and thirst started gnawing at them as well. Again they talked to keep from thinking about it. They reassured themselves that they would *surely* be let out of the cage as soon as the Persians thought it was safe to let them out. Prokles again argued for "acting tame". "They have to put into another port to take on water," he argued now. "That will be our chance—but only if we get out of here."

The discomfort and claustrophobia of this cage made Leonidas agree—even if he was afraid of what would happen between the release from the cage and their arrival at a port in two or three days. The boys sank down to sit on the filthy floor, leaning forward awkwardly because of their tied hands.

Meanwhile the rhythm of the oars and the drum never faltered. Now and again they heard fragments of chanting from the oar deck, but it never lasted long. It died away again, and then there was just the splash-surge-pause, splash-surge-pause and the steady thump-thump of the drum.

Finally a man emerged out of the darkness. It was not the mate. It was a black man. He did not speak Greek. To their questions, he just shook his head and with gestures indicated that he would pour water into their mouths if they held their mouths up to the top of the cage. They had no choice. He poured carefully so they would not choke. He made eating gestures and they nodded fervently.

He seemed to take forever to return, but he eventually brought them bread—which he fed to them through the bars of the cage as if they were wild animals. Clearly his instructions had been not to untie them, let alone release them. That was depressing. The black man disappeared.

"Are we supposed to piss in here, too?" Prokles asked in outrage as the water worked its way through him.

Leonidas nodded miserably. They were captive beasts, he told himself, trying to understand it and believe it. Slaves. They no longer had names or fathers, rights or dignity. They were animals to be bought and sold, fed, watered, and worked all at a master's whim.

The heat was also increasing steadily and oppressively. The only air circulating in this lower deck came down the gangway from the oar-deck, and this stank of sweat and urine. In the stuffy, hot air, Leonidas started to feel as if he were suffocating. It was only partially physical. His brain was telling him he was dead. He was no longer Leonidas, son if Anaxandridas. He was not a future Spartiate, much less an Agiad prince. He was a beast in a cage. The thought was so overwhelming it was numbing. His breathing became increasingly laboured. He started to drift in and out of consciousness.

He was shaken back awake by a volley of shouting from overhead. The rhythm of the drum altered sharply, becoming faster. The oars no longer hissed as they slipped into the water, but splashed. The water rushed by the hull.

At last these changes penetrated to his brain, and Leonidas tried to sit up. "They must be running from something!" he decided excitedly.

"Shhh!" Prokles retorted. "I'm trying to hear something!" Everything had gone still again—except for the drum and the oars beating faster now. Soon, however, they heard the first grunting that indicated the oarsmen were tiring. An order was shouted. Silence returned. Then a new order, and the pace increased again. The whole ship seemed to strain. Prokles and Leonidas just stared at the tarred beams above their cage. Leonidas was certain that at any moment he would see the sweat of the oarsmen seeping through the deck. That was just fantasy, of course, but they did hear the first crack of a whip.

"Slaves," Prokles declared contemptuously. "Greek ships are manned by citizen crews. They never use the whip on them."

"Merchantmen sometimes use slaves," Leonidas reminded him.

"Listen!" Prokles hissed. There was another sound coming through the water. A rushing, slashing, churning sound. "That's another ship!"

Leonidas held his breath, hoping and praying. Another ship that had overtaken this one could surely mean only one thing. Or did it? What if it were a pirate ship? Leonidas had heard Lysandridas talk about what a terrible plague pirates had become. The capture of many Greek cities in Ionia had forced more and more men to take to piracy. And Persian ships, filled with oriental luxuries, were the favourite targets of pirates. But a pirate would bring no relief to the two captive boys. They would still be slaves. And allegedly pirates treated their slaves worse than anyone.

Shouting again.

"Did you hear?!" Prokles asked excitedly. "Did you hear?! Someone said something about ramming!"

Leonidas was not at all delighted by the prospect. He could picture the ram piercing the side of the ship right here, crushing them before sending them forever to the floor of the ocean.

But already an order had been given, and the drum abruptly stopped. Overhead they heard things falling on to their heads, as if men had collapsed over their oars the moment the order came to stop. The ship was clearly gliding to a halt.

As the ship lost forward momentum it started to roll quite unpleasantly, apparently turning its side to the swell. But the shouting overhead was furious, and now it was very clearly in Greek. Although they only caught snatches of it, evidently the demand to board had been made and carried out.

The voice of the mate was easily identifiable. "...But how was I to know? They looked like runaway slave-boys—barefoot and shaved." They could not hear the words of the man he was speaking to, but the mate insisted again, "It was an honest mistake. They gave only shifty answers to my questions—just like runaways. One of them even said his father was dead—"

The other voice was an angry rumble.

"Of course, kings die; but how was I to imagine that you let your king's sons run about unescorted like common street urchins! The sons of even our noblemen would not set foot outside without a dozen servants to pave the very streets with their own cloaks—"

"The sons of our kings grow into men, not women," came the terse reply, and Prokles gasped out, "It's my granddad!"

The gangway darkened, and several figures clattered down the ladder and came toward the cage. The mate led; he unfastened the cage and reached in to help drag the boys out, using his knife to cut the bonds around their wrists as he did so. Their arms at once fell uselessly to their sides, and the dead weights of their useless hands unbalanced them, making them stagger helplessly as they tried to regain their feet. Lysandridas caught Prokles, and the perioikoi mate who was with him caught and steadied Leonidas. "Steady on, boy. You're safe now," the man told him kindly.

At the gangway, Leonidas was horrified to find he could not make his hands respond and grasp anything. The perioikoi mariner had to take him in his arms and lift him up in front of him. The light of the sun hurt his eyes, too, and he had to screw them up. He tried to lift his arm up to shade them from the sun, but the motion sent a stabbing pain through his shoulders, and his fingers looked like blood sausages hanging limply from his raw, red wrists.

But despite the blinding sun, he could make out the silhouette of a trireme. As his eyes adjusted to the light, he could see that her flapping sail bore a single lambda. Leonidas could have kissed it or bowed on to the floor before it—it stood for Lacedaemon. The warship, with her three banks of oars, had easily overtaken the merchantman, but how had she known what course to steer? Around them was absolutely nothing but ocean—not a shoreline nor island nor any landmark at all. Leonidas didn't understand, and that made it seem all the more miraculous. He thanked Castor silently and profusely.

Grapples held the two ships side by side, and an unsteady gangplank bridged the gap between the gunnels of the two ships. "Can you make it?" Lysandridas asked the two boys. They nodded. It was the only way home.

Once they were safely aboard the Lacedaemonian trireme, it backed decorously away, and turned slowly to set a course back for Lacedaemon. The rhythm of the oars that had terrorised them for the better part of the day became a melody.

"How did you ever find us?" Leonidas asked their rescuers.

The perioikoi captain laughed. "The ship had just reported to the harbour master, announcing her departure and declaring her cargo and destination. She was making for Troizen, and there are really only two sea routes. With this wind," he glanced to his sail and indicated the waves, "we could be fairly certain he'd go this way, but Philippos went with a second trireme on the other route just in case. You must be hungry. Why don't you make yourselves comfortable afore the mast, and I'll have my boy bring you something to eat."

They took this suggestion gratefully and sat down on the spare sails rolled up in front of the main mast. The pain was slowly easing in Leonidas' shoulders and arms (if he didn't move them much), but he kept anxiously testing his hands. So far they just flinched and twitched a bit when he tried to get them to open and close.

"You two are going to get the flogging of your lives when you get back to Sparta," Lysandridas warned them, shaking his head. "Launching two triremes with full crews to chase you halfway across the Gulf of Argos cost the Lacedaemonian government a small fortune! And all because you were too stupid to see a trap when it stared you in the face! Thank God, Alkander has more brains than the two of you together!"

Prokles frowned, but Leonidas smiled up at Lysandridas. "Thank you for coming after us."

The remark seemed to catch the old man completely off guard. Leonidas saw him catch his breath, and tears sprang into his grey eyes. He grabbed Leonidas to him and held him in a fierce hug. "Boy, don't you know? I would have searched for you to the ends of the earth. Have you forgotten? I've been there. I would not have rested until I had you home."

———

When he went to the pits for the promised flogging, Leonidas was not afraid as he had been two years earlier. He was proud to be there, because this was not an effort to demean or break him, but his just punishment for foolishness. The alternative was a lifetime of degradation, and Leonidas had never before been so aware of the privileges of citizenship. There were, he was certain, few other cities in the world that would have launched two crack warships just to save two 14-year-old boys from their own foolishness.

CHAPTER 7

Age 15

NEXT TO FIGHTING WELL, SUCCESS IN war depended on marching well; so the youths of the agoge were taken on increasingly long marches as their training in the arts of war intensified with each year. By the time they went on active service, they were expected to be able to cover 35 miles a day for three days at a stretch, 80 miles for two days back to back, and 50 miles in one 24-hour period. [1] They had to be able to cover those distances across the rugged terrain of the Peloponnese—which meant up over mountains and back down them again. The boys of the agoge started to develop their marching skills by taking on "simple" tasks like crossing the Parnon range to the important perioikoi town of Epidauros Limera on the Gulf of Argolis, or marching across the Taygetos to Kardamyle.

The later expedition, traditionally made by 15-year-olds in the late summer or early autumn, was particularly important. For many of them, Leonidas and his friends included, it was their first trip into

---

1   I have chosen to use a familiar measure of distance to make distances meaningful to the modern reader. The Spartan army is known to have covered the distance from Sparta to Athens in less than three days, which is a distance of roughly 120 miles.

the Spartan colony of Messenia. Many of the boys came from families that owned estates in Messenia. Most of these estates, however, were managed by hired overseers because the Spartiate owners were required to live near enough to Sparta to attend their syssitia daily and take part in Assembly or respond to a call-up. The overseers of the Messenian estates were usually Laconian perioikoi, because the Spartiates mistrusted all Messenians profoundly.

And the boys knew why. They had been taught, usually from their mother's knee, about the treachery of the Messenians. Leonidas had been taught along with his fellows that after the First Messenian War the Messenians had been well treated. But only a generation later, they had risen up in revolt. They had killed without provocation and they had violated sanctuaries, in one incident carrying off the virgin priestesses at the Temple of Artemis of the Goats and ravaging them all.

At the agoge, the story most frequently told was how once a band of Messenians, under the ruthless rebel leader Aristomenos, had crept into the agoge in the dark of night and slaughtered the children in their beds. There were many scars on the walls attributed to the weapons of the Messenians. These were carefully pointed out to the children attending the agoge: "Here a boy was skewered to the wall by a Messenian spear," "There a little girl's head was cut off by an axe," and "In that window two youths were cut to pieces as they tried to crawl out into the street." There was also a small monument just outside the main entrance to the agoge, dedicated to the entire class of eirenes who had been butchered in the massacre. Every single 20-year-old at the time of the incident had died trying to defend his charges with whatever weapons they could grab in the darkness. The obvious moral of the story was that the Messenians knew no honour and would not spare even a defenceless child if they got the upper hand.

The Second Messenian War taught the Spartans not only that the Messenians could not be trusted, but also that the only language they understood was force. Since their good treatment after the First War had resulted only in revolt, the Spartans decided after their victory in the Second Messenian War that the Messenians could not be treated like the loyal perioikoi. They must be reduced to helots, tied to a specific plot of land, and carefully watched by overseers.

The children of Sparta were raised to believe, furthermore, that these Messenian helots were not like the peaceful and reliable helots of Laconia. Laconian helots could be trusted as squires and as cooks and messengers for the army; they could be employed without hesitation as servants in homes and as nannies to young children, as Leonidas' own Dido had been. They could be trusted even to run the kleroi of the Spartiates without excessive oversight. But the Messenian helots were different. They remained fundamentally "enemies"—which was why the ephors ritually declared war on the Messenian helots once a year. Before crossing into Messenia, the boys were reminded that the Messenians were sly, insolent, untrustworthy, and lazy. They were warned not to trust any of them.

At first light the next day, five units of 15-year-olds departed together on their first foray into legendary Messenia. Although the distance to Kardamyle was "only" 40 miles, the Taygetos range that stood between Sparta and Kardamyle was a steep range rising to over 8,000 feet at the peak, and the youths found the going rough. The sun burned on their backs as they climbed, so that they were soon drenched in sweat. This being the main highway into Messenia from Sparta, the road was well maintained by details of captives and criminals that worked in chain gangs to shore up any weaknesses and remove obstacles. It also climbed at a relatively steady rate, switchbakking its way up the face of the mountain.

They made good progress at first and soon left the quarries, where the finest marble in all Lacedaemon was won, behind and below them. The vast majority of Sparta's temples and public buildings were built with marble from these quarries. As younger boys they had all visited the quarries more than once, but this was the first time they had ever been able to look down from above on the great swath of white cut into the green of the forest by the vast quarries. A light cloud of dust hung over the quarries in the stagnant air.

By now, however, the boys had no breath for talking. They kept going with sheer determination, their blood pounding in their ears. Their eirenes kept them moving with light mockery. "Come on, you can't be tired *already*! We've barely started." Because the eirenes walking beside them looked dry and relaxed, the boys could hardly protest. So they kept going miserably.

They next passed the Temple to Artemis of the Goats, but they were not allowed to stop and rest. It was from this temple that the Messenians had captured the virgin priestesses, all maidens of Spartiate families in their youth, and subjected them to barbaric degradation. The Messenian action was often compared negatively to a similar incident in the Tegean War. The Tegeans had also captured a number of Spartan maidens in a raid, but these had been held to ransom and returned to their families unharmed.

By noon the boys were reduced to a panting, sweating, dragging band. At last the eirenes allowed the boys to fall out to refresh themselves at a spring built directly into the side of the mountain, with seven spouts in the shape of lion's heads. Instantly the boys fell upon the water in a loud and unruly horde, shoving each other aside, splashing and dunking one another. The eirenes watched it all with tolerant disdain, filling their own mugs with the water spewing from the bronze faucets and then cupping their hands to splash the sweat from their faces. After about a half-hour break, they called the boys to order. The boys had to form up in rank and file; the eirenes inspected them critically; and then at a signal provided by the piper, they set off again.

They did not stop for a light meal until they crossed through the pass, well after noon. Disappointingly, although the eirenes assured them they were now in Messenia, there was nothing that visibly distinguished it from Laconia. The slopes were still heavily forested with outcroppings of white limestone. Furthermore, although they had passed the highest point of the trip, the road at this point only dipped down into a valley and the next mountain was still ahead of them, cutting off the view.

By now all their muscles were aching, and one boy had twisted his ankle and could only hobble along on a crutch. But with the peaks of the Taygetos behind them, they "enjoyed" the rays of the late afternoon sun. This meant that they were still bathed in sweat as they descended along the winding road past the lead mines toward the Gulf of Messenia.

The lead mines were extremely important to the Lacedaemonian economy, and the perioikoi industrialist who held the concession was allegedly one of the richest men in the Peloponnese. He ran the mines with hundreds of chattel slaves that he imported through the port of Pharai on the Messenian Gulf. The bulk of the slaves were barbarians, captured far to the north of the Black Sea or beyond the Pillars of Herakles or in Africa. The boys saw some of these poor creatures being herded along the road, apparently new arrivals just offloaded at the port and being escorted to the mines by a troop of hard-nosed marines. The marines were armed with whips and javelins. The officers rode on little donkeys, their sandals almost scraping the earth; but the agile little beasts moved up and down the edges of the road, enabling the marines to keep a sharp eye on their charges. The slaves themselves were chained at their ankles to one another and wore only loincloths. Their hair and beards were completely untrimmed and unkempt. Their ribs and even their vertebrae showed clearly through their filthy skin. Many had open sores—particularly on their ankles, where the shackles had rubbed the skin off completely, or from the lash. Leonidas found himself looking to see if there were any boys as young as he had been last year.

Some of his fellows were jeering the slaves and even throwing little rocks at them to make them dance. Leonidas was glad when they were called to order by one of the eirenes, who reminded them that they had no right to damage the property of another free man.

At last they reached the famous springs just north of Kardamyle—which, reputedly, never ran dry. These springs were sacred to Persephone, and there was an extensive fountain house built around them with a lovely colonnade. Here a number of merchant convoys travelling between the port of Pharai and other points east had stopped to water their horses and mules and to refresh themselves. The pack animals were watered at a trough lower down the slope, while people went up an elegant sweep of steps to the fountain house. The Spartan boys were told to make do at the animal trough by their eirenes, who were now in a hurry to make Kardamyle before nightfall—or maybe just didn't want their unruly, stinking teenage charges to disturb the other travellers.

The sun had already set by the time they finally reached the town of Kardamyle, with its high acropolis and its little harbour. The sky above the Gulf was glowing pink, and the waters of the bay caught the reflection and turned a dark purple. A few remnants of cloud were silhouetted against the luminous sky, and the rhythmic whisper of the waves on the beach was like the beating of one's heart: subtle and reassuring. Two large merchant ships rode at anchor in the harbour, and a cluster of fishing smacks had been drawn up on to the sand for the night.

Even though the sun had set, the air was still very warm and humid. The boys were allowed to strip and plunge into the bay to wash the sweat and dust of the day from their bodies. Their eirenes selected a place to camp on the beach beyond the harbour, and ordered the pipes to sound muster. The boys, more or less reluctantly, abandoned their swim and formed up. The eirenes made sure that all were present and then gave the order to set up camp, make fires, and cook their evening meal. Each unit made their own fire and their own meal. The eirenes sat a little apart around a fire of their own, and the boys of each unit brought their respective eirene his portion of the meal. A watch was also set and the sentries walked around the perimeter, making sure that none of the boys slipped away and no stranger entered.

The next day the boys were allowed to rest before the return journey. They were told they could go where they liked, but they had to report for muster at noon and at dusk—which meant they couldn't get very far. Anyone who failed to report at either muster would be reported and would face a flogging on their return to Lacedaemon.

Only now did Alkander confide to his friends that he wanted to find his sister, who had been sent here years earlier. As the boys did everything together, there was no question of letting Alkander go off on his own. Alkander knew the name of the man in whose household his sister had been sent to work, and by asking residents they got directions to a house located on the edge of town. It was a very impressive house, with terraces and balconies facing the sea and a fine colonnade along the front. When the boys asked after Alkander's sister, Percalus, they were directed to the back of the house.

The sound of children's high-pitched screaming announced the nursery. A moment later they found themselves on one of the terraces, well protected by a wall and shaded by potted palms and dates. No less than four children of various ages were playing loudly on the terrace, while on the benches against the house one woman rocked a cradle while two others corded and spun. Alkander looked at the women uncertainly, and the woman beside the cradle leapt up with a little shriek. "Alkander! Where did you come from?" She rushed to him and her veil, which she had laid over her head loosely, fell off as she ran. She wrapped her arms around an embarrassed Alkander, who half tried to evade her exuberant kisses while his friends stared in wonder.

Alkander's sister was a voluptuous young woman with bright blonde hair. Prokles' mouth dropped, and then he threw Leonidas a look that betrayed jealousy and lust and confusion. This wasn't what they were expecting.

Percalus was all over Alkander. "Oh, let me look at you! You're so *big*! You must have grown a foot, and so *brown*! Oh, and you must be Leonidas!" she said to Prokles, who shook his head and pointed to Leonidas. She looked at Leonidas, the least attractive of the three boys, and was clearly disappointed. Princes were supposed to be exceptionally handsome, weren't they? But she managed a smile for him. "I can't tell you how grateful we all are to you. It means the world to Mother! And I'm so proud of Alkander!" She looked at her little brother again. She remembered her manners at last and took her brother's hand. "Come, let me introduce you!"

She led the three youths over to the other women. The elder of the women was the mistress of the house and the other was a widowed sister who now lived with them. Percalus was very proud to introduce her brother and even prouder to introduce his friend, "Leonidas, son of *King* Anaxandridas."

"Oh, you must be one of the twins," the lady of the house recognised at once.

"Yes, ma'am."

The woman, who was evidently a very wealthy perioikoi, studied Leonidas intently, and then nodded once. Turning to Percalus, she said, "You may take time off to visit with your brother, but be back for dinner. I can't possibly manage the children without you."

"Yes, ma'am." Percalus dipped her knee and head respectfully as she answered.

They left the house and the incessant noise of the children behind and walked down to the shore. Percalus did most of the talking. She had so much to tell Alkander. Leonidas and Prokles followed behind in silence. Percalus seemed happy enough, and clearly she was better off here than in her mother's hovel, but Leonidas didn't like the fact that she was serving a perioikoi woman. It would have been bad enough if she had been in a Spartiate household.

And then suddenly a young man emerged out of seemingly nowhere and stopped them. He was barefoot and tanned almost black by the sun of the Mediterranean, wearing only a chiton pinned at one shoulder. Longish black hair fell in his face, and black eyes were dark with wrath. "Percalus!" He stopped her roughly with a large hand. The smell of fish clung to him.

Percalus's face seemed to light up—a most inappropriate reaction to his rude treatment of her. "Polybios!" she exclaimed with a big smile.

"What are you doing with these bald Spartiate cubs!?" the young fisherman demanded in an outraged tone.

Percalus's face dropped. Fear came into her eyes. "They—they—Leonidas here is the owner of my mom's kleros. He—he came to tell me about my mother and brother."

The young man's eyes narrowed as his gaze shifted to Leonidas, but he was clearly not convinced. He looked again at Alkander. The resemblance between brother and sister was pronounced. Also, Percalus had been talking too obviously to Alkander rather than Leonidas. "That's not true, is it?" he demanded of Leonidas.

"Who the hell are you," Prokles interceded, adding pointedly, "Messenian?"

"You're damned right I'm Messenian, and proud of it! Who are you and what are you doing here?"

"We're on an exercise," Leonidas answered.

"An exercise? Is harassing helot girls part of training in Sparta?" he sneered.

"We aren't harassing anyone." Alkander pointed out.

"What do you mean, helot?" Leonidas asked.

"You lying bitch!" the young man flung at Percalus. "You're one of them, aren't you? You're a damned Spartiate bitch!" Percalus was already close to tears, and then the fisherman did something terrible: he spat at her.

The fisherman turned and managed to get a couple of strides away before the boys had recovered from their shock. Then they sprang after him like hounds of a pack. They brought the young fisherman down, and while Leonidas got him pinioned, the other two, mostly Prokles, kicked and punched. Percalus was screaming at them to stop, and the young fisherman was defending himself furiously. He was strong and increasingly angry, even frightened, but they were three to one, and they too were furious. Alkander kicked sand in the fisherman's eyes and howled out insults. From farther up the beach other fishermen were running toward them, and from even farther away one of the eirenes had caught sight of the commotion and was sprinting over.

The fishermen reached them first but were afraid to intervene. Instead they formed a circle, shouting at the boys to let their colleague go, ridiculing them for fighting three to one. Percalus had collapsed on to the sand sobbing.

The eirene finally came up, a little winded from running, and ordered the three boys to let go of their victim and explain themselves.

By this point, they had clearly got the upper hand but were tired, winded, and not reluctant to end it. They got up, and the young fisherman at once staggered away, grabbing on to his colleagues for support. They closed around him at once, forming a front against the Spartiates, their stance and expressions openly hostile.

Wiping the blood dripping from his nose with the back of his arm, Prokles answered for all three of them. "That Messenian helot *spat* at Alkander's sister."

The eirene glanced at the little heap of misery sobbing on the sand; his eyes took in the maiden's unquestionable misery—and her charms. He frowned. "What the hell is your sister doing here, Alkander?"

"She's helping f-f-friends with their ch-ch-children, sir."

It wasn't unheard of—and of course everyone knew that Alkander was a mothake. The eirene left it there. He turned his attention to the fishermen. With a gesture he ordered them to separate and expose their comrade. There was only a moment of hesitation, and then they resentfully obeyed. The fisherman was not really hurt. His lips and nose were bleeding, and his eyes were watering to flush the sand out. He was still breathing hard. "Do you deny that?" the eirene demanded of him.

"The bitch lied to me!" he spat out furiously, his eyes filled with hatred.

The eirene punched him hard in the gut, and the fisherman doubled over in pain. "Don't you ever refer to a Spartiate maiden as a bitch again—at least not in hearing of any of us!" the eirene warned. Then he turned his back on the fishermen, who at once started to withdraw, pulling their still doubled-up colleague with them.

The eirene turned his attention to the maiden. He went down on his heels beside her. "Are you all right?" he asked solicitously.

Percalus just covered her face with her hands and cried more intensely.

"Come, let's get into the shade and I'll fetch you some cool water."

The three younger boys could only watch as their superior helped Percalus to her feet, guided her back toward a fallen palm, and then indeed went to fetch water for her. While he was gone, Alkander asked his sister in outrage and shock, "Have you been seeing that Messenian?"

"He—he's—we—you don't understand!" she concluded, starting to cry again.

Silly goose, Leonidas thought; but it really wasn't his business.

She started sobbing out, "It isn't easy to be all alone here. I don't have any friends. The perioikoi treat me like a servant, and I have no time off. Today, this is the *first* free time I've been *given* in three years! Otherwise I have to *steal* it when I get sent on errands. What good would it have done me, saying my dad was Spartiate? No one would have believed me. Polybios was nice to me. He brought fish from his catch just for me. Otherwise I only get leftovers. He was nice to me," she insisted feebly at the end, noting that her brother was no longer looking reproachful—just sad.

It was getting very close to noon, and Percalus would have to return to her duties and the boys to muster. Leonidas and Prokles shifted uneasily, glancing over in the direction of the fountain where the eirene was fetching water.

"You *told* him you were a *helot*?" Alkander asked.

"Not exactly. He—he just assumed it. The Messenian helots are different from our own. They aren't peasants, really. They come from good, Doric stock. Polybios' grandfather was captain of a Messenian ship during the war—"

"Don't talk like you sympathise with them!" Alkander warned, scandalized and frightened by his sister's tone.

"But it's true!"

"How do you know? He was just talking you up! Trying to impress you! You can't know if he was lying!"

"He says he can show me the wreck of his grandfather's ship. It's right out there!" She pointed toward the bay.

"There may be a wreck there, but it doesn't prove it was his grandfather's—or rather that his grandfather commanded more than an oar on it!" Alkander was getting angry, Leonidas suspected from fear. After all, his own position was precarious enough without his sister openly sympathising with the enemy at their backs. Fortunately the eirene was returning now, a goatskin of water over his shoulder and a mug in his hand.

"Don't talk like that to the eirene, will you?" Alkander urged his sister, dropping his voice earnestly.

They stepped back a little to let the eirene through to Percalus and he casually remarked, "You boys better get back down the beach for muster. You wouldn't want to be late."

"No, sir," they agreed obediently, and departed at once. Alkander looked back anxiously once, but his sister seemed to be accepting the water with appropriate gratitude and modesty.

At first the three boys walked in silence, but then Prokles broke the silence. "You never told us your sister was a prize filly, Alkander. She'd rival even Cleomenes' queen! You better find a way to bring her back to Sparta."

CHAPTER 8

Age 16

PERCALUS WASN'T THE ONLY TROUBLE WITH girls that Leonidas and his friends had by the time they reached 16. After consulting their elders, it had been arranged for Percalus to return to Laconia and live with Lysandridas' neighbour Cleitagora. Cleitagora, who had taken in Koiris on that fateful stormy night three years earlier, was a widow with two unmarried sons on active service. She had agreed to teach Percalus her future duties as a Spartiate wife and to "introduce" her to society. Percalus was clearly pleased with the arrangement, although Leonidas and Alkander were both somewhat uncomfortable with it; Leonidas because everyone seemed to assume that he would provide a dowry for Percalus, and Alkander because he found the attention his sister attracted embarrassing. She couldn't go anywhere without young men taking notice of her. Percalus loved the attention and openly encouraged it—in her modest, mincing way.

Meanwhile, however, they had discovered their own interest in the opposite sex, albeit to differing degrees. As so often in other situations, Prokles was the most forward, actively seeking out opportunities to watch the girls of the older cohorts at sports. The fact that Hilaira was still winning every race she entered provided a good excuse for them to hang about the racecourse when the girls competed, but Prokles took little interest in Hilaira herself. In fact, he took no interest in any girl in particular, just "girls" generally.

Alkander had the opposite problem. He was as beautiful in the same golden way as his sister, and it was the girls who took an inordinate interest in him. Whenever Prokles led them over to loiter around girls' events, Alkander would become the object of repeated efforts, by maidens both bold and shy, to attract his attention. No matter how indifferent Alkander acted, the girls persisted. For some his shyness constituted a challenge, and for others it increased his attractiveness. One lithe, dark beauty, Eirana, who was an outstanding rider, openly snubbed Prokles but had only smiles for Alkander.

Leonidas found himself frustrated that his friends were so "obsessed" with girls and less interested in riding about the countryside with him. Once or twice he left them to their "girl watching" and went off on his own—but that wasn't really much fun either, so he ended back with them although he was mostly bored. Until, that is, they found themselves watching some girls wrestling.

On the whole the quality of girls' wrestling was far beneath their own and not really worth watching, but a crowd had been attracted this particular afternoon by a maiden who quite simply defeated every opponent she faced with ease and elegance.

"Who is she?" Prokles inquired, looking automatically to Alkander. Alkander seemed to know all the girls' names.

"Don't you recognise her? That's Lathria, Timon's sister."

"Timon?" Prokles asked, disbelieving. Timon had long been Alkander's most merciless tormentor, and still treated him with disdain, long after most of the unit had accepted him. Timon increasingly challenged Ephorus, too, calling his decisions "stupid" or simply ignoring his directives contemptuously. Since they no longer "ran" as a unit, Ephorus' role as leader was more a matter of courtesy anyway, but Timon was the least courteous young man Leonidas knew. What aroused Prokles' disbelief now, however, was that Timon was a stocky, rather unattractive youth, whereas his sister was as tall as they were, albeit heavyset and not particularly pretty.

Even as they spoke, Lathria defeated her final opponent with the same ease with which she had dismissed the others. Far from tired, she dusted herself off with evident contentment and then declined the linen towel her trainer offered her. Turning instead to address the crowd of youths, she challenged instead: "I bet I can beat any of you, too!"

"Lathria!" the trainer, a widow, hissed in shocked disapproval.

"I can!" Lathria declared, with a scowl to her trainer. And then she reached up to rebind her long strands of dark, curly hair, a gesture that drew the eyes of the entire audience to her naked breasts. These were still rather small, plump and round rather than pointed, but they were definitely *there*. Thus although she had a rather squarish face, her dark brows met over her nose, and there were even little dark hairs on her upper lip, she had put her youthful audience into a state of turmoil. Some of the older youths hissed and turned away, expressing in this way their disapproval of such unseemly boldness and hubris.

This only provoked her. "What's the matter with you?" she called after them. "Afraid to fight a girl? Afraid you'll lose, aren't you?" she laughed. "I knew I could beat any of you, but I didn't think it would be *this* easy!" She dropped her hands to her hips and smiled at the youths remaining. "All a bunch of lily-livered cowards!"

"Don't let her get away with that!" Prokles hissed in Leonidas' ear.

Leonidas looked at Prokles in horror.

"You've got to put her in her place!" Prokles insisted.

"Why me?"

"You're the best wrestler here," Prokles countered.

Leonidas glanced around, and Prokles was right. He could beat any of the others here.

Meanwhile, the others took up Prokles' cause. "Go on, Leonidas! Teach her a lesson!"

"This is ridiculous," Leonidas protested. "Everyone knows I can beat her."

"I don't know it, Little Leo!" Lathria teased, using the adjective that Leonidas hated—and had not heard in years. "Prove it!" she challenged again.

Prokles was literally pulling Leonidas' himation off his back and unbuckling his belt in preparation of removing the chiton.

"This is silly!" Leonidas protested one last time, but it was pointless. The whole crowd of youths, about nine of them altogether from both his own and the 15-year-old cohort, were all pushing him into the ring.

The next thing he knew, Lathria had him in her grip and was trying to throw him to the ground. It was the most disorienting sensation he had yet experienced. On the one hand she was strong and lithe, but on the other he could clearly feel her nipples crushed against his naked chest, and the response of his body was so distracting that she had tossed him on to the sand before he could come to himself.

The shouts of outrage from the spectators brought him back to himself. He sprang up and in a fit of determination that blotted out all acknowledgement of her sex, he caught her in a grip with his shoulder in her crotch and flung her down before she knew what hit her. There was a cheer of approval.

Lathria, evidently surprised, jumped up rapidly and fought back by trying to trip him. They danced around one another for a bit and then Leonidas, determined to get this over with, lunged again, unbalanced her, and after a short struggle forced her down. The crowd cheered again.

Now Lathria was angry. She lashed out more viciously than ever before, but Leonidas was used to violent fights and he deftly got her under control, twisting her arm behind her back and forcing her down on to her knees. She was panting and gasping from effort now, and Leonidas again became conscious of the fact that he was fighting a girl. He let her go and backed off. The crowd groaned and shouted insults at him.

Lathria scrambled back to her feet and spun about on him. Her face was flushed and her eyes flashing. She came for him again, with her favourite "bear-hug" grip, but Leonidas was ready for it now. He gripped her back so hard that she started to struggle to get free even before he started to pull her down with him. Slowly but surely, he forced her down on to the sand. First her buttocks touched, and then he kept pushing her over until her shoulders too were crushed into the sand. He had won.

The youths around him cheered, but Leonidas was lying with his body pressed up against Lathria's. Her face was just inches away. And she was smiling at him triumphantly.

Leonidas jumped up and angrily grabbed his chiton from Prokles. He pulled it on as fast as possible, ashamed of the response of his body and anxious to hide it. Declaring loudly, "That was silly," he jogged away, heading for the cooling waters of the Eurotas.

———

Sixteen was also the age at which the boys of the agoge underwent another ritual, the floggings at the Feast of Artemis Orthia. This ancient sanctuary on the banks of the Eurotas had, according to legend, once been the site of an uneven battle between the early Dorians and the native peoples. The sons of Herakles were worshiping at the shrine and had brought offerings to the goddess when they were attacked by the barbarians. Unarmed as they were, they had only been able to defend themselves with the reeds they tore up from the riverbank. Armed with these canes alone, they had beaten off the attack.

To commemorate this distant victory, it had become tradition for a ritualised battle to take place between the 16-year-olds and the 17-year-olds. The 17-year-olds represented Sparta's ancestors by "defending" the temple with canes against an assault by the 16-year-olds. The assault of the 16-year-olds had been transformed at some unknown date in the past into an act of theft, symbolising the sacrilege of the ancient attackers. The matrons of Sparta made hundreds of small, round cheeses that they laid on the altar of Artemis as an offering. The 16-year-olds, representing the impious barbarians, then tried to steal as many of these cheeses from the goddess as possible in the face of the defenders.

The 16-year-olds were allowed no weapons and no armour. Naked, they had to run a gauntlet of 17-year-olds armed with the vicious canes used for all Spartan floggings. The youths were safe from blows only while inside the temple or outside the perimeter at the tables where they delivered their cheeses. The eirenes kept count of how many cheeses each member of their particular unit retrieved from the temple, and the honour of the day went to the 16-year-old who managed to bring out the largest number of cheeses. The honour was considered great, and for the rest of his life the winner was referred to as a Victor of Artemis Orthia. Between Olympiads, the Spartans kept track of the years by the names of the victors at Artemis Orthia.

Dorieus, of course, had been the victor in his class eleven years ago. He was inordinately proud of the fact, and frequently referred to it when trying to drum up support for his latest adventure: a colony on Sicily. Leonidas knew that many people would expect him or Brotus to follow his brother's example, so it did not surprise him when, on the eve of the festival, Brotus sought Leonidas out.

The twins' paths crossed regularly. They were on the drill fields at the same time, and often worked out in the palaestra or visited the baths simultaneously. They sang together in chorus. They even competed against one another in some sports, particularly in ball games or at broad-jumping, discus, and archery. For the most part they treated each other as they would any other member of the age-cohort. Only rarely did they talk as brothers—usually when there was news about Dorieus or Cleomenes.

Now, on the eve of Artemis Orthia, Brotus turned up at Leonidas' barracks and insisted that he come outside. Once they were alone in the dark alley, Brotus announced, "Leo, I intend to win the honours tomorrow."

"Fine," Leonidas agreed readily. Prokles, Alkander, and he had long ago agreed that three to four cheeses—which meant running the gauntlet in and out a corresponding number of times—was enough to satisfy honour. Prokles felt that anyone who would want to get himself "beaten bloody" for the sake of being able to boast about such a ridiculous achievement the rest of his life was "an idiot". Prokles claimed that his grandfather said the rest of the Greek world laughed at Spartan youth for being so "stupid". Throughout the rest of the world, the whole ritual was seen as an example of the "blind obedience" of Spartan youths. Foreigners snickered at the stupidity of youths willing to endure such a ridiculous amount of abuse just for the entertainment of the whole city, and they made even more unkind comments about what sort of city would find amusement in watching their youths get thrashed by canes—although the number of foreigners who came to watch the ritual was increasing every year.

Leonidas had to admit that he had rather enjoyed watching the spectacle in other years, and presumed he'd find it entertaining in the future. It wasn't really about watching boys get beaten—it was a fast-paced, exciting, rough-and-tumble contest where the winner was always one of the underdogs—one of the naked boys taking the punishment. But Prokles had been so adamant about how stupid the whole thing was that Leonidas had not dared voice his own opinion. In Prokles' words, "Oxen are more intelligent than to want to win a whipping contest!"

This phrase ran in his ears as Brotus made his announcement, and Leonidas decided that Prokles was right after all. Brotus was a bonehead.

"Dorieus is back, you know," Brotus informed him next.

"Oh? When did he get back?"

"Today. He's come extra to see how we do tomorrow."

Leonidas did not like the sound of that. It could only end in another lecture from Dorieus on how he had "failed" their mother's memory again. He was heartily sick of it all—and had been happy when, almost two years earlier, Dorieus had received a Delphic oracle that said his place was in Sicily. The oracle said that he was to found the city of Heraclea to honour his ancestor, who had conquered Sicily but had now been forgotten there. Ever since he received this oracle, Dorieus had spent his time trying to convince others to come with him and found the colony—and to finance him. Although only a handful of Spartiates—his closest friends and supporters—were interested in the adventure, an increasing number of perioikoi appeared intrigued by the prospect of financing it—and then getting the trade monopolies Dorieus promised in return. As a result, Dorieus had recently spent most of his time in the perioikoi town of Anthana, negotiating with key perioikoi merchants to finance his expedition and, most importantly, provide him with ships.

"Why should he care how we do?" Leonidas asked his twin brother, a bit petulantly.

"He plans to make himself king of Heraclea, and he wants us to join him there."

"First he has to establish Heraclea," Leonidas pointed out.

"Do you doubt it? The oracle said it would be his." Brotus then dropped his voice and added, "And you know he still has no heir except that bastard by that African woman." Cleomenes now had two children, a boy and a girl, and his wife was pregnant yet again.

Leonidas understood now. Brotus saw himself as Dorieus' heir apparent. He also finally got around to what he really wanted from Leonidas. "I don't want Timon getting in my way tomorrow."

"Timon?"

"Yeah, he's been going around bragging about how he's going to win tomorrow. You must have heard him?"

"I guess so. I don't pay much attention to what Timon says."

"Well, to hear him talk he's already won, and I want you to stop him."

"What do you mean, stop him?"

"You and your friends could hold him back when he's in the temple—you aren't planning to seriously compete anyway," Brotus added contemptuously, to show he knew all about Leonidas and his plans.

"Maybe not, but I'm not going to cheat, either." Leonidas informed him bluntly.

"I see." Brotus' face became very grim. "Family honour means nothing to you. Sometimes I wonder if you're an Agiad at all!"

"How should I not be?"

"I don't know. Castor and Pollux were twins by different fathers...."

"Sure, our mother the adulteress! Tell that one to Dorieus, if you want to make sure he *never* makes you his heir."

"Maybe she didn't have a choice...." Brotus suggested in a low, ominous voice that conjured up images of brutal rapes in dark mountain ravines; but Leonidas found the whole conversation ridiculous, and broke it off to go get some sleep. The ordeal was going to be bad enough tomorrow as it was.

———

The festivities began in the predawn light as selected maidens departed the Temple of Artemis up in the Taygetos, bearing a magnificent new gown for the goddess that had been sewn during the preceding year. The maidens, carrying the gown and singing odes to the goddess, came down from the mountains in a procession, escorted by selected units of the army carrying torches for them. The maidens were selected for their beauty, virtue, and voices. They also wore "ancient" dress, which meant the tight-waisted, bare-breasted gowns worn in the age of heroes. The procession down from the mountain was joined all along the route by matrons with their cheeses and children, helots, and perioikoi, all dressed in their festive best. They fell in behind the maidens to form an ever longer parade that wound its way through the city as the sun topped the peaks of the Parnos.

By this time the whole city had turned out, and the crowds lined the streets to watch the procession or flooded the temple grounds around Artemis Orthia. The 17-year-olds, in leather training armour and helmets, meanwhile cut their canes from the reeds of the Eurotas. They were in high spirits, and obviously looking forward to giving their juniors as difficult a time as possible. The 16-year-olds stripped down, oiled themselves, and prepared to face the ordeal, as tables were set up and they were shown where to bring their cheeses and shown the "safe area" where they could go after surrender. Clearly, the first youth to seek the safety of this area would face considerable hissing and scorn.

The kings arrived. Demaratus was 29, still on active service and single. He came alone, driving his own light racing chariot, with the team he planned to enter at the Olympic Games later this year. Cleomenes also arrived by chariot, but it was a heavy state chariot with a driver. Beside him was his pregnant wife and his three-year-old son. His infant daughter had apparently been left at home with a nanny. The boy was very active and excited. His high-pitched voice could be heard even above the crowd, and his parents were "outrageously" indulgent. Leonidas looked on with disapproval, remembering his own strict upbringing.

Dorieus stood far apart, surrounded by his tight-knit clique of loyal followers, and made no effort to meet Leonidas' eye.

The singing drew closer and the crowd parted for the procession of maidens, led by the priestesses in high headdresses. Percalus had been selected as one of the maidens, and Alkander groaned at the sight of her. Like all the maidens in the procession, she looked straight ahead or dropped her eyes modestly. She moved with stately slowness and her voice was clear and modulated. There was no flirting and no frivolousness; but Percalus had the perfect figure for the ancient dress. Her waist was small enough to enclose in two hands, while her breasts were unusually full for her 19 years of age. All male eyes, notably those of King Demaratus, seemed to be riveted on Percalus's magnificent endowment, and Alkander felt ashamed.

The priestesses and maidens, followed by the matrons laden with trays of cheeses, disappeared into the temple. When they re-emerged, they joined the crowd and the kings stood and led the paen to Apollo. As the voices fell silent, Cleomenes went forward to offer a sacrifice to the god, pouring wine and scattering seed. After he returned to his seat, he gestured with his hand to the waiting agoge officials that the ritual could begin.

The boys were told to take up their positions and the seventeen-year-olds formed two files, shoulder to shoulder, facing each other on either side of the door. Then with a shout the sixteen-year-olds were told to attack.

Leonidas was surprised by how easy it was at first. There were so many of them that none of the blows seemed to hit directly or hard. He had three cheeses out before he was even winded. He paused to catch his breath and take in the situation. Amazingly, there were already a handful of youths sheltering in the safe area, and a glance at the tables indicated that the most ambitious had already managed to take out four cheeses. Leonidas caught Prokles' and Alkander's eye, and with a nod they made another dash through the gauntlet. It was so easy, in fact, that they did it twice more without too much trouble. By then, however, about half the boys had given up, and the 17-year-olds could concentrate on fewer and fewer contestants. That made it easier for them to strike and strike hard. Alkander had one ugly welt on his cheek, and the side of his neck was bright red and swelling. Leonidas could feel but not see that he had an unpleasant welt on his backside. Reaching around, his fingers told him it was swelling up nastily. "One more?" he asked his friends.

Alkander nodded, breathing hard. Prokles hesitated, made a sour face, and then agreed reluctantly, "If you insist."

They made another dash for it. The blows rained down on them, and Leonidas, holding his arm over his head, took a blow that numbed his entire forearm. It staggered him enough to make him trip on the steps, and at once the canes fell upon him with a vengeance. Alkander shouted to Prokles, who had just made it into the temple. A moment later, they each grabbed one of Leonidas' arms and dragged him up into the temple to safety.

It took half a minute to catch his breath, and Alkander was looking at the damage, while Prokles commented simply, "It was *your* idea!"

It was only now, as they took their time, that Leonidas noticed something else. Timon was stretched out on the floor, apparently exhausted. But he wasn't moving or making any noise. "Timon?" he called out. "Are you all right?"

The others looked over.

"Hey, Timon? Get up! You can't just stay in here." Prokles nudged him with his toe.

He did not respond. They looked at one another, and Leonidas felt icy cold all of a sudden. "Timon?" He went down beside the other boy and shook him hard. His head fell to one side. His eyes were rolled back in his head, and blood trickled out of the side of his mouth and nose.

"My God!" Prokles exclaimed, jumping back. "He's dead!"

"We've got to tell someone!" Alkander decided.

The three youths fled the temple, driven by terror, and hardly felt the blows of the youths outside. They had fled so fast that they had completely forgotten to take a cheese with them. They arrived gasping at the table, and their eirene started to admonish them, "Where are your cheeses, you fools? What—"

"Timon's lying in there! Unconscious!" Leonidas burst out.

"Maybe even dead!" Prokles added.

"What?" The eirene didn't want to believe them.

"He is, sir!" Alkander insisted. "We tried to wake him, but he didn't respond at all."

"You're certain?" The eirene still did not want to believe them, but around him his comrades started to take notice.

"What is it?" they asked, and Leonidas, Prokles, and Alkander told what they had seen.

"Do we stop it?" one of the eirenes asked uncertainly, looking around at the cheering crowd of enthusiastic spectators. The contest was clearly into its last phase, with just a handful of boys still competing. The spectators were cheering on their favourites. Dorieus' faction was shouting for Brotus.

"It's almost over anyway," another replied.

They clearly did not want to disrupt things in front of the entire city. They weren't yet citizens, after all. It was a heavy responsibility.

"Maybe he could be revived!" Leonidas argued desperately. Although he had seen nothing suspicious and had not a fragment of evidence with which to make an accusation, in the pit of his stomach he was certain that Brotus had had something to do with Timon's state.

Before the eirenes replied, one of the officials came over and angrily asked the boys: "Are you still competing?"

"No, sir, there—"

"Then get over there in the safe area!"

"But, sir, there's—"

"Do as you're told!"

They retreated, joining the vast majority of their age-cohort.

Within another five minutes Brotus had won. In the festivities following, no one seemed to take any notice of the fact that Timon had to be taken to a surgeon, comatose. And by the time he died, three days later, the city was back to normal. His death was attributed to over-eagerness on his own part. It was just one of those "tragedies" that the "enthusiasm" of youth produced. Leonidas was left alone with his suspicion of his brother's role, and it was a suspicion no one wanted to hear. Brotus had raised himself from simply being the bigger and stronger of the "Agiad twins" to being a "hero".

Brotus' status was further increased by the departure of Dorieus shortly afterwards. Dorieus sailed away with 14 ships and over 200 men, but only a handful of Spartiates, just a month after the feast of Artemis Orthia. He seemed to have made some kind of arrangement with Brotus, but it was not one to which Leonidas was party. In fact, Dorieus took no further note of Leonidas at all, beyond remarking in passing, "Mother always said you were superfluous. I can see now how right she was. Brotus is the only brother I need."

Leonidas had retorted impudently, "And frankly, sir, Cleomenes is the only brother *I* need."

Dorieus had hit him for that—as he was justified in doing—leaving Leonidas feeling a little triumphant at provoking his elder brother's anger. But he was glad to see the back of him when he sailed.

Brotus was a persistent problem, however. Not only was he now a Victor of Artemis Orthia, he was also attracting attention as a boxer. He was so good, in fact, that the city sent him to the Olympic Games to compete in the youth contests there. To Leonidas' further chagrin, he was successful and returned crowned with Olympic laurels. Fortunately, his victory was eclipsed by the more dramatic victory of King Demaratus in the four-horse chariot race.

After that the Eurypontid king started to become increasingly popular, so much so that young Cleomenes became openly jealous. To counter the popularity of his co-regent, he announced dramatically that he had an oracle from Delphi that ordered the Spartans to rescue Athens from the tyranny of Hippias. This caused a rather large sensation. The Oracle was read and re-read, and it was very—unusually—explicit. Leonidas couldn't forget the Athenians in Prasiai, who had been so interested in Spartan aid. They had been so interested to hear that Sparta would follow the advice of Delphi....

While the Assembly debated, the 16-year-olds drilled and drilled and drilled. They were now expected to master the smallest "phalanx"—a unit of twelve. This meant they were expected to form up four by three or three by four, six by two or two by six, or in files, and of course reverse and alter formation at a signal from the pipe without confusion or loss of defensibility. And now their marches took them to Tegea and on to Corinth, and right across Messenia to Pylos.

Then quite suddenly, Leonidas' voice dropped, and he started to grow even faster. He grew so fast the others joked about the sound of it keeping them awake at night. He had to be issued a new chiton ahead of schedule. The instructors muttered about it being "unnatural". There was, however, nothing that anyone could do about it—least of all Brotus, when he discovered that suddenly his "little" brother was taller than he because Brotus had stopped growing. Brotus was becoming increasingly stocky, while Leonidas was soon topping most of his classmates. At the end of that year, Leonidas finally felt that he was on the way to adulthood. He had withstood ten years in the agoge and successfully passed the two most difficult hardship tests: the fox time and the flogging at Artemis Orthia. He had just four years to go, and he told himself they would be relatively easy.

CHAPTER 9

Ages 17 and 18

AT 17 THE YOUTHS OF THE agoge exchanged their training weapons for battle equipment. They were taught the use of the short swords and long spears for which the Spartan army was famous, and—just as important—to wield the heavy hoplons that characterised Greek heavy infantry the world over. The first day they drilled with the real hoplons, the youths were staggered by the weight of the "monsters". They had thought themselves strong and proficient with their wooden shields, but now they found themselves collapsing from exhaustion. Just a few minutes' drill with the hoplons left them breathless, and soon their shoulder muscles cramped and their knees gave way abruptly. The next morning, their muscles were so stiff they hobbled about like cripples—much to the amusement of their eirenes and drill masters. It took them months before they could handle the hoplons with anywhere near the ease with which they had carried their training shields—and then they started formation drill.

Now they had to work in units of 24, 36, and 48. The manoeuvres were infinitively more complex in these combinations. Drill seemed to last longer and longer; and time for sports, much less loitering around watching the maidens, was greatly reduced. For Leondias, particularly, the time he had for himself was cut to the bone by an unexpected development. When his voice had finally broken in the previous year, the senior choral master had been delighted. Leonidas had always had a good ear for music, but suddenly he also had the voice for it. More exciting still (from the choral master's perspective), his voice was exceptionally deep for a youth, and this made him exceptionally valuable for the next Hyacinthia.

At the Hyacinthia, one of the most popular events was the performance by a youth chorus of a dance in which one or another fable was performed to music. In this traditional event, each participant represented an animal in a musical pantomime before dancing out the fable. In short, each animal performed a short, introductory solo dance that ended with a short, sung text of introduction. Then in a complicated choreographed dance, the fable itself was acted out, and finally the entire cast came together to sing a choral conclusion to the fable.

The choreographing was in the hands of Sparta's senior chorus master, who also selected which fable would be depicted and which youths would perform. The choral master, a certain Hellanikos, was highly respected even beyond Lacedaemon, and had been asked to choreograph plays in both Delphi and Corinth. Hellanikos was not, however, a poet. The actual texts of the songs were written by whichever poet won that honour in a competition at the previous year's Hyacinthia (although many older people felt that "modern" writers could not equal the texts that Aesop had himself composed for the Spartans ten Olympiads earlier). Regardless of what the "traditionalists" thought, the competition for the honour of writing the texts attracted poets from throughout Hellas. Likewise, the music was composed each year by the musician who won the pan-Hellenic competition for that honour as well. This was a key reason why the Hyacinthia was the most international of Sparta's festivals. Musicians, poets, and connoisseurs of both, as well as dance enthusiasts, came to see the renowned Spartan chorus perform the works of Greece's leading musicians and poets—and to compete themselves for the honour of composing for next year's festival.

For the youths participating, the challenge was to pantomime the animal portrayed so perfectly that the audience recognised it before the text was sung. The boys were selected for their voices, but their ability to pantomime was what made their performance successful or otherwise. Depending on the fable selected, there were youths who had to imitate foxes, snakes, hares, dogs, horses, wild boars, deer, bulls, bears, badgers, roosters, and—in Leonidas' case—a lion.

The role of lion was undoubtedly seen as an honour, and reflected the confidence Hellanikos had in Leonidas' ability to sing the difficult text prepared for him, but Leonidas himself was far from happy. While the other dancers were being asked to pantomime animals they had frequently observed, he was being asked to portray an animal he had never seen in his life. In past performances, the occasional lion had usually been portrayed with a great deal of prancing about, bullying, and roaring.

Leonidas did his best to follow in this tradition, but when he performed his introductory routine for his friends, Prokles told him bluntly that he looked "like an ox trying to imitate a bear".

When Alkander finally finished laughing, he pointed out, "Lions are big cats. Why don't you try to act more like a cat than a bear?"

The trick worked, and Leonidas' pantomime soon won the praise of Hellanikos, but Leonidas was still nervous about performing for the whole city and foreign guests. The dance was performed on the dancing floor right in the agora, and there was always a huge crowd. The younger boys climbed up on to the roofs of the buildings to get a good view, and the dignitaries (notably the kings and foreign guests) sat in chairs dragged out for the occasion and set up at the top of the steps to the Council chamber, where they had an excellent view.

This year, Cleomenes was conspicuously accompanied by a number of Athenian guests. He was still trying to convince the Council to introduce a motion to the Assembly calling on Sparta to support the exiled Alcmaeonids in driving the tyrant Hippias out of Athens. Equally notable was the absence of his queen. The infant son she had given birth to in the fall was rumoured to be ailing, and both she and her mother-in-law had stayed home to tend to him.

The absence of the much-admired Agiad queen had the unfortunate side effect of making Alkander's sister Percalus all the more prominent. Although dressed only modestly and not in any official role at this festival, it was impossible to overlook the attention she attracted. One of Cleitagora's sons had already inquired of Leonidas if she had a dowry, which Leonidas had answered in the negative. (It wasn't that he objected to providing Alkander's sister with a dowry if she needed one, but it was obvious to both him and Alkander by now that this was not going to be necessary.) Now that the word was out about her dowry, the young men gathering around her were all suitors who could afford to take a dowerless bride—which meant they all came from very powerful and wealthy families, including the Eurypontid king and his younger cousin, Leotychidas.

Leonidas was preoccupied with his own preparations, of course, and paid little attention to what was going on in the audience. The Elisian composer was fighting again with the Thebean poet. They had been fighting like cats and dogs from the day on which the cast had first come together to start rehearsing. The poet felt that the composer's music was too frivolous for his text, while the composer called the text "ponderous, pompous, and pubescent". The performing youths preferred to call it "putrid". In fact, they had developed their own rather farcical version of the entire performance, which entailed making occasional but key substitutions in the text that gave it decidedly bawdy overtones.

Now, with the entire city collected and the composer trying to talk the boys into cutting certain stanzas that had been agreed on earlier, some demon got into them. Even as Hellanikos gave his final instructions to perform exactly as practised, the boys exchanged a look, and Leonidas knew they were going to do it. They went out on to the dancing floor, and an expectant hush fell across the entire crowd. The musicians started to play the music, and Leonidas minced his way into the centre of the agora like a market cat in the early morning. In the centre he sat down and proceeded to lick his right "paw" and use it to wash his face and behind his ears. The audience was delighted. Cats rarely appeared in fables. The "dog" appeared next....

Hellanikos knew something was wrong almost at once, but it was too late to stop them. All he could do was hold his breath in anticipation. He knew and his dancers knew they would be in serious trouble if they offended their elders. If they were still willing to take the risk, than he could only hope and pray that they would do so for the sake of something worth seeing. By the time they started singing the corrupted text, he was far too amused by the audacity and wit of his charges to be angry with them.

The Thebean poet, however, had not noticed the subtle changes in the pantomimes, and so it was only after they started to sing his text in garbled and wilfully misshapen form that he gasped in horror. "What's happened? What is going on?" he demanded. "What have you done to me? They are butchering my text! They are making a mockery of it! How could you do this to me?!"

Hellanikos threw up his hands. "I had no idea they were going to do this."

"What do you mean you had no idea? Who gave them those insulting texts? Everyone knows Spartan youths always follow orders! You gave them orders to commit this outrage!"

"Nonsense! You heard me give them orders to the contrary. Besides, I've never even heard this text before. They must have written it themselves. They are doing this on their own initiative and at their own risk."

"They are turning the entire performance into a farce!"

They were indeed—and the audience loved it, none more than the Athenian guests of King Cleomenes. As the dance ended, these men leapt to their feet, applauding vigorously. "Magnificent! Brilliant! Bravo! Bravo!" they called out to the performers, before turning to Cleomenes and remarking in obvious wonder and delight, "We had no idea you had comedy in Sparta! What a pity none of our comic playwrights could be here to see this. They would recruit your youths for one of our comic choruses on the spot! And these youths! Where do they get their training? I had no idea you had a drama school here. I thought all your youth just drilled and let themselves get flogged," Isogoras exclaimed in rapturous enthusiasm.

Then a new thought occurred to Kleisthenes: "They aren't really Spartiate, are they? Perioikoi? Surely not helot?"

"Of course they're Spartiate," Cleomenes countered indignantly. "Why, the youth who played the lion is my own brother."

"Your brother?!"

"Well, half-brother. Shall I have him come over?"

"Of course! At once! Such a talented youth! And a magnificent voice! Does he have a lover?" Isogoras asked anxiously.

"Leonidas?" Cleomenes couldn't imagine such a thing. "I shouldn't think so," he answered dryly, and then attracted the attention of one of his helot attendants and told him to go fetch Leonidas.

The performers were towelling the sweat away and gulping water laced with a thimbleful of wine to recover. They were euphoric, mostly for having got away with their mutiny, but also because the applause had gone to their heads. They were cracking jokes and exchanging good-natured insults, and their laughter came in volleys that echoed in the lofty ceiling of the bathhouse that they used as their changing room.

The arrival of the helot with the message to Leonidas that he was to report to his brother was unwelcome. "Do I have to go?" Leonidas asked rhetorically. The others tossed unwanted advice after him as he pulled his chiton on over his head and belted it. Someone threw a himation after him as he left, and he just managed to catch it.

"What is this all about?" he asked the helot as they trotted along the back streets towards the steps of the Council House. It was now getting dark and the crowds were starting to disperse. Smoke from cooking fires filled the air, and the smell of meat roasted over great pits along the waterfront came in on the evening breeze. Leonidas was famished and thirsty. He wanted to find Prokles and Alkander and spend what free time he had left with them. He wanted to know what they had thought of the parody his troop of dancers had performed— or rather, wanted to collect the praise he expected from them. He wanted to have dinner with Prokles' family and drink some stronger wine. Instead, he found himself reporting to his elder brother. "You sent for me, sir?"

"Your own brother has to call you 'sir'?" Kleisthenes remarked with raised eyebrows, while Isagoras exclaimed in shocked amazement that Leonidas, shaved and barefoot, was evidently really a youth from the agoge. (His costume had covered his head, hands, and feet.)

"He doesn't have to; it's just habit." Cleomenes answered the first question with a touch of irritation. "Leonidas, these gentlemen from Athens wanted to meet you. May I present my little brother Leonidas, gentlemen. Leonidas, these are Kleisthenes of the Alcmaeonid family and Isagoras, son of Tisander, of Athens. They were impressed by your little performance today." From Cleomenes' mouth it sounded very patronising.

Leonidas ignored his brother's barb and addressed himself to the guests: "Thank you, sirs."

"Tell us, have you had much training as an actor? We thought Spartan youth spent all their time drilling and what not?" Kleisthenes asked with apparent interest.

"No, sir. We rehearsed almost six months, every day except holidays."

"May I suggest we discuss this over dinner, gentlemen?" Cleomenes interrupted. "A meal is awaiting us at the palace. You'll join us, Leonidas." It was an order, not an invitation. A state chariot had drawn up, and Cleomenes gestured his guests and Leonidas aboard. Resentfully, Leonidas had no choice but to go along.

It was the first time he had set foot in his childhood home since the day Cleomenes had expelled him along with his mother and brothers. It was a strange sensation to return, and even stranger to be taken to the state apartments of his father. These were very ancient and very elaborately decorated with mosaic floors and vivid frescoes on the walls, something not seen in newer Spartan homes. Oil lamps provided soft, wavering light, and music floated into the andron from an adjacent room in which a flutist evidently played. The food was presented upon pottery imported from Athens, as the Athenian guests noted with delight. "Oh, the very best! You must have excellent purveyors in Athens!" They even recognised the names of individual artists on the pottery. At least, Leonidas comforted himself, he was probably going to get a decent meal.

Eventually, after things had settled down, the Athenians focused their attention on Leonidas again. "Just how old are you?" Isagoras asked Leonidas, leaning forward to get a better look at him at close quarters.

"Seventeen, sir."

"And how long have you been training as an actor?"

"I'm not training as an actor, sir. I was selected for this one dance."

"That was your first performance?! Remarkable. Then again, talent usually shows itself young. What will be your next role?"

"I hope there won't be one, sir."

"What? You can't be serious. Why should you not want to act again?"

"It takes too much time, sir. I still have drill and the other classes. Rehearsals robbed me of almost all my free time."

"Seriously?!" The Athenians looked over at Cleomenes for confirmation. "You don't excuse even your best choristers and dancers from drill?"

Cleomenes shrugged. "Of course not. My brother and the others are still in the agoge. They have to learn how to be good hoplites. As Spartiates they must learn the profession of arms."

"But why to the exclusion of all else?" Isagoras leaned intimately close to Leonidas again, and Leonidas drew back instinctively. "Why not give up all that mindless drill and let me adopt you?" the Athenian asked him directly. "You never need worry about marching or sleeping out in the rain or eating your horrid black broth again. I know a dozen comic playwrights who would be delighted to employ you!"

Leonidas shook his head sharply.

"Why not?" the Athenian pressed in a cloying voice. "You can't mean you like being flogged and running around in rags?"

"No, sir, but I like what I *will* be," Leonidas answered far too sharply. It was humiliating to stand here before these wealthy Athenians and know that to them, he was a pitiable creature.

"You mean a Spartiate hoplite? A cog in a military machine? An interchangeable part of the Spartan line? Is that really such an enticing prospect? Think of the alternative: you could be a great actor, a man who brings audiences applauding to their feet. You would be wined and dined and entertained at the best addresses, adored by men and women! I fear you simply cannot imagine the joys of life in Athenian society."

Leonidas glanced at his brother, offended that the Athenians felt free to talk like this in the Spartan royal palace. Cleomenes, however, looked highly amused, as if he were enjoying the exchange. So Leonidas replied simply, "Nor you the joys of mine, sir."

"Joys? What joys do you have in your miserable clothes and barren messes?"

Leonidas glanced again at Cleomenes, resentful for being subjected to this shame. How was he, a youth of 17, supposed to explain to these Athenians what it meant to be Spartiate if the ruling king had failed to do so? Cleomenes, however, simply raised his eyebrows, evidently looking forward to Leonidas' answer. Leonidas had no choice but to reply, and he decided on a single word: "Freedom."

"Freedom?! But you are chased from one exercise to the next. You said yourself you have no free time. You are the least free of all free Greeks. Indeed, I think you are less free than many slaves."

"No, sir!" Leonidas snapped back. The never-forgotten cage on the Persian ship seemed to cramp and suffocate him even as he lounged here in the royal andron. Leonidas had tasted slavery, and he was certain of his answer now: "We are the most free of all Greeks, because we are free of fear. We are not afraid of hunger or cold or pain because we have known them all, and we know we can endure them all. We fear no man, because we know we are dependent on no man's favour and no man's pay, but are the absolute masters of ourselves."

"Fine words, young man," Kleisthenes agreed in a rather sour tone, "but empty, too. You live in constant fear of your instructors, your elders, your own leaders. Why, any citizen can call you to account, report you for the slightest infringement of the rules, cause you to be flogged like a common slave."

"Not so, sir." Leonidas insisted hotly, aware that there was enough truth in the man's words to make it all the more important to protest. In fact, it was the very fact that there was *some* truth to what he said that made Leonidas so agitated. He hated to think of his society in the way this Athenian was portraying it, and he wanted it to be better. He argued: "We obey our elders only as long as we respect them or what they stand for. Take tonight's performance: the text was not what our chorus master had prepared and rehearsed with us. It was our own work."

Cleomenes burst out laughing and slapped himself on the thigh in delight. "I should have known it! I'm beginning to like you, little brother. I thought that pompous Thebean looked like he'd swallowed a porcupine!"

"*You* wrote the text?" the astonished Isagoras asked, in amazement and obvious admiration.

"No, sir, we all did. Everyone in the troop contributed bits and pieces as they occurred to us. It just sort of evolved."

The Athenians seemed delighted to learn this, too, and congratulated Leonidas yet again. "A youth of many talents, indeed!" Isagoras insisted, stroking his shoulder. Leonidas shuddered, and turned on his brother. "May I be excused now, sir? My friends will be wondering where I am."

Cleomenes considered him over the rim of his kylix and then nodded. "Yes, of course; unless *you*, gentlemen, insist that he stay?" he asked his guests.

Isagoras appealed to Leonidas to stay, and when Leonidas insisted he wanted to leave, Isagoras pleaded, "At least let us drink your health!"

This was agreed, and wine was called for. To Leonidas' astonishment, it was poured pure into his kylix, and they all drank it that way—even his brother. It tasted terrible, and he had a hard time swallowing it down. At once he set his kylix aside and stood. "Thank you. I hope you have a pleasant stay in Lacedaemon. Good night." He fled from the overheated, overlighted room.

Outside the andron, the corridors of the palace were cool and dark, lit only by the occasional lamp at strategic corners. Leonidas knew his way out, of course, and he headed toward the back—the kitchen and stables exit where he would draw less attention than at the main front entrance. To reach the back, however, he had to pass through one of the inner atriums, the one around which the private apartments of the royal family were grouped.

Looking up toward that wing of the sprawling palace in which he had grown up, Leonidas noted that light spilled through the second-floor colonnade on to the roof of the peristyle. Counting the windows, he could identify his own nursery. This room was also lit, and he thought he could hear whimpering coming from it. He remembered that Cleomenes' youngest son was sick, and started to hurry away.

Something moved and made a sound in the darkness just in front of him. He stopped abruptly, the hair standing up on the back of his neck—until he realised it was only a child, standing beside the central fountain sucking its thumb. It had to be Cleomenes' little daughter. She gazed up at him with huge, frightened eyes.

He went down on his heels to be at her level. "Nothing to be afraid of, child." He couldn't remember her name. "I'm not going to hurt you. But shouldn't you be in bed at this time of night?"

"Of course she should be in bed." The voice came from the side of the atrium below the nursery, and a moment later a lady stepped out on to the crushed marble pathway and started toward him.

It was "that whore", his stepmother. He had not seen her up close since that horrible storm during his "fox time". He slowly got to his feet again to face her, bracing himself for the worst. She was, he thought with a sinking heart, very like his own mother: tall, slender, grey-haired, and dignified. She was dressed very simply in her own home. Her head and feet were bare, but she wore beaded earrings and a collar of beads as well. She held out her hand to the child, who did a childish thing: she took refuge behind Leonidas, clinging to his knee and giggling, as if this was a game of hide-and-seek.

To Leonidas' astonishment, the "other woman" did not frown or snap her fingers at the errant child; she laughed. Then she raised her eyebrows and remarked to Leonidas, "You seem to have won her confidence instantly, but then she is excessively bold. Now, Gorgo," she addressed herself to the little girl. "Let your uncle go and come with me. You need to go to bed."

"No!" The little girl stomped her foot, shook her head, and continued to cling to Leonidas. "I don't *want* to go to bed!"

The "other woman" still did not get angry. She seemed to think for a moment, and then she asked, "Would you like to sleep with me, in my bed?"

Leonidas could feel the child clinging to his knee nod her head.

"All right. Come to me, and I'll take you up to my bed." Chilonis held her hand out to the child, and this time the little girl let go of Leonidas and ran to her grandmother. The woman bent and swept the two-year-old into her arms. The child nestled her head in her grandmother's neck and closed her eyes in obvious contentment. The "other woman" smiled and stroked her granddaughter's cheek before turning to Leonidas. "It's the sound of her brother's whimpering that distresses her. He cries most of the night. Agis sleeps through it all, but Gorgo is more sensitive." She looked down at the child in her arms with obvious affection. Leonidas wondered if his mother had ever looked at him like that, but he knew better. He doubted if she had ever held him in her arms at all.

Leonidas felt he had to explain himself. "I didn't mean to intrude, ma'am. Your son insisted that I join him for dinner at the request of his Athenian guests, and I wanted to slip out the back rather than attract attention at the main door."

"I never imagined you had just barged in here. After all, you never have before." She considered him long and hard, and Leonidas squirmed inwardly, wondering what she saw. He would never know. "Good night, then," she ended the encounter.

"I hope the baby recovers," Leonidas remembered to say.

She paused already in the act of turning away. "Thank you. I hope so, too.... And, Leonidas, I want you to know that I did not want your mother expelled from here. I was perfectly happy where I was, but Cleomenes felt he had to do it to establish his—position."

"That's all right, ma'am. He was probably right."

She seemed to consider him again, but then she nodded, thanked him, and was gone. Leonidas let himself out the stables exit into the street.

Spartan law forbade her citizens from carrying torches and lighting the streets, so that they would always feel comfortable moving about in the darkness; but at a feast like this there were so many foreign guests who had their own lighting that the city seemed bright. Furthermore, the bonfires built to roast the sacrificial meat were still burning, giving a red glow to the sky in the east. In consequence, the city looked eerily unfamiliar to Leonidas as he hurried back to the river, hoping to find his friends there. It seemed very late, and he feared they would already have headed for home. He was startled when Alkander came out of nowhere.

"Leonidas! Where have you been? I've been looking all over for you! I need your help! Leotychidas, son of Archidamas, has asked for Percalus's hand."

"Who?"

"Leotychidas! You must have seen the way he's been hanging around her!"

Leonidas hadn't particularly noticed. "Well, will he take her without a dowry?"

"Yes; that's not the problem."

"Doesn't Percalus like him?"

"No, she likes him well enough. In fact, she seems rather keen about it."

"So what's the problem?"

"He's a Eurypontid!" Alkander said this as if he thought Leonidas was being excessively dense.

"He is?"

"Yes, he's great-grandson to King Hippokratides and heir to the Eurypontid throne until Demaratus marries and has heirs of his own."

"So what?"

"Leonidas! I'm a mothake! I can't marry my sister to royalty."

"Who says?"

"People will get angry. You know what they're like."

"How can you say 'no'?"

"I can't. You've got to do it."

"Why me?"

"Leonidas!"

"All right, I'll talk to him. It doesn't have to be tonight, does it?"

———

Leotychidas didn't like what Leonidas told him, and he was not very pleasant about it. In fact, the interview was one of the most unpleasant of Leonidas' short life. Leotychidas naturally insisted on the courtesy he could expect from a "mere" youth towards a full citizen; and Leonidas was kept standing with his hands at his sides, saying "yes, sir" and "no, sir" and swallowing insults. Leotychidas kept pressing Leonidas to tell him whom they were planning to give Percalus to, refusing to believe that Alkander simply didn't want "trouble". By the time Leotychidas finally let him go, he was sweating as if he'd just run a ten-mile course, and inwardly very resentful of Percalus and all the trouble she was causing him.

Furthermore, she was soon making Alkander's life miserable by insisting she was "in love" with Leotychidas and *wouldn't* marry anyone else. In tear-laden scenes, she even threatened to sleep with him without the sanction of marriage and force Alkander's hand.

"She wouldn't *really* do that, would she?" Leonidas asked in shock.

Alkander shrugged his shoulders, but wouldn't meet Leonidas' eye. "I don't think so. She ought to know that it would ruin her. But all this attention has gone to her head. She really thinks her beauty makes her more valuable than family ties or fortune."

It was hard to deny that, not at an age when they were themselves so fascinated by female charms. By now, watching the girls of the agoge at sports had become deathly boring. Just when the girls started to get really "interesting", they were yanked out of the agoge and sent home to learn how to become good wives and mothers. The girls running, swimming, and wrestling were thus, at best, in the early stages of puberty; and by the time the boys were 18 going on 28, they looked down on these girls as "babies"—an attitude reinforced by the knowledge that the girls in the agoge were strictly "off limits".

Not so the girls who worked in the large basket factory near the dye works, or the girls who worked in the flax mill, or the helot serving girls working in houses all across the city. Helot girls seemed to mature young, and were often married and breeding before they reached their twentieth year. For them, there was nothing more thrilling than the attentions of a young Spartiate.

Everyone knew the rules of the game. No helot girl expected a Spartiate lover to marry her or even keep her as a concubine. They knew perfectly well that the youths were only collecting experience and would soon turn their attention elsewhere. But these Spartiate youths were young and strong and beautiful in a way that helots never could be. And not only were they surrounded by an aura of future power and strength and status, they also paid well. A youth from the agoge would bring his helot girl the hares and pheasants he trapped or sometimes cured meat, oil, or wine from his kleros (if his mother turned a blind eye to such things). The richer boys might even give the helot girls real gifts—ivory combs, glass beads, pottery, or wooden utensils. The prettier and cleverer helot girls knew how to convert their success with the youth from the agoge into small dowries that made them more attractive to suitors from their own class.

Alkander and Leonidas, as usual, played by the rules; Prokles did not. While Alkander more boldly and Leonidas with considerable hesitation and almost backwardness found helot girls to court,

Prokles was not content to gather his youthful experience with helot girls. He set his sights on seducing a particular perioikoi maiden who had caught his fancy. Leonidas warned him against it. "If her dad finds out, he'll make a stink! He's one of the principal purveyors to the army. He's well connected and he has important friends."

"No one is going to find out," Prokles promised.

And maybe no one *would* have found out if the girl herself had kept her mouth shut, but Prokles was too successful. The girl liked him so much, she wanted to keep him. Since it was obvious to her that he would not marry her of his own free will, she decided she would force his hand. Her reasoning was that if the scandal got out about their relationship, he would be forced by public opinion and pressure to marry her. She therefore went to her father and accused Prokles of rape.

The accusation was extremely rare in Sparta. In fact, the city prided itself on the fact that women were perfectly safe to walk unescorted anywhere in Sparta at any time. In other cities, a woman's safety was the duty of her male relatives, who generally dealt with the risks by keeping their women locked up in their homes. But a society that depended so heavily on women managing the estates and running all aspects of the domestic economy, as Sparta's did, could not afford to have women confined to their homes or afraid to move about on their own. Whereas in other cities, a woman out alone was automatically presumed to be a woman of ill repute and hence fair game, a woman alone in Sparta bore no stigma of impropriety, and matrons and maidens of the very best families and repute moved freely about the city. Their safety was, however, the duty of *every* citizen and *every* youth. Unbelievable as it seemed to foreigners, the system worked so well that the Spartans had no statute punishment for rape; it was too rare to warrant such a statute.

Precisely because it was so rare and because Sparta was so proud of it being rare, the fact that Prokles, the son of a good and respected father, was being accused of this outrage became an instant scandal. Prokles was arrested straight off the drill fields, without being given time to even bathe or change. He was clamped into the jail usually reserved for rebellious helots—not one of the polite cells for minor offences against sumptuary laws or breaches of military discipline.

He was allowed no visitors except his father and the judges appointed to his case. His mother and grandmother publicly stated that "if the charges were true", they would disown him.

Privately, however, Prokles' family pressed Leonidas and Alkander for assurances that it was not true. Leonidas and Alkander found themselves at Prokles' kleros the night of his arrest, facing an inquisition from Prokles' entire family. They were AWOL from the agoge and would get in trouble for it, but after all the hospitality and kindness they had enjoyed over the years, they couldn't just leave. Leonidas, in particular, remembered that he would be a slave somewhere in Asia if Lysandridas had not persuaded the perioikoi fleet commander to send two triremes to rescue him. In the smoky darkness of the kitchen, Leonidas and Alkander tried to convince the distraught grandparents and mother of their friend that Prokles had never used force.

"But her father says he saw the proof of force! He says she's covered with horrible bruises and even cuts. He says any surgeon is welcome to examine her!" Prokles' mother reminded them in evident despair. She was wringing the skirt of her peplos in her hands in distress.

Leonidas and Alkander couldn't explain that, of course, but they kept repeating that Prokles had been seeing the girl for months. "She's crazy about him—more than my helot girl is about me!" Leonidas candidly admitted.

"You know Prokles as well as we do," Alkander reasoned. "You *know* he wouldn't use force. He doesn't need to. If she didn't want him, he could easily find someone else."

"Then why was he pursuing this modest maiden of a good perioikoi house?" Prokles' grandmother wanted to know. Leonidas and Alkander looked helplessly at one another.

"I cannot understand you young men!" the old woman announced with obvious exasperation. "Why do you let your balls rule your brains! It makes no sense to me at all! Prokles' whole future may be ruined, and for what? For a few moments of pleasure that he could have had with any number of other girls!"

"What do you think the judges will decide?" Prokles' mother asked anxiously. She was trying very hard not to sound alarmed, but she obviously was.

"If he is found guilty of rape, the very least they will give him is exile," Lysandridas suggested soberly. "They will not allow a convicted rapist to live in the city."

"Exile!" Prokles' mother was horrified.

"The *least* they will give him?" Lysandridas' wife noted. "You're saying they could sentence him to death?"

Lysandridas drew a deep breath. "Only if they find him guilty. I don't think we should assume that."

But even so, the thought was sobering.

The next day, Leonidas and Alkander were questioned separately by the magistrates. Nobody appeared to question that Prokles and the girl had had an ongoing relationship, but the evidence of force was apparently overwhelming and convincing. The only issue was, therefore, who had applied the force; and if it had been someone other than Prokles, why did the girl lie about it? As no one could come up with an alternative candidate who might have raped the girl, the judges moved to condemn, and his father, Philippos, was warned what his son could expect: on account of his youth, the judges had agreed on exile rather than death, but if he set foot again in Lacedaemon, he would be killed. Stunned, Philippos returned to his kleros to break the news to his wife and parents.

The same news also went to the father of the victim. While the news that Prokles was to be exiled permanently was greeted with satisfaction by the girl's parents, she herself responded with hysterics. It soon became clear that she had expected Prokles would be ordered to marry her. It had never occurred to her that he might be exiled or killed. Her father, in astonishment, pointed out that no one dreamed of forcing her to marry the man who had so violently abused and degraded her. The Spartan judges had from the very first showed understanding for this position. In a flood of tears the girl now changed her story: Prokles had never used force. She had been attacked by a young neighbour, a perioikoi, who was jealous of Prokles. He had got wind of what was going on with Prokles, and knowing that she was no longer "pure", had refused to take no for an answer. The rape had been real enough, but the rapist was not Prokles.

Most of that night her father struggled with his conscience, ashamed to return to the Spartan court and admit that his daughter had lied to them all. He wanted to leave things as they were, but he could not. All the servants had heard his daughter's screaming and wailing, and just next door the young man who had really raped his daughter was smugly waiting for Prokles to be exiled. So, weary and deeply saddened, he made his way to the court the next morning, and was waiting for the magistrates when they arrived. He told them what had transpired, and at once the case was remanded to a perioikoi court. Prokles was released from his prison—and sent to "the pits". It was the opinion of the judges that a youth who had seduced an honest maiden of good family should be punished.

When Prokles' family and friends got the news, they were over-joyed. Prokles' mother and grandmother rushed to bring offerings of thanks to the Gods, while Philippos and Lysandridas went to be at Prokles' side when he endured the flogging. Leonidas and Alkander were given permission to be there, too. Drill wasn't scheduled until the afternoon, and sports weren't quite so compelling.

By the time they reached the pits near the Temple of Artemis Orthia, a large crowd had already gathered. Prokles' case had attained such notoriety, after all, that this sudden turn of events attracted excited attention throughout the city. For many, Prokles was a name only, and they were anxious to finally see the youth who had caused so much scandal in a city usually devoid of it. There was a particularly large crowd of women, curious about just what sort of youth this was who would seduce modest maidens before he was even out of the agoge.

Prokles looked decidedly the worse for wear as they led him to the pits. For a start, he hadn't seen the light of day for days, and his face was twisted up by squinting in the bright morning sun. Nor had he been allowed to wash; and he was dirty. His hair was starting to grow on his scalp, and that gave it a dirty shadowing as well. Leonidas heard women muttering that he didn't look "that irresistible" to them.

Alkander and Leonidas wormed their way as far forward as they could, determined to let Prokles know that he was not alone in a hostile crowd. They did not know if he had been told he was facing exile, but they were certain the treatment he had received would have discouraged him. Only at the last minute, after Prokles had stripped down and turned to hand his things to one of the officials, did he cast a glance in the direction of his friends; but he didn't seem to see them. "Here!" Leonidas shouted out. "We're here!"

Prokles smiled once and then stepped into the sand pit to take up his stance before the bar, his feet and arms well apart. The two officials of the court selected to administer the flogging had already cut the reeds to the appropriate length and tested them on the palms of their hands. One took up a position on either side of Prokles, ready to spell each other if their arms tired before Prokles did. The usual hush fell over the crowd and with a nod from Prokles, the flogging began.

Although he had stood here often enough in the past and been in Prokles' skin twice, Leonidas found himself thinking of his brother's Athenian guests. Apparently everywhere else in the world, Spartan youth was looked down upon for enduring this humiliation, usually reserved only for slaves. No sooner had he thought this than he remembered that Prokles himself had complained about that fact before Artemis Orthia last year. And no sooner had he remembered that, than Leonidas knew in the pit of his stomach what was going to happen: Prokles was going to demonstrate his contempt for the whole ritual. Sure enough, the flogging had hardly started before Prokles raised his hand in surrender and dropped to his knees in the sand.

The crowd broke into a wild chatter of disbelief. Prokles was a strong, well-built 18-year-old—not a little boy enduring the cane for the first time. He was obviously far from physically finished; he didn't even pretend to be in pain. Quite to the contrary: in a voice that carried to the spectators, he impudently announced, "She was good, but she wasn't *that* good."

The commentary of the crowd, which up to now had been baffled and uncomprehending, instantly turned indignant and angry. Women, particularly, were offended by such an attitude, and they starting calling out insults. The judges were so astonished that they hardly knew how to react, and they conferred together hastily. The law clearly stated that a youth condemned to flogging could stop it at will, but youths were supposed to be proud to show what they could endure, not turn it into a commentary on the seriousness of their crime.

Leonidas looked at the angry people around them. He found himself torn between the sentiments of his friend and those of the crowd. He understood that Prokles was furious with his girlfriend for trying to manipulate him. He understood that he felt she had caused him enough unnecessary humiliation. His words were first and foremost an expression of contempt for her. But they were also a challenge to Spartan law and custom. Leonidas saw, with sudden and unsettling clarity, that if youth took advantage of their freedoms— not just by changing the text of their songs, but by challenging the very premises of the system of discipline—the whole foundation of Spartan society would start to crumble. He had only a vague and imprecise image at that moment, but it was a frightening one never-theless.

Alkander had him by the elbow. "We better get Prokles out of here," he urged, "before they decide to lock him up again!" And so together they pushed their way through the indignant crowd and plucked Prokles out of the middle of it, pretending they had orders from their eirene. With his usual presence of mind, Alkander thought to say in a loud voice, "You've got to report at once, or you're going to be cleaning the latrines all night!"

As was to be expected given the mood of the crowd, several people shouted that this was just what he deserved, and others urged that he should be subjected to extra duties and drill for a month, et cetera. And while they all made their suggestions, Leonidas and Alkander got Prokles extricated from the crowd.

CHAPTER 10

Age 19

AT 19 THE YOUTHS OF THE agoge became "meleirenes"—those on the brink of becoming eirenes. As with every other age-cohort in the agoge, this brought with it a unique curriculum and expectations. The most exciting aspect was that for the first time since entering the agoge, they were freed of the control of an eirene. It was recognised that the 20-year-olds just didn't carry enough authority with youths only one year younger, so the meleirenes were placed under the direct authority of the Paidonomos and supervised by his assistants, all full citizens—when they weren't at drill or on "duty".

"Duty" was a new responsibility that, like drill, was under the supervision of the army itself. In addition to standing by as runners for the ephors, Council, and magistrates, duty entailed providing the watch on all public buildings in the city, and patrolling the city at night. Ever since the disastrous raid on the agoge during the Second Messenian War, the city provided a 24-hour watch over its public buildings, including the agoge and the royal palaces, as well as roving patrols during the hours of darkness. Such duty being boring, tedious, and disruptive of normal activity, the army had soon delegated this responsibility down to the meleirenes, who were trained well enough at arms to look impressive to visiting strangers, discourage common crime during the hours of darkness—and raise the alarm if there was a serious threat to the city or her citizens. After all, the days were long since past when Sparta really had to fear an attack by an armed force so far inside Lacedaemon.

Whether by accident or design, Leonidas frequently found himself posted to guard the Agiad royal palace. As there was nothing the least degrading about this duty (even if it was boring), he did not mind particularly—except that it meant he found himself being greeted by people going in and out, which was not entirely correct. The first time it happened, he had been confused as to what his response should be. Technically, of course, no sentry responds to any kind of comment or provocation—except to do his duty of barring entry to an unwanted visitor. But when the queen mother stopped and addressed him by name, Leonidas felt it would be rude not to reply.

"Leonidas!" the "other woman" addressed him with a smile. "How are you doing these days?"

"Well, ma'am."

"You look splendid!" she assured him as if she meant it. "You'll be an eirene next year, will you?"

"Yes, ma'am."

"Hmm." She seemed to find this significant for some reason, and nodded to herself with apparent satisfaction before bidding him farewell and continuing on her way.

After that, she always stopped to chat with him when she found him on duty. She was frequently accompanied by her two grandchildren, six-year-old Agis and four-year-old Gorgo. Agis was an overactive, self-willed boy who couldn't seem to stand still or be quiet even for a second. Gorgo, in contrast, was a curious and observant child who took an open interest in adult conversation and doings. While Agis was impatiently throwing stones at crows or scratching with a stick between the paving stones or some such thing, oblivious to the adults, Gorgo always listened to what her grandmother said. Given the beauty of their mother, it rather surprised Leonidas that neither child was particularly pretty. Agis had his father's large nose even at this age, and Gorgo was red-haired and freckled, which was not considered attractive in any society.

No matter how often he had the duty at the Agiad palace, however, Leonidas only saw the queen herself once. She was heavy with child again, and it was rumoured that she was not well. Certainly her face was pinched and her eyes circled; she spoke in a tart, impatient voice to the women accompanying her, and held a hand to the small of her back as if in pain. She took no notice of Leonidas at all—as was perfectly correct—but Leonidas was left with the impression that she was not a happy bride any longer.

Of course, that might have to do with the fact that her husband had been absent since the previous summer. Indeed, he must have made her pregnant very shortly before he departed on his great expedition to free Athens from Hippias. The appeals of the Athenians, backed by a favourable decision from Delphi, had finally borne fruit. After a compromise proposal that entailed sending Sparta's fledgling fleet had resulted in ignominious defeat, Cleomenes talked the Council into putting a proposal to take the army north to a vote in the Assembly. Here he made an eloquent appeal to restore democracy to Athens. By this time, the army was so bored and fed up with the dithering of the older citizens that Cleomenes won thunderous applause from the younger age-cohorts. Demaratus, sensing the mood of the younger citizens, threw in his lot with Cleomenes and agreed that they should take the active army north.

The kings very scrupulously avoided a call-up of even one class of reserves, as support for the adventure declined sharply among the older cohorts, and many reservists had no desire to disrupt their settled lives. The active units, in contrast, were composed of men who were young and fit and confined to barracks anyway. They were raring for a fight. The youngest age-cohorts, those that had not campaigned at all yet, were particularly anxious to prove themselves.

So the Spartan army had marched out shortly before the summer solstice, and the city expectantly awaited the news of a victory within a month. It didn't come. To be sure, the Spartan army had taken Athens without a fight, but the tyrant Hippias himself had fled to the Acropolis with his most loyal followers, and they remained holed up there still. The Spartans did not dare abandon Athens without having seized or killed Hippias, since he would obviously just re-establish himself as soon as they were gone. But it was equally unthinkable that

Spartan troops would assault the sacred temples of the Gods—even if they were harbouring the tyrant and his men. The result had thus been a siege of the Athenian Acropolis that showed no sign of ending. Apparently Hippias either had vast stores of food hidden in the treasuries of the temples, or he was being supplied secretly by supporters who knew ways up to the Acropolis that the Spartans did not control.

The situation was exactly the kind the Spartans hated. The army was bogged down in a "foreign adventure", leaving Lacedaemon "naked" to her enemies (as the more dramatic opponents of the war liked to word it). Certainly the older men who had opposed the war from the start were unhappy about keeping up the garrison duties usually carried out by the active units. It kept them away from their hearths with winter drawing near, and from their own beds at night. It meant they were away from their kleros and their growing children. With the active age-cohorts in Athens and not at Assembly, the calls for the troops to come home and leave Athens to the Athenians grew and gained support from Assembly to Assembly. Leonidas couldn't help thinking that if his brother Dorieus had only patiently bided his time rather than rushing off to make himself king in Sicily, this would have been his opportunity to turn the citizens against Cleomenes. But with Dorieus in Sicily and Demaratus with Cleomenes in Athens, there was no rallying point for opposition; and so the citizens raged futilely while the strange war dragged on into the winter.

———

One dreary day, roughly three months after Leonidas had become a meleirene, an army runner came down the Tegean road while Leonidas' unit was at drill on the muddy fields beyond the Eurotas. A shout went up, and it was only with difficulty that the officers could force the youths to keep their minds on their drill. As soon as the youths were dismissed they ran, still in their full panoply, over the bridge and back into the city to find out the news.

A drizzle had started, and a gloomy darkness was sinking over the city early, but the streets were crowded. Women and helots, perioikoi, and the boys and youths of the agoge were on the streets asking each other what had happened. The dogs ran about, barking in a frenzy of vicarious excitement. The only thing anyone seemed to know for sure, however, was that the runner had reported to the Agiad royal palace and the five ephors had been summoned. A huge crowd had therefore gathered in front of the Ephorate, as this was where the ephors would make any official announcement. Leonidas' friends and comrades, however, insisted that he seek admittance to the palace. "They won't turn you away!" his friends pleaded. "They can't! Ask to see the queen mother!"

Leonidas had never done that before and he was not entirely comfortable with the idea, but he was no less anxious to learn the news than his comrades. Propelled forward by the others as much as by his own willpower, Leonidas found himself at the gates of the Agiad palace. The two unfortunate meleirenes on duty were clearly uncomfortable with the loud crowd gathered in front of them, and they responded by taking up a defensive position, shields at ready and spears crossed. Most people accepted that there would be no admittance and returned to the Ephorate to await the official announcement.

By now it was getting close to dinner, and after the long afternoon of drill most of the youths were hungry. The immediate excitement of seeing the messenger was past. They noticed how heavy their armour was and how uncomfortable their soggy undergarments, and decided to go back to change and eat before besieging the Ephorate. And so they dispersed into the gathering gloom.

Leonidas and his two friends lingered a bit. "You're plotting something," Alkander observed.

"You know other ways into the palace," Prokles guessed.

Leonidas didn't answer exactly, but after going around to the back of the palace, he passed the kitchen entrance and started up a side alley. Here he stopped abruptly. The clouds had dropped down on to the city and the streets were cloaked in mist. The mist glistened on the paving stones and straw that lay about. A cat trotted over, meowing, and rubbed herself against their legs. Leonidas looked up. The others followed his gaze. There was a window about three feet over their heads.

"What's that?"

"It's the loft of the stables. They load hay and straw through that window. The wagons stop here in the street and hand the hay up to the grooms in the loft. It avoids having to drive the cumbersome hay wagons in and out of the stableyard or lugging the bales up into the loft on the ladders. I used to watch them do it when I was little."

The three youths looked up at the window. "Well, what's stopping you?" Prokles asked.

"I don't know that I want to sneak in like that. The queen mother has always been nice to me."

"Once you're inside, you don't have to tell her how you got there," Prokles pointed out practically. "Come on, get out of your armour and climb on my back." Leonidas hesitated just a little longer, and then turned his hoplon over to Alkander and removed his helmet, greaves, and breastplate. Still wearing the leather jack that was worn under the metal pieces, he scrambled on to Prokles' back and from there got a hold on the ledge of the window. It took two attempts, but he managed to haul himself into the loft. He turned around and called back down to his friends, "Wait for me here!"

"Of course. Hurry!"

Leonidas nodded and slipped deeper into the loft. It smelled of hay and straw above the stable smell from below. He lay on his belly and looked down into the stable to see how many helots were there. Apparently the horses had just been fed. They were all munching contentedly in their stalls, and the helots had left them alone. They were probably getting their own meal, Leonidas calculated, and quickly descended the ladder. The horses were too interested in their feed to take any note of him. At the stable door he hesitated again, looking out into the stableyard, but again all was deserted. The mist was so thick that it all but obscured the buildings. The lamps hanging under the kitchen porch were just blurs of murky yellow. Stepping carefully to avoid the puddles in the yard, Leonidas made his way past the storerooms and work sheds towards the entrance to the kitchens.

Even before he reached them, however, he could hear excited voices. The helots were clearly having their own meal, so he backed away quickly and sought instead the narrow passage that led straight to a stairway. This stairway accessed the rooms on the second floor where most of the helots slept. But beyond those chambers were the rooms occupied by the household officials, and beyond them, the private rooms of the family. Taking this route into the palace constituted a great invasion of privacy, and Leonidas dreaded the thought of running into anyone up there, but he hoped there would be no one in the nursery at this time of day. He hoped he would be able slip down the internal stairs before anyone saw him. Once he was in the main atrium, he would be able to walk into the hall as if he'd come through the main gate.

The corridor in the helots' quarters was darkened, and he heard no one as he advanced very cautiously. In the nursery corridor a single light burned, casting as much shadow as light. Just at the landing to the stairs back down, when he thought he was out of danger, he was taken by surprise. A figure was standing at the top of the stairs looking down, and at the sound of his footfall, it spun about guiltily. It was the child, Gorgo, again.

Her eyes widened at the sight of him, but when he put his finger to his lips, she smiled and ran to him. "You won't tell on me, Uncle Leonidas, will you?"

He just gestured with his finger to his lips.

"News from Papa!" she told him eagerly in a loud whisper.

He nodded.

"Is Papa coming home soon?"

"Maybe," he whispered. "That's what I'm going to find out." He pointed down the stairs.

"Come tell me!" she demanded next.

He nodded. Then, his finger to his lips, he started cautiously down the stairs.

At last he was in the atrium that he would have passed through if he'd come by the back door. That was not so compromising, and he tried to act as if he had every right to be there as he mounted the steps toward the main hall.

At once he encountered a servant carrying a tray laden with wine, water, bread, and cheese. The man started rather violently, but he too was an old helot from the days when Leonidas' mother had ruled here. He started stammering, "Master Leonidas. How did you get in?" but on second thought revised his greeting to: "What can I do for you, master?"

"I understand a messenger has arrived from my brother?"

"Yes, he is with the queen and the queen mother now."

"Would you announce me and ask if I may join them?"

The old helot looked dubious, but he could hardly say "no". He continued on his way and Leonidas waited. It seemed to take a long time before the helot returned without the tray. "Master Leonidas, you may come with me."

Leonidas was led to the representative hearth-room with its heavily painted walls, squat painted columns, and large square hearth in the centre. Leonidas had rarely seen the room used, and on a dark night like this it seemed particularly gloomy. The smoke hung in the air. It rose to the roof where there was a hole where it should have escaped, but the windless drizzle outside sent the smoke back down into the room.

It was, of course, Chilonis who came to greet him.

"Forgive me for intruding, ma'am, but the whole city—"

"Of course," Chilonis agreed. "I quite understand. You will forgive me if I am brief?"

"Ma'am."

"My son has captured Hippias' small children, as their servants were trying to smuggle them to safety outside of Athens. My son is now holding them hostage, and intends to release them only if Hippias and the rest of his family and supporters abandon the Acropolis and promise to leave Athens forever."

Even before Leonidas could express any pleasure at the news, Chilonis had hold of his arm and was escorting him back out of the hall again. "My daughter-in-law is naturally delighted," Chilonis was saying. "She looks forward to her husband's return, and longs for him to be at her side when she is brought to childbed again."

"But of course, ma'am. We are all looking for the army to return."

"Do you approve of the price, then? Using innocent young children as bargaining chips? And what if Hippias calls our bluff? What if he says: 'Keep my children! I can get new sons.'?" She stopped and looked up at him (for Leonidas was now several inches taller than she, although she was a tall woman.)

"But who would say such a thing, ma'am?" Leonidas countered vigorously, unable to imagine it.

She shrugged. "Tyrants are men who have trampled the laws of their cities and the rights of their fellow citizens. How can we know to what lengths they are prepared to go to retain power? I do not like using children as pawns in politics."

"But what would you have your son do, ma'am? He is at war with Hippias. He could kill the children or keep them as slaves. Surely to use them as bargaining chips is the lesser evil?"

Chilonis considered him seriously. "You think like a man already, I see. But that is only natural. And, of course, you are right. Children are always victims in wars—whichever side loses drags its children down into the depths of hell. Indeed, one could even argue that Hippias' children have earned a harsher fate than most children of a lost war. Hippias certainly *chose* tyranny and war. The children of other cities are often the victims of nothing more reprehensible than unpreparedness, poor leadership, or weakness. When I think of the children of the cities of Ionia, exposed to the whims of a Persian despot merely because their father's resistance was crushed by a vastly superior foe, I sometimes despair. Forgive me." She looked up at him again with an apologetic smile. "I am boring you with my old woman's woe. I just couldn't stand to listen to my daughter-in-law's inane chatter any longer. She thinks of no one but herself."

Leonidas said nothing, knowing that he had no business to have heard this. Instead he remarked, "Your granddaughter is anxious to hear news of her father, ma'am. Maybe you could go to her?"

"Gorgo? She's supposed to be in bed. Did you run into her?"

"Yes, ma'am. She was excited to think her father would be coming home soon."

Chilonis sighed, but noted indulgently, "She adores him. He spoils her. He spoils both of them. All right, I'll see to her."

"Thank you for seeing me, ma'am."

"Any time," she assured him, and gave him her hand.

———

The army was back in just five days. Hippias had agreed to leave Attica forever in exchange for the release of his children, and so Athens was again a democracy. Cleomenes was clearly very pleased with himself and quick to point out to everyone that those who now held sway in Athens owed their position "to Spartan spears". The cynics warned that he should not expect the Athenians to be grateful, but Cleomenes clearly thought he had greatly expanded Spartan influence.

Demaratus returned in a far less sanguine mood. There were rumours that returned with the army that the two kings had quarrelled frequently and all too publicly. Certainly Demaratus resented the fact that the Athenians treated Cleomenes as the "real" commander of the army and their special friend, while they all but ignored him. He resented no less the fact that Cleomenes was taking all the credit for their ultimate success—although the unit that captured the children of Hippias was no more under Cleomenes' command than Demaratus'. Demaratus was a year older than Cleomenes; but because his father had lived longer than Anaxandridas, Cleomenes had come to the throne sooner, giving him a "unwarranted" sense of precedence, in Demaratus' eyes. Furthermore, because Cleomenes had been a ruling king he had been free to marry even before turning 21, while Demaratus had lived in barracks with the other men of his age-cohort, and was not yet married. But he was now 32. If he had been an ordinary citizen, he would have been subject to ridicule and sanctions for failing to marry. As king, he had a double duty to marry and produce offspring. It was therefore not surprising that he was visibly displeased when almost the same day that the army returned, the Agiad queen gave birth to yet another son. Leonidas knew all this just from being an alert and observant meleirene, but nothing prepared him for receiving a summons to the Eurypontid palace late that night.

"Where?" he asked the helot shaking him awake in disbelief, while his comrades groaned and cursed about the misfortune of sharing a barracks with an Agiad prince.

"King Demaratus has sent for you," the helot insisted.

"What time is it?"

"Nearing midnight, sir. Please, come quickly. My lord was very angry."

"What the hell have you done *now*, Leonidas?" Ephorus asked in a sleepy voice.

"I haven't done *anything*," Leonidas protested, trying to find a chiton and himation in the dark.

"That's mine!" Prokles snatched his himation back.

"Would you shut up! Some of us need our sleep!"

It was bitter cold in the streets, and Leonidas woke up quickly as he followed the helot along the frosted way in his bare feet. Just nine more months, he told himself, and he'd be an eirene and could wear sandals.

The Eurypontid palace was located near the Temple to the Bronze Athena, and he knew it only from the outside. The meleirenes on watch looked astonished as he passed them, but all he could do was shrug and shake his head to indicate he didn't know what this was about. He was led through what seemed like a maze of corridors, and at last ended in a bedchamber with a roaring fire in which the Eurypontid king was pacing about angrily. He stopped as the door opened and greeted Leonidas with: "There you are! What took you so long? I've been waiting at least an hour." The helot bowed and withdrew rapidly without a word.

Demaratus stared at Leonidas. "Weren't you called 'the runt' once?"

"I wouldn't know, sir," Leonidas replied evenly, wondering where this was going, while feeling his hatred of the Eurypontids rekindle.

"Hmphf! Well, you were, but I can see you've been growing. Look, let's get this over with quickly. I've been kept waiting long enough. I want to marry Percalus, and I expect a respectable dowry. Anything else would look ludicrous after what Cleomenes got his hands on."

Leonidas was reeling from the unexpectedness of the blow. Percalus had successfully resisted all other suitors until Alkander had at last agreed to let her marry Leotychidas last summer. But Leotychidas, like Demaratus, had deployed with the army, delaying the wedding. Leotychidas, furthermore, was still with the army, having been assigned to the rearguard that had been left in Athens to ensure that Hippias complied with the terms of the treaty. Suddenly, Leonidas smelled a rat. "Did you order Leotychidas to remain in Athens, sir?"

"What the hell does that have to do with anything?" Demaratus snapped back.

"Well, Leotychidas has also asked for Percalus. And he doesn't care about a dowry."

"Don't try to bargain with me, boy! You can afford a dowry for the girl."

"She's not my sister. Alkander can't afford a dowry."

"You sponsored Alkander. You're responsible for the girl as well."

"No, sir."

"They warned me you were a stubborn smart-ass!"

That did not require an answer, and so Leonidas said nothing. He was in the right, and both Demaratus and he knew it. After a long pause, Demaratus said simply, "If I ask Alkander for the girl, he can't refuse me."

"That's up to Alkander, sir."

"Get out of here."

Leonidas didn't wait to be asked twice. He was grateful that the helot was waiting just outside the door to lead him back out of the unfamiliar palace.

———

When Leotychidas returned to the city just five days later, it was too late. Percalus had already been removed "by force" from Cleitagora's kleros to the Eurypontid palace and introduced to the city as their new Eurypontid queen. Leotychidas was furious, and he blamed Leonidas. "You planned this all along!" he fumed. "You kept me at arm's length because you knew Demaratus would eventually get hot enough to take her without a dowry. I should have taken her without your consent! I won't forgive you for this, you arrogant whelp! You or your conniving little friend! You'll live to regret playing with me like this!"

"What do you think he can do to us?" Alkander asked anxiously, when Leonidas reported the confrontation.

Leonidas shrugged. He didn't like having an enemy in Leotychidas, but the fact was, he was less dangerous than a reigning king like Demaratus. They really hadn't had any choice once the king accepted the "no dowry" stipulation. Furthermore, the marriage had distinct advantages for Alkander, starting with the fact that his mother moved into the Eurypontid palace and he now stood a good chance of being assigned a viable kleros on coming of age.

The fact that he was the brother-in-law of the Eurypontid king also increased his value in the marriage market. Suddenly girls (and their mothers) who had stopped showing interest in Alkander after

the girls left the agoge and had to be careful about their reputation, took an interest again. Leonidas found it rather amusing, but
Alkander was less pleased.

"I want them to want me for myself," Alkander insisted irritably,
after warding off yet another overattentive approach by a matron and
her daughter in the agora. It was an early spring day, shortly after
the sailing season had opened, and the agora was filled with the first
imported goods of the year. Leonidas and Alkander had gone ostensibly to look at swords. As long as they were in the agoge, all their
equipment was provided by the school, but on turning 21 they would
have to have their own. The city provided each new citizen symboli-
cally with a scarlet himation and a shield embossed with the lambda
of Lacedaemon, but the city did not provide the other essentials of
hoplite panoply: helmet, breastplate, baldric, sword, and greaves.
Each hoplite had to provide this equipment himself.

Swords could be and often were passed down over generations.
Prokles had already been promised his grandfather's sword, which
was of excellent Tegean craftsmanship. But Alkander's father's sword
appeared to have been lost or sold at some stage, and Leonidas' father
had naturally bestowed his own weapons on his eldest son, Cleomenes.

There were several local armourers who had stands on the agora,
and also merchants who sold imported wares. The imported swords
tended to be fancier and more expensive, but they were also longer
than the standard Spartan sword and so not permitted in the phalanx.
They were, therefore, an expensive luxury, since you still had to have
a Spartan sword for active duty. Leonidas knew that Dorieus had
been very proud of the Thessalonian sword he carried about. It had
two bronze rams locked in combat on the hilt and a sheath with
scenes from the life of Herakles. Leonidas had admired it as a boy, but
one look at the prices asked even for more simple swords sent him
back to the local smiths.

The perioikoi merchant smiled when he returned. "Not the kind
for all that vainglorious show, are you, young Leonidas?"

Leonidas shrugged in embarrassment, inwardly aware that he
might have been tempted by the more artistic weapons if he knew he
could afford them. Since he was still not of age, however, he had no

control over his estates (whatever they might consist of) and still had to apply to the Agiad treasurer if he wanted money—something he had scrupulously avoided up to now. His own and Alkander's agoge fees were paid directly, and until now he had never needed more money than he could earn from the sale of skins or meat from the animals he killed trapping and hunting.

"Let me show you a sword I've been saving for a special customer," the perioikoi salesman continued, bending down and removing a sword from under his counter. He held it out to Leonidas on the palms of both hands.

Leonidas cautiously took the sword and drew it partway from its sheath. It gleamed magnificently. He ran his thumb expertly along the edge; it was incredibly sharp. With a glance at the merchant for silent consent, he slipped the baldric over his shoulder so the sword hung at his left hip. The merchant at once came around the table to help him adjust the buckles until it hung just perfectly. "There you go. A good fit," the salesman insisted. Leonidas reached for the hilt again. The sword slipped out of the sheath as if it had been greased—there was no stickiness or friction at all. He slipped it back and drew it again. It made a satisfying but very soft hiss. Leonidas had never handled a sword of such quality before. The merchant laughed, reading his customer's face.

"Look at the balance," the smith urged next, taking the sword from Leonidas and balancing it on his index finger from a point just an inch away from the hilt. He then gave it back to Leonidas, who tested it himself. It was a wonderful weapon.

"What does it cost?"

"Well, you can't buy a weapon like this every day, much less from just anybody," the merchant answered, looking away and fussing with his wares, as if calculating what he could ask of a covetous youth from the wealthiest family in Lacedaemon. "A tetradrachma," he decided at last.

Leonidas removed the sword and baldric and replaced it on the table. "I'm not of age. I don't have money like that."

"You can pay me in instalments," the merchant suggested.

"No, thank you." Leonidas turned away and looked in the crowds for Alkander. He should have known. Alkander was talking to Eirana and her mother. Eirana was the only Spartan maiden that Leonidas secretly fancied. He always had, but she had never paid the slightest attention to him. Even now, as he came up beside Alkander, she acknowledged him only with an absent-minded smile. Her mother was doing most of the talking. Eirana came from a very "good" family. Her father was one of the lochagoi, commanding one of Sparta's five divisions, and he kept a good stable of horses. They were ostensibly discussing horses at the moment, although Alkander gave Leonidas a look that suggested he wanted to be rescued.

Simply by coming up beside Alkander, however, Leonidas had placed himself next to Eirana, and he liked that. She smelled of lavender, and her dark hair was silky and blowing in the light breeze. The breeze also pressed her soft peplos against her body, revealing a figure that was slender but curved in the right places. Leonidas' pulse quickened, and he was so distracted by the sensations pulsing through his body that he couldn't think.

"We really must be going," Alkander said, with a glance at Leonidas to back him up, but his friend remained mute.

"But you will come around and take a look at the colt, won't you?" Eirana's mother insisted.

"It's too soon, ma'am; I won't be able to own a horse for another year."

"He's a yearling. We'd be happy to keep him for you, if you like him. He'll be ready to back just about the same time you get your citizenship."

"I must see what kleros I get, ma'am."

She laughed. "Your brother-in-law will see you properly taken care of, I'm sure. There are a half-dozen vacant Eurypontid kleroi, my husband says."

"I'm not Eurypontid, ma'am."

"No need to split hairs. You'll be uncle of the next Eurypontid king."

"If my sister is fortunate enough to have healthy sons, ma'am. At the moment, I am still a mothake."

The matron glanced at Leonidas, and Leonidas could feel her assessing him. She smiled faintly and patted Alkander on the arm. "Don't feel any obligation to buy. Just come and take a look at the colt. I'm sure you'll like him. Eirana." The young woman smiled and nodded to Alkander and Leonidas in turn, and then followed her mother over to a waiting wagon.

"That bitch is only interested in my connections!" Alkander swore as soon as they were out of hearing.

"Her mother maybe, but Eirana has *always* liked you."

"When she was younger, maybe," Alkander countered. "Now she won't give me the time of day. She's got her eyes set on a citizen. A certain Asteropus."

"Asteropus? Brotus' eirene four years ago? Son of the seer, isn't he?"

"That's right. Anyway, Eirana has been making cow's eyes at him for the last six months at least."

Leonidas couldn't imagine Eirana making cow's eyes at anyone. She seemed so cool and self-possessed whenever he encountered her. She was certainly a first-rate rider and charioteer; not at all like Percalus. "It really is getting late," he changed the subject. "If we want to get a swim in before—"

"Alkander! Leonidas!" It was the rather high-pitched and breathy cries of Hilaira. She was pushing her way through the crowds towards them, harvesting looks of reprobation and irritation. She was now 15 and no longer in the agoge; in short, she had reached an age where she was expected to behave with more "decorum". Certainly she was not supposed to pick up her skirts to her knees as she ran. "Thank God I caught sight of you!" she declared breathlessly as she reached them. "Grandfather's not well! He's got pains in his chest. Come quick! Where's Prokles?"

"Where's your grandfather?" Leonidas countered.

"Just over there!" She gestured vaguely to the far side of the agora. "At the Temple to the Twins. You've got to help me get him home. Where's Prokles?"

They ignored her question again because they did not intend to answer it (Prokles was with his latest girlfriend), and started toward the temple at a jog. Even before they reached it they could see the little crowd collected at the base of the steps. The crowd stepped back and made way for them as they arrived.

Lysandridas was sitting on the bottom step up to the temple, hunched over, clutching his chest, and he was ashen. The youths went down on their knees on either side of him. "Father, what's happened? What's wrong?"

"My chest," he gasped out. "My heart. Get me home. Where's Prokles?"

"I'll go for him," Leonidas offered at once, but Alkander stopped him.

"We need a chariot. You can borrow one from the Agiad stables. I'll fetch Prokles."

Of course, any citizen had the right to borrow another's horse, bull, or dog, but they weren't citizens yet, and Leonidas accepted that he would have an easier time at the Agiad stables. Leaving Hilaira with her grandfather, they both set off. Leonidas sprinted to the back entrance of the Agiad palace and told the meleirenes on duty what he'd come for. They let him in right away and he went to the stables and talked to the head groom, a man who knew him well. At once several grooms started to back out one of the light chariots and hitch up the horses selected by the head groom. Someone must have been sent into the palace as well, however, because just when Leonidas was about to mount up, Chilonis appeared.

"I heard Lysandridas is ill."

"Yes, ma'am. I'm just borrowing this to take him home. I'll have it back before dinner."

"I'm not worried about the damn chariot," she retorted with a touch of irritation. "Why don't you bring Lysandridas here? I'll send for the surgeon at once. If it's his heart, the time it takes to get him to his kleros could kill him."

"He asked me to take him home, ma'am."

"Come on, then." She climbed into the chariot and took the reins herself, leaving Leonidas no choice but to step up beside her and tell her where to go.

The crowd seemed larger than ever by the time they got back, but they promptly made way for the chariot. One of the younger boys stepped out and took the horses without being asked, so that Leonidas and Chilonis could both go to the old man. "Lysandridas, let me take you to the Agiad palace and have the surgeon come to you there."

"No. I want to die at home."

"Who says you're dying? Come—"

"NO."

Chilonis glanced at Leonidas, and he tried: "Father, if you just lie down for a bit. Take something to ease the pain—"

"I want to go home. Leonis—" That was his wife.

"I'll send someone for her at once," Chilonis assured him.

"No. Take me home."

Chilonis surrendered with a gesture of helplessness to Leonidas, and backed away. At once Leonidas bent to lift the old man into his arms. Lysandridas had been small and slight of stature all his life, an ideal jockey and charioteer, but Leonidas was still thankful that a youthful perioikoi came to his assistance. Together they lifted Lysandridas and carried him to the back of the chariot. They wanted to lie him down, but Lysandridas insisted on sitting up with his back against the front of the chariot. Clutching his knees to him, he laid his face on his knees and closed his eyes.

Carefully Leonidas stepped up beside him and took the reins. Hilaira sat on the floor of the chariot behind him. Carefully Leonidas backed the horses, turned, and set off, picking up a trot as soon as they had left the city behind them.

Leonidas had to concentrate on driving the unfamiliar team. They were hot horses, racers really, and they at once sensed that their driver was a stranger and somewhat unsure of himself. They fretted, one even bucked several times, and the further they drove out of the city, the more they wanted to bolt. That made for a rough ride, and Leonidas was grateful for Hilaira, who held her grandfather in her arms. "Please don't die, grandpa," she pleaded with him. "Please." She was openly weeping, but Leonidas didn't think the less of her for that. He couldn't imagine a world without Lysandridas in it—or, rather, he didn't want to imagine it.

The helots saw the chariot from the lower pasture, and Leonidas shouted out to them what had happened. A boy cut across the paddocks and up the stairs from the stables so that by the time they arrived at the house, Lysandridas' wife and daughter-in-law were waiting to receive him. By this time the pain seemed to have eased somewhat, and Lysandridas managed, with the help of Leonidas and his wife, to stagger to a couch in the andron. Within minutes pillows and blankets had been brought. Leonis had removed her husband's belt and convinced him to lie down. She was now very much in charge, giving orders to everyone, and demanding of Leonidas the location of Prokles. Leonidas assured her that Alkander was bringing him, while one of the helots was sent for Philippos, who was helping repair the fencing on the upper paddocks.

Leonidas started to feel superfluous and wondered if he should take the chariot back, but he hated to leave for fear that Lysandridas would die while he was away. Philippos arrived, dressed only in a dirty chiton and dripping sweat. He went in to his father at once, and Leonidas sat on the back terrace with Hilaira, who couldn't seem to stop crying, although she did it silently. She simply sat there with the tears running down her face, and with the corner of her himation she wiped at her eyes and nose. Philippos came out and asked after his son.

"Alkander went for him, sir."

"Is he far away?"

"Amyclae, sir," Leonidas lied. Prokles' parents would be furious if they learned Prokles was seeing another perioikoi girl.

"Would you go in to my father then? He was asking for you, too."

Leonidas jumped up, flattered and frightened both. He had never been with a dying man before—unless you counted his own father. The women were still with Lysandridas. His wife sat on the couch and held his hand. His daughter-in-law was on the couch opposite, her hands in her lap, apparently awaiting instructions.

Lysandridas lay with his eyes closed. He looked ghastly white, and all the old-age flecks on his face, neck, and scalp stood out as they never did when he was up and about. In fact, it was only now that Leonidas noticed how very old he looked. He tried to calculate how old Lysandridas must be, but he wasn't really sure how old he had been when he'd won the chariot race at the 55th Olympics. He had been a citizen, so at least 21, and probably older. That made him close to 73 now, Leonidas reckoned.

"You asked for me, father?" Leonidas asked hesitantly, standing beside the couch and looking down at the old man.

Lysandridas did not open his eyes, but he lifted his other hand,

and Leonidas took it. The old man clasped his hand around it. His hand was icy cold, and the scars from the quarries stood out amidst the dark, purple veins. When he spoke, he spoke slowly with many pauses for breath. "Leonidas, stand by... Prokles. He's too... rebellious. I... understand him. Sparta can be... cruel. It... requires... much of us. But it gives us... much in return. If he had seen... a little more... of the world..." It was too much for him to finish the thought, so he squeezed Leonidas' hand.

Fearing he had been dismissed, Leonidas hastened to say, "Father, I owe my life to you. I would have been a slave and—"

The old man was shaking his head. "Shhh. You do my son... and the entire city... an injustice. They would... have come for you... without my frantic urgings. We have... too few citizens to let... others steal... our children. Let us... waste no more breath... on that. More important: you must know... that you are a youth... of unusual... potential. I know... you will never be... king, but you can be... a peerless Peer—if... you keep to your... present course."

Leonidas was frowning. He didn't understand what Lysandridas was talking about. He didn't think he had ever done anything but just follow the rules and try to get along with everyone. He was not even truly exceptional at anything—not like Dorieus and Brotus. If he just continued doing what he had been doing, he would continue to be a mediocre Peer of no particular interest to anyone. It seemed rude to argue with a man on his deathbed, however, so Leonidas held his tongue and promised instead, "I'll try, sir."

"I know. As for Alkander—"

They were interrupted by the loud arrival of Prokles. Prokles came crashing into the andron breathlessly, looking genuinely shaken. His mother admonished him to be more respectful, but Prokles ignored her as he fell on to his knees beside his grandfather, pushing Leonidas aside.

Leonidas hesitated because Lysandridas had been interrupted, but now he was clasping Prokles' hand and seemed very anxious to speak to him. Leonidas decided it was time for him to withdraw. He nodded to the two women and slipped out, returning to the large back terrace on which he had spent the happiest moments of his life. He remembered that very first evening when he had been allowed to join this family: the starry night, the sound of Leonis playing the lyre, and Lysandridas' raspy voice telling an enthralled eight-year-old audience about his adventures. Leonidas felt the tears in his eyes and blinked them back, and at the same time heard someone crying behind him.

He turned around and saw that Hilaira had finally given in completely to her own tears and started sobbing. She was curled up in Alkander's arms and crying on to his chest. It made sense that Alkander was here, since he had fetched Prokles. The fact that he would be holding Hilaira in his arms like that was less self-evident. They had been like sister and brother for seven years, but this wasn't a "brotherly" hug—or so Leonidas thought. He met his friend's eyes, and they dared him to protest. That said it all.

———

Lysandridas was buried, as he had requested, beside his father and mother below the orchard. The crowd that came was nothing like that which gathered for the burial of kings; it was devoid of ritual and histrionics and motivated by real respect, if not grief. And it was large. Leonidas was astonished by how many men and women walked the seven miles from the city or even further to be there. The entire Council was there, many of the city officials, all other living Olympic victors, and the local horse-breeding community including King Demaratus with Percalus. Leonidas was impressed, too, by the perioikoi and helots. They came not because Lysandridas had been an Olympic victor and councilman, but because he had been a good neighbour and a fair master. That was a tribute, too, Leonidas thought, remembering the way the staff had abandoned his mother in her hour of greatest need.

The speeches stressed that Lysandridas had seen both the heights of success in his Olympic victories and the depths of failure in humiliating defeat, capture, and slavery. They spoke of how he had been "decisive" in bringing down the Tegean tyrant Onomastros, and how his wisdom in Council had only increased with age. That left Leonidas wishing he had paid more attention to the old man and wishing he had asked him many more questions. Only from the eulogies did Leonidas register that Lysandridas had been a protégé of the great

Chilon himself. Only after Lysandridas was dead did Leonidas start to grasp what a resource he had lived beside—and never truly tapped into. He had loved and respected Lysandridas from that first holiday at his kleros, but he had not truly appreciated just how exceptional Lysandridas had been. And now it was too late. He would never again be able to benefit from Lysandridas' advice or his wit or his experience. That was a depressing realisation, and Leonidas promised himself not to let it happen again. Meanwhile he would try to live up to Lysandridas' hopes for him, to be a "peerless Peer" when he came of age—even if he didn't have the faintest idea of what that really was or how he was to attain it.

CHAPTER 11

Eirene

"NEVER AGAIN IN YOUR LIVES—NOT EVEN if you should one day rise to senior command in the army—will you have as much power as you have this coming year." The Paidonomos addressed the new class of eirenes in the agoge auditorium. This square room sank downwards from the doorways in a series of steps on three sides towards the speaker's podium in the middle of the smallish square floor 20-some feet below. The only lighting came from some windows along the back wall, and so it was a rather dim room and—like everything in the agoge—virtually unfurnished. The youths sat on the worn marble seats, but the atmosphere in the chamber was charged with energy.

They hardly needed the reminder from the Paidonomos about the prerogatives of their new status. They were all wearing sandals just to make a point (although the footgear was uncomfortable and caused blisters for most of them) and they luxuriated in the soft wool used for their standard-issue chitons and the real warmth of their black himations. They were looking forward to growing out their hair, and to being freed from cooking, cleaning, learning, keeping watch, and—best of all—drill. For the next year, rather than learning and drilling, they were entrusted with the welfare of a unit of younger boys.

The Paidonomos was only stating the obvious when he continued: "You all remember eirenes that you particularly respected—
and eirenes that you disliked, even disdained. Those memories last
a lifetime. Your behaviour now will not be forgotten like your own
misdeeds as children, but will indelibly leave an impression upon the
boys or youths entrusted to you. They will be your subordinates—or
possibly superiors—in the army one day, your peers in Assembly, or
officials of the city. You will face the boys and youths you have control
over this coming year again and again throughout your life, and you
will always be remembered for how you treated them in this critical
year—no matter what other deeds you may perform or what fame
you may obtain."

The youths were bored. They knew all that. On Leonidas' right,
Prokles was rolling his eyes and muttering "yak, yak, yak". Other
youths were gazing pointedly at the ceiling or using sign language to
one another. (Many boys developed their own private sign language
during their years at the agoge, because it was so practical at times like
this when they could get in trouble for speaking.) They all wanted the
Paidonomos to get on with things—that is, get to the assignments.

"Nor should you forget," the Paidonomos droned on, "that the
entire citizen body will be watching you. Every citizen will be alert for
any indication that you have misused the privileges granted or—far
more serious—abused your power over your charges. If you prove
irresponsible as eirenes, you can be assured you will never hold a
command in the army, much less an elected office. Never forget that.
We are watching your every move."

"So what else is new!" Prokles groaned. "Sometimes I wish I'd
been born anywhere but here!"

Leonidas looked over at his friend and frowned. He wanted to
ask him if he would really have preferred to be a perfumed Persian
wearing make-up and silks, but he was not prepared to talk while the
Paidonomos was speaking. Prokles might ridicule him for being so
"stupidly obedient"; but Leonidas was obedient not out of stupidity
or fear, but out of respect for a system that had made Sparta the most
respected city in Greece.

At last the Paidonomos was handed "the list", and he started
reading off the assignments. The eirenes were assigned on the basis

of an overall assessment of their leadership abilities and placed on the list from best to worst. They were then assigned units in order starting with the 18-year-olds, until the last (read: worst) eirene was assigned to the last class of seven-year-olds.

Leonidas noted stoically that his twin was the second name read from the list, followed by Ephorus; but when his own name came shortly afterwards he was so taken aback, he looked around and then asked the others for confirmation. "Did he say me? For the 18-year-olds?"

The others nodded and hushed him silent. They were listening intently, anxious not to miss their own names. Leonidas was stunned. He had expected to fall somewhere in the middle, like he usually did. He had mentally prepared himself for a class of 13- or at best 14-year-olds. He'd even given some thought to how he'd help prepare the little boys for their "fox time". And suddenly he was faced with the rather terrifying prospect of youths almost his own age and inherently, almost biologically, inclined to challenge their eirene.

Prokles' name fell where Leonidas had expected to be; he was assigned a class of 14-year-olds. Alkander, naturally, was near the end, but—as he noted happily—not at the very bottom. He was given 9-year-olds. "They'll be fun," Leonidas assured him almost enviously, as the session ended and they dispersed to meet with the mastigophoroi responsible for their particular age-cohort.

As they stepped on or over the seats on their way towards the doors, Leonidas was struck hard by the fact that for the first time in 13 years, he and his friends were not going to be spending their days and nights together. They would have different barracks and different schedules. Even now, they barely had time for a hasty goodbye before they had to go different ways.

———

Leonidas reported to a short, round young man by the name of Technarchos. He was an Olympic discus thrower and had been a drill sergeant during his ten years on active service, which had just ended. He was bull-headed, gruff-voiced, and stronger than anyone Leonidas had ever seen. He called the nine eirenes entrusted with units of 18-year-olds to order with a single sharp clap of his hands.

"All right, you're all feeling tickled pink for being in this selection, right? Well, you shouldn't be. You should be cursing the Gods for playing such a rotten trick on you. By the time a week is over, you are all going to be wishing you had some sweet, timid little seven-year-olds. You fools drew the short straw, and rather than having a nice leisurely year, while your adoring boys wait on you hand and foot, you're going to be busting your butts trying to stay one step ahead of your impudent charges. Worse: you're going to be drilling with them and marching with them, and you're going to get up before them and go to bed after them, and your armour had—by all the Gods—better be in better condition and cleaner than any one of your charges' arms and armour or you are going to have hell to pay. Believe me, you are going to get less sleep and be sorer and wearier than you have ever been in your lives before. I could almost feel sorry for you, if I wasn't enjoying this so much."

Leonidas believed him, and he really did wish he was not here. Leonidas had never had command authority over anyone before. He had never been elected leader of anything. And he had never expected to be entrusted with command or leadership in the future, either. He didn't feel up to this task.

The worst thing, Leonidas reflected, was knowing that no method worked equally well with all youth. Leonidas had observed that his brother Brotus, for example, thrived on provocation, and seemed to love being taunted or even ridiculed. For such youths, the more you sneered at them, the wilder they became to prove you wrong—and it was a game that some instructors and pupils understood and enjoyed equally well. Other youths, however, were completely demotivated by such tactics. It made them sullen and resentful—as Leonidas knew he felt himself. He had noticed, too, that many youths thrived on competition, giving their best only if they were challenged or dared. Other youths seemed to function only in a group, as part of a herd, and were able to give their best only if they saw it as part of a collective activity. And then there were loners like Prokles, who hated group pressure and rebelled against any overt efforts to make them do anything just for the sake of conformity. Last but not least, there were youths like Alkander, who lost every competition and soon gave up and stopped trying. The more you made fun of and humiliated weaker boys like Alkander, the *less* they were capable of doing. They needed encouragement, not bullying or competition. In short, it seemed impossible to handle everyone in the best way—to bring out the best in each—without seeming unjust.

What was worse: he had to find the right way of handling them before they lost respect for him and turned on him like a pack of ravenous rats. Leonidas knew that because he knew what his own unit had done to a weak eirene; they had ignored him so completely that the agoge administration had to step in and replace him. Looking back on it, Leonidas cringed, knowing how unmercifully cruel they had been in the delight at discovering their own power.

The next day when he stood before the 14 youths of his unit, he felt as nervous as he could ever remember feeling. They were watching him like hungry hawks, and he could feel them searching for the slightest sign of weakness. He had indeed spent most of the previous night polishing his armour and hoplon. He'd been to the baths and even had one of the bath slaves trim and file his fingernails and toenails. He'd dispensed with the sandals, however, because he couldn't walk in them without limping, on account of the blisters between the toes and at the instep that had developed in the first day of wear. He was infinitely grateful that he was no longer short. He stood several inches taller than all but one of his charges, and his deep voice was an asset as well. When he called for order, they actually obeyed.

In the weeks that followed, Leonidas nearly killed himself to be a paragon of perfection while he tried to take the measure of his unit. The bulk of the youths appeared to be herd animals, content to follow a lead and most happy when working together as a team. They were willing enough to follow orders and easy enough to motivate with competition against other units or if divided into teams against each other. There were two troublemakers, however, who clearly thought of themselves as something special and were always trying to get away with little breaches of the rules. They were the last to get up, the last to fall in, and they laughed and winked at each other and made jokes behind his back. So far, they hadn't taken things far enough that he would have been justified in cracking down on them, but their entire attitude nevertheless tended to undermine his authority. Leonidas did everything he could to set a perfect example (Lysandridas' words about a "peerless Peer" constantly in his inner ear), but aside from exhausting himself, he didn't seem to have much impact on the two troublemakers. So he lived in a kind of fear that a clash was coming and he was going to lose.

His fears were not eased by hearing, at one of the daily eirene briefings, that Brotus had been tied up by his charges and beaten rather brutally. It had been in the dark of night. He had just drifted off to sleep. Suddenly he was rudely awakened by someone clamping a himation over his face as if to suffocate him. Instead it was tied around his neck, blinding him, before he was dragged out to the latrines behind the agoge and beaten until he vomited. No bones had been broken, no irreparable damage done, but a message had been delivered: Brotus' youths weren't prepared to accept his rule, which had been too dependent on his all-too-effective fists.

Although Brotus had his suspicions about which of the youths had instigated his humiliation, because his eyes had been covered and they had not exchanged a single word among themselves, he could not bring charges. He had been furious, sputtering abuse and demanding retribution "against all of them" at the briefing. He kept demanding that the whole unit be flogged "till they whimpered like kittens being drowned". Leonidas had been shocked to see his brother so unnerved that he was still trembling by the time he addressed the briefing.

"The question is, rather, whether you should be relieved of your position," Technarchos countered dryly. "I've never heard of an eirene who aroused so much hatred among his charges that they turned on him like this. None of your unit's previous eirenes had trouble with them."

Brotus blustered like a stuck boar, but he had never been the most eloquent of speakers, and there was a deafening silence from his colleagues. Leonidas was not about to defend him, and apparently nor were the other seven youths. Brotus had friends, of course, but none of them were in this group of eirenes, all having been assigned younger age-cohorts. With the exception of Leonidas, none of the other eirenes in this group even knew Brotus very well—and he was not making a very good impression on them.

Technarchos decided to suspend Brotus from duty and take over his unit himself until the Paidonomos had had a chance to consider the case. Leonidas returned to his own unit, only to notice the smug smirks on the faces of the troublemakers and overhear half-whispered jokes about the Agiads.

———

About a week later, he ran into Alkander on the street. Leonidas paused, letting his own youths continue towards the drill fields, and Alkander stopped, too. It was morning, and Alkander's charges were off on their own. "What's this I hear about Brotus?" Alkander asked at once.

Leonidas sighed. Being a twin could very tiresome. "He was using his fists to maintain discipline, and the 18-year-olds decided to teach him the limits of his methodology."

"And how are you doing?"

Leonidas just sighed. "I don't know. And you?"

"I love it. They are all competing for my favour at the moment. I'm sure it won't last, but it is wonderful while it does. I really can't even think about what I might want without one of them jumping up to get it for me—a mug of water, a himation, a place to sit. I've never had it so good."

"And Prokles? Have you seen him? How are things going for him?"

"Even better than me. I saw them over at the palaestra recently, and the youths flocked around him like he was a demigod. They worship him so much they were even starting to imitate him. You know, the way we did with Erastosthenes."

Leonidas did remember. Erastosthenes had undoubtedly been one of their better eirenes, and they had quite consciously taken to using his expressions and gestures and gait.

Leonidas would have liked to talk to Alkander longer, but as Technarchos had warned that first day, the eirenes of the senior units were required to drill with their units. He had to hurry to catch up with them now, before he got in trouble. Drilling with them had only one advantage: the eirenes were given the role of NCOs and so commanded the smaller units. It was good preparation for future command, for which the selected eirenes were clearly being groomed. Until two months earlier, Leonidas had assumed he was not destined for any future command in the army, and had been looking forward to a year without drill. In fact, he still had mixed feelings about this development. Command in the army would tie him to it even after he had become a full citizen at 31. While other men went into the reserves, moved out of barracks, and took up residence with their wives on their kleros, an officer was still on active duty and was expected to live in the city, if not in barracks. Leonidas didn't like that idea particularly, but he supposed it didn't hurt to have the opportunity open to him.

A couple of hours later, sweaty and tired, they returned from the drill fields to the agoge. Leonidas had only just stripped out of his soiled things when a boy burst in on them, saying that the Paidonomos wanted to speak to him.

Leonidas pulled on clean clothes and reported. The Paidonomos was seated and he looked surprisingly old. "I can remember the day your father brought you and your brother here," he opened in a weary voice.

"Yes, sir. So can I."

That brought a faint smile. "Everyone was so impressed with Brotus."

"He was bigger than I, sir."

"Did he beat you when you were a child?"

"All the time."

"I'm surprised we had no trouble with him before."

Leonidas shrugged. "His eirenes were always bigger than he was. He prefers to tackle those who are smaller."

"But he's an Olympic-class boxer!" the Paidonomos countered in outrage.

"That's different—everyone is watching and there are strict rules."

"But if he is the bully you suggest, why didn't he terrorise the other boys in his unit?"

"He did. How do you think he got elected leader year after year?"

"You're very cynical."

Leonidas could only shrug. Part of him wanted to mention the incident with Timon, too, but he had no evidence whatsoever. And it was now four years ago. People would want to know why he had been silent up to now.

"I have decided I cannot reassign him to the same unit. On the one hand, he is unwilling to admit he is to blame for what happened; and on the other, the youths say they will do it again if he tries to bully them. They claim, incidentally, that they all participated. Whether true or not, they are sticking to that story with admirable solidarity."

Leonidas nodded unconsciously.

"So, I am going to put you in charge of them."

"Sir?" Leonidas thought he had been inattentive. "Who are you putting in charge of them?"

"You. Brotus will take over your unit."

"Sir—I—" What could he possibly say? "I don't think that's fair."

"To whom?"

"To anyone, sir. My unit certainly doesn't deserve Brotus. They haven't done anything wrong."

"Do you think your twin brother is incapable of learning?"

"Sir, you just said he refused to admit he had done anything wrong."

"I think—I hope—that that is mere stubbornness. But if not, and he truly has learned nothing, than we will find out soon enough, and his citizenship will be at risk. Move your things into Room 17B and assume command immediately."

They were waiting for him at attention. They stood in two files in front of their bunks; their armour shone, their chitons were fresh, their heads were freshly shaved, and even their toenails were clean. Leonidas had not been given time to wash and he was lugging his panoply, his change of clothes, and a handful of personal things over his back. He was certain his hair, just starting to grow after 14 years of keeping it shaved, was standing up in tufts on his head. He felt foolish. He stopped in the doorway, brought the heavy hoplon down to rest against his knee, and let the rest of his stuff fall to the floor with a clatter. He looked the ranks up and down; they did not even move their eyes.

"At ease."

They moved their feet apart 18 inches and clasped their hands behind their backs. Eyes straight ahead. Leonidas wondered what on earth they were playing at. Then again, he supposed the last week must have been difficult for them. They had done something unprecedented (at least in living memory) by beating up their eirene, and even if they were not officially being reprimanded, Leonidas did not suppose that Technarchos had been particularly pleasant. On the contrary, Technarchos undoubtedly knew exactly how to make life miserable without opening the slightest flank for complaint or rebellion. Furthermore, Technarchos had taken over the unit with the obvious intention of "shaping it up", and that meant bending them all to his will and squeezing the last drop of rebelliousness out of them.

Then another thought struck him as well. They probably didn't know very much more about him than he knew about them. In the agoge the age-cohorts tended to stick together, with little interaction upwards or downwards. Brotus had attracted attention: he had been an Olympic victor, a victor at Artemis Orthia. He was a celebrity. Leonidas, by contrast, was just his twin brother: the paler, once-smaller, less successful double. They probably expected him to be an almost interchangeable—but less glamorous—version of Brotus.

"Look. I'm not my brother. I'm not going to act like him, and I don't want to be treated like him."

The first of the youths risked shifting his eyes enough to look at Leonidas sideways. He relaxed slightly. The others, sensing that move, also risked looking over and slowly, one after another, they did relax somewhat, but they stayed where they were.

"Where's my bunk?"

"There, sir." It was at the far end of the room under the window.

Leonidas reshouldered his shield and bent to collect his other things. He advanced between the rows of youths to his bunk. He hung his hoplon on the hook provided at the head of the bunk, and quickly put away the other items on the shelves or in the basket provided. Then he turned around again. They were all still in their places, but now looking at him expectantly. "I don't know about you, but I've had enough drill for today and I don't intend to do any more, so why don't we go for a swim and then have dinner down in Amyclae?"

They just stared at him, disbelieving or unwilling to trust him.

"There's a tavern run by a perioikoi by the name of Medon, who serves excellent chicken in olive and goat's cheese sauce. I have credit

with him if any of you are short of cash." That was stretching things
a bit, but Leonidas felt certain he could *get* credit if he asked for it.

The youths exchanged glances. One finally ventured, "Are you
serious, sir?"

"Why shouldn't I be? I've spent all morning on the drill fields.
I stink. My hair is stiff with sweat. I need a bath, and I haven't had
anything to eat since breakfast."

It was not until after dinner, when they were walking back in
the dark, that they finally ventured to trust him a little. By then they
were all slightly inebriated. (The perioikoi tended to mix less water
in the wine, no matter what the Spartiates told them.) The bolder of
the youths fell in beside Leonidas and started trying to explain things
to him.

"It's not that we can't take discipline, sir. Or even a little bullying."

"I'm sure you can. You put up with Technarchos for a whole
week."

They laughed a little uncertainly. The experience was too fresh in
their minds for true levity.

"But you have to understand, sir, that your brother wasn't being
fair. He was picking on Euryleon."

Leonidas glanced over his shoulder to where this youth was
among his comrades. Euryleon was clearly weaker than normal. He
had been left short-sighted after an illness and suffered from short-
ness of breath as well. Perhaps because his illness had developed after
he was in the agoge, his comrades had not shunned him as Leonidas'
unit had Alkander. On the other hand, Euryleon seemed to have
earned the affection given him. He readily made jokes about himself,
his blindness and incompetence—so much so that Leonidas thought
he was a bit of a clown. But he wanted to reserve judgement until he
knew him better. So Leonidas just nodded for now, and thanked his
informant.

———

By the spring equinox, Leonidas was thoroughly enjoying life
as an eirene. He reckoned that, more from gratitude at getting out
from under Brotus and concern to show that they weren't inherently

troublemakers, the youths of his unit had decided to be loyal and dedicated to him. Not that they didn't try to get away with things individually from time to time, but Leonidas found that he could rely on them not to take things too far—and above all, respect him when he drew the line. They knew, in turn, that he would turn a blind eye to certain things, no matter what official policy was, and that he would accept honest excuses—if he didn't think he was being taken advantage of. In exchange, they covered for him when he wanted to stretch the rules for one reason or another.

One reason he often wanted to stretch the rules was any opportunity to "run into" Eirana. Not that she appeared the least bit interested in running into him; but Leonidas couldn't help but hope she would change her mind about him if she got to know him better. After all, other people—from the Paidonomos to his colleagues—*had* changed their opinion of him over time. Exploiting the fact that Eirana was an accomplished horsewoman and her father had his own stables, Leonidas pretended an interest in purchasing a colt that he did not really want. To be sure, he intended to buy a least one horse, and possibly two, when he came of age, but he planned to buy them from Philippos; first of all, Prokles' family needed the money, and secondly, Leonidas knew the entire stables well. He knew which of the young horses he really wanted to buy. But the feigned interest in Eirana's father's horses gave him an excuse to visit her kleros.

Leonidas was always warmly received by Eirana's mother. She was gracious and welcoming and, although she understood perfectly well that Leonidas wasn't primarily interested in livestock, she played along splendidly, often coming up with excuses for him to return. Leonidas was less certain how Eirana's father, Kyranios, felt about him. Kyranios was a divisional commander and a man who appeared aloof, severe, and certainly unapproachable to mere eirenes. Leonidas generally tried to keep out of his way, timing his visits to the kleros when he did not expect Kyranios to be present.

It was late in the spring during an Assembly that Leonidas mistimed things badly. Kyranios galloped up straight from Assembly and caught Leonidas standing beside Eirana and his wife while leaning on the paddock fence watching the yearlings frolic about.

The lochagos drew up sharply. "Shouldn't you be in the palaestra with your charges, eirene?"

Caught red-handed like that, Leonidas was candidly honest. "Yes, sir."

The commander considered him. "Well, don't expect me to close my eyes just because you may turn out to be my future son-in-law. Duty is duty."

"Yes, sir."

"Why are you back so early, dear?" Eirana's mother interceded, coming to take the lathered and winded horse from her husband.

He jumped down, pulling his helmet off as he did. "We're mobilising again," he announced. "Cleomenes has talked the Assembly into letting him return to Athens to drive out Kleisthenes."

"But we helped put him into power less than two years ago," Eirana protested with open alarm.

"Yes, and he never showed the slightest gratitude for what we did for him!" her father countered angrily. "Now he has whipped up the rabble and started a completely radical program. He has increased the tribes of Athens from four to ten—thereby swelling his own following—and with this false majority he is pursuing Athenian hegemony. He's become a threat to us."

"But what about the oracles?! They told us to restore the Alcmaeonidae to power," Eirana pointed out, incredulous.

"Oracles! I should have known you would quote oracles to me!" There was a sneer in Kyranios' voice that Leonidas could not overhear. "Bought! That's what those oracles were! Bought with Alcmaeonidae bribes! That should show you the measure of priests and seers. Nothing but corrupt cowards who write their oracles to suit the highest bidder!"

"Kyranios!" His wife was shocked. "Don't talk like that!"

"Well, it's the truth. Cleomenes had proof of it. The Alcmaeonidae had bribed Delphi to give judgments that pushed us to support them. And once they were placed in power by our spears, they laughed at us for fools and imbeciles, so easily bamboozled by the 'cheap sayings of corrupt priests'. Well, they'll soon see what fools we are! Demaratus refuses to support the war, but Cleomenes got approval for taking 'volunteers'. They jumped up on the spot. So we're deploying the equivalent of two lochagoi to drive Kleisthenes and his priest-bribing family and their pack of upstart followers out! The sooner we march, the better. And the sooner you get back to your charges, eirene, the better for you, too! Be off before I decide to report you!" He flung the last at Leonidas, who was more than happy to comply.

———

By the time Leonidas was back in the city, the mobilisation had been announced, and the streets were filled with agitated people: the volunteers were making a quick trip home to take leave of loved ones and collect their personal provisions, while their helot attendants were making last-minute purchases and repairs to their own and their hoplites' equipment. Meanwhile, the army's purveyors were delivering supplies, and the state helots were loading up the wagons from warehouses. Trains of horses and mules were being led to the blacksmiths to have their feet trimmed and shod. An unusual number of people could also be seen going in and out of the temples, from which the smoke of sacrifices was rising.

Leonidas had only to stop the first eirene he saw on the street to learn that the march-out was set for the following dawn. "Why the rush?" Leonidas asked.

"It's either tomorrow or the moon will be waning—and you know how inauspicious that is. No one wants to risk starting a campaign during the waning moon. Some of the old men said it was against our laws to do so, but then some of the others said it wasn't a law, just 'advice' from Chilon. And they fought about it for a long time, with the old men getting all worked up about it, while the young men kept trying to get things focussed again on the campaign against Athens." (His informant had evidently attended the Assembly as an observer, something the eirenes were encouraged to do.) "Finally Cleomenes made the suggestion that he leave tomorrow, and he got support for that from the younger cohorts that had volunteered to follow him, and so the decision was made—although Demaratus said he wanted nothing to do with this campaign and announced he would stay home."

"Cleomenes alone will be commanding? Is that legal?"

"Apparently, as long as it's just volunteers—not a regular deployment." (Many of Sparta's laws were not written down, resulting in ambiguity on the fine points, particularly on issues that did not come up every day.)

Leonidas thanked his informant and continued on to the palaestra, where he found his charges in excited discussion. "Have you heard the news, sir?" they asked him eagerly.

"Unfortunately, from Kyranios himself. How can Cleomenes be so certain that 2,000 troops is enough? Last time he took almost 5,000."

Whatever their source, the 18-year-olds were well informed: "He is in contact with Isagoras, who assures him that many Athenians will rally to their cause. Indeed, Cleomenes has sent an order to Athens, warning them that if they do not throw Kleisthenes out, we will come and throw him out. The troops are there to give credence to our threat, but Cleomenes says they will not have to fight."

Leonidas was not sure what to think of all this, so he said nothing, and waited to see what would happen.

———

The first thing that happened was that as soon as Kyranios left Sparta, Leonidas started encountering Asteropus at Eirana's kleros. Usually, he ran into him on the road coming or going. Once he found Asteropus already there when he arrived. On the road they merely greeted each other, but at the kleros they were forced to make polite conversation.

Leonidas could not see what Eirana saw in the man. Although tall, he was overly thin, and his skin was marred with several unsightly pockmarks. His response to Leonidas' presence was to start lecturing him on how disrespectful his entire family was towards the Gods. First his brother Dorieus had set off on an adventure without so much as consulting Delphi, and now Cleomenes was manipulating oracles and provoking the Gods with his ill-advised campaign against Athens.

"What do you mean about manipulating oracles, sir?" Leonidas asked defensively, as he watched the way Eirana gazed admiringly at Asteropus. It wasn't exactly "cow's eyes" as Alkander had claimed, but she seemed to take every word he uttered unduly seriously—or at least more seriously than she took the things Leonidas said.

"Well, first your brother brings us the oracles that suggest we must support the Alcmaeonidae. Then he brings us evidence that they were false—bought with Alcmaeonidae bribes. But my father says the signs are completely against this campaign. He says it will end badly for us. He says that the claims of bribery might be lies. Or even if not, still we should have waited until the signs were good. Cleomenes is arrogant. He does not think he has to wait on the will of the Gods."

Leonidas remembered that one of the adjectives his mother had coined for the hated "bastard" was "impious", but he did not think it would serve any purpose to mention that now. On the other hand, he also remembered the eager way the Athenians at Persiai had learned of Sparta's willingness to comply with Delphic advice. He tended to think the oracles had indeed been bought. But if oracles could be bought, how trustworthy were they?

———

At all events, the signs Asteropus' father had seen proved right. Within two months, Cleomenes and his 2,000 volunteers were trapped on the Acropolis of Athens, surrounded by a hostile mob. Kleisthenes had fled even before the Spartans arrived and Cleomenes had entered Athens triumphantly, but he had then set about trying to impose a new constitution on the Athenians that would have institutionalised the power of his friend and host, Isagoras. The Athenians had no intention of letting the Spartans dictate their form of government to them, and they had taken up arms against the Spartans. Cleomenes and his entire army had fled to safety on the Acropolis, where—fortunately—they found the vast stores that had been feeding Hippias and his supporters when they had been the besiegers rather than the besieged.

Clearly this situation was even more ridiculous and humiliating than the stalemate of two years earlier. The news therefore created outrage, lamentation, and confusion in the city. While Demaratus and others who had opposed the campaign (including Asteropus, Leonidas noted sourly) appeared almost smug, the majority of the citizens were distressed by the "humiliation". Furthermore, it seemed obvious that unless Cleomenes negotiated, the food stores found on the Acropolis would eventually run out, and then they would all starve or be forced to surrender—an appalling thought to the proud Spartans.

Leonidas went to Eirana's kleros to express his concern over the fate of Eirana's father Kyranios, trapped on the Athenian Acropolis with the others, but unfortunately her mother was absent on some errand and his reception from Eirana was outright cold.

"It's his own fault," Eirana told him, as she vigorously clipped roses from a vine in the garden behind the kleros and laid them in a flat basket for arranging in the house. "He shouldn't have been so eager to go against the Gods and fight this war that has nothing to do with us." Eirana was dressed in a very fine peplos that fluttered about her as she worked in the light breeze that came off the Eurotas. She had looped her long hair on to her head, and her lovely long neck was exposed. Everything about her was both beautiful and graceful; but Leonidas could hardly overlook her hostility to him, either. She avoided looking at him whenever possible, and she never smiled for him. He was beginning to despair.

"How can you be so sure it was against the Gods' wishes?" he asked cautiously.

"All the signs were bad," Eirana insisted.

Leonidas could not stop himself from remarking bitterly, "No doubt you heard that from Asteropus."

"Yes, I did," Eirana declared, stopping her work and looking him straight in the eye. "I don't know why you don't accept that I love Asteropus, and I don't want your attentions. As long as you insist on coming, my mother hopes she can marry me off to an Agiad. She likes the idea of being related to one of the kings. But if you just stop coming, then she'll let me marry the man I love."

Even though Leonidas had long sensed Eirana's feelings, now that it was out in the open he found himself saying, "But what about Asteropus makes him better than me?"

"It's not a matter of being better!" Eirana protested, adding the complaint: "Why do you men always see everything as a competition!? He's not better; he's just special *to me*. He's intelligent and learned. He's not only interested in sports and war."

"I'm not only interested in sports and war," Leonidas tried to tell her, but it only exasperated her.

"Maybe not, but you aren't the same as Asteropus! You're one of
them! Like my father! You'll be an officer one day, and Sparta will be
at the centre of everything! I don't want to marry a man who's more
interested in his troops than his children!"

Leonidas, who had neglected his duties to spend so much time
with Eirana, felt the accusation was very unjust; but he also felt he
couldn't take any more rejection. "All right. I won't ever bother you
again," he told her and departed.

He didn't hurry back into the city as he should have. Eirana's
father, after all, was trapped on the Athenian Acropolis and could not
surprise him here, and his unit was diligently training for the cham-
pionships in the ball games. They were very good as a team and stood
an excellent chance of being a finalist this year, so they took training
seriously and could be counted not to get in trouble. As a mediocre
ball player himself, Leonidas was not much use to them even as a
coach, and it was this which had turned their training afternoons
into his opportunity to go to see Eirana. With a glance towards the
afternoon sun that was still above the Taygetos, he was confident that
they were still at training and he need not rush.

Instead he lingered along the road, feeling sorry for himself. He
really didn't understand why he was so unsuccessful with women.
He was no longer the ugly duckling he had been when younger, and
with his assignment to the 18-year-olds he had demonstrated that he
could earn responsibility. But unlike Alkander and Prokles, none of
the maidens took any particular interest in him—except that hussy
Lathria, and he detested her.

He dawdled all the way, and the sun was behind the mountains
when he reached the bridge over the Eurotas. He was startled to find
Euryleon waiting for him there. He called out: "Leonidas, sir! Come
quick! Something terrible has happened."

The guilt was almost paralyzing. Something had happened to one
of his charges while he was off indulging himself on a futile courtship.
He sprinted over the bridge and reached Euryleon. "What is it?! Has
someone been hurt?"

"They're saying the boy is dead, sir," Euryleon told him over his
shoulder, even as he started jogging back toward the ball field beyond
the acropolis.

"Dead? But how? Who?"

"Oh, I don't know the details, sir, but your friend Alkander is there. He knows more."

Now Leonidas was completely confused, but the only thing to do was to keep running. He was sighted before he reached the ball field where, astonishingly, a game appeared to be in progress as if nothing had happened. (Euryleon didn't play because his bad eyesight made him useless.) Alkander, however, rushed to meet him. "Have you heard?!"

"No. What?"

"One of Prokles' boys died—drowned—in an accident last night. Prokles has been arrested again. This time for neglect of his duties, negligent homicide—and drinking. He was drunk, Leo. He and two other eirenes were drinking off by themselves after turn-in during a four-nighter. They were camping on the beach beyond Gytheon and had gone behind the dunes to be by themselves. The boys of their units decided to take advantage of their inattentiveness to "borrow" some fishing boats and go out for a moonlight sail. One of the boats capsized in a sudden squall; and although the other boys roused their drunken eirenes, they were unable to get out to the capsized boat in time to save one of the boys from drowning."

Leonidas was staring at Alkander. He felt a horrible chill, knowing that he too had been neglecting his charges just now. "What about the other eirenes?"

"They've been arrested too, of course; but it's Prokles who's in the most trouble. It's not just that the boy who died was from his unit; it's that after the rape incident, there are a lot of people who think he needs to be taught a lesson."

Leonidas knew it was all too true. He knew also that he wouldn't be allowed to see Prokles. "Do his parents know?"

"They must. They would have been sent word. I only found out about it by chance—we happened to be near the jail when Prokles and the others were brought in. I got the story from the meleirenes who assisted with the arrest. Prokles is in a bad state, Leo. He *looked* terrible."

Leonidas was remembering Lysandridas begging him to stand by Prokles, warning that he was too rebellious. He remembered all the times Prokles had chafed at the rules, broken them surreptitiously. But what else had *he* been doing just now at Eirana's kleros? "How can we possibly help?" Leonidas asked in genuine distress.

Alkander shook his head in perplexity. "I don't know exactly, but I'm sure we'll be questioned. Did you ever know Prokles to drink? I mean, drink *excessively?*"

"No," Leonidas answered honestly; and yet he knew that Prokles could so easily be tempted by anything that was forbidden.

———

As Alkander had predicted, they were questioned separately by the magistrates. The horrible thing about the interrogation was that everyone knew Leonidas was not a witness to the incident: he was being questioned exclusively about Prokles' character. The last time he had been interrogated about Prokles, he had been able to swear with conviction that Prokles would never have used force with his girlfriend, that he had no need to, and that it just wasn't in his nature. But now, asked if he thought Prokles respected Spartan law, Leonidas' brain was filled with all the phrases of contempt and impatience that Prokles had uttered over the years.

He squirmed and wriggled and tried to find a way to defend his friend. He tried to make Prokles' rebelliousness seem harmless, but each time the magistrates confronted him with: "A boy is dead! Is that harmless?!" Of course it wasn't. It was terrible, and Leonidas felt partially guilty—because he had been at Eirana's kleros so often when something *could* have happened to one of his charges.

"A young life has been snuffed out before it even had a chance to show the world what it was capable of. Do you want to face the boy's mother and tell her that it was all just a harmless little breach of discipline? Drinking oneself into a stupor so profound they did not hear the boats being dragged down the beach and launched? Did not hear the shouting of the boys when the boat capsized? And when woken by the survivors, were still too drugged to be able to respond promptly and effectively?"

Leonidas wanted to put his hands over his ears to block out the words, the images.

"There are reasons for our laws!" the magistrate hammered into him. "We prohibit drinking for exactly this reason: it incapacitates us. Makes us slaves of wine rather than masters of our own bodies! Prokles is a strong youth! A good swimmer! If he had not been drinking, he would very likely have been able to save the boy. He would have dived into the water right away and reached the capsized fishing boat in time. Instead, he was hardly able to drag himself to his feet, vomited several times before he even seemed to grasp what had happened, and then staggered down to the shore and plunged into the water so uncertainly that the boys thought he was likely to drown himself."

Leonidas could think of no excuse for or defence of what his friend had done. He found himself whispering hopelessly, "I'm sure he's learned from his mistake, sirs. He's intelligent and—"

"The boy who's dead doesn't have a second chance, does he?"

Leonidas looked down miserably.

"Does he?" they pressed him cruelly.

"No, sir."

————

Almost as bad as the certainty that Prokles was going to be punished in some terrible way was the malicious commentary of some of the townspeople. To Leonidas' horror, he overheard citizens making slurs about Lysandridas. "What could you expect of the offspring of a coward and traitor?" they murmured self-righteously. Coward and traitor? Just a year ago, most of the city had turned out to honour him as a man of wisdom and courage. Leonidas wanted to spring at the throats of these people who implied that Lysandridas had "spent too long in Tegea" and failed to raise his offspring to be "true Spartans". They conveniently forgot that the other two eirenes had been no less guilty, really—just luckier.

Leonidas and Alkander both tried to comfort Prokles' parents; but Prokles' mother refused visitors, and Philippos seemed to blame them for what had happened, implying they had been a "bad influence" on his son. Hilaira had to run after the youths, catching them up on the road and throwing herself into Alkander's arms. "They've all gone mad!" she wailed miserably. "The whole city and now Dad, too! If only Granddad were still alive! He'd have knocked everyone's heads together."

Leonidas felt as if he'd just been thrown out of his home a second time. This time it hurt more than the first time, because it had been the only home he consciously loved—his refuge for the better part of his life. He was only months away from turning 21, and he felt as if he had no one at all in the world that he could turn to for comfort, advice, or support—except Alkander. And Alkander had a maiden. Leonidas distanced himself a little and turned his back so they could kiss and whisper together "in private" for a few minutes. Then Alkander joined him.

They walked in silence through the star-studded darkness, both burdened by what had just transpired. It had been Alkander's home, too, after all, and he now had to fear that his suit for Hilaira would be rejected.

———

The judgment came shortly afterwards: the other two eirenes were sentenced to be flogged and then degraded to meleirene. They would be held back not just one year but two, because they were told they would not graduate with the others at the solstice but remain meleirenes for a full year afterwards. Then a decision would be made about citizenship. Another "command", however, was ruled out.

Prokles was condemned to 20 years' exile.

Leonidas was stunned. He did not know what he had expected. At the darkest hour of the night, he had sometimes feared they would sentence Prokles to death: a life for a life. But exile was almost as bad. Leonidas could not imagine being sent away from Lacedaemon— cut off from family, friends, and the society that had nurtured and shaped them. Lysandridas had suggested that Prokles would benefit from seeing other cities and their customs, implying that the comparison would make Prokles appreciate Sparta more. But 20 years? It was a lifetime—literally as long as they had already lived. And how could he live outside of Lacedaemon with no property, no income, no trade, no profession? He had been trained intensively for almost 14 years for only one thing: to be a Spartan citizen. And they were denying him that. They might as well have killed him.

Yet when Leonidas waited at the door to the jail for Prokles' release, he went with a different message. He wanted to assure Prokles that he and Alkander, who was with him, would welcome Prokles back. He would always have a home under Leonidas' roof. But Prokles' parents and Hilaira closed around the youth as he emerged from the jail, and Leonidas hardly got a glimpse of his friend. The glimpse he did get was terrible. Prokles looked as if he had not slept or washed in the entire month of his confinement. He looked aged and dazed and lethargic. There was not a spark of defiance left in him.

Philippos had brought him a fine young stallion and a pack mule, the latter laden with a full panoply of arms and armour and also baskets full of provisions. There were bags heavy with other provisions over the withers of the horse. More importantly, Prokles was given the names and addresses of contacts throughout the Greek world— horse traders and horse breeders, merchants of grain and shippers of livestock. Leonidas was thus reminded that Prokles' family had friends in the wide world. He decided that things might not go so badly for Prokles after all.

In fact, as Prokles mounted and set out, Leonidas could almost envy him. He envied him for breaking free of all the rules and regulations and rigid expectations of self-righteous Spartan society. Prokles could go anywhere he liked in the whole world, be who he wanted to be, do what he wanted to do—while Leonidas had no choice whatever about his profession, his clothes, or even where he was to sleep at night; he was confined to barracks for the next ten years. When he thought about it like this, he was less free than the helots! But Prokles would soon see the whole world, and as he watched him ride away he wished he were going with him.

Chapter 12

Farewell to the Agoge

As THE WINTER SOLSTICE APPROACHED AND the time came when the age-classes would move up a grade, the eirenes were faced with preparing for the most profound transition in their lives since entering the agoge: the transition from "youth" to "young man" and the award of citizenship. "Young men", those citizens aged 21 to 30, were on active service and excluded from public office, but they were nevertheless required to belong to a syssitia and take part in the nightly mess, as well as being full members of a military unit. Because they had to contribute their portion to their syssitia, it was on becoming citizens that they were assigned a state kleros and inherited any other estates due them. Last but not least, since they were expected to report for duty in the army, ready for combat, the day after the festivities ended, they had to be in possession of the full panoply of armour and attended by a body servant or attendant.

Most young men had fathers and extended families who made sure the transition of status went smoothly in all respects, but Leonidas and Alkander had to fend for themselves. They decided that the first step was to find a syssitia that would accept both of them. Officially, every member of a syssitia had to approve a new member: a single veto meant that a youth was rejected. In reality, family and friends lobbied hard to ensure their sons were accepted—if not always to the syssitia of their first choice, certainly into one dominated by their clan. But despite the fact that both Leonidas and Alkander were now related to a ruling king, neither of them liked their royal relatives, and both were determined *not* to have to dine the rest of their lives with either king. They were equally determined to join the same syssitia, and had long since decided which of the syssitia they liked best. Still, it had accepted new members since they had served in it as boys, and they couldn't be sure that no one would object to either of them. They therefore decided to seek out the chairman, a certain Nikostratos, and ask him "unofficially" if he thought their applications would be received with favour.

Nikostratos was a man in his mid-50s, distinguished less for his military career than for his remarkable ability with figures. He had been a student of Pythagoras in his youth and had travelled to Samos and Tarentum to meet with the philosopher on separate occasions. He had been elected treasurer of the city for the last ten years, and many unofficially sought his advice and assistance—even the architects working on new public works, because of his understanding of geometry.

Leonidas and Alkander sought him out in his office behind the Ephorate. A man with thinning grey hair and hunched shoulders from days spent behind a desk rather than out on the drill fields, he was not a stereotypical Spartan. But Leonidas and Alkander knew that the syssitia he headed offered some of the best conversation possible—and it had never once ridiculed or belittled Alkander for his stutter as a boy.

Nikostratos' face lit up at the sight of the two eirenes lurking outside his door, the many creases around his eyes deepening as he gestured them in. "Come in, come in! What a sight for tired eyes you are! Leonidas, you've grown another two inches since the last time I saw you! Alkander, how do you keep the girls off you?"

"He doesn't," Leonidas answered, laughing to his friend's discomfort.

"Sit down!" Nikostratos offered. "Just put those tablets on the floor. They won't be the worse for it. You must be upset by what

happened to your friend Prokles," he surmised as the youths did as
they were bid. "You will miss him, I know, but it is not such a bad
thing to see something of the world."

"I envied him that, sir," Leonidas admitted, adding hastily, "I
mean, if the circumstances had been different. How did you get permission to travel?"

"I didn't—until I was off active service. Pythagoras was here, a
guest of your father for several years, you know. That was how I got to
know him, and he invited me to visit him after I was off active duty.
Your stepmother's mother was one of his most brilliant students, did
you know? A truly remarkable woman, and a worthy daughter of
Chilon himself. You don't harbour fantasies about going after Prokles,
do you?" He asked the last in a concerned tone.

"No, sir. Alkander and I don't have the resources or the connections."

Nikostratos raised his eyebrows at that, and then leaned forward
and fixed his sharp grey eyes pointedly on Leonidas. "Have you
spoken to the Agiad steward lately?"

"No, sir. Should I?"

"You're due to come into your inheritance. It's time you found
out what it is." Then, leaning back in his chair, he added in a lighter
tone, "Have you decided on a syssitia, by the way?"

"That's what we're here about, sir. We—" Leonidas glanced at
Alkander and got a slight nod—"we would both like to join your
syssitia, sir, if you think there would be no strong objections—"

Nikostratos had broken into a wide smile long before he got that
far. "I was hoping you'd say that! Nothing would please me more!
Just last night we were discussing this year's crop of eirenes, and your
names came up top of the list. Of course there will be no objections!
We'd be delighted."

The eirenes were taken aback by the official's enthusiasm. "Are
you sure, sir? Not even from the newer members?"

"We choose our members very carefully. Besides, what have they
to object to?"

"I'm a mothake, sir," Alkander reminded him.

"With citizenship, that status ends. You'll have a kleros of your
own—and although I'm not supposed to reveal details, I can assure

you, your brother-in-law has been most insistent that your lot not "disgrace" him. He doesn't want an impoverished brother-in-law, nor the responsibility of paying your debts. Your kleros will be one of the best. Yours, in contrast," he turned to Leonidas, "is one in a deplorable state of disrepair—ravaged by a fire about four Olympiads ago—that no one without independent means can afford to rebuild and replant. You'll need to divert some of your private resources to restoring it."

"Maybe I should just renounce it?" Leonidas answered, thinking he was going to have enough on his plate while on active service without a kleros he couldn't look after without a wife.

"No. You can't do that. It could be interpreted as a renunciation of citizenship itself," Nikostratos warned. "It's a first-class property right on the banks of the Eurotas not far from the Menelaion. Once you've got it fixed up, you will enjoy its proximity to the city and the view of the Taygetos."

Leonidas caught his breath as he realised that someone must have been looking after his interests. "Do I have you to thank for that, sir?"

"Not just me, Leonidas. You have impressed the Paidonomos and others along the way. You may be an orphan, but you are not without mentors."

"Or enemies."

"If you mean your brothers and Alkander's brother-in-law, you are right. Managing to get both reigning monarchs on your bad side is almost unique in the history of the agoge; but if anyone should be able to live with the consequences, it is you. What I—"

A citizen emerged in the doorway, and both eirenes dutifully sprang to their feet, hands at their sides and eyes down.

"Ainetos, come in!" Nikostratos addressed the citizen. "I've got everything ready for you." Turning to the eirenes, he smiled and added, "We'll have plenty of time to talk in the future!" This was clear reaffirmation of their place in his syssitia, and so they thanked him and departed, much relieved that this key hurdle to citizenship was now removed.

Only two days later, Leonidas was asked to attend upon the

Agiad steward in the offices at the back of the Agiad palace. Because Leonidas suspected that Nikostratos was behind the summons, he was a little surprised to find Brotus already waiting.

The twins rarely spoke to one another anymore. From being rivals as children and indifferent to one another as youths, they had become hostile ever since Leonidas had been given command of Brotus' unit less than a year earlier. Leonidas could not exactly follow his twin's logic, but Brotus made it very clear that he viewed Leonidas as some kind of "traitor".

Brotus was displeased to see Leonidas. "You, too?" he asked in obvious annoyance.

The Agiad estate steward, a fastidiously dressed perioikoi with a receding hairline and an aquiline nose, quickly reminded him, "Of course. I have summoned you both today to explain the dispositions your parents made for you and settle your estates on you."

The estate office was a room completely clothed in narrow, divided shelves designed for the storage of scrolls. It gave Leonidas the feeling of being inside a honeycomb. The steward had prepared well for this long-anticipated meeting. Survey charts were already spread upon the table, showing Laconia and Messenia, respectively. A variety of other documents were piled up under a chunk of marble, apparently the last will and testament of King Anaxandridas and Queen Taygete. On the survey charts, neatly drawn little squares were delineated all across the landscape in blue or green ink, like scattered mosaics. The steward invited his young guests to sit.

"First let me explain the terms of your parents' testament," he suggested.

Brotus and Leonidas nodded.

"Your father ordered that his personal estates—those not part of the royal estate that went to his heir Cleomenes—be divided equally among his three remaining sons in such a fashion that all three would possess property yielding as closely as possible the same revenues. He left the actual parcelling of his properties and the assignation of properties to the trustees of the estate. Your mother, in contrast, left the bulk of her estate to Dorieus and only designated one small estate for each of you. Dorieus, however, had to renounce all claims to property in Lacedaemon before setting out for Sicily. Since his departure, his estate—both that derived from his father and that from his mother—has also been held in trust and also divided equally between you."

That sounded perfectly fair to Leonidas, but Brotus objected at once. "But Dorieus much preferred me! I can bring you a dozen witnesses who can attest to his contempt for little Leo!" He nodded his head contemptuously in Leonidas' direction and pronounced "little Leo" with a sneer.

The steward appeared unimpressed. "I'm afraid that is immaterial."

"My mother said Leo was 'superfluous' and should have been killed at birth."

"Perhaps; but since he was not, he will become a Spartiate Peer and will be treated as such." Leonidas kept a straight face, but he found himself rather enjoying the perioikoi's utter indifference to Brotus' (not entirely unjustified) objections.

"That isn't what either my mother or Dorieus would have wanted!" Brotus insisted, getting agitated.

"Dorieus hasn't been heard from for over a year, and his wishes are irrelevant," the Perioikoi insisted. He had long, elegant fingers with rings on both ring and index fingers. He was undoubtedly a wealthy man in his own right, Leonidas noted mentally. The steward was continuing out loud to Brotus, "As you are generally said to be the firstborn twin, Brotus, the only concession I can offer is that you may select first, which of the two portions—carefully balanced to ensure the maximum comparability—you wish to assume."

Frowning, Brotus leaned forward to see the charts. The steward pointed out the properties scattered across Laconia and then the even larger properties located in Messenia. "These symbols," the conscientious steward tried to explain, "indicate shares in enterprises as opposed to actual landholdings. For example, this is a 12.5% share in the marble quarries. This here is a 7.75% share in a dye factory. This here is a 24% share in an iron foundry. And this here is a 50% share in a lumber mill."

Leonidas wasn't listening closely, because he was unsettled by the number of properties, many deep inside Messenia, and at the same time unable to really relate neat little squares on a survey chart with land. There was no topography on the chart—only roads, rivers, and boundaries. He could not tell if a piece of land was steep or flat, barren or fertile. He could not tell from the chart if the lands in question were barley fields or orchards, pasture or vineyards. As for buildings, although little squares indicated structures of some kind, from the chart there was no way of knowing if they were barns or fine houses.

Brotus was frowning, apparently having the same difficulty relating the squares on papyrus to rocks and soil and crops. At last he asked in an exasperated voice, "Where is the estate where my mother is buried? I want it in my portion!"

The steward glanced at Leonidas; but when he made no objection, the steward replied evenly, "Very well. Then you have selected the blue share. All the properties outlined in blue are yours."

"But I don't want any of these silly shares of things!" Brotus protested, with a contemptuous gesture towards the symbol of the quarries. "Spartiates aren't supposed to engage in trade! That is perioikoi business. I don't know what my father or mother was doing with them in the first place!"

"The laws prohibit Spartiates from *engaging* in any trade other than that of arms; it does not prohibit holding shares in perioikoi businesses. I believe your ancestors at some point deeded the lands or provided the initial labour for the businesses involved in exchange for the shareholdings. As it is—" The steward would have been happy to explain more, but Brotus waved him silent.

"Well, I don't care what they did. I want nothing to do with activities that would demean me! Give them to Leonidas. Everyone knows he is not likely to amount to much as a hoplite, and if he wants to spend his time with perioikoi, then let him! I want estates in Messenia instead!"

The steward looked over at Leonidas in alarm, as if expecting a violent—or at least angry—response. Leonidas just shrugged. "That's fine with me. My only request is that I be granted at least one estate suitable for horse-breeding."

"That would be this farm, here." The steward pointed to a square on the peninsula south of Asine.

"If he gets to keep that, then I want these four estates in exchange for the shareholdings!" Brotus demanded.

"That's not necessarily fair," the conscientious steward warned, glancing towards Leonidas and twisting one of his larger rings with the thumb and forefinger of the other hand. "We have to look at the actual yield of the individual—"

"Go ahead and give him what he wants," Leonidas decided. What he saw was that estates in Messenia would be almost impossible to visit, much less control, for as long as he was on active service and hence required to live in barracks in Sparta. Although some holidays were long enough for trips to Messenia, these allowed for only occasional, short visits—not nearly enough time to properly manage even one of all the estates shown. Shares, in contrast, would bring income without requiring personal attention in the same way. The perioikoi majority-owners of such enterprises had an even greater interest in turning a profit than he did—and certainly more than Messenian helots, who were widely known to be lazy, resentful, and untrustworthy.

The steward gazed at Leonidas for a moment, glanced at Brotus, and then took a deep breath and noted the changes on the map, remarking, "So be it, then. I will have the changes recorded and inform the respective estate managers of your official status as owner—once you gain citizen status, of course." The steward looked among his papers until he found a roll, which he opened. He very carefully scratched out several items and noted others at the bottom of the roll before handing it to Brotus. "Here is the complete list for your records."

Brotus nodded, still frowning, mumbled something that could have been a comment or a complaint or a farewell, and was gone. The steward gazed after him for a moment and shook his head. Leonidas just waited. Then the steward turned his attention to a second roll, where he recorded the corresponding changes and then handed it to Leonidas. As he did so their eyes met, and Leonidas noted that the steward was smiling slightly. "You are not only taller than your twin, young sir; you are head and shoulders above him in brains. With the exception of the quarries, which have not been performing well lately, the value of the shares far exceeds the properties you just deeded to your brother. The lumber mill, particularly, is benefiting from the ever-increasing demand for shipping, while the iron foundry has a lucrative government contract that cannot be cancelled."

Leonidas was somewhat uncomfortable with the compliment. He had been motivated more by convenience than recognition of relative value. "I'm going to need the income. I've been warned my state kleros is in deplorable condition and I'll have to invest money into repairing it."

"Yes, sir. Nikostratos mentioned that; but, you see, it is located right here." The steward leaned over the map and with his manicured index finger indicated a longish property backed up on the east bank of the Eurotas, almost directly opposite the Temple of Artemis Orthia. "It is a very fertile piece of land, young sir. Suitable for barley or even wheat, and it has a beautiful stand of olives here and a small apple orchard here. You can easily walk the distance to barracks or syssitia—or with a horse, be in the city in less than 20 minutes."

Leonidas liked the sound of this very much, and tried to imagine it all from the neat square on the survey map. He couldn't. "Could I have a copy of the map, sir? Or someone who can show me around the various properties?"

The man now smiled outright. "It would be my pleasure to show you around myself, sir. As soon as you have your shield and some spare time, let me know and we can ride to all of the nearby properties. Your Messenian properties will have to wait until the spring. If you want recommendations for a good steward, I would be happy to give you some names as well."

"What did you say your name was?" Leonidas asked, embarrassed that he had not noted it at the beginning of the interview.

"Eukomos, sir."

Leonidas held out his hand.

The perioikoi was taken aback for a second, and then extended his own with a smile. "I will look forward to showing you your properties, young sir."

The only property Leonidas had noted mentally was the kleros that was going to be his. Most young men were assigned kleros that had been in their own family in one way or another. Often they had lived on their kleros, if their father had since died, or had at least visited their future kleros when they visited grandparents or aunts and uncles. Hence most of Leonidas' age-cohorts knew exactly where their future kleros lay, what it looked like, and what sort of accommodation it offered. Leonidas was anxious to visit the kleros selected for him. He thought it would enable him to dispel the sense of homelessness that the abrupt banishment from Prokles' home had induced. And so it was with considerable youthful enthusiasm that he set off at once to visit this kleros, since his unit had been warned he might not be back until dinner.

It was a clear, crisp day, quite typical of this time of year, when the sun could be hot and the shadows freezing. As he walked at an easy marching pace south from the drill fields, Leonidas was full of plans for "restoring" this kleros, and feeling rather pleased with himself for being so clever in trading income for land with Brotus. The income from other sources could now clearly be funnelled into the repairs needed on his state kleros, which was within an easy ride of his barracks and syssitia. He was feeling as if a benevolent god (Castor, perhaps?) had planned things out for him.... And then he came to his kleros.

Or rather, he walked past it. When he came to a deeply rutted cross-road used by timber wagons headed for the lumber yards on the Eurotas, he knew from the steward's map that he must have gone too far. So he retraced his steps, increasingly suspicious that the field now to his left, which he had blissfully dismissed as a fallow pasture, must in fact form the core of the neglected property. The problem was that he could not see any house on the land at all—unless there was something lurking amidst the man-high reeds and stunted trees along the banks of the river?

It was with growing trepidation that he struck off through the tall weeds towards the grove of trees. The weeds, dry and grey and brittle at this time of year, came up to his waist and crackled under his sandals. Little patches of ice had formed on the muddy puddles that dotted the field. Field mice by the dozens scuttled for cover.

As he got closer, Leonidas could see that there were charred tree stumps amidst the weeds, and over to his left, vineyards had run wild. Gradually the ruins of what had once been a house became visible. Or rather, he could see a high wall, torn open at one end to reveal a courtyard surrounded by gutted chambers into which blackened

beams had collapsed. All were roofless and filled with debris. One of
the ruined buildings had evidently been two stories high, and a blak-
kened chimney reared up from it into the sky from a naked hearth.
The very sight of that shattered symbol of warmth and comfort sent
a chill through him.

By the time Leonidas stepped through the collapsed gateway into
the courtyard, he was cursing himself for a fool. What had he been
expecting? They had told him there had been a fire. But somehow he
had not pictured anything as ruined and overgrown as this. Directly
in front of him three steps led up to what had once been a fine portico,
but the blackened pillars stretched out like rotting corpses into the
courtyard, and the tile roof was now a carpet of tile fragments amidst
the weeds. Behind these, a passageway in the blackened wall led to
what appeared to be a second courtyard.

Leonidas hesitated, but then mounted the uneven steps, walked
cautiously across the uneven flooring of broken tiles, and started
into the passage. Just when he reached the darkness, the sound of
something behind him made him spin about in alarm. A stray dog
was standing at the entrance to the passage, wagging its tail tenta-
tively. Annoyed at his own alarm, Leonidas continued quickly into
what he expected to be the inner atrium. Instead he emerged in a
second courtyard enclosed only on three sides. Two-storey buildings formed an "L", and the building ahead of him had an outside
stairway leading up to what had once been a wooden gallery. This had
burned in the fire and lay like a blackened corpse along the foot of the
wall. The shutters on the upper stories had burned, and the windows
loomed black and empty like the eye sockets of a skull. But the open
side of the courtyard, if you looked beyond the thicket of river reeds
encroaching on the patio, offered a splendid view of the Taygetos in
all its majesty. Even at this time of year, the view was breathtaking.

Turning away from it, Leonidas cautiously made his way around
the edge of the courtyard, looking into the downstairs chambers.
These were vacant but untouched by the fire, which had apparently
gutted the upper storey only. A large loom, encased in cobwebs, stood
in one long hall. There was what had once been a pretty little bath
chamber (now filled with decades of dirt and debris), backed by a
laundry. And beyond the right-hand wing there was a walled orchard

in which almond and lemon trees embraced one another in an almost grotesque fashion above the layers of unharvested, rotting fruits. They all but obscured a little temple at the far side of the garden, and Leonidas realized it was these trees that had hidden the house from view when he was on the road.

Leonidas couldn't imagine where one would start to repair this mess. He turned his back on the orchard and returned to the courtyard. The stray dog was waiting for him, ears half cocked and tail wagging slowly in cautious hope.

"You're out of luck," Leonidas told the bitch, speaking as much for himself as for the stray.

The dog, however, interpreted the words as friendly, and her ears lifted a little more as she took a couple of steps closer. Her big eyes were focused intently on Leonidas' face. "You must be an unreformed optimist," Leonidas concluded as, feeling overwhelmed by what he'd found, he sank down on to a rickety bench backed against the wall and gazed at the view of the Taygetos.

He noticed now that the walkway around the courtyard was paved in marble mosaics of white and black in a simple but attractive pattern. Once upon a time, this had been a lovely house. He also noticed that the second storey of the right-hand wing appeared to be intact after all. So he got to his feet again, and carefully mounted the outside stairs to enter the end room.

He found a series of three small rooms, all with shuttered windows and doors, each of which opened on to a balcony overlooking the walled section of the orchard. Although the rooms were dusty, the shutters were in ill-repair, and cobwebs clogged the ceiling beams, they were inhabitable. In fact, Leonidas could almost picture them being a wonderful refuge from the crowded barracks.

He descended back to the courtyard and at once the stray reappeared, wagging her tail and looking up at him expectantly. Leondias pulled his knapsack off his back and reached inside. From well-trained habit, he was carrying water, bread, and sausage. He took his knife and cut off a chunk of sausage, which he tossed to the young bitch. She caught the offering in mid-air, gulped it down, and took a step nearer. Her tail was wagging with decided enthusiasm now.

Leonidas cut a second piece of sausage for himself, and the bitch moved closer still. She fixed her eyes on him as if he alone could save her from starvation. Leonidas considered her. She was clearly a dog of excellent breeding. The so-called Castorian hounds bred in Lacedaemon were valued throughout the world, and there were not a few citizens who maintained large kennels. Leonidas judged this bitch was the product of an unplanned coupling when a bitch escaped while in heat, or a puppy discarded for some imperfection such as the white patch that half covered her face. Pure-coloured dogs were more prized and brought higher prices.

Leonidas cut another piece of sausage. The bitch tensed in order to be ready to catch, while wagging her tail furiously in anticipation or pleading. Leonidas held the piece out to her in his fingers. She reached out her neck as far as she could, but would not move a step closer. Instead, she drew back and looked up at him reproachfully. He let the piece of sausage fall and she snapped it up gratefully.

"We're both just a couple of strays, really," Leonidas told her. She lifted her ears expectantly and wagged her tail more furiously. Leonidas laughed and cut her another piece of sausage. She only had to lift her nose and stretch her neck to snap it out of the air. "But we're both still here, aren't we?" Leonidas concluded, and looked at the house again. It was growing on him. It was smaller, much smaller, than the house his mother had inhabited and which Brotus had claimed, not to mention being smaller than the royal palace. It was even smaller than Prokles' house. But from the broken shards, Leonidas knew that once upon a time, potted plants had graced each step of the staircase, and the charred trunks of palms told him that once their lacy leaves had framed the view of the snow-capped Taygetos. If he cleared away the reeds, he would have a view of the river, too.

Leonidas reshouldered his knapsack and made his way cautiously back to the south portico and the gutted outbuildings. Here he stood for a moment, surveying the damage again. The bitch had come to stand right beside him, and he cautiously reached out his hand—empty—and let her sniff it. After a moment she licked it and then looked up at him. He petted her, and she closed her eyes in contentment at each stroke. When he stopped and straightened up, she pawed him for more. She was craving attention more than food, he concluded, but turned his attention back to the house. He would have to consult with Nikostratos. The experienced financier would know what it would cost to repair this house and how to go about it. This thought formed, Leonidas turned and left the courtyard, heading back for the city. It was getting close to dinner time, and he dare not be away from his unit any longer.

As was to be expected, the bitch followed him, trotting about three paces behind him. As he got closer to the city, however, she lagged more and more, and he expected she would soon give up and return to her familiar territory. Instead, just as he reached the bridge, she sat down on her haunches and howled.

Leonidas turned around and called to her. "Go on back to the wild, girl. This city enslaves all her inhabitants." Then he resolutely turned his back on her and continued on is way.

The bitch let out another long, wailing howl. This time Leonidas went back and down on to his heels, to pat her and explain. "Out here you have your freedom, girl. If you come with me, I will expect you to serve me. I'll get you cleaned up and get rid of those ticks and see that you have plenty to eat, but you'll have to come and go at my bidding and share the fruits of your hunting with me. You'll never be your own mistress again. Are you sure you want that?"

She panted happily as long as he was petting her. But as soon as he turned his back on her and started for the city again, she howled as if he'd stabbed her. This time Leonidas ignored her and kept walking. A few moments later something cold and wet touched his calf, and he looked down to see the bitch at his heels. She gazed up at him desperately. He shook his head at her. "It's your choice, girl," he told her and kept walking. She clung to him, almost tripping him in her determination to stay beside him and to be protected by him. Leonidas resigned himself to his fate. She had adopted him, and short of killing her, it was obvious he was not going to be rid of her.

His attendant also found him, rather than the other way around. Less than a week before the official ceremony that would mark his transition to adulthood and citizenship, Leonidas still lacked a body servant. Most young men received the services of an attendant who had been trained by their fathers for several years. Others, like

Alkander, were told about suitable squires by brothers or brothers-in-law. (The Eurypontid king had recommended the brother of his own trusted squire.) Most young men recruited from the helots working on their family estates. Leonidas, however, had not dared recruit from Agiad royal properties, and had not known what his private estate would be until his talk with Eukomos. He had then requested that Eukomos spread the word on his properties that he was looking for an attendant; but contrary to expectations, there had been no eager flood of applicants.

The problem, as Nikostratos explained, was that Leonidas' private estates were too prosperous. As long as they provided a high standard of living for the helots working them, there was no incentive for the young men to take up a life of army discipline and hardship. The situation was aggravated, according to Eukomos, by the fact that in the decade since his father's death, the helots on Leonidas' estates had been doing things pretty much the way they wanted, and this included building up cottage industries from tanning and leather making to oil and wine pressing on a commercial scale. Such industries added to his wealth, but they also kept the younger sons employed on the estates. A helot working and living on an estate could have a wife and family. One with the army could not.

With his transfer from the agoge to the army just a fortnight away, Leonidas had resigned himself to the need to go up to the slave market in Tegea to look for a likely candidate. He'd even gotten permission from the Paidonomos for two days' leave; but shortly before he was scheduled to depart, the old helot concierge at the gymnasium stopped him as he tried to enter. "There was a young man here asking for you," he told Leonidas, "but I didn't like the look of him, so I told him to wait at the *Golden Fleece*."

"Did he say what he wanted?"

"No. Shifty character and rude for such a young man. I wouldn't trust him if I were you." The porter lowered his voice before adding, "Messenian, if you ask me. Keep a lookout!"

Leonidas looked at Alkander, who shrugged. "Best find out what he wants," his friend advised, adding, "I'll start warming up," and went inside, leaving Leonidas to go to the *Golden Fleece*, his bitch at his heels. The *Golden Fleece* was a run-down tavern frequented mostly by off-duty helots who worked directly for the army or for individual hoplites. At this time of day, when a hot meal was offered, it was also populated by rural helots who had brought goods to market or were in town on errands. It was neither clean enough nor its food and wine good enough to attract better-class clientele; and the arrival of a Spartiate, even if only an eirene, raised everyone's head.

Leonidas stepped inside and announced: "I'm Leonidas, son of Anaxandridas. Someone was asking for me?"

A young man who had been sitting crouched in a corner on a bench at once got to his feet. He had evidently not ordered anything, since the table before him was empty. While he squeezed his way around the tables and past the other customers, Leonidas had a moment to assess the stranger. He appeared to be roughly Leonidas' own age, and like Leonidas he was tall and broad-shouldered. He was dark-skinned with almost black hair and eyes, which gave him a decidedly "foreign" appearance. He was wearing no less than two shabby himations over a short chiton, and carried a large but very worn and frayed knapsack, which hung off his shoulder as if very heavy. Although he wore old, dirty sandals, his feet looked as if they had gone unprotected most of their life. Furthermore, although the man was clean, even clipped and shaved as if he had just come from the baths, his hair was shoulder length and unbound—a style that looked very unkempt in a society where the boys were shaved, the young men had to keep their hair shorter than the edge of their helmet, and even grown men, who were allowed to wear their hair long, wore it neatly braided. Altogether the stranger conveyed an impression of poverty and general neglect, combined with an expression and pose of almost belligerent self-confidence.

"Mantiklos, son of Isthmios. I heard you were looking for a squire," he announced as he came to a halt just a couple of feet in front of Leonidas, using the antiquated term of "squire" for the personal attendant position Leonidas had advertised.

"Maybe. Come out in the fresh air where we can talk." Leonidas did not intend to have this conversation in front of everyone in the tavern, all of whom were staring at them. He turned and stepped back out into the street.

Of course, the street was hardly the ideal place for a conversation, either, and Leonidas' stomach was grumbling. He made a snap decision. This was going to take too long for him to get to the gymnasium before he had to collect his unit at the ball field, so he suggested instead, "Let's get something to eat in the agora." He set off in that direction with the young stranger keeping pace beside him. Without pausing, he asked as he went, "How did you hear I was looking for a squire?"

Mantiklos shrugged, "Everyone's talking about it."

"Everyone?" Leonidas challenged.

Mantiklos shrugged again. "On your estate at Koroni."

"Koroni?"

"Near Asine."

That was in Messenia. So the porter was right, and Mantiklos was Messenian. Leonidas didn't think he wanted a Messenian squire. A squire had to be someone a man could trust with his life and his secrets, and he had been raised to view the Messenians with great suspicion. Indeed, he wondered if it was even legal for Mantiklos to be here. After all, Messenian helots weren't supposed to set foot outside of Messenia—or was that Lacedaemon? Leonidas wasn't quite sure, because although he had learned the laws about Messenian helots in the agoge, they were very complicated, and Leonidas hadn't paid more attention than was necessary to get him through the exams.

Lost in his own thoughts, he did not speak again until they reached the agora, where Leonidas went over to the stall selling meat pies that he had patronized since he was seven. The old man smiled and greeted him, as he always did. "Ah, my best patron! What will it be today? Lamb, beef, or chicken?"

"Lamb," Leonidas answered; and then as an afterthought, he turned to his companion while the pie-man started to wrap his pie in a square of burlap. "Hungry?"

Mantiklos shook his head sharply, but the look on his face as he gazed at the steaming hot pies belied him. Leonidas told the pie-man "two" and paid for both. He took the pies and went to sit on the steps of the Temple to the Twins. "Beware of my bitch," he warned the visitor as he handed him a pie; "she'll steal it right out of your hand if you don't watch her." She was indeed standing expectantly beside him, wagging her tail in anticipation.

Mantiklos gave her a wary look, but she was concentrating her attention on her master. Mantiklos bit into the pie, and in seconds it was gone. The dog didn't have a chance. Leonidas was gazing at Mantiklos, only two bites into his own pie. "You *were* hungry," he observed.

Mantiklos looked down and mumbled something, wiping the crumbs away with the back of his hand as he did so.

"So why do you want a lousy job like 'squire' to a Spartan hoplite?"

Mantiklos looked up sharply. "Why do you call it a lousy job?"

"Because it is, and no one else seems to want it. You have to live in barracks as long as I do—which is another ten years. When we go out on manoeuvres or campaign, you'll have to accompany me, marching and sleeping in the cold and rain or the blistering heat. You get nothing but army food and will sleep in the open—"

"Isn't that what you have to do?" Mantiklos challenged.

"Of course, but—"

"Do you think I'm not up to it? Just because I haven't gone through your agoge? You're wrong! I walked all the way here in four days. And I can use a bow and a slingshot." He brushed his himation aside to reveal the latter weapon. "I would be a hoplite, too, if it were allowed, but the laws deny us the dignity of men! So, no, I have not trained like you, but I have the blood of warriors in my veins," he told Leonidas hotly. "As much as you do! I, too, have the blood of kings, Messenian kings, of the great Aristomenes himself—"

"This isn't the place to brag about it," Leonidas remarked dryly, with a nod towards the monument honouring the eirenes who had died defending the children of the agoge slaughtered by Aristomenes 150 years earlier.

Mantiklos caught himself and held his breath. He looked towards the monument, but could not see from here what it said—assuming he could read, which was unlikely. When he looked back at Leonidas, however, his eyes held a mixture of fear and confusion and defiance. "I just want you to understand that I am as good as you are; but if you don't want my services, then I guess I'll go somewhere else!" Mantiklos got to his feet so rapidly that Leonidas' bitch, who had settled down with her head on her master's lap, jumped up in alarm.

Mantiklos hauled his rucksack on to his shoulder and started down the stairs in a rush.

"I didn't say I didn't want your services. At least, I'd first like to see what you can do with that slingshot."

Mantiklos stopped, looked back at Leonidas, set down his rucksack, removed his slingshot, and then opened his purse and removed a pellet. Leonidas noticed that his purse was otherwise empty. Either he had a second purse, or he had no money whatsoever. He looked around and then pointed to some pigeons on the far side of the agora, pecking at something that had fallen amidst the cracks of the paving stones. "I'll kill one of those."

Leonidas nodded and waited. He'd heard enough empty bragging when growing up to take no one at their word in something like this. But a moment later, there was one less pigeon pecking at the cracks of the agora. Leonidas sat up straighter. "Do you know anything about horses and dogs?"

"Koroni is one of the best stud farms in all of Lacedaemon— and so the world," Mantiklos answered. Eukomos had said much the same thing. Leonidas needed at least two horses, and now that Philippos was so unfriendly...

"Give me a day to think about it," Leonidas said aloud to Mantiklos. "Wait for me at the *Golden Fleece* tomorrow, at noon or thereabouts."

Mantiklos nodded, his expression unreadable; and Leonidas set off to get some advice on the legality and advisability of employing a Messenian.

Leonidas found Nikostratos first, who assured him that it was perfectly legal to employ anyone he liked—slave or freeman, helot or perioikoi, Messenian or Laconian or Athenian, for that matter. Whether it was *wise* to give a Messenian so much opportunity to slip a knife in his heart was another matter.

"But surely they aren't *all* murderers," Leonidas protested.

"By no means, but it only takes one. And why is this young man so keen to serve an Agiad prince?"

Leonidas shrugged. "He seemed to think it was more honourable than farming."

"Honourable?"

"Dignified."

"Leonidas, I think you should be very cautious, but I would not rule it out altogether. In fact, there might even be real advantages to you." Nikostratos leaned back in his low chair and brought his fingers together. Leonidas, who had been standing, sank on to a bench to listen.

"Messenia is the source of our wealth, and so the base of our power. Without the taxes and resources we draw out of Messenia, we could not maintain the army we do—much less toy with building a fleet, as Cleomenes and now Demaratus are both keen to do. In other cities, each citizen is responsible for providing his own panoply, horses, servants, even supplies. Athens' entire fleet is financed from *private* resources! Wealthy citizens are 'asked' to grant to the city the costs of building a trireme, or they build them directly and turn them over to the city in a grand gesture of generosity. We are the only city-state in Hellas that uses state resources to outfit our armed forces with a minimum standard and provides the entire logistical support for our fighting forces at public expense.

"Because the city assumes the costs for the army, we can ensure a minimum quality of equipment and weapons, which is not an insignificant factor in our successes on the battlefield. We are generally the best-outfitted, best-fed army in the field; because while individuals among our enemies may have better weapons or armour, the poorer elements may have nothing but makeshift or ancient kit—a factor that seriously undermines their confidence and so their steadfastness in the line. It's all very well for young men to think they defeat their enemies by virtue of their superior courage, but old men can't afford to delude themselves with such rubbish. Every city has brave men, but if you don't give them the tools or the training they need, they will rapidly lose heart.

"All of which is a very roundabout way of saying that the Spartan army would not be the feared machine it is, if we didn't have Messenian resources to spend on maintaining it.

"The problem is that Messenia isn't secure. For whatever reasons—and believe me, the reasons are debated and debated and debated—the Messenians (or at least a substantial portion of them) have not accepted their subject status. They still long for their independence, and so they are always looking for opportunities to stab us in the back. We can never risk taking the whole army far away, for fear the Messenians will revolt if we do. We cannot risk denuding our garrisons here, for the same reason. So despite having a large standing army, we are restricted in our ability to deploy it far from its base.

"All the cities and tyrants that come to us for support look objectively at our disproportionately large army and the fact that it is idle, and assume that we can send it anywhere in the world. They assume we must be waiting only for the opportunity or the offer, gilded with sufficient incentive. They don't understand that we cannot send our army anywhere at all without being afraid.

"Imagine, then, what the advantages of a secure rear would be for Spartan influence in the world! If we did not fear a Messenian revolt every time we turn our backs, then we *could* deploy our army anywhere we liked, anytime we liked. We could afford to engage in several campaigns at once. We could keep our young men busy, their skills honed and their minds open, while supporting—and so securing—friendly governments throughout the civilized world.

"No doubt you are wondering what all this high politics has to do with whether you hire a Messenian helot to clean your kit and care for your horses. Well, it has to do with getting to know Messenians better. Because our laws require that every citizen eat in a mess in Sparta each night and be ready for muster within 24 hours, we do not live on our Messenian estates, and we tend to leave the business of managing them to perioikoi—or even Laconian helots. The Messenians have remained strangers to us. Yet nothing would increase our security and potential for power projection more than a thorough understanding of Messenians. If we could really understand how they think and why, maybe we could adjust our policies in such a manner as to win their loyalty, just as we gained the loyalty of the Laconian helots and perioikoi."

"So you think it would be a good thing if I hired this Mantiklos?"

"Only if you are certain he does not intend to slit your throat the first time he is alone with you on a hunting trip."

"How can I be sure of that?"

Nikostratos shrugged. "You can't, really, but try to find out more about him."

So Leonidas sought out Eukomos again. The steward's first reaction was that he had heard something about the youth, but couldn't remember what. When he checked the records of Koroni, however, there was no Isthmios or Mantiklos on the estate records. In short, he was not who he said he was, and under the circumstances the steward felt the young Messenian ought to be arrested at once.

It was by then dusk and nearly dinner time, however. Leonidas had to hasten back to collect his unit at the ball field and join them for dinner. It was the next day after drill before he could give a further thought to Mantiklos—or whoever he was. By then Mantiklos had already been arrested. He had been picked up by the watch for sleeping in a temple after curfew, and by the time Leonidas could slip away from his duties, the young man was in the stocks.

The stocks were located on Eunomia square, before the courthouse. There was also a temple to Athena and a monument to Lycurgus on this square. By the time Leonidas arrived, there was a large crowd of little boys and youths gathered around to mock the Messenian. Taunting anyone unfortunate enough to be put in the stocks was a fairly routine entertainment for the boys and youths of the agoge. When they were "little boys", with time on their hands, Leonidas and his friends had frequently dropped by to see if there was anything "interesting" in the stocks. He understood that for the boys of the agoge, a Messenian of uncertain origin was first-class amusement. But there were also unspoken rules about how far anyone was allowed to go in harassing the victims.

Since the person in the stocks might even be a Spartiate (one who violated certain laws), it was generally inadvisable to be too offensive. A Spartiate would find it all too easy to take his revenge on the boys who tormented him after his release. And even with helots (perioikoi were always turned over to their own magistrates and never punished publicly in Sparta), certain rules applied—first and foremost, that no one was allowed to do any physical harm to the victim. It was strictly forbidden to throw rocks or stones, for example, much less draw blood with arrows, javelins, or spears. Likewise, while it was not uncommon for the boys of the agoge to throw waste material (rotten eggs or spoiled vegetables) at the victim, it was a well-established rule that the tormentors had to keep their distance and could not poke, prod, or otherwise have physical contact with the offender under-going punishment.

When Leonidas arrived in the square, however, he saw something he had never seen before. While the crowd of boys hung back as usual to about ten feet away from the stocks, a slender boy, who looked about seven but had to be younger because he was not shaved or in the chiton of the agoge, was standing very close to Mantiklos and very deliberately poking him in sensitive areas in an openly malicious manner.

"Stop that!" Leonidas ordered in a loud, clear voice.

The little boy spun about in surprise, while the rest of the crowd of boys fell expectantly silent. Leonidas registered that the tormentor of Mantiklos was his nephew Agis. Although he was already seven, indeed nearly eight, as heir to the throne, he was exempt from the agoge. Agis, meanwhile, had recovered from his surprise and he stuck out his tongue and declared: "You can't stop me! I'm not in the agoge! I'm an Agiad Prince!"

"So am I," Leonidas told him; and before his nephew knew what was happening, Leonidas had hold of him and had slapped him hard twice. "Don't you ever demean the Agiads again by setting a bad example to your peers."

Agis was staring at Leonidas in utter disbelief, his mouth literally open. It occurred to Leonidas that he might very well never have been hit before—a suspicion confirmed by the fact that Agis next broke into tears, and would have run away if Leonidas hadn't still had hold of him. Leonidas yanked him back and pulled his arms behind his back so he could hold his wrists together. Agis was struggling furiously and screaming: "Let go of me! Let me go! Get your hands off me!"

His screams brought his parents, who had apparently been in the courthouse. The queen appeared first, and at the sight of her, Leonidas released Agis. The boy ran crying to his mother's arms, accompanied by the hoots and catcalls of the agoge boys, still clustered around and watching avidly.

Cleomenes, who had followed his wife out of the courthouse, came to confront Leonidas. "What the hell do you think you're doing?"

"Defending the honour of our House, which your son debased by his behaviour."

"Well, don't. It's not your place."

"No?"

"No."

"Did you never wonder why my brother Dorieus had such a strong following?"

"Your brother Dorieus was a madman—the product of incest, just like you!"

"He had a large following because he lived by our laws and proved he was the equal of his peers."

"I am a king, not a Peer."

"Only for as long as you uphold our laws."

"What are you? A prince or a revolutionary?"

"Have you forgotten your *mother's* heritage?"

"Thank you, Leonidas." The voice was that of Chilonis herself. She put her hand on her son's arm, and to him she said simply, "It is time to go. Your son and you have made enough enemies for the moment."

Cleomenes turned on her furiously, but he did not rebuke her in public. He let her lead him away behind a still sobbing Agis, who was being comforted by his mother.

Leonidas watched them depart for a moment, uncomfortable with what had just transpired so publicly. He started when Eukomos addressed him. "I knew the name was familiar. Mantiklos is from the royal estate beside Koroni. We know nothing derogatory about him; and his father, Isthmios, has a record of long, honest service. He is a younger son, and your brother has no objection to you taking him into service. If that's what you want."

Leonidas had completely forgotten about Mantiklos, and he twisted around to consider the young man sagging miserably in the stocks. It was clear to him that he had been caught sleeping in a temple simply because he could not afford the price of lodgings; and Leonidas had a guilty conscience, because he had known Mantiklos had no cash when he'd said he wanted a day to think about employing him. Besides, he needed an attendant, and who was to say a slave he bought in Tegea would be more loyal than this young man who had gone to so much trouble to apply for the job? "If I take him on, will they release him?"

"Probably. Go talk to the magistrates."

And so Leonidas acquired his squire just in time before he was officially granted his citizenship.

———

The festival surrounding the graduation of the age-cohorts was an internal affair. In contrast to the high feasts of the Hyacintha and Gymnopaedia, which drew large crowds of visitors from around the world, this festival was more a family affair. For the great feasts, Sparta not only invited foreign poets and musicians to compete for the privilege of writing the songs and choreographing the performances, the performing choruses and competitors were selected for their superiority. But at this winter festival everyone had a part to play, even the weakest, slowest, and youngest.

For the eirenes, the festivities actually started the night before. They were all required to sacrifice a puppy to Artemis—a custom Leonidas found both incomprehensible and hard to perform. He found himself wondering if his own bitch (whom he had christened Beggar because she never seemed to stop begging) had been an intended victim from the year before who had somehow escaped. What a loss it would have been for such a loyal and intelligent young animal to have had its life extinguished before it could be of use to anyone! What could be the point of this slaughter? Hunting was completely different. It was natural—an eternal contest between predator and prey in which both had a chance. And the usual sacrifices—cattle, sheep, goats, and even fowl—provided meat and entrails that could be read for prophecy. But the slaughter of puppies, whimpering and helpless, provided nothing of value at all. It was symbolic only, he had been told, of the slaughter of innocence itself, just as the transition to manhood was considered an end of innocence—as if any of them were innocent any more....

Leonidas had no stomach for the ritual, but he was surrounded by his age-cohort and the stony, heartless priestesses of Artemis. Was he supposed to believe that Artemis, so often portrayed with hounds at her heels, really wanted whole litters of puppies slaughtered in her honour? In the age of the *Iliad*, the Gods had required human sacrifice, Leonidas reminded himself. He gritted his teeth and got it over with.

But that had been last night.

On the day of the solstice each age-cohort, male and female, had their own special event, attended religiously by relatives and friends of those taking part. The first events of the day were for the youngest children, and the day progressed towards the climax of the graduation of the eirenes. By late afternoon, when the best two teams of ball players from the class of eirenes competed brutally for the last honours they could gain as "youths", the sun was well below the Taygetos. In fact, on this particular day, the cloud cover had descended on to the valley and blanketed it in mist. The gloom closed in early, and the moisture made the ball field a morass of mud long before a soggy and battered team of youths was declared the annual winners. Leonidas, never good at the game, was just as glad he hadn't needed to compete. Alkander and he had been able to stay on the sidelines, cheering their favourites of the "Lycurgan" team, without the bruises, cuts, dislocated joints, and bone fractures that the competitors endured for the sake of honour.

After this event there was a pause for the players to clean themselves up, during which people could get refreshments in the agora. The perioikoi catered to the event by selling a variety of specially baked goods, and some of the surrounding kleros made it a point of honour to offer cheese and other produce, including wine. Jugglers, acrobats, chained bears, and cockfighting provided light entertainment, while the eirenes prepared themselves for the most important moment of their lives so far.

The torches were lit in the barracks, and around him Leonidas' comrades, fresh from the baths like himself, nervously joked and teased one another as they put on fine-spun, soft chitons for the first time in 14 years. Mothers and sisters had sent these garments, often adorned with family emblems or personal names and symbols. The youths pretended to find them silly or "girlish"—but none of them scorned them. Even Alkander had a chiton with a lovely border of horses woven and sewn for him by Hilaira. Leonidas felt like the orphan he was to have nothing but a plain, if well-woven, chiton bought at a stand in the agora.

With even greater excitement, the youths started to don their armour. For the first time in their lives they did not help each other, because their attendants were allowed into the agoge barracks for the first and only time to help the youths who had retained them. They brought with them the breastplates, greaves, swords, and helmets provided to the youths by proud fathers and grandfathers. Some of these were so ancient they were no longer practical for war, but they represented one's ancestors and the great deeds performed in the past. Others were the very latest in fashion—expensive, embossed breast-plates and helmets fashioned by the best armourers in the world and imported to Lacedaemon at great expense—such as Dorieus had worn.

But again, Leonidas had only what he had been able to buy locally. He had bought that simple but perfectly crafted sword in the agora, but he had indulged his vanity to the extent of buying an imported breastplate with a lion etched upon it. He had feared it might be too "ostentatious" until he saw what his classmates were donning. As for his helmet and greaves, they were hardly better than "standard issue". (The army did maintain stores of equipment for youths whose families could not outfit them, and to replace lost and damaged equipment during manoeuvres and campaigns.)

The pipes were already calling, and the eirenes jostled one another as they formed up in the courtyard. Notably, none of them wore himations. The black ones denoting their status as eirenes had been flung into a large basket by the wall. These would be collected, inspected, and those still serviceable cleaned and given to another eirene tomorrow. It was dark outside, and in the cover of darkness they risked whispering and jostling one another as they had not done since they were much younger. It was chilly, too, without any himation, and some of the youths stamped their feet and blew on their hands to draw attention to the fact.

The Paidonomos, his assistants, and the instructors were already gathered. It took longer than usual for them to get the ranks to settle down and for silence to descend. "Tonight," the Paidonomos announced, "my authority over you ends. Tomorrow you are citizens, subject only to the laws of Lacedaemon and the orders of your officers and kings. I have done my best to make each of you worthy of that honour. I can do no more. Good luck."

He stepped down from the raised platform he had been standing on, and after a stunned moment the eirenes realised he really *was* done with them, and they let out a triumphant cheer that echoed off the buildings all around them. The cheer was silenced by a short order to "March out!"

The pipes started playing and they automatically took up the tune, singing in the harmony they had been taught and had practised for as long as they could remember. They made their way down the relatively narrow alley leading out of the back of the agoge barracks, and up the street running beside the main administrative building of the agoge that faced the dancing floor spread out between the Council House and the Ephorate. They marched in a narrow column of four abreast until they reached the open area of the dancing floor and then, as one rank after another stepped into the wide agora, the rank stretched out the length of the open area, and only when it was filled did the first rank step forward while a second rank was formed behind it. Neatly and without hesitation, just like water pouring from a channel into a basin, the agora filled with the over 200 young men about to receive the symbols of citizenship.

Torches not only surrounded the dancing floor itself, they also burned along the front of the Ephorate and Council House, and the temples were lit as well. The torchlight glinted off the armour of the young men filling the square, and revealed the packed crowds flowing off the steps of the buildings and choking the streets that ended on the square. Some bolder or more agile boys had climbed on to rooftops to call out and wave to their relatives or eirenes.

Leonidas' eyes were drawn to the chairs set up on the Council House steps for the two kings. Both kings were accompanied by their wives. Percalus looked stunningly beautiful in a diadem, and Leonidas found himself remembering the way she'd looked on the beach at Kardamyle—so simple and unspoilt—and liking her better that way. Cleomenes' wife was still attractive, but her sour expression was like tarnish upon silver.

Immediately behind the kings sat the rest of the Council of Elders in two rows, fourteen persons wide. Below the kings were the five ephors. They too sat, and were dressed in chitons rather than armour. Then, two steps below them, the five lochagoi in parade panoply stood well spaced out. At the foot of the steps, two ranks deep, stood the oldest age-cohort of young men, the age-cohort that would go off active service tomorrow. They each held one of the heavy, standard-issue hoplons with the lambda of Lacedaemon on its face.

They were now all in place, drawn up by clan. The pipes ceased. A hush fell over the entire agora. A scroll was passed to the first ephor, who read off a name and patronymic. The youth took a step forward, walked between the rows, and presented himself at the foot of the Council House steps, facing the kings. The ephor announced the military unit to which the young man had been assigned, and the hoplite opposite him stepped forward and deftly spun the hoplon around to present the concave inner side to the ex-eirene. Inside the hoplon, looped through the arm-brace, was a scarlet himation.

The eirene took another step forward, withdrew the himation, and slung it over his back before slipping his arm into the braces on the inside of the shield. Then he raised it once in salute to the kings and ephors, before going to stand at the back of the formation while the next name was called.

They had all been given very precise instructions, and formed up in accordance with the order of the names on the list. As there were well over 200 of them graduating this year, the ceremony would take hours if they didn't keep up the pace. In fact, the next youth was always into position to go forward even before the youth before him had received his shield.

As was only to be expected, Cleombrotus was called just ahead of Leonidas, and Leonidas moved into the waiting position, where he could clearly see his brother's spectacular, embossed breastplate and his modish helmet with hinged cheek-pieces. The latter were also elaborately embossed, although Leonidas could not see exactly what was depicted.

At his name, Cleombrotus strode forward confidently, and Leonidas thought he had his eye set straight on Cleomenes, rather than down at the hoplites in front of him. His demeanor was defiant, and his salute with the hoplon more a gesture of threat. Leonidas sighed, hoping he wasn't going to start acting like Dorieus now that he was a citizen.

"Leonidas, son of Anaxandridas."

Leonidas stepped on to the well-worn stone, facing the kings, Council, ephors, and lochagoi. Leonidas felt as if all eyes were upon him. He was acutely aware of his simple armour after Cleombrotus' panoply. The himation and hoplon were offered to him. He stepped forward and took both gratefully. The himation seemed no different in the dark from the one he had just discarded, but the hoplon was welcome because it covered his body from shoulder to knee—offering protection not just against the weapons of his enemies, but the preying eyes of the crowds.

Leonidas was torn between a pride in his city's ethos of equality and dismay at the weight of tradition that the shield symbolised. In other Greek cities, indeed in Sparta itself until only a handful of Olympiads ago, each man carried a shield with his individual device upon it. But in Sparta nowadays they were turned from individuals into anonymous, interchangeable pawns. Peers. Equals in rights and duties, in dress and diet.

But we *are* still individuals, Leonidas insisted to himself as he followed Cleombrotus to stand at the back, while others took their place in the front and center of the agora. They remained individuals even if they wore the same himations and carried the same shields. They were no less individuals than they were equals.

From this day forward, Leonidas reminded himself, he would be one of the body of Peers that raised the boys of the agoge and defended the city, that voted on public policy and elected the city officials. He was one of "them". The responsibility seemed as heavy as the hoplon on his left arm. Everything up to now had been preparation for this—a long, slow, agonising process of making himself worthy of this privilege.

He could hear Prokles mocking him in his head. Privilege? What privilege? Being confined to barracks and drilled half to death? Eating simple food and weak wine every night of his life? Being forced to steal a bride in the dark of night...

The last of the names had been called, the last shield presented. The pipes started up and they all sang together, new citizens and city officials and spectators, a paean to Zeus.

No sooner had the last note died out in the fog, than the crowd broke in from around the edges. Mothers, fathers, friends, and siblings rushed amidst the disintegrating ranks to congratulate the new citizens. Sweethearts embraced openly, defying their parents to separate them. Leonidas turned to find Alkander and saw Hilaira throw herself into his arms. He turned away to let them be together and came face to face with Cleombrotus.

"Couldn't you play the part of the prince just for *once*?" Cleombrotus sneered. "You look worse than that mothake of yours!" He gestured contemptuously toward Alkander. Now that he could see it up close, Leonidas noted that Cleombrotus' armour was little less than a claim to the Agiad throne—covered with images of Herakles in his various trials.

"We hardly need yet another Agiad prince, do we?" Leonidas answered his brother. "Between you, Dorieus, and Agis, there are more than enough Agiad princes to damage Sparta with disgraceful behaviour or ill-judged adventures! I, for one, will be content if I can be no more—and no less—than a Spartan Peer."

Cleombrotus just snorted contemptuously and turned away, but Leonidas comforted himself in the mist by vowing he would indeed become a peerless Peer. Because, he told himself, being a good Peer—one who always put Sparta's interests first—was surely a worthy goal. Wasn't it?

HISTORICAL NOTE

THE SPARTAN AGOGE WAS THE OBJECT of great admiration in the ancient world and the subject of endless debate, speculation, and misinformation ever since. In his meticulously researched study, *Gymnasium of Virtue*, Nigel Kennel demonstrates that the overwhelming bulk of information we have today describes the agoge in the Roman period. This agoge was a "reinvention" of the Hellenistic agoge almost 40 years after the latter had been disbanded. Furthermore, the Hellenistic agoge was itself a new institution founded in the reign of Cleomenes III (235-222 BC). Cleomenes III styled his reforms as a "restoration of the ancient customs", but there is very little evidence that they were, in fact, a return to old customs. Indeed, others of his reforms, such as the abolition of the ephorate, were clearly in contradiction to Spartan law as it had been exercised in the archaic and classical periods. Furthermore, as Kennel demonstrates convincingly, Cleomenes' agoge was consciously designed and structured by the stoic philosopher Sphaerus of Borysthenes.

Sphaerus had his own theories on education that he set about implementing when given the opportunity by Cleomenes. For example, the emphasis on endurance at the expense of aggressiveness and initiative is clearly evidenced by the transformation in this period of the Feast of Artemis Orthia from a lively battle between youths of different age-cohorts into a pure "whipping contest", in which youth passively allowed themselves to be flogged until they collapsed.

Thus, as is so often the case, the only authentic source for the agoge in the fifth century BC is Xenophon and, to a lesser degree, Plutarch, because he is known to have relied on lost classical works on Sparta. But even these sources describe the agoge roughly 100 to 130 years after the period described in this novel. There is no source whatsoever that describes the Spartan agoge of the archaic period. Yet it must be assumed that, like any institution, the agoge changed over time and had distinctly different characteristics at different periods— or even simply under different influential headmasters.

Nevertheless, there are some features of the agoge that can be inferred from Herodotus, Xenophon, and archaeological evidence, and that appear to have been consistent over time. First and foremost, it is clear that even in the archaic period, Sparta alone of all the Greek city-states had public education for its youth, both male and female. It appears that parents paid fees (in kind) to support the public schools. This public education apparently started at age 7 and ended at age 21, when a youth became a "young man", or Hebontes. Thus Spartan education differed from the education of youth in other cities not only by being public, but also by its unusual length. Second, Spartan education, apparently alone in the ancient world, stressed austerity and discipline over intellectual content. It appears most likely that the youths were given uniforms and fed rather too little rather than too much. The ancient sources do *not*, however, support the claim put forward by so many modern commentators that the youth of the agoge were fed so little that they had to steal to survive, that they had only one garment in all weathers, or that they had no kind of education beyond physical sports and drill.

Kennel's study demonstrates convincingly that Spartan youth *at one stage in their training* were expected to live outside society, and during this period had to live by their wits and skills—these meant primarily hunting and trapping, but theft was tolerated if they could get away with it. This period was known as the "fox time", or Phouxir. There is no source that tells how long or at what age this "survival training" occurred. I have placed it at the critical transition from "little boy" to "youth", because anthropology suggests that a period of exclusion from society is often an important rite of passage to adult-hood, and in primitive societies this often occurs at 13 or 14—that is, the onset of puberty.

I have also assumed that the duration of the Phouxir was long enough to represent a hardship for the boys, but not long enough for widespread theft to be disruptive in a very ordered society. It is simply not reasonable to imagine that every Spartan wife on her kleros and every craftsman and merchant vital to the survival of the city had to live in constant fear of theft by the hordes of youth in the agoge. This is why I do not accept the interpretation of other historians that suggest the youths of the agoge had to live outside society for an entire year. If that were the case, one age-cohort would always be in the Phouxir, and society would be dealing constantly with thieving youth rather than getting on with making a living. Instead, I have chosen to limit the Phouxir to 40 days and 40 nights, at that time of the year when the harvest would already be safely in and the slaughter taking place, thus minimizing the potential for desperate youth to disrupt society by their theft.

The tradition for set classes with distinctive names dates from the Hellenistic agoge. However, schools all over the world are organised into "grades" by age. It is the exception—and almost always seen as a serious disadvantage—when children of different ages are mixed together. There can be no doubt that although children develop at different rates individually, on the whole the differences between children belonging to one age-cohort are less than the differences between age-cohorts. Furthermore, it is generally unfair to pit young children against older children at sport. Since there can be little doubt that the Spartans placed considerable emphasis on physical exercise, it is reasonable to suppose the Spartans always segregated the boys of the agoge by age-cohort—whether or not they gave them discrete designations.

The unique status and role of eirenes is one of the few features of the agoge that can be found in Xenophon. Unfortunately he does not define the term, and so we cannot be sure what age his "eirenes" were. However, we do know that throughout the Greek world, youths on the brink of citizenship went through intense military training and performed key military functions such as guard and garrison duty.

While in a sense the entire agoge was a form of military training, it is nevertheless reasonable to suppose that the eldest classes were gradually given greater and greater responsibility. Xenophon himself stresses that at the very age when "youths become very self-willed and are particularly liable to cockiness", Lycurgus decreed that Spartan youth "be loaded with the greatest amount of work and contrived that they be occupied for the maximum time." This description fits perfectly for 18-, 19-, and 20-year-olds. I certainly cannot accept Kennel's argument that all young men on active service (ages 21 to 30) were "eirenes", because once Spartan men were on active service their duties—and the possibility of being called up on campaign and so away from the city for months on end—would have made it impossible for them to act as instructors and drill masters in the agoge. Lastly, there is no reason to believe that *nothing* in the agoge of the Hellenistic period came from an earlier tradition; and so I have projected the Hellenistic tradition, in which the eirenes were 20-year-olds and meleireines 19-year-olds, backwards to the period of this book.

The evidence for elected leaders and "herds" of boys is also quite ancient. In addition to Plutarch's description of the boys being organised into troops with elected leaders at age seven, many inscriptions at sacred sites in Sparta suggest the importance of various kinds of groups, possibly teams, and their leaders. The terms used mean nothing to us today, and it seems most probable that there were a variety of different teams or groups that might well have intersected in various ways. Given the confusion, I have chosen to keep it simple, in this case following Plutarch.

Many readers may be surprised to see no description of institutionalized pederasty in this book. This is not an oversight, not ignorance of the fact that many noted historians stress its importance, nor coyness with a theme thought distasteful. Rather, it is my considered opinion that there is absolutely no evidence of pederasty in the agoge—or in Spartan society generally—at this period or in the centuries before. Like many other of the most offensive aspects of the agoge, I believe it is a later development. As noted above, Xenophon, the only historian with first-hand experience of the agoge, states explicitly: "...[Lycurgus] ...laid down that at Sparta lovers should refrain from molesting boys just as much as parents avoid having intercourse with their children or brothers with their sisters." It is hard to find a more definitive statement than this, and from the most authoritive of sources. To dismiss this evidence simply because it does not suit pre-conceived ideas is arrogant. Xenophon even goes on to add: "It does not surprise me, however, that some people do not believe this, since in many cities the laws do not oppose lusting after boys." And this is the crux of the matter. All of our written sources on Sparta come from these other cities, where pederasty was rampant, in short from men who could not imagine a world without it. But then, they could not imagine women who were educated, physically fit, and economically powerful who were not also licentious and lewd either.

Modern readers ought to be more open-minded and admit that pederasty is not inherent in society—particularly not in a society where women are well integrated. My thesis is supported by another ancient authority, Aristotle, who blamed all of Sparta's woes on the fact that the women were in control of things, a fact that he in turn attributed to the *lack* of homosexuality in Spartan society generally. Finally, I would like to call on the archaeological evidence. To date—in sharp contrast to other Greek cities—no Spartan homoerotic artwork has been found. Since the Spartan legacy of artefacts is somewhat less numerous than that of Athens, Corinth, or other cities, maybe something will still turn up; but until that happens, the evidence is very strongly against institutionalized pederasty in the agoge of the archaic and early classical periods.

There has also been endless scholarly debate about what clothing the boys of the agoge were allowed. Xenophon stressed only that in contrast to the spoilt boys of other cities (who had vast wardrobes of himations), the Spartan boys were given only one per year. At no time did he imply they wore no undergarments, although this is the inter-pretation of many later scholars. Again, I follow closely the research of Nigel Kennel.

Of greater significance is the fact that Spartan education did include literacy and music, the primary subjects of ancient education. Starting with the circumstantial evidence, Spartans could not have commanded the respect of the ancient world, engaged in complicated diplomatic manoeuvring, and attracted the sons of intellectuals like

Xenophon to their agoge if they had been as illiterate and uneducated as some modern writers like to portray them. Clearly Spartans knew their laws very well, they could debate in international forums, and their sayings were considered so witty that they were collected by their contemporaries. Furthermore, Sparta is known to have entertained leading philosophers and to have had a high appreciation of poetry, as evidenced by the many contests and festivals for poetry, particularly in the form of lyrics. The abundance of inscriptions and dedications found in Sparta are clear testimony to a literate society; one does not brag about one's achievements in stone if no one in your society can read! Likewise, Sparta sent written orders to its commanders, and anecdotal evidence suggests that mothers and sons exchanged letters.

Certainly, ancient sources stress the Spartan emphasis on musical education and on dance. Most importantly, ancient sources not only concede that Spartan youth learned to read and write, but claim that "devotion to the intellect is more characteristic of Spartans than love of physical exercise." (Plutarch, *Lycurgus*:20)

Last but not least, while everyone agrees that Spartan education was designed to turn the graduates of the agoge into good soldiers, I have tried to point out that the skills needed by a good soldier included far more than skill with weapons, physical fitness, endurance, and obedience. A good soldier also had to be able to track, to read the weather from the clouds, to navigate by the stars, to recognise poisonous plants, to apply first aid, to build fortifications and trenches, and much, much more. Far too little attention is paid by most commentators to this simple fact. I am confident that while the ages at which certain things were taught are fictional, the total picture provided here is closer to reality than the one-sided and unidimensional depiction of most modern writers.